# A Hobo's Wish

## Connie Lounsbury

2020© Connie Lounsbury

Published by Scrivenings Press LLC
15 Lucky Lane
Morrilton, Arkansas 72110
https://ScriveningsPress.com

Printed in the United States of America



Paperback ISBN 978-1-64917-032-3
eBook ISBN 978-1-64917-033-0

Library of Congress Control Number: 2020940050

Cover by Diane Turpin, www.dianeturpindesigns.com

(Note: This book was previously published by Mantle Rock Publishing LLC and was re-published when MRP was acquired by Scrivenings Press LLC in 2020.)

All characters are fictional, and any resemblance to real people, either factional or historical, is purely coincidental.

All scripture quoted from the King James Version of the Bible.

Published in association with Jim Hart of Hartline Literary Agency, Pittsburgh, PA

❀ Created with Vellum

*I dedicate this book to my daughters Laura Lounsbury, Elaine Perry, Lisa Lounsbury, and Cindy Johnson, as well as my grandchildren Hannah and Jordan Aasen, Hayley Elken, Jennifer Happ, Monica Happ, Ryder Fedyk, Kate Ford, Jack Ford and Emily Ford. Also my great-grandchildren Ashton Aasen and Aaliyah Aasen.*
*I pray none of them will ever face homelessness.*

# ACKNOWLEDGMENTS

My heartfelt thanks to God for providing guidance for this book every time I sat at the computer to create this work of fiction.

My deepest love and appreciation go to my husband David who provided love, support, and patience as I focused on writing this book, and who was always on hand to answers my many questions about farming practices during the 1930s.

I am abundantly grateful for my literary agent Jim Hart who sent this work to Mantle Rock Publishing. It has been a pleasure working with publisher Kathy Cretsinger and her staff. My very special thanks goes to editor Monica Mynk who taught me more than I thought I still needed to learn about writing, and made me look good.

I owe much to Dr. Tom Hagerty, Dr. Peter Poss, and Dr. David Wright, who took time to answer my questions and educate me on veterinary practices in "the old days."

I could not have written this book without so many loving friends who have offered me wisdom and answers to my many questions. While I shudder to think that I might overlook someone, I especially want to thank Connie Lee, Vickie Williamson,

Darlene Anderson, Cindy Johnson, Lorraine Newkirk, Pastor David Hibbison, Ken Rudolph, Brenda Olson, Mike Bregenzer, Bill Fiedler, Nancy Latham, Walter McIntire, Floyd Thompson, Lila Fenske, Helen Quanbeck, Marilyn Gordon, Mildred Shadduck, Lorraine Benson, Chris Lantto, Stanley Lantto, Arlan Larson, Lisa Lounsbury, Rick Ingham, Delores Lanz, Jed Zimmerman, and Donald Streich.

Thank you, my many wonderful friends.

Pete Walters swung down from his buggy and shook away tears as he hitched his team to a post in front of the café. Couldn't cry now. He needed to get a grip.

He stroked Maddie's velvet nose and patted Mike's neck. "Just one more call and then we can go home, but first I need coffee to keep me awake."

The bell over the café door jingled, and Ruby looked up, her gold star-shaped earrings brushing against her neck. "Merry Christmas, Doc. Coffee?"

She set a cup of steaming liquid on the lunch counter and displayed a more-than-friendly smile.

Pete shook snow off his cap and heavy gray jacket and hung them on a hook. He waved to the other customers. "Merry Christmas, Bill. Happy Holidays, Arthur." Each time it became harder to say those words. He cleared his throat once again. Today, Rose would have turned six years old.

Garish glittering ropes of red and green garland cluttered the window frames. "Oh Tannenbaum" blared from a small radio behind the counter. Pete cringed.

The folks in Grand Island, Nebraska liked their mid-afternoon coffee and noisy conversation in the café. Too noisy.

He downed his coffee in three quick gulps.

A bell over the door jangled as someone came in, ushering another burst of cold air to his back. A large hand clasped Pete's shoulder from behind, and a ruddy-faced man slid onto the red vinyl-covered stool next to him. "Coffee's on me today, Doc."

"Nice to see you, Ray." Pete shook hands with the local butcher.

"I just can't thank you enough, Doc. If you wouldn't have noticed the symptoms so soon and treated my team, my horses would be dead like so many others around here." He nodded his thanks as Ruby set a cup of coffee in front of him. "I hear this encephalitis epidemic has spread throughout all of Nebraska. How're you holding up through all this?"

"Every horse I can't save feels like a kick in the ribs." Pete wrapped his palms around the warm mug Ruby refilled. "I spent most of the night at Donaldsons' and got called out early this morning to Volbrechts'. Don't expect any of those horses will make it. I don't know what those farmers will do. With this depression and drought, most of them don't have two nickels to rub together."

"I know what you mean. I hope the economy improves in '35. It should pick up now that Roosevelt is in office." Ray rested his elbows on the counter. "I heard that he…"

Pete traced his thumb over the rim of his mug, making a low whistle, same as he'd done for Rose on many occasions. She'd have enjoyed hearing about Roosevelt. *When I'm six, I'll learn everything in school.* Her sweet little voice echoed in his head. That was just weeks before she died.

Ray swiveled his stool to face Pete. "I got in some of those ribs that you like. Stop in and pick up a slab."

"Thanks, Ray. I will." Pete pushed away his empty cup. "I've got to ride out to Otto Madison's to bring him some Kramechu powder. His calves have a bad case of scours." He reached into his pocket.

Ray held up his hand. "No, no. Coffee's on me. And you better hurry. If the wind keeps picking up, this could turn into a nasty storm."

"Thanks." He shook Ray's hand, adjusted his earflaps over his ears, and opened the door against the biting snowflakes.

*Lord, thank you for the good health of my own team.* Pete jumped into his buggy. Rose had loved riding in the buggy. The pain, momentarily lifted in the café, returned like a punch to his stomach. Her face swam before his eyes. Such a sweet little voice. *"That's okay, Daddy. I'm not cold."*

Had it been his fault she died?

A sob shook his body, and tears burst forth. He gave the reins a shake and clucked to the horses. In the old days, he would have belted out hymns as they trotted along. God might have smiled down on him through the swirling snow. But the hymns rang hollow now, and he hated the sound of his own voice.

A twenty-minute journey brought him to the Madison farm-yard, where their black lab barked a welcome.

Otto's grin brought a measure of warmth to Pete. "Good day to you, Doctor Walters. God bless you for coming out in this weather. My poor calves are suffering."

Pete handed Otto the powder. "Mix about a tablespoon with a cup of warm water, shake it good to dissolve it, and give it to the calves in a bottle. Three times a day should do it. Keep feeding it until the scours are gone."

Mildred waved to him from the kitchen doorway. "Coffee's ready. I made it strong, the way you like it. Come on in."

Mildred had laid out a fresh tablecloth and used her festive Christmas cups and saucers. "Have some rusks, Doctor." She moved the plate of cinnamon toast closer to him.

"Thanks." A surge of longing washed over Pete. His own wife Betty had taken such pride in her Christmas dishes.

"The doctor looks half-froze, Mildred." Otto poured a generous shot of strong-smelling whiskey into Pete's cup of coffee. "Here, Doc, this will keep you warm on the way home."

Pete opened his mouth and raised his hand, but stopped halfway. Maybe today he needed that comfort.

After two cups of doctored coffee and as many slices of the crusty, sweet bread, Mildred presented a pint of apple butter to him, what she had to give.

Otto offered his hand. "I apologize, Doc, for having no money to pay you."

Pete shifted the apple butter to the crook of his elbow and patted Otto's arm. "It's okay."

He slid onto the black leather seat of his buggy and placed the apple butter next to him. How good it would taste with the loaf of bread from the Volbrecht's, the ham from the Donaldson's, and the eggs he'd received the day before. Cash was hard to come by, but he got fed. This depression couldn't go on forever. How long before farmers yielded good crops again? They'd soon see the end to this drought. They had to.

Freezing snowflakes stung his face. Even the horses kept their heads down as they plodded through deep snow. Daylight turned to darkness, but the horses knew the way home without watching the road.

They arrived at the livery stable, and Pete relaxed his shoulders. His numb feet and fingers tingled as he hopped out of the buggy.

"You go on home, Doc." Henry, the livery owner, unhooked the buggy. "You look froze to the bone. Don't worry. I'll take good care of Mike and Maddie. Start a good fire and stay close to home tonight. This is turning into a real blizzard."

Pete hurried the short block home, but his steps dragged as

he got closer, knowing he'd have to walk into that cold, lonely house again.

He let himself in the side door, left his boots on the mat, and carried his coat to the front room to dry. As he stuffed paper and kindling into the stove and lit it with a long match, he licked his lips. He could still taste the whiskey from his coffee. A little more would help him forget.

He pulled out a chair to reach into a high cupboard. Reaching past the Thanksgiving platter, canning kettle, and Christmas plates, he took out the quart of Colonel James B. Beam bourbon he'd hidden from himself a year ago.

After the double funeral, when he'd buried his wife and daughter on the same day, Pete hit the bottle pretty hard. Then one day, Pastor Jim and his wife came over. "Betty wouldn't want you to ruin your life like this," Karen had told him. "Let us help you."

For weeks they'd brought food and spent evenings with Pete, playing cribbage and talking, until he'd abandoned the crutch of alcohol. This last unopened bottle had sat in the cupboard since then.

Pete opened the bottle, inhaled the bitter sweet scent, and poured a generous portion of the amber fluid into a glass. He sat and propped his feet close to the stove, facing the empty corner where Betty always stood the Christmas tree.

*I didn't deserve them, did I, Lord? My two beautiful ladies. You trusted them to my care, and I let you down.*

Pete finished his drink, poured another, and brought the bottle with him when he returned to his chair. People thought he should be getting on with his life. How could he? Just when he got his grief under control, something always triggered a memory. A bolt of pain took away his breath.

He refilled his glass.

As much as he dreaded these cold, lonely evenings, he couldn't imagine spending Christmas elsewhere. He had lots of invitations, but how could he impose on families who could barely feed themselves?

Get on with his life? Taking part in festive activities evoked no interest, nor did the idea of dating again, although he knew a few women eager to be asked. He just wanted—no, needed—his family back.

Like the numbing effects of laudanum, the smooth, intoxicating whiskey whittled away at his piercing pain until their deaths and his guilt became distant memories.

Pete fell into a drunken sleep in his chair. He dreamed of his beautiful wife and precious daughter laughing beside a decorated tree laden with gaily wrapped gifts. A loud pounding interrupted his dreams. He blinked his way through the fog and thrashed in his chair.

The pounding persisted. What was it? His eyes burst open. Someone was knocking at his door.

## 2

Pete stumbled to the door, and a fierce swirl of white powder entered along with a snow-covered farmer.

Alvin Thomas rushed in, his almost frost-bitten face surrounded by his fur-lined cap with earflaps tied beneath his chin. He removed one glove and wiped the water from his wind-burned eyes.

He'd ridden a long way to get there. The phone must be out.

"I'm sure sorrowful to bring you out in a blizzard, but my best work horse is down, Doc." Alvin stomped the snow off his boots. "I stopped at the stable and saddled one of your horses. The roads are drifted too much for your automobile or buggy. Gertie is bad, Doc. Real bad. She needs you."

"Okay, just a minute." Pete grabbed his coat and cap, dashed outside, and vomited in the snow. His head pounded with each retch of his stomach, and when he reached the shelter of the outhouse he took several deep breaths.

Alvin was here. He needed Pete to go with him. He'd better shape up.

After relieving himself, he waded back to the house through the deep snow. "Okay, I'm coming." He staggered to the stove and closed the damper and draft with shaky hands. Then he went into the kitchen. Had to check the damper and drafts on the cook stove, though it hadn't been lit all day.

"What are you doing?" Alvin paced by the door.

Pete gritted his teeth. The scars on his neck and arm weren't the only ones he lived with since being trapped in a burning house as a child. He still couldn't shake the fear of chimney fires.

As he stepped into his office, he grabbed the whiskey bottle. After taking a long swig to clear his head, he dropped the bottle into his medical bag.

Pete's head pounded with Maddie's every step. The howling wind made it difficult to talk to Alvin, leaving him alone with his muddled thoughts. Did he close the stove drafts? Yes. Yes, of course he did. He checked them twice.

He and Betty had argued about few things in their happy marriage, other than his obsessive fear of fire. She'd begged him to keep it burning during the night. Instead, he allowed the flames to diminish to almost nothing during the evening.

In the mornings, Pete woke early to build new fires in both stoves, but on the coldest days it took hours for the house to warm. After Rose's birth, Betty tacked a heavy bedspread over the kitchen door, trapping all the heat from the cook stove. The smaller room heated faster and stayed warmer, so she spent many days in the kitchen with Rose.

Being a loyal wife, Betty had tried to understand Pete's fear, but how could she? She'd never seen a house on fire, with flames racing through the rafters, turning a safe, solid home into a death trap in a matter of minutes. She'd never watched flames creep closer, and closer, until they grabbed a pajama sleeve and moved up her arm, the pain of the burn almost unbearable.

He gripped Maddie's reins tighter. *Rose, I was only trying to protect you.*

Up ahead, Alvin's outbuildings emerged through the blinding snow. Pete slowed his mare and patted her head. "Alvin, I'm going to stable Maddie in the machine shed. Don't want her to contract an encephalitis virus."

"Okay."

Inside the barn, Gertie lay on her side, wheezing with labored breath.

Pete inserted a thermometer and held his stethoscope to her chest. Lots of snaps and crackles. When he removed the thermometer, it registered one-hundred and three degrees. He clenched his jaw. "Gertie has pneumonia."

"Thank God it isn't encephalitis." Alvin exhaled.

"Pneumonia is a difficult illness to treat in an animal, and she has a bad case." Pete stood. "Good thing you came to get me. We've got to get her breathing better."

Alvin squared his shoulders. "What do you need me to do?"

"Bring me a big kettle of boiling water and some turpentine. Do you have an old feed bag you can sacrifice so I can make an inhaling tube?" Pete ran his hands along Gertie's flank to comfort her. "Also, bring all the mustard Emma has on hand. Oh, and a pillowcase and a big kettle, so I can make a mustard plaster. Gertie may or may not make it."

By the time Alvin returned with the requested items, the mare's wheezing had grown louder. "Abby's got two teakettles on to boil. I'll find you a feed bag."

Pete grabbed a nearby milk pail and made a mustard plaster. He reached for the dusty canvas bag Alvin offered but held up his palm. "Wipe that down as best you can. We don't want her inhaling that feed dust."

Before long, Pete had a makeshift turpentine inhaler in place and a mustard plaster on Gertie's chest, and Alvin returned to the house for more water.

Pete knelt beside his patient. "You're going to get well,

Gertie." He ran his hands along the mare's body. "Keep fighting. You're strong. You can do it."

But Rose couldn't. Such a terrible night when he'd tried so hard to cure her of pneumonia. It still gripped him so hard it sometimes blocked his breath. He reached into his medical bag for his bottle and took a long, slow swig. He had to forget.

Alvin returned with another teakettle of boiling water and a quilt. "It's going to be a long night."

Pete pushed the bottle deep into his bag and snapped the clasp. "I'm doing everything I can for her, but I won't lie to you. She's bad."

"I don't know what we'd do if we lost Gertie, Doc. We're just hanging on by our fingernails as it is, we're so far behind. We've already had notice. I'll sell most of the pigs next week so we can make a part payment." Alvin passed him the kettle. "The paper reported that hog prices went up to as much as $7 for feeders. That will help, but if we can't come up with some more money soon we'll lose this place."

"I'm sorry to hear that. If you can hang on a little longer, things have got to start turning around soon." Pete poured water into his pan then handed the kettle back to Alvin.

"Well, I don't know if it will be soon enough for us. But, enough of my problems." Alvin flipped over a milk can and sat. "You've had worse, I know. Isn't it about a year now since Betty and Rose died?"

Pete nodded. "I buried them on the 23rd."

"A terrible loss." Alvin shook his head. "Little Rose. Such a sweet little girl." He kicked the snow off his boots. "Well, I'm going to try to get some rest before I come back for milking. The blizzard's gotten so bad it's hard to get from the house to the barn. We'll be drifted in by morning." He grabbed the blanket folded over Gertie's stall door. "Emma sent this quilt out for you. You'll spend the night here?"

Pete accepted the quilt. "I'll stay in the barn with Gertie. You go get some sleep."

After Alvin left, Pete took Gertie's temperature again. Good. Her fever had dropped a few notches.

He checked the mustard plaster, moved it a bit, and soothed her body with his hands. "C'mon, Gertie. Please get better."

A throb pulsed between his temples. Oh, his headache. He fumbled for his medical bag and took a drink of whiskey.

"Better check on the pigs, Gertie." He lifted the lantern from its hook and staggered to the pen. "Aren't you a healthy-looking lot? Alvin should do well in his sales."

Around the corner, the hens all roosted comfortably in their coop attached to the barn. Emma would be in early to gather eggs to barter for food at the general store.

Pete circled the barn, passing the cows Alvin had brought in from the blizzard. He gave several of them affectionate pats. How long would it be before the milk trucks could get through the drifted roads?

Outside the window, the blustering snow swirled furiously, obscuring the view of Alvin's fields. Soon, it would be time to plow again. Gertie's death would be a devastating loss to Alvin. Surely she'd pull through.

Pete checked the horse pen at the far end of the barn. At least Gus slept comfortably. He followed the small path of light from his lantern back to Gertie. He checked her over again and settled into a soft pile of hay with Emma's quilt. *Heal Gertie, Lord.*

The wind howled around the barn and blew cold air through every crack as Pete huddled under the quilt, clutching his bourbon. Would he ever be warm tonight? And would God listen to his prayer?

He'd prayed for both Rose and Betty to recover. But God had let them die. Did Rose get pneumonia because Pete kept the house too cold? Did grief cause Betty's heart to give out a few days later? Did he cause their deaths?

He took another swig from the bottle.

A bad storm like this one had prevented him from reaching the doctor a year ago when Rose's cold turned to pneumonia. Like with Gertie, he'd done everything he could, using a steam tent and mustard plasters. He had stayed at her bedside for two days and nights while the storm railed against the small house. Before they could dig out from the deep snow, Rose died.

Pete remembered Betty sitting in her rocker by the stove. Following Rose's death, she worked her needles with fingers flying as if she couldn't finish that sweater fast enough. She refused to eat the soup Pete made for her. Instead, she knitted day and night, without a word.

Long after the storm, Pete shoveled a path to the street, the doctor came and left, and the undertaker took Rose away to prepare her for the funeral. Then, Betty ate some soup and a piece of bread. When she finished, Pete touched her shoulder. "Why don't you go to bed?"

She glared at him. "If you would have kept it warmer in this house, Rose would still be alive."

The next day, Betty suffered a heart attack. Again, Pete had prayed fervently that God let Betty recover. But she died before the doctor could get there. Did he deserve to lose his family?

The furious wind amplified Pete's heartache. He sat up, cried out in anguish, and reached for the whiskey bottle once more.

---

INTENSE HEAT and frantic cries from the animals shook Pete awake. Fiery flames licked the door and walls across the whole back of the barn. His heart thundered as smoke stung his eyes. He had to get the animals out.

Animal shrieks pierced his ears. His nostrils filled with the nauseous stench of burning flesh. He raced to the front door and lunged as hard as he could. The door would not open. Too much snow.

Pete's pulse rate doubled amid the trampling mayhem. Was there any way to save the animals? Any other way out?

Thick smoke roiled through the barn in choking billows, burning Pete's lungs. Not only the animals... He had to get out. How?

## 3

The window. Pete searched along the wall for a pitch fork, and then broke out the glass. As he tried to wriggle through the small opening, Alvin appeared through the waist-high snowdrifts and pulled him the rest of the way out.

"Are you all right?" Alvin dragged him away from the barn.

Coughs shook Pete's body. "I... I..." Was he all right? He sensed no injuries, yet his legs collapsed beneath him. He crawled away, gagging and vomiting.

The fire roared like a freight train, lighting up the farmyard as Pete retched in the snow. Angry, orange flames shot from the windows, doors, and every crack in the barn walls.

The cries of the animals stopped. The horses. Gertie. Gus. The cows. The pigs. The chickens. All gone. The hay and the feed. Everything. All of it. Lost.

How could this happen?

Sparks drifted along a northward wind. At least the fire wouldn't spread to the machine shed or the house.

Emma tugged at his arm. Her mouth moved, and her hands waved in motions, but what was she saying? Deep grief consumed him.

She pointed toward the house and pulled him to his feet, the sharp wind stinging his forehead. Had he lost his cap? And his hands… he held them out in front of his chest. Why were his hands bare and bleeding?

He waded after her through deep snow drifts into the warmth of the kitchen. She took off his coat and tended to his hands. "The wind is dying down now…"

A tremendous crash drowned the roar of the fire, and they rushed to the window. The roof had collapsed onto all the dead animals. Emma's hands flew to her face, and she sobbed.

Alvin barged into the house, tears streaming his cheeks. He shook Pete's shoulders. "How did this happen?" He jerked back, his mouth twisted into a snarl. "You smell like a brewery. You were drunk! How could you do this to us? Why? Oh, God!"

Emma ran to Alvin's side and collapsed in his arms. "What will we do?"

The two cried as one while the flames consumed their livelihood. Pete collapsed in a chair, cradled his head, and wept.

Surely he wasn't that drunk. And he didn't wake up sooner because he had so little sleep the night before. Rubbing his eyes with the heels of his hands, he sucked in a deep breath. He didn't do this. He couldn't have killed all those animals.

Emma showed him to a bedroom upstairs, where he tossed and turned. Did the lantern cause the fire? It had to be. He'd carried it to the other end of the barn and brought it back. Did he hang it on the hook? Certainly, he must have.

He balled his fist, gathering the quilt in his fingers. He was careful with fire. He wouldn't have set the lantern down.

After hours of replaying the scene, his body ached almost as bad as his head, but his heart ached even worse. The truth was, he didn't remember.

Dawn broke though darkness before he fell into a fitful sleep. He woke to the smell of coffee and made his way to the kitchen. Alvin got up from the table and took his coffee into the front room.

"Sit." Emma's flat voice gave Pete chills. She poured him some coffee and placed a plate of cold eggs and fried potatoes in front of him. Then she, too, went into the front room.

Pete forced the food down. He went outside and shoveled a path to the barn. Midway, he frowned. Why was he doing this? The barn no longer existed.

He stood at the edge of the remains—the ghostly foundation, smoldering coals, metal, and bones. Moments later, he lost his breakfast, and dropped to his knees in the snow.

Gertie and Gus. The cows. The pigs scheduled for market. The chickens. No more eggs for buying groceries. How would they live? What would they do?

The scrape of the snowplow in the distance grated his spine like nails on a chalkboard. At least the milk truck would get through. Wait… No more need for the milk truck. No more cash flow for Alvin. New sobs shook Pete's shoulders.

He went back into the house, and Alvin withdrew to the front room again. Emma tended the whistling teakettle. "Thank you for shoveling the walk."

"What else can I do?"

"The driveway has to be cleared." Her voice dropped to a near whisper. "Could you ride over to the Henderson's and ask them to plow after they've cleared themselves out?"

"I'll do that. I feel so bad for you." Saliva caught in his throat.

Emma turned away, and he headed out toward the machine shed. He mounted Maddie and slogged through the deep snow to Henderson's.

"How could the barn burn down with all the livestock when you were in there?" Ron Henderson shook his head. "And we didn't see or hear a thing other than that howling wind."

"It went fast once it started." Pete removed the heavy cap Emma had handed him as he went out the door. "The fire blocked the back door and the snow drifted against the front door. I couldn't push it open. By the time I got out a window, the whole barn erupted in flames. It was too late."

"The poor devil doesn't even have a horse to get to town anymore," Ron slid his feet into his boots, "or the money to buy more. He sold his car to make a farm payment. Sure, I'll get over there as soon as I can. Thanks, Doc."

Pete urged Maddie through the snowdrifts onto the plowed road where he rode in a daze back to the livery.

"I wondered where Maddie had gone to." Henry took the reins from Pete.

"Feed and water her, Henry. She's had a tough night."

"Looks like you had a tough night, too, Doc." Henry studied Pete in the semi-darkness of the stable.

Pete nodded. What more could he say?

Back home, he fell into bed wearing his coat and cap. He piled several quilts over him and closed his eyes.

A short time later he awoke to his own screams.

## 4

After dark Pete woke with a racing pulse.

Grief gripped him like a heart attack. With trembling hands, he lit a fire in the stove.

He sliced some homemade bread, made a ham sandwich, and carried it to a chair near the stove. When he brought the sandwich to his lips, his throat constricted. The ham—that putrid smell!

Holding his nostrils, he took a small bite, chewed it, and forced a swallow.

The poor, dead pigs. Alvin and Emma's farm. They'd lose it for sure.

His own parents had struggled after losing their house to a chimney fire. His mother used to say, "All we lost were *things*. At least we still have each other, and the Good Lord will provide." Through faith and hard work, they had recovered from the fire.

As a youngster, Pete claimed his parents' faith as his own, honoring God by being kind to others. A good student, he worked his way through college and vet school, believing God wanted him to prepare for a useful profession. When Betty came into his life, Pete thanked the Lord for leading him to such a wonderful lifetime partner.

The birth of perfect little Rose offered further proof of God's loving care. Pete put his heart into his veterinary practice, serving God by ministering to his community and supporting his family. And so he had brimmed with hope, confidence, and gratitude.

But since Rose died, nothing made sense anymore. Pete continued through the motions of daily life, but his purpose departed. As for God, Pete could only say, "I'm sorry." Sorry for not taking better care of his family, for not keeping the house warmer, and for letting fear cloud his judgement.

Was Betty right? Did Pete cause Rose's death? Her accusing tone and the scorn on her face remained fused in his memory like smoldering ashes. Alvin wore the same look yesterday. He blamed Pete for the fire.

Pete's chest constricted. And, why shouldn't Alvin blame him? He was there when it started. Why didn't he wake up in time to stop it? How could he possibly have slept through all that noise?

He tossed the remainder of his sandwich into the trash. What could he do to make amends? Was there a way to save Alvin and Emma's farm?

Pete sat by the stove until his eyelids grew heavy. He closed the dampers and drafts and went to bed in his coat and cap again. He woke screaming many times.

The morning sun crept above the window sill, exposing his grief with its blinding rays. The walls of the room closed in on him. He had to get out of there. See people.

Dizziness overwhelmed him as he stood. His heart pounded and his stomach churned. Shame he didn't have another bottle of whiskey.

He traced his fingers over the frigid iron then abandoned the stove. He didn't need a fire for such a short time. Quivering with chills, he took a quick sponge bath without shaving, and changed into jeans and a blue flannel shirt. He walked with a light tread toward the café. Perhaps his friends would comfort him.

With a sincere smile, he opened the door.

"I suppose you want coffee?" Arms crossed, Ruby frowned as "Jingle Bells" blared in the background.

"I'd like coffee and some eggs, potatoes, and a biscuit, please."

"You would, would you?" Ruby dipped her chin, and glowered.

"What's the matter, Ruby? What's wrong?" Why couldn't she turn off the radio?

"*You* are what's wrong, Doc." The creases in her forehead deepened. "You were drinking, weren't you? That's why the Thomas's' barn burned with all their animals. Henderson said Alvin smelled it on you. 'Strong,' he said. 'Real strong.'"

How could he deny that? Everyone in the café glared at him. He put on his cap and left, head hanging. He walked home to no holiday greetings or friendly waves.

Did everyone know?

<hr>

JENNY HOWE PLANTED her palms against the bedroom windowsill. Light snow drifted to the streets. She loved this rented room on the second floor of a large, white, corner house, across from the Catholic Church. The big window gave her a fine view of the wide streets and canopies over wooden boardwalks.

Cozy Kathleen Creek, Minnesota held enough small town charm to make her feel safe, yet offered many opportunities. The perfect place to make a fresh start in life. If only she could convince her parents of that.

"Your mother is right, you know." Her father had lectured

her during that awkward journey to her new community. "You're our only child, and you should stay closer to us than some god-forsaken nothing town a hundred miles away."

Jenny had ached with guilt. She'd left her poor teary-eyed mother too sick with a migraine to accompany them. Yet she'd made a wise decision and stuck to her guns.

"Father, with so many schools closing, there were no jobs in Minneapolis. And giving up the one I had to get married..." When her father opened his mouth, she gripped his arm. "Besides, I want to get away from all the gossip about me and Gerald."

"That gossip won't go on forever. Your mother and I don't like it either, but we're not going to move away because of it. Neither should you."

Even now, the terrible disgrace sickened Jenny. How embarrassing to have been engaged to a man arrested for embezzlement just two days before the big wedding her parents had planned for them. How could she not have known that Gerald was a thief?

*I wanted to have a nice house and car.* He'd fallen to his knees as she stared in shock. *I did it for you. I wanted you to have the finer things in life.*

His values differed so completely from hers, yet she hadn't seen that. How could she have been so blind?

Even worse, she'd been just as blind when engaged to Jed two years earlier. Head-over-heels in love, she would have done anything except quit her teaching job in the middle of the school year.

She shook her head. She'd enjoyed her students and her first teaching job. But those children... Most of their fathers couldn't find employment in that depressed area of the city. The children came to school in rags. They had no breakfast, no noon lunch pail, and no warm winter clothes.

Jenny used her own money to bring food to school, and

she'd bought clothes for some of them. They loved her, and she loved them. She'd refused to walk out on the ones who'd needed her so.

She cringed. What a rainy day when Jed told her he wanted to marry someone else, a girl who wanted to be a wife and mother. How could she have missed Jed's feelings and Gerald's dishonesty? She did want to be married and have children of her own. Someday.

But could she ever trust her choices again?

---

AT HOME PETE tossed a bundle of kindling into the front room stove and struck a match.

He held it between his fingers and thumb. The dancing light, eating away at the timbers of the barn. The screams and wails. Gertie, so sick and helpless, meeting her bitter end when he should have saved her. Emma's sobs, and Alvin's aloofness.

A jolt of pain surged through his hand, and he flicked the match. When it landed in the midst of the kindling, the flames leapt and grew, taunting and teasing him. *You were drinking, weren't you?*

Gulping, he added two chunks of dry oak, then put kindling to the kitchen cook stove, this time averting his gaze from the flames. He fried ham and eggs and served them with toast and apple butter. It made an attractive plate, the sort of meal Betty would have prepared.

The smell of burning flesh constricted his lungs. He gagged and threw his breakfast in the trash.

*Alvin smelled it on you.* How could he stop those words from running through his mind? Pete gripped the rim of the trash can. Why, oh why did he drink that night?

Better grab his medical bag and dump out what is left in his whiskey bottle. He opened the door to his office then felt a punch to his gut. His bag had burned, too. He clutched his chest. *Could* it be that his drinking caused the fire? He dropped into the nearest chair, his legs unable to hold him upright. *Was* he responsible?

That impressive leather bag had been a gift from his parents upon his graduation from the Iowa State College Veterinary School. Gone. Like Alvin's barn and all the animals. He put his head in his hands and moaned.

He tried to read the *Journal of the American Veterinary Medical Association,* but the words blurred on the page. If only he could block out the memory. Nothing worked, and his day and night filled with anguish. The next morning, the walls of the house smothered him yet again.

Where could he go? Not the café. No way could he face Ruby. He scratched his thick, matted locks. Perhaps the barber shop.

The familiar brown leather chair gave a comforting sense of normalcy, and the musky smell of after shave cleared the fire-stench from his nostrils. Pete's spirits lifted despite the loud Christmas song on the radio. Bob, the barber, gave his cape a sharp, angry shake and wrapped it around Pete in a brusque manner.

Pete grimaced. Should he address the reason for Bob's obvious disdain? He tapped his fingers against his pants leg. No sense in hiding it, he supposed. "You've heard of the tragedy at Alvin's?"

"Heard you were drunk as a skunk. And you tipped over the lantern, burned the barn and all the animals, and only saved yourself, if that's what you mean."

Pete's mouth turned down. "Sounds like I better get out of this chair before the target of those scissors is more than my hair."

Bob whipped the cloth from around Pete's neck. "If that's

what you prefer. Have a good day, if your conscience will let you."

Pete rushed out of the barber shop, bumping into someone coming in without looking to see who it was.

Did everyone in town feel the same?

No calls for his veterinary services. Did no one trust him? Without the distraction of his work, he could only wait in the empty house. Sleep eluded him, and food only made him nauseous.

After a dark three days, Pete emerged into bright sunlight and mild weather, a stark contrast to the violent storm. Maybe he should ride out to see if the Donaldson's and Volbrecht's' horses had survived. He made an early start and rode out on Mike, leaving Maddie to rest.

At the Volbrecht's' farm, Pete tied Mike to a tree at the edge of the property and entered the farmyard on foot. Volbrecht's son Billy greeted him with a smile. Finally, someone who trusted him… or, who hadn't heard yet. "I came to see how the horses are doing."

"The rendering truck came for them yesterday." Billy lifted one foot to rest on the shovel he had stuck into the snow. "Pa went to town. Do you want to talk to Ma?"

Pete's stomach lurched. He never got used to losing a patient. "No, Billy, just tell them I stopped by to check on them. Tell them I'm sorry. This epidemic has taken horses by the thousands, and there's not much we can do about it until it runs its course. You take care."

"Merry Christmas, Doc."

Heart heavy, Pete waved and mounted Mike. He leaned close to the horse's ear. "Let's get out of here before you get encephalitis, too."

Pete's shoulders slumped. He had done everything he could to save those horses. Such a terrible loss. At least the Volbrecht's didn't have a financial situation as dire as many of the others.

Like poor Alvin, collapsed in the snow in front of the burning embers, convulsing in sobs. A man down on his luck about as far as he could go.

Except for the loss of family, of course. Pete, too, had sobbed for weeks, until he had no tears left. He knew that kind of grief.

He prodded Mike into a gallop and rode on to the Donaldson's' farm.

Mr. Donaldson's piercing glare hit Pete in the face like a bucket of ice water. "I'll not be calling on you no more, no, siree! And to think you spent a whole night in my barn. Not one farmer will trust you now. Not a drinking man who doesn't know his responsibilities. No, siree! You got no business here. Go!"

Pete rode away as if chased by the devil. His chest burned, and heat spread over his face. Like a stuck needle on his Victrola, the angry words played again and again. *"Not one farmer will trust you now."*

He reached town at mid-morning. If only he could find a friendly face and a cup of coffee.

Subdued chatter and the smell of fragrant roasted beans filled the busy café. Pete found an empty stool at the counter, and the chatter stopped.

The radio announcer gave the weather report and introduced the next song. The café patrons remained silent, their gazes directed toward Pete.

Pete snagged Ruby's arm. "What's going on?"

She jerked away. "Alvin and Emma have to be out of their house in sixty days. They got a final notice of foreclosure."

"Oh, God!" Pete bolted up and staggered out the door. He zigzagged down the street until he reached the church. Sobbing, he found his way to the back pew.

For a long time, he wailed in the empty sanctuary. He cried for Alvin and Emma. For Gertie and Gus and all the animals he had loved. For the trust he had lost in the community.

He cried for Betty and for Rose. For his own loneliness. After emptying his tears, he lifted his head and reached into his pocket for a handkerchief.

Next to him, Pastor Jim cleared his throat and scooted closer down the pew. "You had a good cry, Pete. You must have needed one."

"You might say that." Pete blew his nose into his handkerchief.

"You have troubles." The pastor patted his arm.

"You might say that, too." Pete wiped his eyes, blew his nose again, and put his handkerchief back into his pocket. "You must have heard what happened."

"Yes, and everyone blames you."

"Wasn't my fault. Second night in a row sleeping in a barn. I spent the night before with the Donaldsons' horses and didn't get a wink. And then, I slept so sound in Alvin's barn. Didn't hear the fire until it blocked the back door." Pete's shoulders heaved. "The front door wouldn't open because of the drifted snowbank. No way to get the animals out. They screamed and ran around and..." He pinched his nose. "I smelled burning flesh. Couldn't breathe because of the heavy smoke. Thought I was going to die in there with the animals."

Pastor Jim folded his hands over his knees. "Well, Pete, God spared your life. He has plans for you."

"But don't you see? No one trusts me anymore. I doubt if anyone will call on me for their vet needs now. The Thomases have lost their farm." New tears stung Pete's eyes, and he wrung his hands. "Where will they go? They have nothing! People blame me."

"Why don't we pray together, Pete?"

Pete wiped his face with his hands and bowed his head.

Pastor Jim put his hand on Pete's shoulder and prayed, "Father God, Pete comes to you today a broken, fallen man, but he seeks forgiveness for his transgressions. Give him the courage to face life amidst the antagonism surrounding him and the strength to never drink again. Show him the way, Lord. In Jesus name we pray. Amen."

Pete chewed his lower lip. "I think..., I'm pretty sure..., I might have started the fire. I took the lantern from the hook, and I don't remember hanging it back up again. Must have set it on the floor and that's what happened." He rubbed his temples. "I don't know how else it could have gotten started. I was drinking. I shouldn't have been drinking. God forgive me, I must be responsible for Alvin losing his barn and all his animals."

Pastor Jim held Pete as he sobbed again. "You are forgiven, Pete. Now, it's up to you to go to God every time you're lonely or troubled. God will always give you peace and comfort and courage and strength. Whatever it is you need at that time. We have an awesome God, Pete, and He loves you."

Thin-lipped, Pete shook his head. "No one loves me now. No one trusts me."

"God loves you. And I love you, Pete. Always have." Pastor Jim scooted away and faced him. "You don't realize this, but you're like a son to Karen and me. From the time we came to town when you were a teenager you've done so much for us. We pray for you every day."

"How can God love me when I've done such a horrible thing?"

"God's love is not contingent upon good deeds, Pete. God forgives you this transgression. Now you must forgive yourself."

Pete drew in a deep breath and slowly released it. "That won't be so easy. What do I do now?"

Pastor Jim rose and leaned on the back of the pew in front of them.

"It might be good to go somewhere else for a while. Do you have family in another city or state that you could go visit?"

"No. No one. My parents are gone, and I'm an only child." Pete stood and shoved his hands in his pockets. "Betty has siblings, but they're all far away and I barely know them. I don't know where I'd go. But there's nothing here for me anymore."

"You don't deserve the troubles you've had, but most of us don't." Pastor Jim patted Pete's arm. "But we don't deserve the grace God gives us every day, either. In spite of your losses, you've been blessed as well. Count your blessings, Pete, not your problems. Go in peace. God bless you."

A huge Christmas tree, decorated and glittering, filled the front corner by the piano. Pete wrinkled his brow. Who'd brought it in? He used to do that before Betty and Rose died. He'd hardly been to church this past year. Memories of the funeral were too painful.

Pastor Jim shook Pete's hand, and they left the church together.

His heart a touch lighter, Pete crossed the yard back to the café to get Mike. Did he really start that fire? He must have. Pastor Jim said God forgave him.

But how could he ever forgive himself?

5

Back home, Pete let himself in and wandered through the dark kitchen. Pastor Jim thought he could make amends to Alvin. But how? He picked up his Bible. Maybe he'd find an answer there.

He flipped through the pages as he had on the evenings when he used to read aloud from it while Betty knitted. Rose played quietly at their feet, or sometimes sat on Pete's lap and listened.

Where should he start? The Bible said God would forgive him, but where did it say how to forgive himself? How to make amends? How to get people to trust him again?

Tight-chested, he put the Bible aside and bowed his head. "Lord, I don't know what to do. What should I do?"

Of course, no answer. Pete got up and built a fire in the cook stove. When it snapped and crackled, he put on a pot of coffee and made a sandwich. "Lord, what should I do?"

Still no answer.

*Foreclosure notice. Sixty days to vacate. Not even a horse to ride into town.*

Pete could give them Mike or Maddie. Could he get by with

one horse? How could he break up his team? Which one could he part with?

Neither.

A splash of coffee hissed on the stove, and its aromatic, nutty scent wafted to his nostrils. What was he thinking? Was this the answer from God he was looking for?

He pulled the pot away from the hottest part of the stove before it boiled over. *Give them one of my horses?* With a slight tremble, he carried his sandwich and coffee to his chair by the front room stove.

God had forgiven him. It was time to stop looking backward. He needed to make amends no matter the cost.

*Give them one of my horses?*

Pete returned to his chair. He chewed the dry ham and forced himself to swallow "But one horse for a whole barn full of animals is hardly making amends, is it?"

He tore off another bite. "I don't have enough money to build them a new barn or replace the livestock. Besides they've lost the farm anyway. They don't need a new barn."

They needed a place to live.

Pete sat straighter. They could live in his house. He could give them his house!

But where would he live? He'd have nowhere to go. "Lord, what should I do? Please tell me what to do."

Pete carried his plate to the kitchen, poured another cup of coffee, and put more wood on the fire. *Give them my house?*

Betty's bright floral plates blurred as he washed them. Where could he go? At the least, he needed an office for vet supplies and equipment. Where could he go?

Out the window, Rose's tree swing squeaked as it swung in the wind. A lump formed in his throat. She'd laughed hard as he pushed her, her long dark hair blowing about her cherub face.

How could he leave all these memories here? Betty smiling

as she took out a pan of hot biscuits from the oven. The smell of her that still lingered in her closet. How could he leave?

He closed the draft and damper on the kitchen stove and did the same in the front room. Then he bundled up and walked over to the livery.

Henry grunted. "Doc."

"Just want to talk to Mike and Maddie." Pete's frozen breath danced around his face.

"Ain't many people around here you can talk to, I suppose." Henry stroked his white beard.

"What am I supposed to do, Henry? Even if it was my fault about the barn, what can I do about it?"

"That's not for me to say, Pete. I don't know what Alvin and Emma can do about it, neither. Henderson brought Alvin into town yesterday looking for work, but there ain't no jobs to be had, you know that. Henderson said the neighbors are helpin' them out with milk and eggs." Henry untied a dusty, brown burlap bag of oats and emptied it into a wooden barrel. "I don't know where they'll live when the time is up. Everybody likes the Thomases."

Pete cringed. "How are Mike and Maddie doing?"

"Nothin' wrong with Mike and Maddie." Henry replaced the cover on the barrel, turned, and shuffled away.

Maddie nickered and Mike whinnied when he approached their stall. "I missed you, too." He caressed both their faces. "Is Henry taking good care of you? How could I ever give you two up?"

Maddie nuzzled his shoulder.

"No way. It would be like tearing out my heart."

After a few minutes with his team, Pete strolled toward the general store to buy coffee. "Good afternoon, Mrs. Wilson."

Emma's close friend held his gaze as she came out of the store. "Hello, Doc. How are you?"

He lifted his chin. Why had she not turned away from him? "Okay."

She put her hand on his arm. "Pete, I've always liked you. Right now, I'm praying for you." She reached for his hand and gave it a squeeze. "I know Alvin won't talk to you, but Emma is a Christian woman. She knows it was an accident, and she forgives you."

Pete's breath caught. Emma... forgave him?

"She hasn't shared this with anyone else, but you should know, after waiting for so many years, they are expecting a baby. She fears this stress might cause her to have a miscarriage. Please pray that won't happen. I'm concerned about her. I'm praying for all of you." Mrs. Wilson pressed a small bronze square into his palm and folded his fingers over it. "Merry Christmas, Pete."

Pete clutched the gift, a wave of dizziness passing over him. He muttered syllables that might have passed for thanks and stumbled backwards, steadying himself against the building.

Sometime later, he staggered into his own home. How had he gotten here?

He unfolded his fingers, the bronze square cold against his palm. Prayer hands. Carved by Alvin, no doubt. Perhaps a gift meant for one of the Wilson's children.

Alvin had always been affectionate with Rose and often discussed his desire to have children. He and Emma married young, and after twelve years, remained childless. Now, worry over the loss of their farm marred their wonderful news. Losing this baby would be the last straw for them. That mustn't happen.

Pete fell to his knees by his chair. "Lord, I have to do something. I can't let them lose a child, too. You want me to give them my house? Yes, I'll give them my house." He gripped the upholstered arm, brushing his thumb over the stitches where

Betty had once repaired the chair. "Shall I give them one of my horses?"

He imagined a younger Betty with her swollen belly, standing next to Maddie when she carried Rose. "But Emma can't ride a horse in her condition. I'll give them my buggy. And one of the horses to pull the buggy."

To part his team? How could he? "No, I'll give them both Mike and Maddie. I'll still have my car." His shoulders heaved. "They need this more than I do."

Before he could change his mind, Pete hurried to the attorney's office on Main Street. In an hour, he returned. Still in his coat, he hurried to Betty's writing desk. He uncapped the ink and dipped a pen.

*Dear Alvin and Emma,*

*There is no way to make up for what I did, but perhaps this will help. Please accept this gift-- the deed to my house, now transferred to your name. I have also enclosed the key. The mortgage is paid. If you encounter any problems, the new attorney Clarence Routio can answer your questions.*

*Feel free to do what you want with the furniture and other things in the house. I will be gone before you get this letter.*

Pete dipped the quill again, tiny drops of ink trailing as he moved it across the page. *I also want you to have my buggy and team. I trust you'll take good care of Mike and Maddie.*

*Alvin, Emma, please forgive me. I hope you and your family will find the same happiness that Betty, Rose, and I had when we lived in this house. I'll write when I can.*

Pete reread the letter, his chest constricting.

*Sincerely, Dr. Peter Walters.*

Once he'd placed the letter in the envelope, he added the house key. Teary-eyed, he scanned the room one last time then carried the letter to the door.

6

Pete found Pastor Jim at the parsonage. "I need a favor." His hands shook as he held out the envelope. "Will you please go out to the Thomas's day after tomorrow and deliver this to them? It contains the deed to my house, my key, and a letter stating that I give them the house and everything in it, my buggy, and Mike and Maddie."

Pastor Jim's eyes widened. "Pete. God chose to keep you alive in that fire. He must have plans for you. You have to stop feeling sorry for yourself and ride this out. Don't give up."

Pete pressed the envelope into Pastor Jim's hand. "Maybe God has plans for me, but it has to be somewhere else. I don't know where yet, but I don't belong here anymore. I'll let the Lord direct me, I guess."

Pastor Jim tucked the letter in his coat pocket. "You can't up and leave with nothing more than a car. Where would you go? Where would you live?" He gripped Pete's shoulder. "Do you have any money?"

"A little. Not much."

"It's the middle of winter, Pete. It's too cold to be traveling. You'll freeze."

Pete tugged at the collar of his coat. "No worries. I'll head south where it's warmer."

"Do you know how dangerous it is out there? You should hear some of the stories about tramps." Pastor Jim pointed toward the end of town, where drunks huddled next to the saloon. "Desperate men kill for warm clothes and something to eat."

"I won't be traveling in the company of tramps, Pastor. I'll be okay."

"You're like my son, Pete. It would kill Karen to think of you wandering around homeless. I'm sure we can find another way for Alvin and Emma. And what will this community do without a vet? We need you, Pete."

Pete clenched his jaw. "Well, nobody's needed me since the fire."

"That'll die down in time. People forget."

Forget that he'd destroyed everything? That he'd left Alvin with nothing? "I've got to do this. I can't live with myself if I don't. This doesn't begin to cover it, but I have to make amends."

"Will you at least wait another week? Think this thing through? Let me see what I can do for Alvin and Emma. Please?"

"I don't know, Pastor. The papers are ready." Pete backed toward the door.

Pastor Jim handed the envelope back to Pete. "Please, Pete, just take time to think this through. You're moving too fast."

Pete drummed his fingers against his thigh. Finally, he accepted the envelope. "Okay, I'll wait a week."

"God bless you, Pete. Your heart is in the right place, but there has to be a better way."

If this wasn't the way, then what was? Pete left the church and glanced at a looming gray cloud blocking the sun. "Lord, help me know what's right."

He put the thick white envelope into his inside coat pocket

and trudged through the afternoon twilight with shoulders hunched against the wind. Maybe he shouldn't give away his house, buggy, and team. Maybe there was another way.

The snow crunched beneath his feet as he passed several houses, colors swirling into blurs. Where would he sleep if he left? Some towns were a long way apart. He could be robbed and then what would he do?

"How are you doing, Doc?" Henry waved from the doorway of the livery. "You look like you're lost."

Pete stopped and blinked at Henry. "Lost in thought, I guess."

"Come on in and have a cup of coffee. You look almost froze, too."

Pete gaped. Was it possible Henry had forgiven him, too?

"Sit down, Doc. How are you, really?"

His brow creased, Pete followed Henry to an old oak chair next to the wood-burning stove. He removed his gloves and accepted a mug of coffee, breathing in the wonderful aroma. How could he answer?

Henry had always been a good listener and not one to gossip. "I guess it's tough to have people down on you like they are." He took the chair next to Pete.

"It's worse to be down on myself."

"It's not like you did it on purpose."

"Nonetheless, I did it." Pete gritted his teeth. "I'm responsible for the Thomas's losing their farm. Thinking I could give them my house and my horse and buggy, but it still wouldn't make up for it."

Henry rubbed the back of his neck. "Well, it would give them a place to live and a way to get around."

"Should I do it?" Pete sat forward.

"When Alvin came in here asking for work, he looked like the world sat on his shoulders. Never saw a man so down." Henry's jaw twitched. "Then I heard today that Emma's in the family way. She's had two miscarriages. If she loses this baby, I don't know what they'll do. They've tried to have a family for more than twelve years, now. If anyone deserves children, it's them two."

"Henry, this afternoon I went to see that new young lawyer, Routio and transferred ownership of my house to Alvin. I brought the papers to Pastor Jim to bring to Alvin and Emma, but he asked me to wait a week. He thinks he can find them somewhere else to live."

"I don't know where that'd be. And even if they found an old farmhouse, how'd they get around?" Henry got up, paced in a circle in front of the stove, and shook his head. "They don't have a horse or a buggy, and Emma in the family way."

"I don't know what I should do." Pete gripped his head in his hands.

"Son," Henry sat, "You're young, and you don't have a family, and I'm sorry 'bout that but it's a fact. If you feel in your heart that you want to donate what you have to them, and if it makes you feel better for doing it… then you should follow your heart and do it. You could be saving the life of that little baby."

He stroked his beard. "Not that I don't care about you, 'cause I do. But, you'll find a way to make out on your own. You're strong and you've got a trade you can practice anywhere you go. Follow your heart, Pete. And I wouldn't be waitin' too long on it, neither."

Pete took the last swallow of coffee, put his mug down on the wide tree stump Henry used as a table, and gave Henry a rueful grin. "Do you have any empty boxes? I need to pack."

"No, son I don't. But you should be able to get some at the saloon." He offered a wide smile as he patted Pete on the back.

"I'll go back and ask Pastor Jim to come get my buggy and horses day after tomorrow and deliver them, along with the deed and key to my house. Have my bill ready tomorrow. And include the next couple months feed and board for Mike and Maddie. I'm sure it'll take at least that long for Alvin to get on his feet." Pete extended his hand. "And thanks for helping me sort this out. You're a good man, Henry."

*Thank you, Lord.* Pete hurried the three blocks back to the parsonage.

Karen answered the door.

Pete waved the envelope and rushed in past her. "Hi Karen. I need to speak to Pastor Jim. You, too."

Pastor Jim came into the living room with a furrowed brow. "What's the matter, Pete?"

"I'm sorry, but I have to go back on my promise to wait a week. I need to do this now. I've thought about it, and I've prayed about it, and it's what I have to do and I have to do it now."

Pastor Jim opened his mouth.

"Wait, wait." Pete held up his hand. "I've made my decision, and it stands."

"Jim told me what you want to do, Pete." Karen sighed. "I'm as concerned about you as he is, but I can see that you're determined to do this, so I can only pray for your safety and wish you well, even though I'll probably cry every day."

"Pete, what changed your mind? I thought we decided to wait a week." Pastor Jim stepped closer.

"It's the right thing to do. I know you're worried about me, but I'll be okay. So will you please go out day after tomorrow with my team and buggy to give these to the Thomas's? I'll be gone by then." Pete handed the pastor the envelope.

"What shall I tell Alvin and Emma?"

"That I wish them all the best in the world."

"They'll want to thank you."

"I don't need thanks. It still doesn't amend all they lost. Alvin is a farmer. I don't know how he'll earn a living in town, but it's all I have to offer. I hope in time Alvin can forgive me. Now I just have to find a way to forgive myself and earn people's trust again."

"Do you want to stay with us for a while?" Karen faced her husband and quirked her brow.

"Yes, why don't you stay here, at least until warmer weather?" Pastor Jim nodded.

"No, but thank you both. I need to get away."

"Then God bless you wherever you go. You'll be in my thoughts and prayers." He put his arms around Pete and held him.

"Thanks Pastor. I appreciate that you're doing this for me. I'll write to you."

He pivoted, bracing his shoulders for the great sense of loss. Instead, a wonderful sense of peace came over him. *Peace? How?*

Of course. The peace surpassing all understanding. "Thank you, Lord." The wind carried his whisper. "I will follow where you lead. Keep me safe."

Yet, after only a few more steps, cold creeping fear washed over him. What would he find out in the world?

## 7

Pete admired the Christmas decorations gracing the gaslights along Main Street. With a smile, he picked up empty boxes from the saloon and drove home.

Alvin and Emma would find happiness with their baby in the house that lost its joy when Betty and Rose died. He'd done the right thing.

By the time he got home, Pete's excitement waned. Betty's face appeared where he'd tried to imagine Emma's, and their faceless child's features shifted into Rose. How could he leave them behind?

Shivering, he built a fire with the last of the kindle wondering how long the dreadful flames would haunt him. He placed an empty box near the silent telephone in his cold office, next to rows of brown medicine bottles and his collection of herbs. He picked up his hoof knife and put it in his pocket.

After emptying his desk and bookshelves, he filled another box with medicines and arranged some veterinary supplies in two more boxes. Then he carried the boxes to the Ford. His larger pieces of equipment already rode in the trunk. Once back in the house he paced, his heart creeping up into his throat.

He had to keep busy.

Next, his stethoscope and thermometer. He might need them on the trip. He reached for his medical bag and then smacked his forehead. Oh, the fire. "But that's *all* I lost." Poor Alvin and Emma.

Still, his instruments… What could he put them in? He pulled Betty's carpetbag out of the closet and placed them into the bottom.

His eyes misted. His wife, his daughter, and his profession. His home, his team, and his buggy. He had nothing left.

In the bedroom, he crawled under the covers with his clothes on and fell into a troubled sleep.

Another nightmare woke him. He blinked several times as the fog in his brain lifted. When he closed his eyes, snaps, crackles, shrieks, and screams filled his mind once more. Pete twisted the thick wool blanket around him. If only sleep would come. He needed the escape.

The next morning, the telephone remained silent. He forced down breakfast and then sorted through the items in the bedroom and kitchen. Betty's clothes. Rose's little outfits. Betty's dishes. He'd leave them all.

Pete put an extra set of underwear, a shirt, four large handkerchiefs, and three pairs of socks into the carpetbag for quick access during the trip, and then packed the rest of his clothes in one of the boxes.

Was there anything else? Rose's beloved Raggedy Ann doll lay on her bed. He held it close, then put it into the carpetbag.

The sweater Betty had been knitting for him lay in a heap of yarn, unfinished. He breathed its scent. If only he could smell her in the yarn.

He only smelled wool.

He added it to the carpetbag, with Betty's small scissors, a couple of needles, and black thread from her sewing box.

Betty's favorite poetry book. Edna St. Vincent Millay's *A Few*

*Figs from Thistles.* He tucked it into the carpetbag with his Bible and then grabbed his toothbrush, razor, bar of soap and a towel.

He'd better bring fishing line, hooks, bobber, lures, and sinker. He could always cut a pole. As he dug through the tackle box, dust scattered. His fingers landed on an old fly Father had tied to his line when he was only a boy. Father often rewarded him with fishing excursions in the Platte River, a special treat for doing his chores.

Oh, to go back to the times he and Father leaned against trees and shared a silent lunch while the water flowed past. The river had crept into his soul with a warm feel of comfort and security. Later, picnics with Betty drew him even closer to the water as their love poured that music into his heart.

"My harmonica!" He gripped the cool metal and brought it to his lips. Betty had loved it when he played for her and read poetry. He had to bring it.

When had he last played it? Before Rose's illness, for sure. He sounded out a few tunes. Oh, those memories. They hurt so much.

He used to be so happy—the apple of his parents' eyes and the one true love of Betty's life. What would they think if they could see him now? A loser. A falling-down, barn-burning drunk.

Pastor Jim's voice came back to him, *"God spared your life. He has plans for you."*

What a miracle he'd survived the barn fire. The lantern must have sat close to where Pete lay sleeping. How had the flames not touched him as they spread along the hay-strewn floor?

Pete's mailbox squeaked. He opened the door as the mailman took the Sears and Roebuck catalog from his satchel.

"Here, Pete. Merry Christmas."

"Thank you, Caleb." No Christmas cards. No personal letters. Just a catalog. He waved to Caleb, shuffled inside, and tossed the catalog on the table.

"What am I doing with my life?" He returned to his chair and slammed his fists against the arm. "I've wasted a year on self-pity."

When had he last felt gratitude? When had he been glad to be alive or set goals for his future? How long since his veterinary practice shone with meaning?

The practice had been his mission, his duty, his life's work. During this past year it had served as an escape from his remorse and loneliness. Like a rat in a flood clinging to a floating log, Pete kept a tight focus on his daily tasks. Afraid to face the long, bleak, empty future that awaited him. Afraid to admit that he longed for a second chance at happiness with a loving wife.

He had no right to hope for such a thing, but he could live out his years as a competent veterinarian.

"But now my veterinary degree isn't worth the paper it's written on." Pete scuffed his feet across the wood floor. "This town wants rid of me. No one trusts me."

"No one!" He stood, raising his voice. "So what are you going to do about it, Pete Walters? Can you make good use of the life God gave you? Can you be a veterinarian people trust? Can you make up for your mistakes? Can you make a life for yourself again? A meaningful life? Can you do that?"

How could he? Tears streamed as he collapsed back into his chair.

"How can I do that, Lord?" Pete covered his face with his hands. "Do you have plans for me, like Pastor Jim said? How can I make amends in my life? How can I find trust again? Please forgive me and help me to forgive myself. In Jesus' name, Amen."

His heart still weighed more than an anchor. He needed to keep busy. What did Betty always say? Idle hands were the devil's tools or something like that. What would Betty do?

He picked up a broom and swept the floors, kicking up a

year's worth of dust. They needed it. Then he washed the few dirty dishes and wiped down the furniture. Why hadn't he noticed all this dust before?

Next, he heated water for the car radiator. Had he forgotten anything else? Oh, his pistol. He put the gun and all his bullets in the carpetbag.

He patted his jacket pocket. Was his new folding hoof knife still there? It was. He could use the different blades for many tasks.

Pete couldn't put it off any longer. He had to do his errands and say goodbye to Mike and Maddie.

He closed the stove, dressed in warm clothes, and brought the heated water to pour into the radiator. The engine sputtered, steadying as it warmed. Along the driveway, fresh snow diminished under the beating sun. He drove along, his breaths heavier with each turn of the wheel.

First stop, the bank. He approached the teller, his stomach churning. "I'd like to close my account."

"Close your account?" The pretty brunette's face twisted into a frown. "This bank is safe."

"I know it is, but I'm, ah, moving away."

"I'm sorry to hear that, Dr. Walters. How would you like your cash?"

"A hundred ones, a hundred fives, a hundred tens and the rest in twenties."

She stuffed bound stacks of bills into two canvas bags and pushed them across the counter. "That's an awful lot of cash to carry with you."

"It is." He scooped a bag under each arm and headed back to the car. Next, the gas station. In the blustering cold, he filled his tank and bought a gallon of alcohol to keep his water from freezing.

He set off for the electric and telephone companies. Then, at the post office, he waited in a short line. When he reached the postmistress, he drew in a deep breath.

"May I help you?" She continued stamping envelopes.

"Please hold my mail for further notice. I'll send a new address… well, I'll send one whenever I can. And I need a few three-cent stamps."

Finally, he drove to the livery. Henry nodded to him as he added a huge piece of wood to his barrel stove.

"Is my bill ready?"

Henry stirred the embers with his poker and then moved to his desk. "Here it is." He passed Pete a yellow paper.

"And here's the cash." His chest heaving, he handed Henry several folded bills. "I'm going to go see my…" He cleared his throat. "Alvin's horses."

Henry lowered his head and shook it as Pete shuffled to Mike's stall.

"M-m-mi…" Pete pressed his damp cheek against the horse's face.

Mike lifted his head and whinnied. In the next stall, Maddie nudged the door a couple times. *God, please keep them safe.*

He staggered back out to his car.

"Wait a minute." Henry chased after him. He handed Pete an old, worn rawhide leather cape. "My uncle did a lot of wandering around the country. When he came home to stay, he gave me this cape. Said it was the best thing to take when you're traveling. I know it don't look like much, but Uncle Cliff swore by it. "

Pete held the coarse, brown cape up in front of him, hiding his misty eyes. He gulped back a sob. "T-thanks, Henry. I appreciate it."

"Well…" Henry scratched the back of his neck. "I never did do no traveling and I ain't about to start now. Good luck to you, Pete. God bless you."

They shook hands, and Pete drove home. His last night in Grand Island, Nebraska.

At home, Pete shivered. Cold, quiet and lonely, the same as it had been since Betty and Rose died. Would he ever have a family to love again?

The clock chimed five times as the room darkened. The gloom of the cloudy day had brought the dusk early. What else should he pack? What would he need on the trip? And for that matter, where was he going? Would he be safe?

He patted the bags of money. How could he keep them hidden? With one of Betty's scarves, he fashioned a money belt. Then he ate and closed the stoves, then checked them again before going to bed.

The next morning, he awoke in the dark. Something was wrong. He patted the sheets next to him and sat up in bed. Then he remembered. Today would be the last day in this house. For a moment he couldn't breathe. Would he regret giving it away?

He dragged one foot after the other onto the frigid floor, forcing himself to face the day. After breakfast, he wrapped the remaining ham and put it, along with a sharp knife, into the carpetbag.

What else could he take? The rest of the bread and the apple butter would sustain him. And, he'd need another knife.

He filled his wallet and money belt with enough cash to keep him for a few days. He would hide most of it in the car, in case of robbery.

Better scan the house one last time. Clean dishes, neat kitchen, the wood box half-filled, and the winter's supply stacked behind the house. Pete's breath caught. *I'm really doing this. God help me.*

He donned his cap and fumbled with the buttons on his coat. With shaking hands, he carried a teakettle of steaming water outside. The eastern sky glowed almost as fiery as those flames in Alvin's barn. But like the Phoenix, the sun rose in a slow, majestic arc through the red horizon in a glorious bright yellow orb, warm and welcoming.

In the silence of the dawn, tears rushed to the surface. The moment… almost holy. The wind no longer stung his face as he lifted it to the sun. A peace washed over him like he'd never felt before, an assurance that he would be okay.

He lifted the hood of the car and poured the hot water into the radiator, adding the alcohol so he wouldn't have to drain the radiator while traveling. The engine sputtered to life when he turned the key. "Good girl, Lizzie!" He patted the hood and brought the kettle back into the house. Then he emptied the cook stove of hot coals and brought the pail outside. The embers sizzled in the cold snow, and he smiled. No chimney fire today.

He set the pail back inside and bowed his head. "Show me where to go to make amends, Lord, and let me find a place where people will trust me again." His chest heaved.

"And Lord, please keep me safe along the way."

Pastor Jim's words played in his mind, and he shuddered. *"Desperate men kill for warm clothes and something to eat."*

8

As Pete drove south, high banks lined the roadsides. Snow-packed gravel surfaces made headway slippery and slow. The sun shot up in the clear blue sky, casting glittery diamonds on the mounds, creating a fairy-land atmosphere.

How lucky was he to have given away most everything he owned, and yet to revel in such luxury while riding along in his nice car? His parents deserved thanks for the sizable inheritance they'd left him, their only heir. His richness exceeded most others in Grand Island, especially during what their newspaper editor had dubbed The Great Depression of 1934. He was blessed beyond measure.

Pete idled at a crossroads and wiped a spot from his windshield. He caught his reflection in the mirror, just as he had when he first bought the car. Such a fun day. After considering many makes and models, he had decided on the new Ford V-8 Standard Tudor Model 18 in blue. A reliable vehicle, with space for a growing family. The trunk in the back served well for carrying his veterinary equipment and supplies. The white sidewall tires and the side mounts made it aesthetically pleasing. Though the $490 price tag took much of his inheritance, he had never been sorry for buying it. And now, it was only thing he had left.

How he ached for Mike and Maddie. They had been part of his life ever since he began his practice. Advanced in age, they still performed admirably. Would they miss him?

Alvin would treat them well, but Pete would grieve for a long time. Would he ever find another team like them?

Though he wore long woolen underwear, thick woolen socks, heavy work boots and rubber buckled overshoes, his feet remained cold. Where could he find warmer weather?

Dallas, Texas?

As a child, Pete had met a family from Dallas while visiting friends. Their accent intrigued him. They seemed other-worldly, and the mystique stayed with him.

"We'll be seein' ya. Y'all come-n-visit Texas sometime." The father, a broad-shouldered boisterous man, had engulfed him in a hug.

Pete drummed his fingers on the seat. Texas. It should be warm there. And they must need vets. "Think ah'll go to Dallas, Texas."

Pete settled against the back rest and relaxed his grip on the steering wheel. He'd consult his maps at the next stop. Texas. It'd be a long trip. Plenty far enough to leave the fires and guilt behind him.

He made a restroom stop in southern Nebraska and a few hours later a small café at the Kansas border. He enjoyed his solitary meal of crisp fried chicken, mashed potatoes, and gravy. His shoulders relaxed as he returned smiles and nodded to other customers. No one there knew him or what he had done.

After eating and checking his maps, he laid 25 cents on the counter in front of the cashier.

"Thank you, sir." The twiggy redhead pressed a key on the embossed bronze cash register, and the drawer popped out.

"Oh, here." Pete took out another nickel. "Give me one of those Powerhouse candy bars for the road."

She traded him the nickel for the candy, and he tipped his hat to her. "Have a nice day, miss."

A few miles farther, he stopped at a gas station.

The young attendant sprinted to his car, cranked the handle on the pump, and filled his tank. "Goin' far?"

"Texas." Pete brushed dust from the window seal.

"I'll get that for ya." The lad washed his windshield with a flourish and wiped a damp rag across the seal. "That'll be one dollar, and ten cents. Eleven cents a gallon, sir."

Pete gave the attendant his money, used the restroom, and continued southward.

After a while, flat plains became steep slopes as Pete passed into Kansas. He drove along miles of hills and sand dunes and crossed the North Fork River. Soon, he encountered farmland and then rugged hills.

Deep grooves from the snow plows exposed dark soil. Pete had only seen such black earth when dust storms passed through Grand Island during the summer. It had traveled so far.

Such varied terrain. Who could have thought such a place would be so interesting? Little Rose would have been fascinated.

He closed his eyes, picturing the calendar he'd left on the corner of his desk. Pain pierced his heart. The funeral, one year ago today… no, he mustn't think of that. He'd only think good things about Betty and Rose. Good things like Betty on their wedding day, her white gown trailing on the floor as her father walked her down the aisle. Her dark hair fell over her shoulders, long, shiny, wavy and beautiful. He loved to run his fingers through it as they lay in bed at night. Her lips so soft.

Enough! Remembering Betty only worsened his pain. He'd think about Rose instead and the time when he bought her a little red tricycle.

She'd feared it at first, but after Pete pushed her around on it, she loved it. She delighted in peddling by herself. A glow warmed his heart. That beautiful smile. How blessed had he been to have her for more than five years. He must remember to cherish the time he shared with both Betty and Rose.

The sunny day turned to nightfall. Pete found a small boardinghouse in Salina to spend the night. He paid the owner and accepted his key. "Thank you, Mrs. Jacobson."

"You're welcome, Pete." Mrs. Jacobson tucked a graying wisp behind her ear. "I hope you enjoy your stay."

When he finally slept, he dreamed about being trapped in the burning barn with shrieking animals. He awoke to his own screams and sat up in bed.

Mrs. Jacobson rushed in, her eyes wide and darting. "Is everything okay?"

"I'm so sorry for disturbing you, Mrs. Jacobson." Pete massaged his temples. "It was only a nightmare."

"It's no matter." She pulled the door closed behind her.

Pete tossed and turned in the bed, wrapping himself in sweat-drenched sheets. Those horrible sounds... The putrid stenches... Even now, his irresponsible actions affected more than just himself. Would he ever stop reliving that fire?

After a tasty breakfast of hot biscuits and gravy, Pete paid Mrs. Jacobson 50-cents. "Again, ma'am, please accept my apologies for disturbing you."

"Be safe, Pete." She squeezed his hand.

"Will do." He stepped outside into a blustery wind. Looming gray clouds prevented the sun from peeking through. Hopefully he wouldn't soon be driving in a blizzard. The unpaved, snow-packed roadways already had treacherous spots.

The sun reappeared by lunchtime, shining over a beautiful landscape, with many sandstone hills. After a brief stop, he resumed his journey through town after town.

On occasion, he encountered a passing train on their outskirts. Men rode inside and on top of boxcars. Near the inn and stores, hobos shuffled around with their long hair and beards, wearing old clothes and a variety of packs. Housewives sometimes stood in open doorways passing out food.

Every sight of the hobos deepened his sorrow. They fared much worse than he did. His homelessness would be temporary.

Many of the men and women trudged along with shoulders slumped, heads hanging. As they huddled around trash can fires with their bony, wind-burned faces, their lips quivered.

*There, but for the grace of God go I.* Pete patted his money belt closer. He would be okay.

At his next gas station stop, an old Model T pulled up behind him. A mother and little girl headed toward the restroom while the father filled his tank. The gaunt man wore a coat that had seen too many days. His hands shook as he paid the attendant.

As the mother and daughter returned to the car, the little girl whined. "But how will Santa Claus find us if we're not home?"

"Santa won't be able to find us this year, honey." The mother closed her eyes as though holding back a flood of tears. "We'll be in the car. But next year he'll have even more presents for you." She turned away and wiped her cheek.

"But I asked Santa for a dolly," the little girl cried. "I want a dolly."

Pete palmed the handle of his carpetbag, Rose's doll tugging at his heartstrings.

The mother ushered the child into the back seat and got into the front as the man returned from the restroom.

Pete dashed to intercept him. "I overheard that your daughter wants a doll from Santa. I… I have my daughter's doll in the car. S-s-she can't use it anymore." His chest heaved. "I'd like to give it to you so Santa can bring her a doll."

"Why would you do that?" The man frowned.

"My daughter passed away last year." Pete extended his hand, then withdrew it when the man remained rooted to the spot, arms hanging limp from his shoulders. "I know she'd be pleased for your daughter to have it. It's in my car. Come on. You can put it under your jacket so she doesn't see it until Christmas morning." He walked back to his car.

The man looked over both shoulders then followed from a distance. Pete reached into his carpetbag and pulled out the Raggedy Ann doll. He shielded it with his body.

"That's the doll she saw in the catalog. That's the one she wants," the man whispered. He clenched his jaw. "I can't pay you."

"I don't want anything for it." Pete held the doll out to him. "I'm just happy your little girl will have a doll on Christmas morning."

Trembling, the man slid the doll inside his coat. Tears escaped from the big man's eyes.

Blinking away his own tears, Pete took the man's hands in both of his and squeezed hard. "God bless you and your family. Merry Christmas."

For the first time since he lost Betty and Rose, he really meant it.

*Yes, Lord God, this is your holiday. Your day of birth. It should be a merry Christmas.*

But, would he ever feel happy again?

9

As she packed to celebrate Christmas with her parents, Jenny hummed the melody to "The First Noel." Last night's program had gone wonderfully. Her students gave their best efforts while their beaming parents cheered and clapped. In the few short months since becoming Kathleen Creek's elementary school teacher, Jennie had worked hard to win the affection of her students and the respect of their parents.

The success felt like a seal of approval.

She folded the green dress she had worn last night and placed it in the leather suitcase lying open on her bed. She would wear that on Christmas Eve with the black ankle-strap heels she had already packed. Her stylish brown wide-leg pants… no, the navy pair with the matching shawl-collared sweater would serve her well for any daytime event she might attend. She wrapped the soft wool over her fingers. Such a luxurious feel, and the patch-pockets would come in handy. Then, she added her walking oxfords to the case.

What else should she bring? Her red sweater would be nice for the holiday. She tucked in her small clutch evening bag and her favorite pajamas, but left room for the gifts she had wrapped.

How lucky she was to bring her classy new boyfriend home for Christmas. Meeting Mark would surely put her parents' minds at ease. In addition to his polite and charming demeanor, he walked about well-groomed and well-funded. As son of the town banker, Mark had a sterling reputation surpassed only by his family—a fact that would not be lost on her parents after the fiasco of her disastrous engagement.

She slipped into her winter coat and hat and then carried her suitcase downstairs by the door. Mark would be here any minute. How gallant he would look, striding up the walk in his tailored, wool coat, ready to offer her his arm and carry her bag to the car.

Her shoulders slumped. The image didn't stir her heart the way she wanted it to. Maybe her heart was dead. Those ugly memories of failed romance could stay far away. It was all in the past now. She squared her shoulders and raised her head. *New town, new life, new me! I will make this work.*

Mrs. Dixon, her landlady, came out of the kitchen. "Are you off, dear?"

"Yes, as soon as Mark gets here." Jenny hugged her. "Thanks, again, for everything. I hope you and Mr. Dixon and the boys have a beautiful Christmas."

"Well, here comes Mark now." Mrs. Dixon rubbed a spot from the window with her handkerchief. "My, my, my, will you look at his new car!"

Mark whistled "Jingle Bells" as he sauntered up the walk in his chocolate-brown overcoat and tweed newsboy cap, swinging his car keys. He offered his arm and carried her suitcase.

"I like your new car." Jenny stepped aside as he held the door for her. She ran her hands over the soft leather seats and settled in to enjoy a pleasant ride to Minneapolis.

"Gotta' look good for the clients." Mark cast a sideways grin at her. "You gotta' look successful to be successful, Dad always says."

There was more to it than that. Jenny parted her lips, then smiled.

He slid into the driver's seat and glanced at himself in the mirror. Mother would like him because he was a handsome apprentice banker, and Father would like him because his rich family owned the bank, although the bank's success rested partly on the misfortunes of those who had lost homes and farms to foreclosure. Father might not like that.

Still, Mark would be on his best behavior to charm them. Why was she not as impressed with him as she knew they would be? A pang struck her heart. Because she wasn't a good judge of men. Maybe others saw what she couldn't see.

The snowy landscape raced past the window as they drove out of Kathleen Creek, the town she had begun to love. "I think the Christmas program was a success, don't you?"

"If you like that sort of thing." Mark looked over his shoulder for traffic and then turned left. "Kids who forget what they're supposed to say, singers who can't carry a tune, parents watching their kids on stage as it they're little angels, and that old Santa suit that Hank Knobbe wore sure has seen better days. As if no one recognized him with that hitch in his step." He chuckled.

"How can you be so critical, Mark? It was sweet! The little kids get nervous with all those people watching. Didn't you love little Janet Ross, who lisped so much when she recited her piece? She remembered every word."

Jenny faced him. "Her parents had a right to be proud. Those children work hard to learn their parts and all those songs. Don't you remember how you felt when you went to school?"

"That was a long time ago, and I didn't have a teacher as pretty as you." Mark put his arm around Jenny and pulled her closer. "Did I tell you that I got the biggest buck last week when I went hunting up north with Dewey?"

He'd already told her all about it. And he'd tell her again. She tapped her fingers on the arm rest.

"Your dad will want to hear about this..." he continued.

Jenny sighed. Why didn't she feel closer to him? Everyone else thought he was such a good catch. What was the matter with her? Was she afraid to let herself fall in love again?

Every time she saw little Janet Ross, her heart yearned for a daughter like her. She was already twenty-five. She had to get married soon. But she didn't want to make another mistake. How could she trust her own choices?

Mark droned on. Jenny blew her warm breath against the glass, and it faded to a small, wet drop. Father had been so protective last fall when he brought her to Kathleen Creek. He hadn't wanted her to teach in "the middle of nowhere."

Mark cleared his throat.

Jenny sat straighter. "I'm sorry. What did you say?"

"I asked you if you're warm enough."

"I'm fine, thank you for your concern." Jenny fingered the turned-up brim of her slouch hat.

"This Roadster is supposed to have the best heating system made. It's powered by a fast, new Ford V-8 engine. It has power to spare."

Poor Mark. How many times had he told her this already? At least she had the scenery. Was this really the same highway she'd travelled with her father? Everything looked different beneath the blanketing snow.

During her first weeks in Kathleen Creek, it pleased Jenny to forget about men entirely as she organized her classroom and got to know her pupils. Like her Minneapolis students, many shared raggedness and hunger. She often brought food to school for them, just as she had back home.

One day, she handed out apples first thing in the morning.

The young boys and girls gobbled them up almost in ecstasy. The following week she put together a stew in a pot on the heating stove prior to the children's arrival.

By mid-morning the spicy meat and vegetables had the students turning their heads toward the back in anticipation of their meal. By noon, they all ate with vigor and appreciative smiles. It warmed Jenny's heart to meet their current hunger. If only she could do more.

She announced that she would make stew every Monday and Friday. Perhaps they could provide better for themselves in between, which, of course, many of them couldn't.

Jenny made charts and diagrams to illustrate arithmetic lessons. She drew colorful maps and decorated the classroom with magazines to use in various history lessons.

She often stayed long after they left to grade papers and prepare lessons. She'd first met Mark during one of these after-school work sessions. At the end of a day, about a month into the school year, the well-dressed young man had strolled in.

"I hope I'm not disturbing you." He removed his hat and stepped toward her. "I'm Mark Weston. Welcome to town."

"Why, thank you, Mark. My name's Jenny Howe. It's a pleasure to meet you." Jenny erased the blackboard and offered her hand.

"The pleasure is all mine, Miss Jenny." The handsome Mark held her hand longer than necessary. "Would you allow me to escort you to a Halloween party at the fire hall this Saturday evening?"

"I would be pleased to attend with you." She pushed back a loose strand of hair. "I've been so busy with school that I haven't gotten out to meet many people, except for church."

"You'll meet lots of people at the party. You don't have to dress in costume, but some people do. I don't, but you can if you want to." He fingered the brim of his tan felt hat.

"I wouldn't know what to wear." She brushed chalk dust from the front of her dress. "What time is the party?"

"I'll pick you up at your house at eight o'clock."

"Okay, eight o'clock. I'll be ready. Thank you for the invitation."

Mark asked her out every week, and before long everyone assumed they were a couple. Jenny wasn't sure how she felt about that. Was it dishonest to continue seeing him when she had no real feelings for him?

She couldn't think of a polite reason to decline. Who could find a man with more impeccable manners? He brought her to only the best places, and he treated her with respect. Her role, in Mark's eyes, must be to look attractive and listen attentively. Not the deep romance she'd always dreamed of, but romance had already burned her twice. She would be a kind and gentle companion to her stable, reliable, and pleasant Mark. She'd appreciate the nice things he did for her.

Jenny sometimes mentioned Mark in her letters home, and Mother wrote back with questions. Where did they go? What did they do? Father's letters questioned her safety. How far did she have to walk to the schoolhouse every day? Had she met the school board yet? Was she comfortable in her room? Did the landlords treat her well? He wrote even more often than Mother.

When Jenny complained she earned less than in Minneapolis, Father suggested she should come back home. She learned to not complain about any aspect of her new home or her new job. But there was no need. She was happy in Kathleen Creek, and happy in her work.

"Jenny." Mark's voice interrupted her thoughts. "Where would you like to eat?" He slowed the car. "I'm getting hungry."

"I'm hungry, too. Anywhere is fine with me."

He adjusted the rearview mirror. "Dad told me about a nice place on the way to Minneapolis where he once met a client. He said a lot of rich-looking businessmen ate there. I think it's just ahead."

"That's fine." Jenny squelched a sigh. Mark always wanted to be with the rich or successful business men. Had to maintain that status.

When they arrived at Jenny's home mid-afternoon, Mark carried in the bags. He shook hands with both her parents and complimented their lovely home. Then, he presented them with packages of venison and a bottle of champagne.

Jenny cringed. Would Father drink too much again? Many past Christmases, he'd turned the evening into loud arguments resulting in her mother's tears.

Father gripped the bottle. "We'll put this away until later."

She relaxed as he stowed the champagne in the corner cupboard.

Mark regaled them with stories of his many hunting, fishing, and traveling adventures. After dinner, he attended Christmas Eve service with them and impressed Mother even further with his beautiful tenor voice.

After they returned home, Jenny's father lit the candles on the Christmas tree while Mother found Christmas music on the radio. They all settled in the living room to open gifts.

"I hope you will like this, Mrs. Howe." Mark handed her a shiny red package with a huge bow.

She lifted the pink scarf from the tissue paper and looked at Mark with a smile. "I'm especially fond of cashmere." She pressed the soft fabric to her cheek. "Thank you, Mark."

When Father opened the box of Cuban cigars from Mark, he drew in a long, satisfying sniff. "You've got good taste, my boy." He chuckled and offered Mark one before putting a cigar in his own breast pocket "for later."

"Last, but not least." Mark flashed his most charming smile as he presented Jenny with a silver box. When she lifted the gold locket, he took it from her and fastened it around her neck.

"You'll have to find just the right pictures to put into it." He winked at her.

"Mark, I'm touched at your thoughtfulness." But did she want to wear his picture around her neck? She handed Mark the gaily wrapped woolen socks she had knitted for him and then went into the kitchen.

"Here." Mother handed her a platter of decorated holiday cookies. She carried them to the living room while her father extinguished the burned-down candles on the tree.

Mother stood in the hall. "I'll make some eggnog." She beamed as Mark followed her into the kitchen.

"In Kathleen Creek I am well-known for making egg nog." Mark grabbed the apron hanging on a hook and grinned as he tied the strings behind him and reached for the bottle of milk Jenny's mother, Madelyn, had removed from the refrigerator.

Jenny sat with Father in the living room while laughter from Mark and Mother erupted from the kitchen. "Hark the Herald Angels Sing" played on the radio. Soon Mother came out with a tray of eggnogs.

Father clapped. "Lovely, Madelyn."

The next day, they enjoyed a leisurely brunch and then Mark left.

Mother rested a hand on her shoulder. "You've got a good catch this time. He's wonderful."

But was he the right man for her?

## 10

On Christmas Eve day, Pete's chest hollowed. He should be celebrating this holy and festive holiday with family instead of driving alone in the cold, deserted countryside. He ate a lonely breakfast in an otherwise empty café. By lunchtime, all the other cafés along the way had closed.

At noon, he parked alongside the highway with the heater on full blast and ate the rest of his ham. Somehow the heat didn't reach the chill sitting deep in his stomach.

As he neared southern Kansas. he sought a boardinghouse. Town after town, each one had closed.

After a couple hours of darkness, Pete's shoulders ached, and desperation crept in. But finally, he came upon a boardinghouse without a closed sign.

An elderly woman came to the door dressed in several sweaters, heavy stockings, and slippers much too large for her. "Yeah, we have a room. Fifty cents." Her flat voice held no warmth.

"I appreciate that you're open on Christmas Eve." He handed her the money.

The woman snorted. "Christmas Eve. Bah, humbug. Follow

me." Her very appearance and the total grayness of her countenance seemed so reminiscent of Scrooge, Pete couldn't help but smile.

She showed him to a small room with a bed, chair, night stand, and dresser. "Will take a bit for it to warm up. Didn't expect guests tonight. You're welcome to sit in the parlor by the stove. Would you have a cup of tea?"

His jaw dropped, and he faked a cough. This woman who'd vehemently spoken about Christmas found graciousness to offer him tea? And perhaps a few moments of companionship? He drew in a deep breath. "Tea would be nice. Will you join me?"

She pivoted and shuffled out, dragging her large slippers along the floor. A few twists of her gray hair still held tight in a bun, but most of it hung loose. Pete put his carpetbag and hat in the room and went into the parlor. Soon, the woman brought a tray with two cups and a large teapot.

"I guess I forgot my manners." She blew a wisp of hair from her face. "I'm Mrs. Kolb."

"Well, it's nice to meet you, Mrs. Kolb." He took the tray from her. "My name is Pete Walters.

"You can set it there." She pointed to the low table and pulled it closer to them. "Why you out all alone on Christmas Eve?"

"I'm just traveling through, trying to get to Texas." Pete dropped into one of the two matching, stiff-upholstered chairs and stretched out his feet.

"What's in Texas?" She picked up a book from the other chair and placed it on a nearby shelf.

Pete rubbed his neck, where his stethoscope would sit. "I'm starting a new veterinary practice in Dallas." A small gray and white cat trotted into the room and jumped into his lap. With a chuckle, he made small circles beneath her chin. "Oh, hello, little lady."

"That's Misty." Mrs. Kolb sneezed, sending a scatter of dust about the shelf. "You got family in Texas?"

"No." Pete sat straighter as the cat climbed up his chest.

Mrs. Kolb moved to the curtain and adjusted the sash. "You a single man, then?"

Pete lifted the cat down into his lap. "Widowed."

Mrs. Kolb placed a light hand on his shoulder. "How long ago?"

He swallowed. "A year."

Mrs. Kolb approached the low table and gripped the handle of the tea kettle. "So this your first Christmas alone?"

Pete nodded as the cat purred.

The woman's mouth curled into a sympathetic frown. "The first is hard. I lost my husband nigh on twenty years now and it's still hard." She poured tea into each cup and handed one to Pete. "I got no sugar or milk."

"I like mine black." At least for tonight. Pete wrapped both hands around the warm cup.

The steaming cup soothed Pete's hands, and the hot tea warmed his insides.

And how blessed he was to rest with such a kind woman in a nice, warm room. Well, a warm room, anyway. The boarding-house must have been elegant at one time. The red flocked wall-paper and the furniture had seen better days. The room, in fact, resembled its owner—haggard and faded.

"This hits the spot. Thank you," Pete said.

"It *is* nice to have company on Christmas Eve." She gave him a rueful smile. "It occurs to me that everything is closed. Maybe you haven't ate supper. You hungry?"

His stomach growled, and he grinned. "Yes, I am hungry."

"I'll make a sandwich." She stood with a hitch, one hand on her left thigh. Limping on her right foot, she inched forward. She winced and turned toward the kitchen.

"Do you need help?" He dropped the cat to the floor, rose, and moved to her side.

"No, but you might put more wood in the stove. I'll keep Misty in the kitchen." She nodded to her tiny wood pile.

The fire. His jaw twitched, but Pete moved the coals around with a poker. He put a couple of pieces of wood into the stove and opened the draft to generate more heat. Before long, Mrs. Kolb returned with a fried egg sandwich.

Just the smell made him salivate.

She passed him the plate.

He set the plate on the table and refilled their tea cups. "Thank you. I didn't realize I was so hungry."

Mrs. Kolb sipped her tea in silence while he ate.

Pete finished the last bite and drained the cup. "My room must be warmer by now, so I think I'll turn in. Will you be staying up or shall I close the draft on the stove?"

"No, I'm going to bed now, too. Please close it." She set her cup on the tray.

"Well, good night, then." Pete carried the tray to the kitchen. He checked the dampers once more and went into his room.

Shivering, he undressed down to his long johns and got into the cold bed. *Thank you, God for Christmas and the birth of your Son, Jesus. Thank you for Mrs. Kolb, and the food and bed she's provided.*

After a long, eye-watering yawn, he fell asleep on the thin mattress, and awoke early in the morning.

Christmas. He patted the bed beside him. "Merry Christmas, Betty."

A mournful moan caught in his throat, and his breathing quickened. He scooted back against the headboard and wrapped his arms around his knees. At least he hadn't awakened with a nightmare.

A bit later he slid his pants on, buttoned his shirt, and crept along the dark, quiet hallway leading from his room. Tiptoeing, he built fires in both the kitchen and parlor stoves.

Would Mrs. Kolb mind if he made coffee? He searched the

kitchen, but found only an empty coffee can, so he put a kettle of water on to heat and went outside for more wood.

The woodshed held only a few large pieces. He picked up the ax and split some chunks. Then, he carried in an armload and put it in the box.

"There you are." Mrs. Kolb limped up behind him.

"Is that all the wood you have?" He added a couple pieces to the stove.

She nodded. "Needs splitting."

He frowned. "I've split some of it, but it still isn't enough to carry you through the winter."

Mrs. Kolb turned and shuffled into the kitchen. "I'll make tea. Eggs and toast for breakfast."

Pete followed her. Did she have the money to buy more wood? Was there any family to help her? "Do you have children, Mrs. Kolb?"

Her eyes hollowed. "Never did. Mister and me wanted children, but that never happened. After Mister died, I turned this into a boardinghouse. No other way. Business stayed good for years, but not many people traveling through what needs a bed for the night anymore. Nobody's got money. Don't know what I'll do when the wood's gone. There's no money for more."

Pete's heart went out to the poor woman. He accepted the plate of eggs and toast. "Where did you get firewood before?"

"Mr. Burns, who lives in that big blue house on the corner over there." She pointed toward the northwest. "He sells firewood, but it's in big chunks. The young man next door comes over and splits it for me when he can, but he's been looking for work and he's not around much."

Pete downed his toast in four bites. "I'll finish splitting the rest before I leave."

"I can't pay you." She took several dainty bites of her own.

"That's okay. It's my Christmas present to you."

Mrs. Kolb, faced the window and wiped her eyes with the

heel of her hands. "That's more than kind of you, Pete."

He put on his coat, hat, and gloves, went back to the woodshed, and split the rest of the wood. When he carried it into the house, both the parlor and kitchen wood boxes stood heaping full, but it would only last another week, at best.

She met him with a teacup. "Here. Warm yourself before you go." Her hand quivering, she laid the 50-cent payment on the table. "Take this. You've more than paid by splitting the wood."

Pete pushed the two quarters toward her. "No, ma'am. It's my pleasure." He downed the tea. "Thank you for your kindness, Mrs. Kolb. I wish you well. Merry Christmas."

"And I thank you, Pete." She squeezed his shoulders. "Merry Christmas."

If only he could have done more to help her. But maybe... He drove to the big blue house on the corner and dug into his cache of money. Clutching the bills in his fisted hand, he knocked on the door.

A bulky man with a stubble-covered face opened it a crack. "What do you want?"

"Mr. Burns?" Pete stood straighter. "My name is Pete Walters. I'm Mrs. Kolb's nephew, and I want to order a full truckload of dry oak firewood to be delivered to my aunt as soon as possible. But it must be split. Can you do that?"

Mr. Burns scowled, and Pete held up the cash. "I'll more than pay you. And I will be visiting again soon to make sure you've given her the good, dry wood, split just as I've asked."

"I'll take care of it." Mr. Burns glanced over his shoulder. "Noah, get out there and cut Mrs. Kolb some firewood. A full load of oak. The best we have."

"Thank you." Pete handed him the money and headed to the car. He sat for a few minutes while a younger man split wood from a large pile of chunks.

He left with a satisfied smile. "Merry Christmas, Mrs. Kolb." Now, to Dallas.

The further south he drove, the warmer the weather. Soon he crossed bare ground with no snow and found the red dirt that traveled to Nebraska in dust storms. And so many oilfields in Oklahoma. It must take thousands of people to work the huge rigs. Large storage tanks sat alongside the roads, and many tanker trucks came along to transport the oil.

When he reached Texas, he yelled, "Hallelujah!" and waved his arms in the even warmer air. Tall hills surrounded him. He'd always imagined Texas as flat, dry, desert.

As he drove further south, he passed small homesteads with a few animals, but not the large cattle ranches that he had imagined. Soon, he came upon flatter terrain with oak and willow trees, but still not the wasteland he'd imagined. Like Oklahoma, lots of oilfields.

Early New Year's Eve day, he stopped and stepped out of his car next to a dust-covered road sign. "Welcome to Dallas!"

He fell to his knees and kissed the ground. My new home.

The sun shone bright, and the air warmed his face. But where were the many horses and large ranches? Were there enough clients for a veterinarian practice? His joy faded. Had he made a mistake coming here?

A few miles down the road, he pulled into the drive of a small food stand.

Two brown-skinned women waved as he approached. "Próspero año!" The taller, barefoot woman smiled, deep furrows forming in her face.

"Happy New Year." Pete reached into his pocket. "Three tacos, please."

"Fifteen cents," came the smiling reply from the second woman.

"Fancy car you got." A small man wearing a large western hat moved up beside him, too close for Pete's comfort.

As he stepped back, the man spit tobacco to the side and wiped his mouth with his hand. "Where you from?"

"Nebraska." Pete accepted his tacos. "Thank you, ladies." He inched toward the car.

"Sit here and tell me about Ne-bras-ka." The man blocked him and pointed to a picnic table.

"Thanks, but a nice, shady little spot I passed a few miles back is calling to me. I thought I'd eat my tacos while I read. It's such a nice day today. But thanks for the invitation. Happy New Year."

"You sure you won't sit with me to eat?" The man glanced from Pete's car to the picnic table and back.

"No, thank you." Pete yawned. "Might take a little nap after I eat." He got back into his car.

A few minutes later, Pete pulled off the road alongside a shade tree he'd spotted when he'd driven into town. Betty's thickly-padded carpetbag made a nice pillow, and Henry's leather cape provided a comfortable mat. He ate the tacos sitting against the tree and then stretched out on the cape, pulling the carpetbag under his head. As birds chirped around him, he promptly fell asleep.

When he woke, he blinked several times. Darkness? And such a headache. When had the sun gone down? He couldn't have slept that long. Struggling to sit up, he reached for his head. A large lump stung as he touched it.

He patted his money belt and his shoulders relaxed. The contents of his pockets had not been rifled. Still, why would someone have hit him on the back of the head? Wait…

"My car! Where's my car?" He stood up and ran to the spot where he'd parked it. Or, had he parked further away? Was he dreaming?

He rubbed his lump again. Not a dream. His car had been stolen. Along with everything he owned, except what his carpetbag contained. Most of his money. All his vet equipment. His clothes. Everything!

Pete palmed his forehead. "What am I going to do now?"

## 11

What time was it? Pete lifted his wrist, but the darkness obscured his hands. His head throbbed, and he felt the knot again. Did he need to see a doctor? Who'd hit him? Did the odd little man from the taco stand steal his car? Most likely. How stupid to mention he planned to take a nap!

Pete sat straighter and rubbed his temples. He needed to speak to the authorities. Should he report to the Dallas City Police, since he'd parked inside city limits? Where were they located? How would he get there?

No traffic moved along the highway, but he'd have to hitch a ride into town. Would anyone pick up a hitch-hiker this time of night? And on New Year's Eve? He couldn't ride with a drunk. It might be safer to wait out the night and find a ride in the morning.

He settled against the tree on his leather cape, clutching the handle of his carpetbag. Even if the police retrieved his car, everything in it would be gone. All his vet equipment and supplies. His clothes. His money. He patted his money belt and wallet. At least the thief didn't get all of his money. He'd rent a room for a few nights. But, what then?

The shrill caw of blackbirds woke him at dawn. When had he dozed? He relieved himself in the bushes and then stood by the highway to wait for a ride. With a grimace, he tied the cape around his waist and held onto his carpetbag. He must look like a hobo.

The third passing car pulled up on the shoulder. A bald man with a snake tattooed on his neck poked his head out the window. "You gettin' in or not?"

Pete wiggled his toes in his shoes. Other than the weird tattoo, nothing seemed amiss. He put his carpetbag in the back seat and got in.

"You an Okie?" The driver looked him over.

"An Okie?"

"A hobo."

Pete offered a wry grin. "Oh, I see. No, someone stole my car yesterday."

"Holy Smokes! How'd that happen?"

"I took a nap under a tree, and several hours later, I awoke with a lump on my head the size of golf ball. My car with all my belongings had disappeared."

The driver put the car in gear and accelerated. "Good thing you ain't an Okie. Cops hard on hobos 'round hereabouts. You ain't from here?"

"Nebraska."

"Where you going?" Ducking his head, the driver glanced toward the rear view mirror.

"Right now I need to report my car stolen. I sure hope the police can find it."

"Don't count on it. Been in the papers lots lately. Professionals." The driver waved his hand in the air, his large ring glinting. "Seems they tear 'em down and sell 'em piece by piece. Cops can't find 'em."

Pete groaned. His beautiful car! Surely they'd find it. "Where's the police station?"

"Downtown. I'm not goin' that far m'self, but I can take you there."

"I sure appreciate it."

After a long span of silence, the driver reached his hand to Pete. "My name's Carl Beckland. I deliver mail."

"Nice to meet you, Carl. My name's Pete Walters." He gripped the man's hand. "I hoped to move here and start a veterinary clinic. That won't happen unless I get my car back with my vet equipment and supplies."

"We got us a few vets here in Dallas." Carl signaled and made a left-hand turn. "You might do better out in western Texas where the big cattle ranches are. Mostly small ranches 'round hereabouts. Couple cattle and a horse."

"Good to know."

Pete shook hands with Carl again when he dropped him off at the police station. "Thanks for the ride." As he opened the station door, someone muttered, "If I have to deal with one more psycho before my shift is over, I'll…"

Facing Pete, the young officer approached the desk. "I'm Officer Gates, what can I help you with?"

The carpetbag clunked as Pete set it on the floor. "My vehicle was stolen yesterday afternoon."

"What time?" The officer pulled a form from a tray and scrawled across the top with a pen.

Pete fingered the knot on his head. "Sometime after three."

"Where was the vehicle?

"Parked along highway 423 north of the city." He folded his arms and rested them on the counter.

"Make and model?"

Pete's eyes lit up. "1932 Ford V8 Sedan, blue. License number N8064."

"Your name?"

"Dr. Peter Walters, Grand Island, Nebraska."

"What's your address?"

How could he explain not having an address? "I just vacated my home in Grand Island and I'm relocating to Dallas."

"So you have no permanent address?" Officer Gates' brow quirked.

"Not at present, no."

"Driver's license, please." The inquisitive stare continued.

Pete passed it over.

Officer Gates held it up, flipped it, made some notations, and handed it back to Pete. "As you might be aware, it's a holiday today and we're short staffed. It's been a hectic night. Tomorrow, most of our staff is still on holiday hours. We have all the information, but I'm not sure we can do much for you until Wednesday."

Pete leaned toward the officer. "By Wednesday my car could be in Florida or New Jersey. Can't you get the word out to other state police to be on the lookout for my car?"

"Like I said, we're short-staffed and overloaded from so many drunk and disorderly arrests tonight." Officer Gates added the form to the stack in a wire basket. "We can't attend to a simple car theft right now."

"This isn't a simple car theft to me." Pete clenched his jaw and tightened his fists. "My whole livelihood is in that car, and I need all of it. My veterinary equipment, supplies, money, and clothes. I'm in the process of moving. Don't you understand?"

"You'll have to come back tomorrow. Better yet, the day after tomorrow." Office Gates folded his hands on the counter. "That's all I can tell you."

What else could Pete say or do? He'd never felt so helpless.

"Is that all, sir?"

Pete's shoulders slumped. "Is there an inexpensive place to stay nearby?"

"There's a hotel two blocks east 'o here. Clean. Not expensive."

"Thanks." Pete dropped his voice to a murmur. "For nothing."

Outside on the sidewalk, the warm sun beat down on his shoulders. Heat waves wafted over the roofs of houses and a line of trees along the horizon. So this was Dallas. Not the welcome he'd expected.

He turned east toward the hotel, paid the fifty-cent fee for the night, and climbed up to a sparse but clean second floor room. At least the bed looked comfortable. He set his carpetbag on the floor and faced the window.

January 1, 1935. A new year. A new town. A new life. He bowed his head. *I thought this would be exciting, Lord. Please let them find my car and my belongings. I'm almost penniless and in a couple weeks I'll be totally broke. Am I being punished for my mistakes?*

Maybe he should explore downtown Dallas. He locked the door to his room and approached the reception desk, where a tall, brown-haired man with a mustache flipped through a leather-bound book.

Pete pasted a smile on his face. "Where might I buy some breakfast?"

"Well, being New Year's Day, most places are closed." The man stroked his chin and furrowed his forehead in thought. "You know, I bet that little Mexican place south of here will be open today. Taco Mama's. Go about four blocks south and you'll see it. A pink stucco place on the right."

*Taco Mama's? Could it possibly be owned by the same man who stole... who might have stolen his car?* "Thanks." Pete walked back into the sunshine and headed south.

Loud Mariachi music faded in as he approached Taco Mama's. Women in bright skirts and men sporting light colored suits danced in the street, laughing and talking in loud voices. As he worked his way through the crowd to the door, he watched for the man at the taco stand. People clapped him on the back. "Próspero año!"

"Próspero año!" How many times could he utter the phrase before reaching the café? When he stumbled in, he blinked, adjusting to the dim light.

"Welcome." A short, heavyset woman in a flowered sundress approached him with a smile. "Just one?"

"Yes." Pete followed her to a lacquered table, continuing to watch for the little man.

She handed him a menu. "To drink? Perhaps one of our fine whiskeys or tequilas?"

Whiskey. Pete gripped the menu in his fisted hand. "Coffee, please. And eggs and cheese wrapped in a tortilla." Who could tolerate this loud music with the headache wrought by alcohol?

By the time they served his breakfast he, too, tapped his feet to the music.

Pete pushed his chair back from the table. He hated to leave the festive atmosphere and friendly people, but he didn't belong here. He paid his fifteen cents and another nickel tip.

With each step away from the fading music toward the hotel, the air chilled, and the sky grayed.

Pete wandered around Dallas most of the day. Disconnected. Disoriented. Lost. Dallas offered little more than Grand Island except its western appearance and largely Mexican population.

Where cars had parked in Grand Island, hitching posts and horses stood in front of most of the Dallas stores. Their shop windows featured western clothing, saddles, harnesses, and tack for horses. Men wore cowboy boots and spit tobacco in the streets. Even some of the women wore trousers, something he never saw in Nebraska.

He passed a group of women sitting on the open porch of large red hotel.

They called to him.

"Want to party, gringo?"

"I have what you want, honey."

Not a hotel. He cringed.

The scantily-clad women stood and waved, bangles clanging on their arms and big hoop earrings swinging from their ears. "Come on over." "Start the new year right, baby."

A pouty-lipped redhead swayed her hips down the steps toward him, beckoning with her hands. Pete hurried down the street. Was prostitution legal in Texas? Dallas certainly differed from Grand Island.

Hours later, Pete's stomach growled again. He'd explored most of Dallas, but he hadn't seen another open café other than Taco Mama's.

When he returned, the music still played, but no one danced in the streets. The same woman welcomed him with a wide smile and seated him next to parrots painted along the wall.

Pete liked the colorful Mexican people. And for the first time in a long time, he'd found a place where he could be comfortable. He ate rice and refried beans and drank coffee, listening while the other customers spoke in Spanish. If only he could understand their language, he could visit with them.

How he longed for a conversation.

The day dragged on. Pete napped in his room and read from *A Few Figs from Thistles*. That only made him miss Betty more, so he went downstairs to find a newspaper. Sold out. At five o'clock, he returned to the police station. The changing of the guard might make a difference.

An older officer at the desk asked, "May I help you?"

"My name is Dr. Peter Walters. I reported earlier that my car had been stolen yesterday afternoon. Have you had any success finding it yet?"

"What did you say your name is?" The officer thumbed through a large stack of forms.

"Dr. Peter Walters." Pete drummed his fingers on his trousers.

"Ah. Here it is." The officer took the document from the bottom of the stack. "Well, we have all the information. We just have to find the time to telegraph other agencies. It's New Year's Day and we're short staffed."

"How long would it take to do that? My whole future, my livelihood, is in that car. I have to get it back." Pete leaned over the counter, meeting the officer's gaze directly.

"We have a lot of other complaints that come before yours, sir." He picked up the stack of forms. "You will just have to wait your turn."

"And when will my turn come up, do you think?" Pete spoke between clenched teeth.

"Can't say for sure. Tomorrow is still holiday hours. Short staff. Maybe by Wednesday?" The officer's eyebrows lifted, his mouth shaping into a grimace.

"Wednesday is not acceptable." Pete pounded the counter. "By then my car, and all my belongings, will probably be in Timbuktu."

"Most likely in a hundred different pieces." The officer shrugged. "That's what these guys do. They don't drive stolen cars to another state. They find some shop, only God knows where, and take them all apart. They sell the parts to other guys operating out of scattered shops. Best not get your hopes up. I'm sorry, but that's reality."

Pete groaned. "How long until I'll know anything?"

"Can't say. From my experience, I'd say forget your car. It's history. Putting out your report is futile, anyway. We're never going to find it, because it no longer exists." The officer returned the forms to the basket.

What could he do? "I'll be back tomorrow, and the next day, and the day after that, if I have to." He stomped out of the police station and strode toward his hotel, his arms swinging. If he could just punch someone.

Several blocks later Pete stopped dead in the middle of the street. He should have reached his hotel long ago. Of course. In his anger, he'd turned west instead of east. The sun had set and darkness had settled around him without notice.

A group of men stood ahead of him drinking beer and talking loudly. Evidently not their first beers of the day.

One faced Pete. "Hey! Gringo! This here's our street. *Fuera.* Get out of here!"

Pete stuffed his hands in his pockets and walked faster.

"Gringo! Get back here. Nobody comes on our street without a fight."

Pete's pulse quickened. What should he do? Could he outrun them? Could he reach the police station? He ran straight forward, fast as he could. At the end of the block, a hand jerked him to the ground. A skinny, young man stood over him while the rest of the gang caught up. *"Lo tengo, Manuel."*

"Gooood." A tall, muscular man with a goatee sauntered up to Pete.

Groaning, Pete rolled to his side and sat. Manuel? Leader of the gang?

"Lookie what we got." Manuel slurred. "A little gringo." He gave Pete a swift kick.

Pete yelled, and gripped his side.

"Oh, did that hurt, gringo?" Manuel sing-songed. "Get up and cry for you mama.

Pete stood, and Manuel shoved him. "Alberto?" He barked something in Spanish, and a young man came forward with raised fists.

Pete squared his shoulders and raised his own fists. Did they plan to take turns beating him up? He didn't know how to fight.

Alberto swung, but Pete ducked. A deep snarl spanned Alberto's face.

The onlookers jeered at Pete. "Pégalo."

When Alberto swung again, Pete jerked his arm back and came up with a hard right swing that connected with Alberto's jaw, laying him flat on the ground. A hint of a smirk formed at the corner of Pete's mouth. How about that?

"So, you like to fight little guys." Manuel nodded to a small man with his arms and shoulders bulging like those of a lumberjack. "Carlos, eres el próximo."

Carlos's first swing caught Pete unprepared. He struck on the side of his jaw, almost knocking him down.

Pete recovered and grabbed Carlos around his middle. They both tumbled to the ground. Pete quickly got the upper hand, but Carlos flipped him over and pummeled his face.

"Ya, Carlos." Manuel tugged on the man's jacket. "Déjanos algo. Hector, hazlo llorar."

Another one? Pete wiped blood from his nose and cheek.

Hector, the tall skinny man who had outrun him, ambled up to Pete and towered over him. "I could just peeck you up, gringo, and throw you across the street."

Pete punched him in the stomach as hard as he could. With Hector doubled over, Pete stood and shot a sharp upper cut under his chin. This time, Pete allowed himself the smirk. Not bad for a Nebraska veterinarian.

"Okay," Manuel said. "Luis?" The tallest, broadest, and ugliest-looking of the bunch, stomped toward Pete with legs wide apart, arms out at his sides and lips in a snarl. He meant business.

The crowd went wild. "Dale más." "Písalo fuerte." "Písalo fuerte." "Get the gringo goood, Luis."

Pete grimaced. He was in for it now. The other victories being flukes, his luck had run out.

Luis landed a punch to Pete's jaw, another to his stomach, and a third to his temple.

Pete collapsed onto the ground.

"Can't you take more, gringo?" Manual sang in mock politeness. "Get up and fight like a man."

Pete stayed down.

"Get up, gringo. You not hurt yet. "Ayúdalo a levantarse, Luis."

When Pete finally steadied enough, Luis hit him again and again until Pete collapsed, bleeding and groaning.

"Now you stay off our street." Manuel scowled. "Look at you, bleeding all over our nice clean sidewalk. Ain't you ashamed? Didn't you mama teach you no better? Now, what do you want to give us, to tell us you sorry? "Alberto, revisa sus bolsillos."

As Alberto rifled through his pockets, Pete closed his eyes. *Please, God, not my money belt. Don't let them find my money belt.*

Alberto took his wallet, his watch and watch chain, and all the change he had in his pocket.

"Fuera. Get out of here. And stay away." Manuel gave Pete a final kick and sauntered away, his gang following him with loud laughter.

Sharp needles of air pierced Pete's body every time he inhaled. "Thank you, God." They hadn't found his money belt, and they hadn't taken his life.

After several long minutes, he found strength to sit. Blood ran from his split lip into his mouth. He stood, staggered to a tree, and leaned against it. Dizziness swarmed him, and every part of his body cried out when he moved. One eye had swollen so much he couldn't see.

He shuffled onward to the police station and collapsed in front of their office. "Help." His voice barely rose above a raspy whisper.

The same officer from earlier rushed out. "What happened? Can you stand? Can you hear me?" He yelled for another officer. "Let's get him into a squad. He needs to get to the hospital."

A third officer pulled a squad car to their side.

"What all's wrong with him, Doctor?" The older officer stood, hat in hand, next to where Pete lay on a table.

Pete blinked his one good eye.

The doctor patted Pete's stomach while he spoke. "Well, you have a few broken ribs, a possible concussion, possibly some internal bleeding, and those bruises on your face don't look good. We'll keep you overnight."

Pete's heart sunk. He'd paid for a night's lodging. Now, he'd have to pay for a night here at the hospital. At least he was alive and not hurt worse.

The next day a police officer came to his room to take his statement. "You want to press charges? Who beat you up?"

Pete ticked off with his fingers. "Manuel, Alberto, Carlos, Luis…"

The officer stopped writing. "Oh, I see." He put his pen back in his pocket and folded up his notebook. "You should have stayed away from that area. Manuel Diaz runs that part of town and he doesn't like anyone he doesn't know coming around. You can press charges if you want, but it won't do any good. It will be your word against theirs, and they always win." The officer crossed his arms and shifted his weight. "Well, do you want to press charges?"

What's the use? Pete gritted his teeth. Obviously it would just be another hassle that he didn't need. Even if they found his car, he wouldn't stay here.

Dallas had not been good to Pete.

13

During his three weeks in Dallas, Pete washed his clothes in the bathtub, ate as frugally as possible, and visited the police station twice a day. His hair hung well past his collar, but he didn't dare pay for a cut until they found his car.

The police sent a report to other states, but nothing turned up. Every day, the red-faced officer's voice grew edgier. "I've told you again and again, your car is most likely sent off in pieces to all over God only knows where."

"I don't know what else to do." Pete lifted his hands. "All my cash is gone. I'm totally broke. What am I going to do?"

The officer only shrugged.

As Pete bent to pick up his carpetbag, young Officer Tom came from the back with a husky, pockmarked man carrying a bedroll.

"Thanks for your hospitality, Officer." The tall man laughed and tipped his hat to Tom.

Officer Tom slapped the man on the back. "Stay out of trouble now and I won't have to see you in here again."

"Your detectives are pretty sharp. I might see you again." His hearty laugh boomed again.

As Pete walked out of the station, the released man followed him. "Excuse me. I'm Railroad Randy. Couldn't help overhearing. I've been there, man. I know how you feel. Maybe I can help."

Pete blinked. What did he say? Didn't matter. His car was gone forever. His vet equipment and supplies. His money. His clothes. He had hit bottom.

"I can help you out, show you the ropes." The man waved in Pete's face.

"What?"

"When you have no money, you have to do what we hobos do. Ride the rails, or hitchhike, and find work wherever we can. When we can't find work we ask for handouts. We do whatever we have to do."

Pete furrowed his brow. A hobo? Ask for handouts? Never! He'd never stoop low enough to ask for handouts!

"I could take you along to show you the ropes," the man said. "It helps at first to have someone teach you a few things."

"What did you say your name is?"

"Railroad Randy. But you can call me Railroad."

How many times had this man's face been pulverized? His kind smile balanced the one banged up ear, large, thick hands, and a bedroll thrown over one shoulder. Maybe Pete should hear him out.

"Let's sit." Pete motioned to a bench where he had sat waiting for a changing of staff at the police station.

They sat half-facing each other.

Pete stretched out his legs, flexing his toes in his shoes. Beside him, Railroad's big toe poked out of his worn leather boots. His face bore few wrinkles, putting him somewhere around forty-five, a decade older than Pete. And his kind eyes... perhaps he could be a friendly companion.

He leaned closer. "Tell me about yourself."

"My name's Pete Walters." Pete held out his hand. "I came to

Dallas to start over. Lost my wife, my daughter, my house, and my team all over the past year." Goosebumps prickled his arm as he envisioned the flames licking at the barn beams. "Drove here with my veterinary equipment and all the money I had in the world. Now, someone's stolen my car. Left me with a little change in my pocket, the clothes on my back, another set in my carpetbag, and a leather cape."

Railroad patted his pouch. "You're rich compared to me. This bindle only contains a gun boat. That's an empty coffee can used for cooking. And I have this beat-up old deck of cards." He pulled the cards from his shirt pocket.

Pete scratched his chin. "What did you do before you, you know, started traveling around like this?"

Railroad bellowed out a hearty laugh.

Pete laughed, too, but then he cocked his head. "What was so funny?"

"Pete, my boy, stop being embarrassed by your station in life. You can't even say the word 'hobo.' Let me educate you. A hobo is a man who wanders and works. A tramp is a man who wanders and *will not* work. A bum is a man who sometimes wanders but *cannot* work."

Railroad shuffled the cards. "Sometimes they're women, too. I'm a hobo. Now you're a hobo. Get used to it. It can be a permanent situation or a temporary situation. Right now the hobo population gets bigger every day. Maybe you won't have to ride the rails for long."

"I never thought I'd be in such a bad situation." Pete kicked at a small rock near his feet.

"I didn't either. I made good money as a prize fighter for several years but I drank it all up. Never saved a dime." Railroad put the cards back into his shirt pocket. "Lost my first and second wife. Washed up as a fighter. It took me a long time to realize what a mess I'd made of my life. By then, I was dead broke. So, here I am."

"How long have you been, ah, a hobo?"

Randy laughed again. "You'll get used to saying that. I've been riding the rails for about three years now."

"That's a long time."

"I'm still alive and well." Randy wiped his hands over his face. "I've seen most of the whole United States of America. Some parts I never want to see again, and other parts are too beautiful to believe."

"Where will you go from here?"

"Arizona. It's warm. That's where I was heading when I caught it from a yard dick."

"A yard dick?"

"Scoping a drag—that's looking for a good ride on a freight train as it slows down. I got ready to make the jump, but a railroad detective, called a yard dick, caught me by the hem of my jacket and yanked me back. I got 30 days in jail for that. If I would've been caught on the train by a cinder bull I might 'a been dead by now. Some of 'em are brutal, I tell you. Some only arrest you, but others beat you or throw you off a fast moving train."

"Doesn't sound like much fun being a hobo." Pete sat up straight and shivered.

"It has its good times." A wistful shadow crossed Randy's face. "The jungles are the safest."

"Jungles? Where?"

"Hobo camps where they share food and information. You can be safe for a while before moving on."

"Like Hoovervilles?" Pete had read about the shanty towns made from junk and cardboard named after President Hoover.

"Not quite the same thing." Railroad turned his head and sneezed. "Homeless people live there. Jungles are short-term camps for hobos."

"I've seen a few jungles, then, mostly along rivers. They build fires and cook and sing like happy people."

"Well, when they're in a jungle they know they're safe. They look after each other." Randy rested his hand on the back of the bench. "You can leave your pack in a jungle and go out to town and nobody'll even touch it. It'll be there when you come back."

"So, you're leaving for Arizona now?" Pete bit his lip. Was this truly his only option?

Randy tapped his finger against his temple. "You want to hook up with me for a while?"

"Guess I need someone to show me the ropes if I'm going to be a… hobo." Pete cringed. Could he ever say the word without it bothering him? "I'd appreciate the help."

Railroad snickered. "Where do you want to go?"

"I got beat up pretty bad a few weeks ago and they broke some of my ribs. I'm not sure I could jump onto a moving train yet." Pete rubbed his ribcage. "But Arizona sounds good. I want to be somewhere warm for now."

"Okay, partner. Let's head west to Arizona. We can hitch hike until your ribs heal. What about tonight? Do you have any money left? I'm flat broke."

Pete pulled two quarters, one dime and a nickel from his pocket. "That's it."

"I know a decent flophouse in El Paso where we could sleep for a dime each. Last time they didn't have lice." Randy scratched his coarse brown hair. "That's the problem with most flophouses. 'Course, I can't guarantee this place is good as it was a couple of years ago."

"Okay, let's head over there."

"First, you'll have to fix your baggage." Railroad pointed at Pete's carpetbag. "You'll have to carry it on your back, both when you hitch and when you jump a train. Can any of that stuff go?"

"I need it all." Pete clenched his jaw. It was all he had left in the world.

"Okay, I'm not taking it away from you. Don't get defensive.

I'm just saying that weight can slow progress hitching and makes it harder to jump a train. But you'll have to carry it on your back."

Pete lifted the carpetbag. "How?"

"Sew some straps on it and cut off those handles." Railroad stroked his chin. "I wonder where we could get some straps."

Pete frowned. Nothing he owned would work for straps. "Wait a minute, Railroad. I have an idea. One of the police officers has an uncle on a nearby ranch. Maybe I can do some vet work in exchange for some harness straps. I still have my hoof knife. Let me go talk to him."

"Don't let him know you intend to ride the rails. The cops around here are death on hobos. They won't even give us a courtesy call."

"A what?"

"Some police stations or sheriff's offices will give a hobo a night in jail with a meal if a guy needs it. But, not here. Not Fort Worth, either. They're tough here."

"I'll be right back." Pete headed into the police station. Good. Tom had started his duty.

"Tom, good to see you." Pete set his carpetbag on the counter.

Tom tipped his cap. "How are you doing, Pete?"

"This bag is difficult to carry with my broken ribs. I want to turn it into a backpack." Pete nudged it closer for Tom's inspection. "But, I need some straps I can affix to it. Wonder if your uncle would possibly have some old harness straps he'd give me if I cleaned up his horses' hoofs or anything else I could do to help him. I still have my hoof knife. As you know, I've spent all my money."

"Let me call my uncle. If he agrees, we could leave at six when I get off work and stay there tonight." He made the call and arranged it.

Beaming, Pete returned to Railroad. "I'm going to work for the uncle. I'll get the straps and maybe a little extra money."

"Then we can meet tomorrow night, or even the following morning if need be, down at Taco Mama's." Railroad said. "Do you know where that is?"

"Yes, I've been there." Pete could almost taste the salsa. "Nice place."

"Okay, kid, what shall we do until six o'clock?" Railroad shuffled his cards. "Do you play poker?"

"Sure. Where can we play?"

"I know a place."

Railroad led Pete to a table in a park and dealt them out a hand.

After the first hour, Pete warmed his hands in his jacket pocket every so often. Later, he turned the collar up to keep the cold breeze away from his neck. By mid-afternoon Railroad said, "Are you getting as hungry as I am?"

"I'm hungry all right." Pete rubbed his stomach. "But I only have sixty-five cents to my name."

"Here's your first hobo lesson, kid. Follow me."

Railroad put his cards in his pocket and picked up his blanket. "We call this a bindle."

"A bindle."

They walked to a nearby grocery store, where Railroad greeted the clerk with an open, friendly smile. "Good afternoon, sir. Would you have any specks today for my friend and me? We sure would appreciate anything you have."

The grocer drummed his fingers on the counter. "Hold on a minute." He returned and handed them each a pear and a peach.

"God bless you. We do thank you." Railroad smiled. "Have a wonderful evening."

Pete nodded to the grocer and trailed Railroad out the door.

"Now, that wasn't so bad, was it?" Railroad handed Pete half of the take.

"You asked for specks."

"Specks are fresh fruit with spots on 'em, like they're starting to go bad." Railroad turned his pear to reveal a large bruise. "Most of it's still good, but they can't sell 'em. They're usually happy to help out a fellow human being down on his luck by giving 'em to the hobos who ask for 'em."

They ate their fruit as they continued along the sidewalk.

"In here." Railroad turned and entered a bakery, where a young brunette stood behind the counter.

"Hello, young lady. I hope you've enjoyed this beautiful day." Railroad clasped his hands to his chest. "My friend and I are wondering whether you have an abundance of something that might not sell anymore today since it's almost closing time. We could use something to tide us over 'til morning."

The young woman smiled. "I do."

She bagged several donuts and handed them to Railroad. "Here."

"God bless you with a wonderful life, young lady. We do thank you." Railroad tipped his hat to the girl and did a soft-shoe shuffle just outside the door.

Pete smiled. Railroad's exuberance reminded him of a child.

"Now, kid, both the fruit and the donuts are referred to as 'lumps' in the hobo world. Food to be taken away and eaten." Railroad reached into the bag and passed Pete a cake donut. "If someone gives you a dish and you sit outside and eat it on your lap, it's called a 'knee-shaker.' If someone asks you to eat in the house, that's called a 'sit-down.' But that doesn't happen very often."

Pete's stomach burned from the fruit. He sunk his teeth into the sweet dough and chewed. It stuck in his throat as he swallowed. If only he had a bit of milk to wash it down. But still, how could he not feel blessed to have the food? "Do you have a nickname for everything?"

"And everyone. The jungle is a world unto itself. We have

codes, even. But you don't need to know that yet. I'll feed it to you a little at a time so it sticks."

Pete grimaced. Hopefully he wouldn't be out of work long enough for it to stick. He wasn't really a 'hobo.' "I appreciate that. I'm beginning to feel dizzy with all this new information."

"Remember that bakeries are good places to get a handout, as well as grocery stores and meat markets." Railroad passed the bag to Pete. "I'll tell you more about meat markets later."

"I'm not crazy about asking for handouts, though." Pete reached in for another donut.

"I'd rather work for it, too, but sometimes it isn't possible, like now. We can't get a job here because we're leaving in another day. This will hold me until tomorrow. You'll most likely get fed at the ranch." Railroad took the last donut, flattened the bag, and handed it to Pete. "If you can do it, pocket a bit of food for the next day for us. We'll have to watch out for each other on the road from now on. That's what hobos do, they watch out for each other."

Just before six o'clock, as Railroad turned to say goodbye, Pete offered him a quarter.

Railroad shook his head and opened his mouth.

"Hobos watch out for each other." Pete closed Railroad's fingers over the coin. "This will hold you 'til I get back."

Railroad nodded.

Pete walked away grinning. Now, Railroad could find a flophouse for the night or get a meal.

Who knew what tomorrow might bring?

14

Officer Tom smiled and waved when Pete approached the front of the station. "We'll eat, then head out to my uncle's. Don't worry, I'm buying."

"I… thank you." Pete climbed into Tom's car and set his carpetbag in the floor. Scrubby-looking scenery flashed by as Tom's Model A bumped over uneven roadways. When they reached a little building with a sign over the door that read, "Cantina," Tom pulled his car alongside other vehicles and a few horses tied to a post. "Best burgers in town."

Pete drew in a deep breath, the savory spices seeping through his nostrils and stirring up his hunger.

"Hi, Tom!" Two bulky men waved from the counter.

"Tom, great to see you." A middle-aged man at a square table tipped his hat.

They made their way to a booth, and Tom motioned to the waitress. "Let's have two burger meals."

The men enjoyed the hamburger, fried potatoes, and coleslaw accompanied by jukebox music. Then, strains of *Sweet Georgia Brown* faded as moonlight led them back to Tom's car. Another hour of driving brought them to the ranch. Pete dragged his fingers through his long hair. Did he look presentable enough?

At least, he looked more presentable than Railroad. Dirt had caked on the poor man's clothing and a musky, rank odor emanated from him. How did a hobo keep clean? Where did hobos bathe and wash their clothes? How would one wash his clothing if he doesn't have a spare to put on?

Pete's chest heaved. How long until he could find permanent work?

Tom swung the Model A onto a long, gravel drive, and they bumped along toward a two-story brick house. "Here we are."

Two dogs announced their arrival, and a tall, slim, curly-haired man opened the door before they reached it. "Welcome."

They bounded up the steps. The man shook Tom's hand and then Pete's. "Name's Winslow. Come on in."

Inside, Tom hugged a young boy and a tall, thin woman. "Pete, this is Becca and Jason, Winslow's wife and son."

"Have you eaten supper?" Becca smoothed her sandy hair.

"We have." Tom crouched in a mock fight stance and moved toward Jason with a grin. "We stopped at the Cantina."

Becca reached for her apron. "Well, let's have coffee and dessert, then."

At the table, Winslow stirred cream into his coffee. "Never saw it so dry in all my years. If this keeps up, we won't be able to feed our horses. How is it where you're from, Dr. Walters?"

"It's about the same." Pete shook his head and curled his hands around his cup. "The farmers are butchering their cattle because they can't feed them, their crops are so bad."

As they continued to discuss the weather, horses, and Jason's future plans, Pete smiled. He'd missed friendly conversation in a kitchen. He didn't feel like a hobo. He felt like himself again—a veterinarian.

Finally, Becca said, "You two must be tired. You'll have

Jason's room, Tom, and I've made up a bed in the spare room for you, Dr. Walters. Jason will sleep on the sofa."

Pete stood. "Thanks for hosting me tonight. And please, call me Pete." He fell asleep quickly and didn't stir until a rooster crowed at sunrise. How long had it been since a rooster had awakened him? Smiling, he dressed and followed his nose to the kitchen.

Becca handed him a cup of coffee. "Cream or sugar?"

"No, black is fine. Thank you." Pete swiped at his hair with his hands. He must look like a mess.

Becca moved a pan from the hot part of the stove to the warming oven. "Did you sleep well?"

"I sure did. I liked being awakened by a rooster." Pete crooked his neck to look out the window.

"Winslow and Tom are in the barn. They'll be in as soon as I call them, which is going to be right now." She rang a bell attached to the side of the house, and the men came immediately.

Pete chuckled as the men strode toward the house. Nothing like a call to breakfast to make a man obey.

"I haven't had pancakes, eggs, and bacon in a long time, Becca. This was wonderful." Pete patted his stomach as she refilled his coffee cup. Soon, the men finished their meal and headed for the small side yard where Winslow had corralled his horses. "That mare started limping yesterday, but I didn't even check it with you coming today."

Pete slipped a halter over the mare's head and led her, limping, to the rail. "She has a problem in her right hoof or forelock. There, there girl." He tied her to the rail and lifted her foot. "She has a crack in her hoof, right here, see? And infection has set in. I'll clean it out. I don't suppose you have pine pitch?"

When Winslow shook his head, Pete pointed to the woods in the distance. "Do you have pine trees on your property?"

"We have a few north of here."

"This infection will heal much faster if I can pack it with pine pitch. Can one of you go and scrape some off those trees? I only need about a tablespoon."

"I'll go." Tom raised from his crouching position. "I know where they are. I'll get a jar from Becca."

He trotted off while Pete took his hoof knife from his pocket and scraped out the infection. "What's her name?"

"Red." Winslow stroked the horse affectionately. "Jason named her Little Red Riding Hood when we got her years ago, so we call her 'Red.'"

Pete grinned. "Okay, Little Red Riding Hood, we're going to fix you up so you don't hurt anymore. Okay?" He patted the horse and went back to digging with his hoof knife until Tom came back with the sticky, wonderfully fragrant pine pitch.

Red tried to pull her leg away as Pete worked, but he hung on. "Okay, girl, only a little more work and I'll be done with this hoof. Just be patient with me." He cleaned off the knife, folded it back into its place, and slipped out a different blade, which he used to pack in the pine pitch.

When he put her leg down again, he faced Winslow, who had watched his every move. "There. She'll be good as new in about a week. Now I'll take a look and see if she has any rocks or twigs stuck in any of her other hoofs."

When he finished, he stroked her mane. "Red, I thank you for your patience." He slipped off the halter and let her go. "She's a nice horse."

"One of my best." Winslow accepted the pine pitch jar from Pete. "I sure appreciate what you did for her. I never heard of using pine pitch for healing infection. That really works?"

"It's worked for me for years. What have you used?"

"Vets around here use turpentine mixed with hog's grease or tincture of iodine."

"I've used that, too, when I had nothing else, but pine pitch is better. Since you have access, you might want to keep a jar on hand."

"I might just do that."

Pete checked the other horses' hooves and cleaned out the troublesome imbedded debris.

Winslow leaned against the stall beam, chewing on a piece of straw. "Tom said you're looking for some harness?"

"I need two straps so I can remodel my carpetbag to carry on my back." Pete held his side. "Had a run of bad luck with my ribs. Hurts too much to carry it by hand."

"Let's take a look at what I've got. I'm afraid everything will be too thick."

They went into the tack room, and Pete twitched his lips. Winslow was right. Nothing there would work.

"I'd sure like to help you, but I don't have any thin leather. What you need is about the thickness of the cape you have around your waist."

"My cape! Why didn't I think of that?" Pete lifted the hem. "I could just cut off a strip along the bottom about, what, two inches wide? I wouldn't lose much of it. But how will I attach the leather to this rug-like material? I have needles and thread, but they wouldn't be sufficient to get through this."

"Tell you what, Pete." Winslow stroked his chin. "The guy who owns the harness shop in Dallas is a friend of mine. I'll give him a call and tell him to sew the leather straps on for you. He owes me a favor."

"That's sure nice of you, Winslow. That should set me up great. Who knew it would take so long for ribs to mend?"

"Have an accident, did you?" Winslow closed and latched the yard gate.

"Yeah, an accident with a few fists. Then they robbed me. Not proud of it."

Winslow clucked his tongue. "Well, I hope they heal soon for you, Doc. I think Becca might have something ready for us to eat. We don't always have to wait for her to ring that bell." With Winslow's hand on Pete's shoulder, they followed the smell of fresh coffee and cinnamon rolls.

Real appreciation and true veterinary work. How long since he'd experienced that? And how many more weeks, or months, would pass before he could care for animals again?

How could he find vet work as a hobo?

## 15

Pete and Tom left the ranch after their noon meal so he could get his carpetbag work done before the day ended.

"I want to live in the country someday." Tom put his hand over his mouth as he yawned. "My fiancé has a son. It would be better to raise him in the country, you know."

Pete nodded. "Boys have more to do in the country."

"This looks like the harness shop." Tom parked the car. "What was the guy's name?"

"Santana." Pete grabbed his carpetbag from the back seat and joined Tom on the boardwalk. The smell of new leather met him just inside the door. Two men stood talking toward the back of the shop.

The older man smiled. "Afternoon. I'm Santana."

Merchandise stacked on shelves. Counters uncluttered. Edges of the old wide wooden plank floor showed visages of varnish but little dust. Santana seemed well organized and friendly. Salt-and-pepper hair, weathered face, subtle stoop to his shoulders. He patted the second man on the back. "Thank you for coming in, Bill. See you soon."

Santana faced Pete. "You are Señor Winslow's friend, no?"

"Yes. Pete Walters." He held up his carpetbag. "Winslow said you could transform this into a pack to carry on my back. We can use a strip of leather from the bottom of my cape."

Santana rubbed his finger and thumb over the carpetbag fabric and then the cape hem. "We don't take from your good poncho. I got leather."

"I can't pay you, so I thought…"

"No, no. Senor. No pay. Senor Winslow good friend. I fix." He reached under the counter and produced a basket. "Put everything here while I fix."

Pete laid the empty carpetbag on the counter. Santana returned from the back of the shop with a strip of leather and waved it at Pete. "How you want to carry this?"

After measuring both Pete and the leather, he cut, sewed on the straps, and repaired a rip in the seam of the bag.

"Try on." Santana handed the finished product to Pete.

Pete settled the pack on his back. Moved his arms up and down. Turned around. Bent over. "This is perfect, Santana. How can I thank you?"

"No thanks. I do for Senor Winslow. Good friend."

Pete removed the pack and returned his belongings to it. He offered his hand. "You did a great job, Santana. Thank you."

Santana lowered his eyes and bent his head. "You are welcome."

Pete smiled most of the way back to the city. It would be so much easier to travel now. He ran hands over his tender ribcage. And he wouldn't lose his belongings when he jumped into a moving train.

A moving train… He grimaced. Something in his stomach recoiled. He closed his eyes. Be a man, Walters. Other men, even women, jumped into moving trains. He could do it. He took a few deep breaths. He'd be able to do it when he had to.

Tom dropped Pete off at Taco Mama's with a wry grin. "I'll probably see you at the office again."

"I'll keep coming 'til you find my car." Pete tried to be jovial as he shook Tom's hand, but sadness filled him. He was leaving behind the only friend he had in Dallas.

As he walked into the restaurant, his stomach growled. He removed his hat. How long would he have to be penniless?

Railroad waved from the back table where he talked with the woman who had seated Pete earlier. "Pete, come and meet Corrina Torres. She owns and operates this place. We've been friends for a couple years."

"Nice to meet you, Corrina." Pete smiled.

Corrina reciprocated. "Sit down, and I'll bring you a cup of coffee on the house."

Pete slid into the booth across from him. "Railroad, you make friends easily."

"I like people." He shrugged. "What's not to like? Most people are good. Did you get what you needed at the ranch?"

"I sure did. Here's my new pack." Pete lifted his carpetbag from the floor.

Railroad traced his fingers over the stitches. "Professional work. Who did it? I thought you went out to a ranch to find some used harness."

"Tom's uncle only had thick old leather, but he called a harness maker who owed him a favor and asked him to help me." Pete returned the pack to the floor. "He did a great job."

"He sure did." Railroad lifted his coffee cup and took a long, slow sip. "See what I mean about people being good? If you treat people well, they usually treat you well."

Pete unbuttoned his jacket and folded it on the bench beside him. "Did you find a good place to sleep last night?"

Corrina appeared with a coffee mug and set it in front of Pete.

"Thanks. I appreciate it."

She waved away his thanks. As she left, Railroad leaned closer. "I stayed here."

"Overnight?" Pete's eyes widened.

"Corrina lets me sleep on a cot in the back whenever I'm in town. Her son was a good friend of mine on the road." A sad look crossed Railroad's face. He pressed his lips together and looked down. "Rafael was a sweet kid, but a bit strong-willed. I told him more than once to never hang his legs out over the side of the boxcar. But Rafael always did what Rafael wanted to do."

Railroad ran his hands across his eyes. "When..." He cleared his throat. "When... ah, I tried to stop the bleeding by making tourniquets with my handkerchiefs, but by the time the train stopped and I got him off, it was too late. He bled to death."

Pete reached his hand across the table and patted Railroad's arm.

Railroad wiped his face with his dingy handkerchief. "I haven't talked about it for a long time. He was such a spirited kid. Always happy. Wanted to change the world, he said." Railroad blew into the hanky.

"I'm so sorry." Pete's eyes misted, too.

"It was real tough on Corrina, especially with Rafael being her only child. She lost her husband years ago." Railroad took a deep breath. "Your last lesson for the day, Pete." He tipped up his cup and drank the last of his coffee. "Never hang your legs out over the side of a boxcar. You don't know when the train will pass by some structure that can cut your legs off. Understand?"

"Understand."

That night Pete stayed with Railroad at Taco Mama's. Corrina laid a heavy quilt on the floor and handed him another to put over him. "Sleep well, mis queridos." She turned the lock on the door and closed it behind her.

In the morning, they got up early and ate the cold burritos she'd left for them. "God bless you, once again, my dear friend,

Corrina." Railroad kissed his fingertips and touched them to the table.

"Amen." Pete held the door open for Railroad. The sun peeked over the horizon, and a cool breeze blew. When he stepped outside, Pete tugged his jacket tighter.

"Today we head toward Arizona, right, amigo?" Railroad swung his arms as Pete walked alongside him at a brisk pace.

"Arizona it is." Pete would have to hustle to keep up with him.

"We want to get over to Highway 10." Railroad pointed toward the right. "But just about any vehicle going southwest will be heading for 10, so we'll just find a spot and start hitching. You get in front of me. They'll see you first. You're more of a clean-cut, trustworthy sort of guy." Railroad laughed then pointed to a corner. "Over there looks like a good spot."

"Okay."

They darted across the street in an opening of traffic. Blackbirds cawed on the treetops, mocking them as they waited, thumbs up. After many futile minutes, Pete shoved his hands in his pockets. "This is doing no good at all."

"Let's stand on that other street." Railroad pointed even further south. "Maybe we'll have better luck there."

Even more futile minutes passed, and Pete plopped on a sidewalk bench. "This is useless."

Railroad nodded. "Maybe we should keep going. You up to walk a bit?"

"What else can we do?" Pete pulled his already weary body from the bench and followed Railroad to the city limits, his pack heavy on his shoulders. His ribs hurt.

Railroad faced Pete and walked backward. "Let me carry that pack for a while."

"Why should you carry my stuff?" Pete hitched the pack higher on his shoulders.

"When will you learn that hobos take care of each other?

Now give me that pack so we can get to Arizona." He slipped the straps off Pete's shoulders and hefted them onto his own. With his height, the pack didn't sit as well on Railroad's back, but he moved forward with apparent ease. "Now, Pete, tell me about that fight you had. What did the other guy look like?"

"Which one?" Pete moved his shoulders up and down, forward and backward, stretching them.

Railroad's brow creased. "There were two?"

"Try five, although the leader of the gang only kicked me in the ribs." Pete tried to chuckle, but it came out as more of a cough.

"Ouch!" Railroad shook his head. "Did you get any licks in?"

"A couple of lucky shots, but I don't know how to fight." Pete raised his arms and let them flop back down. "Maybe you can give me some pointers."

"Be happy to do that, kid. A man needs to be able to protect himself, especially hitching and riding the rails."

A horn blared, and an old pickup truck full of Mexicans pulled over just ahead of them. Railroad darted to the truck, and Pete raced along behind him.

"Adónde vas?" The man closest to the open window poked his head out.

Railroad peeked in at the driver. "El Paso."

The man jerked his thumb toward the bed of the truck.

When Pete and Railroad had safely settled, the driver took off with a rattle and a roar.

Seven other men sat in the bed with them, different ages and sizes, but all Mexican. Some stared toward Pete, and others averted their gaze. Pete faced the man next to him. "Do you speak English?"

"No English," he said.

"Where are you going?" Pete frowned as the man's brow furrowed. What had the driver said? "Adónde vas?"

"Méjico." Pete nodded. El Paso was near the Mexican border. They were going the right direction.

Railroad wiggled position. "You okay, Pete? All this jostling can't be good on those ribs."

Pete reached behind him and adjusted his pack. "I'm grateful for the ride. And I'll be even more grateful when we stop."

A while later, the truck pulled into a gas station. Everyone jumped off and headed for the outhouse and the bushes. The driver motioned to Railroad. "Tienes algo de dinero."

Railroad pursed his lips. "Dinero?" He pulled out an empty pocket, and took Pete's quarter out of his other one. "Here."

He handed it to the driver, who waved his hand.

Railroad returned the quarter to his pocket.

Pete gave him a wry grin. People were good. Better than he'd thought. He shuffled to the outhouse line. Hopefully the guy ahead of him would hurry.

They reached Big Spring, Texas shortly after noon. Pete's stomach growled, and the sides of his stomach stuck together. The rough ride had pulverized his bottom. Leaning against his backpack helped cushion some of the bumps, yet his ribs ached. As soon as they stopped at another gas station, he got out and stretched his legs.

The driver filled the tank and moved the truck to the side. He pointed up ahead and said something to one of the front seat passengers. Then he trotted off in that direction.

The passenger turned to the others. "Diego, él traerá tortillas."

Tortillas? Would the driver bring something back for them as well? Pete could only hope.

Soon the driver returned with a paper bag and twelve bottles of soda pop. The men found a grassy spot and sat beneath a tree. Pete and Railroad shuffled along behind them. The driver handed out a bottle of soda for everyone, even Railroad and

Pete. Then he pulled a plain tortilla out of the bag for himself and passed around the bag.

"For us?" Railroad asked the driver.

"Sí, yes." The driver waved his hand toward them. "Coma una, por favor. Eat."

When everyone had one tortilla, they passed the bag again and all had seconds.

Food had never tasted so good. Pete raised his eyes heavenward. Who would have ever thought of eating a plain tortilla? And the root beer soda washed it down to satisfaction.

Pete rubbed his still-hollow stomach. He should be grateful. *Dear God, thank you for this unexpected meal. While I could have eaten more—and all of these men would want more—I am grateful for what you've given me.*

When he raised his head, he walked over to his host. What was the word for thank you in Spanish?

Railroad came up next to him. "Gracias."

Pete nodded. "Yes… um…Sí, gracias."

"De nada." The driver motioned for them to get back into the truck.

In a few more hours, they reached Highway 10, having made two more gas and toilet stops. The gray light of dusk descended upon them, and the driver turned on his lights.

They kept going, mostly in silence, though some of the men spoke to each other in Spanish. A few times, Railroad talked to Pete against the roar of the faulty muffler, but he seemed more bent on sleeping. Evidently they'd have no more meals.

When they reached El Paso, Pete sat up, hungry, tired, and sore. At the edge of town, the driver stopped, and Pete and Railroad jumped down to the ground.

The man on the outside passenger seat waved. "Good luck, amigo."

Pete nodded to the driver. "Gracias, sir. Gracias."

"De nada." The driver tipped his hat and drove off.

Railroad switched his bindle to his other shoulder. "Well, kid, we've finished the first leg of our journey to Arizona. What do you think about being a hobo?"

"I..." Pete rubbed his sore buttocks. His tongue stuck to the roof of his dry mouth, and his ribs ached. His stomach rumbled, loud and angry.

Grinning, Railroad nodded. "I suspected as much. Let's find something to eat."

Railroad led Pete to a trash bin, digging until he found a half-rotted potato. "Here, you take the first bite."

Pete nibbled a bit off the raw edge, wincing. Not like the boiled ones Betty used to make. He passed it back to Railroad, who took a big bite close to the rotten spot.

"Good eats, but we're going to have to ask for a handout, kid." Railroad started out at a brisk pace. "It's too dark to find anything more."

They passed through a neighborhood of small modest homes with streetlights on every corner.

"What time do you suppose it is?" Railroad looked up at the stars.

"'Bout ten, I suppose." Pete hitched his pack higher. "It's been a long day."

"Look!" Railroad pointed to the bottom step of a house. The street light shone on a scrawled outline of a cat. "See that?" He knelt, tracing the figure with a gnarled finger. "It means a kind lady lives here."

"How do you know that?" Pete peered closer at the design.

"It's hobo code to let other hobos know that they might get

something to eat here." Railroad bounded up the steps and knocked on the door. An elderly Hispanic woman pulled the door open a few inches and peered out.

"Good evening, ma'am." Railroad removed his hat. "My friend and I are on our way to spend the night about an hour from here. We haven't eaten all day, and we're awfully hungry. Might there be some chores we can do in exchange for something to eat?"

The woman squinted.

"My name is Railroad Randy and this is Dr. Pete." Railroad put his hand on Pete's shoulder. "Someone stole his car with all his veterinary equipment, belongings, and money. He was in the process of moving from Nebraska to Texas."

Pete toed the floor of the porch.

Railroad nudged Pete closer. "He's new to this hobo way of life, and I'm trying to teach him a few things. Fella's still too shy to ask for a handout, but we'd sure appreciate something."

The lines in the woman's face deepened as her smile reached her almost black eyes. She picked up the hem of her calico apron and smoothed it with bony fingers. "You boys sit there on that bench and I'll find you something." She closed the door.

Railroad lowered his bindle to the ground, and Pete dropped his pack beside it. They sat on the bench she'd indicated. Such a nice lady. How many hobos had she fed on that bench? In no time at all, she returned with a plate of food for Railroad.

A young girl with a ponytail followed with a plate for Pete.

"Thank you." Pete accepted the heaping mound of food. He hadn't dared hope for so much.

"Yes, we thank you so kindly, ma'am." Railroad bobbed his head. "And we'd be more than happy to help you with whatever you need."

The woman waved away his offer. "It's too late in the day to be working. You boys have a long walk ahead of you, so don't be worrying about us. You can leave the dishes on the bench when you're through. God bless you, now." She led the young girl back into the house.

Tantalizing odors wafted from Pete's plate. Dim light revealed baked beans and fried potatoes. Pete bowed his head. "God, I thank you for this meal." He forked a bite of the savory potatoes, chewing longer than needed before he swallowed.

"And I thank this wonderful woman who prepared our food." Pete scooped up some beans, letting the sauce roll over his tongue before swallowing them whole.

He took another bite of potatoes. "And I thank the hobo who scrawled the cat on the step."

Railroad chuckled, stuffing his mouth with beans. "Sounds like you're thankful for this knee-shaker." Railroad shoveled in more, the sauce dribbling down his chin.

"Sure am!" Pete grinned. "And we don't even have to work for it."

Railroad laughed.

They left the plates on the bench as she'd requested. After walking forty-five minutes, Railroad stopped in front of a crumbling brick building.

"Ah. Here's that flophouse I remembered."

Railroad walked up to the clerk and returned with a grin.

"We're fortunate they had vacancies." Pete held his ribs as they climbed up the stairs to their room.

"Vacancies." Railroad swung open the door and waved Pete in.

Around the room, wall to wall, men slept on the floor.

"Are there any empty mattresses?"

Railroad craned his neck. "I see one over there and another in this corner."

Pete's shoulders slumped. "Guess I'll take the one over there."

"Keep your pack under you." Railroad hooked a thumb under Pete's strap. "See you in the morning."

His eyelids drooping, Pete set his carpetbag beneath the

pillow. The man close to his left snored, and Pete's ribs ached, but he fell into a deep sleep.

———

"READY TO GO?" Railroad stood over him, waving his hand over his face.

Pete sat up, wide-eyed. He smoothed his trousers and tugged at the hem of his shirt. "Guess since we slept in our clothes, it won't take long to be ready." The corners of his lips slid up in a wry grin.

"Let's head west and see what we can find for breakfast." Railroad slung his bindle over his shoulder.

When they left the flophouse, they passed a grocery store. Railroad went in to ask for specks and came out shaking his head. "The grocer said he was out. We're too close to the flop-house. The others got it already."

They kept going until a little café appeared on the horizon. "We've got enough money for a small breakfast." Railroad put his hand in his pocket. "Should we go for it?"

Pete jiggled the coins in his pocket. "Yes."

For fifteen cents each, they had a filling breakfast of eggs, potatoes, toast, and coffee. "I don't know that I'm cut out for this hobo way of life." Pete pushed back his plate from the table.

Railroad sucked his teeth. "Got a choice?"

"I guess not." Pete tapped his fingers against his thigh.

"Then it's onward and upward. If we can catch a ride soon we'll be in Arizona yet today." Railroad picked up his cap from the seat next to him.

As they paid their bill, another man stood and followed them to the counter. Pete went out the door and started down the sidewalk, but Railroad whispered, "Wait."

When the man came out of the café and started toward a large truck, Railroad caught up with him. "My friend and I are heading to Arizona. We'd appreciate a ride if you're heading that direction."

Pete had slung his carpetbag over his shoulders and stood behind Railroad.

The man raised his eyebrows. "Y'all in trouble with the law?"

"No." Railroad laughed. "'Course, I just got out 'a the pokey. Thirty days for trying to hop a train."

Frowning, the man faced his truck.

Pete shoved his hands in his pocket.

Railroad grabbed Pete's elbow. "My friend here, Dr. Pete, had his car stolen with all his veterinary equipment and clothes and money, so he's as broke as I am." Railroad beckoned Pete forward. "And worse yet, he's new to this Okie lifestyle. Poor boy's not used to hopping into moving trains, so we're hitching. We're trying to get to Arizona to find jobs."

The driver smiled. "Well, you is either an honest man or a good storyteller. I'm not supposed to take on hitch-hikers, but since I didn't see y'all hitch-hiking, I guess I can say y'all are just friends tagging along with me. Right?"

"Sounds right to me." Railroad gave Pete a hearty slap on the back.

"Well then, it'll be tight, but climb on in. Wait. We'll have to put your luggage in the trailer." They all walked toward the back. "My name's Marshall Bill Duncan. My friends call me Marsh."

"I'm Railroad Randy, but you can call me Railroad, and this is Pete."

Marsh opened the door, and Railroad and Pete tossed their packs inside.

Pete climbed into the cab and straddled the gear shift and emergency brake. It was not comfortable in the middle, but he was grateful nonetheless.

Marsh pulled out onto the highway and settled into an even speed, apologizing to Pete every time he shifted gears. "Y'all are in luck because I'm going right through New Mexico and into Arizona, and on into California. I'm hauling Red Wing boots to Sacramento, California. Got a truckload of nothing but boots. Can y'all believe that?"

"Don't they make boots in California?" Railroad brushed dust from the dash.

"I guess these are some special kind or something." Marsh said. "Picked 'em up in Minnesota. So, you're a vet, Pete?"

"Yes, I am." Pete removed his straw hat and fiddled with the brim. "But I feel as if I can't even call myself that with no equipment or supplies to work with."

"We got a blacksmith in South Carolina that calls hisself a veterinarian." Marsh glanced both directions, then entered an intersection. "But he never went to no school to learn to be a doctor, doing what he claims to know how to do, because I grew up with 'im. What do you say about that?"

Pete worked the crease of his hat. "It's not unusual for some men to become what we call, 'Empirics.' They learn from observation, or perhaps from another vet, and set up a practice due largely because no other professional is available. If they have the right equipment, even the farmer can do a lot of his own vet work." He flipped his hat over in his lap. "The problem is that most don't have the equipment they need. Even I can't do what I might need to do in many cases without the right equipment."

"So, he's not doin' nothin illegal?" Marsh leaned forward and flicked his gas gauge, setting the needle to twitching.

"Not as long as he doesn't try to pass himself off as a trained, licensed veterinarian." Pete craned his neck to look at the gauges, too. Would the truck even get them to Arizona? "Has he been helpful to sick animals?"

Marsh nodded. "People keep coming back to 'im."

"Well, I always say, 'If it ain't broke, don't fix it.'" Railroad snorted. "So if nobody's complaining, he must be doing something right."

"Yes, he must be providing a good service." Pete nodded. "I wouldn't worry about it, but he could end up in trouble if someone thought he did a disservice to them."

Marsh shrugged. "Hey, either of you listen to the New York Giants/Chicago Bears game last month? No? Those Giants beat the pants off the Bears when they won the NFL championship. I'd sure like to see one 'a them games in person someday." March looked right and left. "I'm just waitin' to get a truck run to the right place, on the right date, so I can buy a ticket and see a game right there on the field. Wouldn't that be somethin'?"

"I'm more interested in baseball. I always watched our local team play during the summers." Pete sat up straighter. "I listened to the All-Star game last July when the American League won nine to seven. That was a good game. Then when the St. Louis Cardinals won the World Series last year defeating the Detroit Tigers four games to three—that was really exciting!"

"Nah, I never got into baseball, m'self." Marsh shook his head. "Guess it's what you grow up with. Me and my three brothers always played football in our back yard with the neighbor kids. Sometimes my dad even played with us, but he didn't play well. Too old by then."

"Football's a young man's game." Railroad patted his knees. "When the knees go, the ability to play football goes along with it."

After riding along in silence for a bit, Marsh cleared his throat. "Either of you like the ballet?"

Both men turned in unison to Marsh.

He burst into laughter. "Thought that would get you."

Railroad and Pete joined in, and then they quieted again.

Both Marsh and Railroad rode with their elbows out the window, the hot breeze blowing in their faces. Still, the cab grew terribly hot. Marsh cranked open the windshield for a much-needed breeze on Pete's face.

Oh, for a cold drink of water. He yawned. And a comfortable place to lie down for a nap. Where would they sleep tonight? What was that verse from Matthew? Foxes had dens and birds had nests, but Jesus himself was homeless. The Son of Man had no place to lay his head. Such a comforting thought, that Jesus experienced the same thing.

They got through New Mexico with only one toilet stop and long stretches without passing a single home. But then, who would want to live out here with towns so far apart? What if someone got sick and needed a doctor? Pete's heart skipped a beat. What if *he* got sick and needed a doctor while hitch-hiking or riding the rails?

## 17

Railroad raised a fist in the air when they passed into Arizona. "We'll find jobs here, kid. Unless you want to go all the way to California."

"I don't know." Pete scanned the dry, sandy terrain. "What do you think? What kind of job do you want?"

"Do you travel through here a lot, Marsh?" Railroad leaned over Pete.

"I get through here a few times a year, yeah." March glanced toward his rearview mirror. "What do y'all need to know?"

"Are there any fruit-picking jobs in Arizona yet?" Railroad looked hopeful.

"Fruit, vegetables, and herbs. Yeah, Arizona is where the Mexicans and Okies come to work," Marsh said. "Those fruit tramps have jobs all year from picking strawberries to shaking walnuts. So many harvesting jobs. Y'all never been to Arizona?"

"Nope." Railroad jerked his thumb toward Pete. "He hasn't, and I've only come through later in the fall."

"Well, there's somethin' to harvest year-round in Arizona." Marsh tapped his steering wheel.

"Good to know." Railroad faced Pete. "We'll just have to stop when we see something we'd like to harvest, right?"

"I guess so." After a lull in the conversation, Marsh pointed in their direction. "Y'all should try to find a place to pick fruit. It'd be a lot easier than bending over all day pulling carrots out 'a the ground, or breaking cauliflower off the plant."

"That's a good point, Marsh. Thanks," Pete said. "You know any orchards we could apply to?"

"Not acquainted with any, but I'll ask around when we stop for gas." Marsh signaled a lane change.

Farther into Arizona, after passing through mountains and rocky hills, men and women bent over picking vegetables in the fields. "That looks like back-breaking work, all right." Railroad craned his neck to continue watching them.

Pete grimaced. "Yes." Just outside of Mesa, they stopped at a station and stretched their legs.

Railroad ambled up to the attendant. "You know of any fruit picking jobs in the area?"

The attendant removed his cap and wiped away a bead of sweat. "I know of an orange grove just north 'a here. It's been so warm that I think they'd be picking pretty soon, if not even now."

"What do you think, kid?" Railroad bumped Pete's arm. "Should we get off here and give it a try or keep going for a while yet?"

Pete scratched his head. If he stayed, he might make enough money to settle somewhere. But, if he went on he might find something better. "Are there more plentiful orchards between here and California?"

"Oh, yeah. Lots more orchards over there."

"Then, let's keep going, Railroad." They needed to earn money soon. Hunger gnawed at him. He only had 15 cents left, and Railroad had none.

"Fine by me. Besides, I like the company." Railroad laughed and slapped Marsh on the shoulder.

Back in the truck, Marsh faced them. "I don't know about y'all, but I'm getting' mighty hungry."

Pete bit his lip, and Railroad fidgeted in his seat.

"I'm also gettin' the feeling y'all don't have money to buy a meal." Marsh quirked his brow.

Railroad nodded.

"Well, I've been down on my luck more than once, too. Know the feeling." Marsh slapped his knee. "Guess I could spring for a meal for all of us when we get to Mesa. I know a place that serves the best prime rib this side of the Mississippi."

Prime rib? Pete's jaw dropped. Could Marsh afford prime rib?

———

LONG PAST SUPPER TIME, Marsh pulled into a little café on the edge of town. He ordered prime rib for all three of them, and Pete thanked God with every succulent bite. People were good.

They walked back to the truck by the light from the café window.

"If you want to spend the night at the truck, we can try to make that work." Marsh burped and excused himself. "There's a little Mom and Pop gas station not far from here that lets truckers park in the back. I usually string a hammock under the trailer. One of you could curl up on the seat and the other can stretch out on top of those boxes of boots in the trailer." He raised his eyebrows. "I've got a couple extra blankets."

"We'd be obliged to do that." Railroad spoke for both of them.

Pete stepped in front of him. "I'll take the cab. Railroad, you're too tall. You'd never get comfortable."

"The trailer sounds good to me." Railroad motioned toward the back.

With a full stomach, his ribs feeling somewhat better, and a long day on the road behind him, Pete settled himself as best he could on the bench seat. Hopefully they'd find an orchard soon, so he wouldn't have to work in a field.

Sleep came quickly. When Pete awoke, he rubbed his tender, healing ribs. *Thank you, God for the ride from Marsh.*

After they started on their way again, Marsh announced, "The next stop will be Blythe, California, unless y'all want to get off sooner."

"What's it like in Blythe?" Pete hadn't seen any place he wanted to stop in Arizona so far.

Marsh shrugged. "Not much in Blythe, but the big Colorado River is close by."

A river! Pete placed his hand over his heart. How wonderful it would be to stop and sit by a river. To hear the song of rushing water. Should he go on as far as Blythe? Would Railroad?

Before long, fruit trees stood in long rows on either side of the road. "Want to get off anywhere around here, just let me know." Marsh waved toward the orchards.

"Think I'd like to go on." Pete pressed his palms against his trousers. He had to get to the Colorado River. It could change everything. The river always gave him peace and comfort. He could think better. Make better decisions. It would feed his very soul.

As more and more orchards came into view, Railroad kept his face pressed to the window. "Pete, I think we need to get out and get a job at one of these orchards. What do you think?"

"I don't know." Pete hesitated. "How far to Blythe, Marsh?"

Marsh's nose twitched. "We'll be there before suppertime."

"Railroad, I feel like I need to go to Blythe." Pete let out a long, slow breath. "That river is calling to me."

"Okay, kid. I sure hope you get along well." Railroad patted Pete's shoulder. "Marsh, you can let me off at that fruit stand up there. I sure do appreciate what you've done for me and Pete."

Marsh braked and pulled to the side of the road. Railroad reached past Pete and shook Marsh's hand while Pete gaped.

"I… Railroad…" Pete cleared his throat and squeezed Railroad's palm. This was happening too fast. How could Railroad leave him?

"Sorry I never gave you a fight lesson, kid, but you'll be okay." Railroad picked up his bindle. "Just think: bob, weave, jab. Like this: bob, weave, jab." He made the motions, then laughed. "Take good care, my friend."

Pete swallowed hard. Another friend gone. "Thanks for everything, Railroad. God bless you."

With that, Railroad hopped off the truck. He waved and walked off toward a distant fruit field. Pete stared after him until he disappeared.

"So, you like the river?" Marsh pulled back onto the highway.

"I don't know why, but it's where I need to be." But, how would Pete get along without Railroad showing him the ropes?

"There's a place where hobos hang out along the Colorado just before we reach Blythe." Marsh studied Pete for a moment. "We'll be going right by it. Maybe you want to get off there?"

"Sounds good." Pete turned back to the window.

Field after field raced past. Pete wrung his hands. What would it be like in a hobo jungle? Would he be welcomed? Would he be safe?

Should he have stayed with Railroad Randy? Guess it was too late to worry about that now.

## 18

Pete shook his head. Each step should bring him closer to the hobo jungle. But where was it?

"Be careful now." Marsh had issued the warning as Pete climbed out of the truck, alone in the world. How far had he walked? Had he missed the jungle?

A light breeze tickled Pete's nose, carrying a faint hint of smoke. He sneezed, his eyes widening and his throat constricting when the smell grew stronger. Fire! Where had it come from?

His heart slowed as he turned right. A confined fire lay ahead. Was that the hobo jungle?

With slow, unsure steps he entered into a gathering of men who slept, sat, and milled around. A savory aroma overcame the smoke, and his stomach contracted. Food.

A stout, scruffy man sat on an overturned pail, stirring a large can over an open fire. He stood as Pete approached. "What do you have for the pot?"

"I don't understand." Pete removed his pack from his back, but slung it over one shoulder.

"You come into the jungle, you bring something to add to

the Mulligan stew." The man plopped back down on the can. "Where you been?"

Pete shifted his weight. "I've never been to a jungle before.

The man rubbed his coarse hand over his head. "Welllll," he scratched his mustache, "newcomers get a freebie the first time. You got a dish in that pack you carrying?"

Pete gripped the strap of his pack. The clothes, the fishing gear, his Bible... Nothing would hold a dish of stew. "I guess not."

"You got to carry a dish and spoon and a can to cook in. You don't always got a jungle handy. You can use mine tonight, but get your own next time." He reached into his bindle and handed Pete a bowl and a spoon. "I'm Stubby. Help yourself."

"Pete." He laid his pack beneath a nearby tree, sat next to it with a bowl of thick stew, and ate with gusto. Was it appropriate to take seconds? Maybe he could at least chance it. He stood.

"I'll wash 'em myself." The man reached for the empty bowl.

Pete's shoulders slumped as he passed it over. So much for seconds.

"Thanks for the use of them." Pete sat leaning against a tree. Guitar music filled the air, and the lively chatter quieted.

A younger, skinny blond man with red suspenders played mostly old favorites. Not half bad. He launched into the first few notes of *I Got Rhythm.*

Pete's lungs constricted. How many times had Betty sung that song as she cooked or ironed clothes? The weight of her loss pressed on his chest until each breath stuck in his throat. After a while, his eyelids grew heavy. He removed his cape, spread it beneath the tree, and lowered his pack. As he reclined, he lay his head on the bulky pack.

The sky spread wide overhead, and the stars shone with brilliance. So many of them, more than Pete had ever seen. Close enough that if Pete stretched his arms out as far as they would go, he could almost reach one.

It'd be nice to have the blanket from the truck cab, but his jacket and cap would have to keep him warm enough. Would Marsh and Railroad sleep well tonight? He would miss Railroad the most. He should have stayed with him long enough to learn about fighting. Hopefully, he wouldn't ever have to fight again.

The rising sun awoke Pete, and the camp came to life as the men got up one by one. They relieved themselves in the bushes and helped themselves to a bowl of stew. Someone had built a fire under it, but grease still congealed around the edges of the gray and unappetizing gruel. Though his stomach growled, he headed toward the gurgling river to wash up.

A dog's yip set his heart racing. Was it in pain? He rushed to the sound.

A huge man hunched over, taunting a roped dog with the red-hot end of a stick. As Pete got closer, the man laughed as he jabbed the dog with the stick.

The dog jerked and cried out in pain.

"Stop that!" Pete ran toward them. "Stop torturing that dog!"

"It's my dog. Why do you care?" The man jabbed again. The dog strained to get away from him and cried out when the hot end pressed into his side.

Pete dropped his pack, sprinted to the big, crouching man, and belted him in the jaw.

The man dropped the end of the rope and stumbled backward several steps. He landed on his rump with a snarl that curled his lip and revealed rotten teeth.

As the man stood, Pete squared his shoulders. The man towered over him and weighed a great deal more. He didn't have a chance.

Feet shuffled as men from the jungle surrounded them.

This wouldn't take long. Pete locked his jaw and held up his fists. The muscles in the man's arms flexed. His huge, dirty hand curled into a fist, which came forward in a flash.

In only a few seconds, Pete fell flat on his back. He was right. It didn't take long.

"You want some more?" The man swung a few air punches in front of Pete's face.

Pete drew in a labored breath. Where was the dog? Not here in this patch of trees. Maybe it got away. He shook his head and sat up.

"Stick to your own business from now on." The man spit at Pete's feet. "Look what you done. My dog's gone. Well, good riddance. Stupid thing ate too much anyway." He stomped off.

A tall gray-haired man with a dirty mustache helped Pete up.

Pete patted down his ribs. Good thing the man hadn't hit him there. He eased his jaw open and closed, wincing as bolts of pain shot through the bone. Was it broken?

"Stay away from Killer," the older man said. "He's the most sadistic son of a gun I've ever seen. I'm surprised he let you go so easily. He must be having an off day."

Pete rubbed his jaw. "I'm Pete. Thanks."

The man lifted his bindle to his left shoulder. "They call me Birdman. Stubby said you're new to this kind of life."

Pete brushed dirt from his pants "And I have a lot to learn, I know."

"Well, the rules of the jungle are pretty simple. One free meal." Birdman took a few steps. He looked back as Pete followed. "After that, you have to contribute to the pot if you want to eat. If you're the last man in the jungle, you make sure the fire is out and the pot is clean before taking off again."

"Clean pot and fire out." Pete listed them on his fingers. "Got it."

"Turn the pot upside down. It's up to everyone to keep the jungle clean." Birdman faced Pete. "And everyone respects the other guy's belongings. This is our sacred place. Anyone who doesn't respect the rules of the jungle is asked to leave. They're handed a match. That means 'leave, you are not welcome here.'"

"A match? Why a match?" Pete frowned.

"No one knows how that got started, but it's good because no one has to put anything into words. There's no room for argument." Birdman wagged his finger in the air. "If someone hands you a match, you just pick up your stuff and go to the next jungle. Simple as that."

"Okay, thanks. What else should I know?"

"Men usually stay in a jungle for no more than three days unless they're recovering from an illness or something. Some jungle buzzards stay longer." Birdman tossed long gray hair from his face. "Not much more to know. Every jungle is your home when you're there. It's safe."

"What's in Blythe?"

"Not much." Shrugging, Birdman slowed his pace.

"You think there might be work around here? Any orchards?" Pete wiggled his fingers in his pocket and fingered his quarter. It would be nice to have a little money again.

"Not so close to the jungle. The orchards might already have all the help they need. They're just starting their harvests." Birdman gathered his hair and tied a ponytail. "Some aren't even ready for harvest yet. But, give it a try."

"I see a mirror over there." Pete pointed to a nearby oak tree. "Does that belong to anyone, or can I use it to shave?"

"It's there for all of us to use. There's a Gillette razor too, but, why bother shaving?" Birdman stroked his long, scraggly beard with a grin and followed Pete to the tree.

"Old habit, I guess. Thanks." Pete picked up the razor hanging by the mirror. "This doesn't have a blade in it."

"A hobo carries his own blade in his wallet." Birdman patted his back pocket.

So much to learn. Pete shaved with his own razor. He combed his hair, grabbed his backpack, and took off for Blythe. Or an orchard, whichever he ran into first.

Hot, dry sun beat down overhead. Although Pete's ribs still

hurt and his jaw throbbed, his spirits soared. California, here I come.

Who would have thought he'd end up in California, so far from Alvin and Emma and all his friends? So far, he liked Arizona, but the Colorado River hadn't brought the satisfaction he expected. Last night, the darkness kept him from seeing it. This morning, too many other things kept him from finding a quiet spot. He didn't want the busy jungle by the river. He wanted to be alone.

But it was okay. He'd come back later today.

The long walk overheated Pete's feet. His stomach growled, and his dry throat ached. He should have filled his canteen before he left. Big mistake. The heat shimmered in waves before him, and a small café materialized in front of him. Might it be a mirage?

He stumbled into the door of the quaint stucco building, his mouth so dry he could hardly spit. Empty tables filled the room, and a young brunette girl stood at the counter.

Pete shuffled forward. "Water."

She passed him an ice-filled glass, and he drained it. After taking a sip from the second, Pete smiled. "Thank you so much. I needed that. How much is breakfast?"

The girl pointed to a faded yellow menu. "Fifteen cents for eggs and potatoes. A nickel more if you want bacon."

Pete gripped the nickel and dime in his pocket. "Eggs and potatoes are fine."

He'd have no money left for a tip. Then, he'd be flat broke. Totally broke. Dead broke.

He needed a job.

Pots and pans clanged in the kitchen. "I don't have to put up with your crap anymore. I warned you. Now get out of here. GO!"

The loud voice held a strange high pitch. Someone got fired. The cook? Not the cook! Pete really needed to eat.

In a few moments, the young girl brought him a plate of steaming eggs and fried potatoes. Tears brimmed her puffy, red eyes. Had she just been fired?

"Are you all right?" Pete reached for the plate. "I couldn't help overhearing."

"My boyfriend just got fired." She wiped a tear with her finger.

Pete stroked his chin. Would the café need a replacement? "What did he do here?"

"Washed dishes." She wailed and rushed back into the kitchen.

Dishwasher? Pete sat straighter, gripping his fork tighter. He could wash dishes.

He took small bites of the eggs, glancing over his shoulder at the swinging kitchen doors several times. When the girl appeared with the coffeepot, Pete drew in a deep breath. "Could I perchance talk to the boss?"

She looked toward the kitchen. "It's only me and the cook here right now."

"Can I talk to the cook?"

"I'll see." She disappeared behind the doors again.

## 19

By the time Pete had finished breakfast, a young kid not more than sixteen emerged from the kitchen.

"I'm Cookie." He twirled the end of a dishtowel he had tucked into this waist. "You wanted to see me?"

Pete's eyes widened. This kid was the cook? "My name is Pete Walters. I'm looking for a job. You have an opening."

"Yeah, for a dishwasher." He stopped whirling the towel and put his hands in his pockets.

Pete smiled. "I can wash dishes."

Cookie quirked his brow. "It only pays a quarter a day plus meals. You may—"

"I'll take it." Pete slapped his hand on the table then drummed his fingers. Should he negotiate for more money? Did he accept too soon? "When can I start?"

Cookie folded his arms across his chest. He pursed his lips and narrowed his eyes. "How long will you hang around here?"

"That depends on how good the food is." Pete snickered.

Cookie snickered, too. "Okay, Pete. The noon rush will be coming in pretty soon, and I need a dishwasher, so I'll give you a try. Bring your stuff into the back room. I've got to finish prepping, so find an apron in the cupboard and get acquainted with the kitchen."

Pete beamed. When had he last felt this happy? He didn't mind washing dishes at all. He worked to the hum of conversations in the dining room, the order calls from Rita, and Cookie's efficient steps as he moved between the grill, the cook stove, and the counter. After the rush, Cookie tapped his shoulder. "Time to eat, Pete. What'll you have?"

"What are my choices?" Pete removed his apron.

Cookie lifted the covers of several pans. "Macaroni and cheese, meatloaf, and mashed potatoes. I could make you something special, but the boss wants us to eat what's left over."

"Makes sense." Pete pointed to one of the pans. "I'll have macaroni and cheese. I haven't had that in a long time and it looks really good."

"My choice as well. My mother taught me how to make good mac and cheese when I was just a kid." Cookie grabbed two plates.

"Please don't be offended, Cookie, but you're just a kid now."

Cookie chortled. "I'm not offended. I started riding the rails at sixteen, but I got this job over a year ago. Been here ever since."

"You were a hobo? How old are you, now?"

"Seventeen, and I'm still a hobo at heart. I want to see the world."

Cookie finished scooping the remaining macaroni and cheese on the plates, and Pete asked, "What about Rita?"

"Oh, she eats after I'm through, then she goes home until the supper rush." Cookie added a couple slices of garlic toast to each plate. "I wait on anyone who comes in during the afternoon."

Pete nodded, and they sat at a table next to the kitchen. "I'm impressed that you can cook at your age."

"I grew up in the kitchen of my parent's café watching my

mother cook and bake. Mom let me help even when I made a mess."

"That's wonderful." Pete swirling his fork around in the thick cheese sauce. "Your parents must miss you."

Cookie only nodded. "I'm saving enough money to go to Hollywood to see John Wayne. He's my favorite movie star. Did you see him in *The Big Trail* or *Riders of Destiny*? He's so tall and he has this deep voice. I can't wait to meet him! I've been ready to leave here a few times already, but then I go on down to the Colorado River and just can't seem to walk away."

"You like being by the river?"

Cookie sprinkled salt on his food and stirred it with his fork. He tasted it, frowned, and added more. "Yeah, I can spend a whole day there and not want to leave. Fishing is good there."

"I like being at the river, too." Pete took a napkin from the table dispenser and wiped his mouth. How many times had he thought the same? And, he'd only just arrived. "It just seems to call to me."

Cookie leaned forward. "I know a place in Kathleen Creek, Minnesota where there's this big old maple tree right at the river's edge. You can sit there and lean against that tree trunk and fish or sleep or read or just think. The best place in the world." He forked some food into his mouth, chewed, and swallowed. "'Course, there's lots of lakes around there, too. And in the middle of Indian Lake there's this fancy place called Grand View Island Resort where rich people come to fish. You have to take a ferry to get to the island and they have fishing guides and everything. The fishing is good there, but the Colorado is almost as good. But, I still like sitting by the Crow River in Kathleen Creek the best. Do you like to fish?"

"I do like to fish." Pete bit into his toast. Was Cookie from Minnesota? "So, Cook—"

The bell signaled another customer. Pete and Cookie both took their plates and disappeared into the kitchen.

Pete worked in the café every day and walked back to the jungle each night. He never ate there, but he often brought an aging piece of meat or vegetable for the Mulligan stew. Most nights passed pleasantly enough, but sometimes alcoholics joined the mix, either drinking themselves into quiet oblivion or making loud, obnoxious demands for more alcohol. Only one man earned a match. Grumbling, he picked up his gear and left.

Pete and Cookie became good friends, spending their breaks together and fishing together on Sundays. He even found "pearl diving," as hobos called washing dishes, enjoyable.

The owner of the café showed up once a week to take inventory, pay the employees, and do the ordering. Otherwise, Cookie handled everything. An old man came in every night to clean, and Rita came in for the three mealtimes.

One day, she burst into the café in the morning, her hair twisted in a loose braid and an enormous smile spanning her rosy cheeks. "I'm quitting. I'm going to get married and move to Arizona."

"When?" Cookie glanced at a clock on the wall.

"We're leaving now." Rita reached under the cash register counter and grabbed her sweater.

"Now?" Cookie raised both hands in the air. "Who's going to serve the customers?"

"That's not my problem. Jimmy said I shouldn't even tell you I'm quitting. He's still mad that you fired him." Rita stuffed her sweater in the bag she'd brought in. "But, you've been good to me, so I told him I had to stop and get my sweater. I'm sorry to just quit like this, but Jimmy says we have to leave today. So, goodbye."

Cookie stared after her as she left. "What am I going to do during the rush?"

"I can serve and wash dishes both." Pete put his hand on the young man's shoulder.

Cookie cocked his head. "You can?"

"Sure, I know the menu, except for the prices, but that's easy to learn." Pete reached for a menu. "I can handle it until you find someone else."

After a few days, Pete no longer felt awkward and clumsy, and he did the job to people's satisfaction. He washed dishes during the lulls when Cookie served customers and cooked. Because he worked longer days, Cookie let him sleep on a sofa, a big relief as the long trip back and forth wore on him. Cookie slept in a small alcove next to the back room.

Cookie always had prep work to do for the next morning, so Pete often fell asleep before Cookie finished working. Their personal hygiene consisted of wash-basin-baths in the restroom, and both men stayed clean. Over time, the place felt more and more like home, even though Pete hardly recognized himself behind all his facial hair.

Pete settled back into reading his Bible in the evenings again, as he had done before Rose and Betty died. He sometimes quoted Bible verses and read certain passages to Cookie when he felt the young man needed to apply them to his day, so Cookie started calling him "Preacher."

"What's your real name?" Pete asked Cookie one day.

"Ben. The guys in the jungle called me Cookie because I always carried herbs and spices with me, and I make the best Mulligan Stew. My reputation as a good cook just took off and soon the name stuck."

Another day, a hobo came in looking for work, and Cookie put him on as dishwasher. That left Pete with only having to serve the customers. He liked that just fine, although the owner lowered his 50 cents salary back down to 35 cents a day.

A month had passed since Pete left Grand Island. He held the change he had just been paid. What was he doing here? He wasn't a waiter, but an educated, licensed, experienced veterinarian.

He needed to find a community where he could gain the trust of the people, make a home for himself, and start a new vet practice. Dare he even hope to have his own family again someday? Did he even deserve that much happiness?

As much as he wanted all that, Pete had a long way to go before he deserved love and respect. For now, he should be grateful for three meals a day and a safe place to sleep. Shoulders heaving, he put the money in his pocket and tied on his apron.

One day in late February, Cookie tapped Pete on the shoulder. "I'm ready to head west to Hollywood. Do you want to go with me, Preacher?"

Pete jingled the change in his pocket. He'd saved all the money he earned. He liked Cookie's company. It was time for a change. "You know I'll go with you."

"I'm leaving tomorrow." Cookie banged the frying pan on the stove. "The old man won't give me a raise, so he can just close the place until he finds someone else to be chump enough to do everything I've done for his wages."

"We can't leave without giving notice, Cookie, even if you're sore at the old guy." Pete carried a box of salt to the table and uncapped the shakers. "It's not right."

"Who are you all of a sudden? My dad?" Cookie smirked.

"Well, I've lived longer than you, Cookie, and I've learned a few things. One is you always treat the other guy the way you want to be treated." Pete poured in the salt and screwed on the caps. "You didn't like it when Rita left you in the lurch without giving notice, did you? The Good Book says to love your neighbor. Loving people is treating them right."

"Okay, okay already." Cookie waved his hand. "We'll give notice, Daaaaad."

Two weeks later when they packed for riding the rails, Cookie still sometimes called Pete 'Dad.'

Pete bought a bowl and spoon from the café and saved an

empty coffee can. This time, he'd be better prepared to live the hobo life. He shaved once more, washed his clothes, and tucked them in his pack.

But... Pete had never hopped a train. Cookie said they'd jump on while it moved down the tracks. Would he be able to do that with his pack on his back? Would he be arrested by the yard dicks, or worse, by the cinder bulls Railroad had mentioned?

Or even worse than that, would they be robbed or killed by the jack rollers Cookie had said robbed hobos on the trains? Would they make it to Hollywood safely?

Pete tossed and turned for hours. He finally fell asleep with the first gray light of dawn, only to dream of ugly, angry men chasing him, their heavy feet one step behind him.

## 20

All morning Cookie instructed Pete on the safety issues of hopping a train. "Always jump on the ladder at the front end of the car. The rungs go clear up to the top. Swing up and climb on. If you miss it, you'll be thrown back against the car or away from the train, but you can swing back again and get on. If you grab the ladder at the back end of the car and you miss, it throws you under the train."

"Good to know." Pete exhaled loudly.

"The train engine builds up steam so they get going slowly. You have time to jump on after it leaves the station and before it gets up speed. The same with stopping. You have time to jump off before it reaches the station. That way you avoid the yard dicks who'll arrest you, or worse."

"How do you handle your pack when you jump?" Pete rocked on his heels. How on earth could he remember all these things?

"Make sure it's over your shoulders and it'll come along with you. Some guys throw their pack in first and then jump, but they're the seasoned hobos who know they'll make the jump okay. I tie my bindle around my waist so it's no problem for me."

The closer they got to the rails of the Atchison, Topeka, and Santa Fe Railway the more Pete's nerves rattled. "What if I can't do it?"

"Do what?"

"Jump."

"We'll get as close to the station as I dare, so the train won't have time to get going very fast. When I point to the car and say go, run up and grab the handle. Put your feet on the lowest rung of the ladder and hop into the car. Do it quickly, because I'll be right behind you."

They stood close to the track, next to the cold, hard, gleaming metal strips of rail. A shrill train whistle blew twice. Thick, black smoke and white steam escaped into the air. Thudding sounds of couplings grabbing. Chugging sound of iron wheels creeping closer. Then the huge, black locomotive rumbled past, spewing hot air along its sides, so noisy it drowned out everything else. Pete's stomach churned

The train inched past him. He stood straighter, took a deep breath, and watched Cookie for the sign.

"Go!" Cookie pointed to an open car. Pete ran, but a horde of other men, all running for the train, appeared out of nowhere alongside him. With Cookie right behind him, giving him a shove at the right moment, Pete grabbed the handle, lifted his feet to the rung, and flung himself in the car.

Cookie landed right behind him.

Pete's hands hurt from scraping them on the rough, gritty boxcar floor. He pushed to sit and re-adjusted his backpack as he wove from side to side with the movements of the train. The darkness clouded his vision, and the stench of several men overpowered the small, crowded space.

"You did it! That wasn't so hard, was it?"

Pete leaned over the edge of the car and vomited. Cookie howled along with many of the other seasoned hobos in the car.

While Pete recovered, they sat with their backs against the front of the boxcar. He flexed his toes and stretched his hands overhead. "Now all I have to do is jump off again. Is that easier or harder?"

"It's scary the first few times you do it. You'll get the hang of it. Did your pack feel too heavy? Do you need everything you have in there? And how about that leather cape tied around your waist? Did it feel like that got in your way when you jumped?"

"The cape didn't interfere at all, and I don't know what I'd get rid of."

"Just something to think about." Cookie shifted to face the countryside. "I saw the desert as ugly when I first came here, but it's grown on me."

"How far are we going in this boxcar?" Pete turned toward Cookie's view. The many different kinds of trees, the clear blue sky… so beautiful. All moving past too quickly to take it all in.

"I don't know. When you live the hobo lifestyle, you go with the flow. If the train stops, you stop. You get off and on when you want to." Cookie tightened his thick bindle around his waist. "We'll probably have to change trains a few times before we reach Hollywood. As long as it points in the right direction, we'll stay on it."

Pete huffed. They needed a better plan. But for now, he would trust Cookie's experience.

They traveled with incredible speed, making a brief stop at Riverside while Pete and Cookie, along with the others, stood silently in the darkest inside corner of the boxcar. They breathed a sigh of relief when the train pulled out again.

When they reached Palm Springs, Cookie stood. "Let's get off here. Jump and roll then run for cover." Cookie grabbed

Pete's arm and tugged him close to the edge. "Watch me. I'll go first."

When the wheels had almost stopped, Cookie jumped. Pete followed, doing a decent job of rolling. They took off running for a cover of palm trees.

"There. So far so good, Preacher." Cookie peered from behind a thick tree trunk. "No one saw us. "

Palm Springs, California sure didn't look anything like Grand Island, Nebraska. Long jagged branches on the top of palm trees swayed in the hot breeze. Low, pastel colored adobe buildings stood baking in the sun. A subtle pungent odor wafted toward Pete. Lemons?

"I need a toilet." Cookie turned a full circle. "Then, we'll find something to eat."

"Oh, look. Is that a gas station?" Pete pointed to their left.

"Yes, and with a restroom." Cookie took off in a fast jog.

They used the facilities, cleaned up, and then strolled down the street toward a restaurant.

Pete caught his reflection in the pristine glass windows. A clean place, but could they afford it? He followed Cookie inside to the counter, where a chalkboard menu covered the top half of the wall behind it. Ah, good. Inexpensive.

A young, gum-chewing blonde beckoned to them with long painted fingernails, and led them to a booth. "Newcomers, right? Let me tell you all about Palm Springs." She turned over two upside-down glasses and reached behind Cookie's red leather bench for a pitcher of ice water. "There's a lot of movie stars around Palm Springs. Many stay at the La Quinta Resort." Her cheeks flushing, she tapped Pete's arm. "I saw Loretta Young once. Oh, she's so glamourous! I almost died when she got out of a shiny, big, black car and went into that fancy El Mirador Hotel. She wore blue-ish high, high-heeled shoes, and had on a white coat that swirled when she turned. Oh, she's so gorgeous!"

She put her hand over her heart. "You'll just love Palm Springs!"

"Maybe John Wayne is here in Palm Springs!" Cookie raised from his seat. "Where is this fancy hotel?"

Pete chuckled. That Cookie… so eager to meet his hero.

"The El Mirador." She took a small white pad from her apron pocket and scrawled across the page. "Here's directions. Now, what'll it be?"

After their stomachs were filled to the brim, they walked to where the beautiful, white building stood, topped with a red-tiled roof and a bell tower.

"Maybe we can get jobs here!" Cookie folded his hands together, a wide grin bursting across his face.

Pete smiled. Nice to see his too-mature friend exhibit child-like exuberance over the movie stars. "Let's go ask and see!"

They dashed to the entrance, where a receptionist directed them to a tall, wispy man in a crisp pinstripe suit.

"Excuse me, sir." Pete extended his hand. "Do you have any jobs available? We're looking for work."

"You and five hundred others like you." The man sniffed. "We have no openings."

Pete winced. Did he see them as vermin when he looked down that long nose at them?

Outside, Cookie leaned against the white brick, his shoulders slumped so much they might have touched the ground. Poor crestfallen chap.

"That went well." Pete flung his backpack on his shoulder.

Cookie straightened and brushed imaginary dust from both shoulders. "Let's try that other place where movie stars live. What is it called?"

"The La Quinta Resort." Pete took a few steps forward. "Maybe we have to tell them right away that you can cook before they have a chance to tell us no."

"Okay, but what will we say you do?" Cookie frowned.

"I'm willing to do anything." Pete stepped in front of a passing middle-aged couple. "Excuse me. Can you tell us how to find the La Quinta Resort?"

Armed with directions, they walked forty-five minutes due west. When they reached the many sprawling Spanish-style haciendas and casitas nestled together at the foot of the mountains among beautiful palms and fruit trees, Pete grinned. The branches, heavy with yellow and orange fruit, sent off heavenly aromas that made Pete's mouth water. Those luscious oranges and grapefruit. Would anyone mind if he just picked one? His chest tightened. Probably so.

"Look, Pete. A swimming pool." Cookie dragged him around the corner of the building. "Can you believe it?"

Pete's jaw dropped. The green grass, aqua water, blue and white front doors set against the red tiled roofs of the white buildings… Certainly only rich and beautiful people lived like this! Was it right for Pete to even stand on this ground? Was he clean enough? And, how should he act? He trudged on, a knot growing in the pit of his stomach.

As they passed the front of the resort, a beautiful team of horses trotted around the curved drive to the front door, pulling a shiny black carriage. Behind them, a couple on horseback tugged on their reins, her hair shining like polished brass and curls bouncing with every toss of her head. His crisp white pants and perfect polo shirt starkly contrasted the midnight black horse he rode. The laughing man and woman dismounted.

"Be right back!" The woman tossed her luxurious blonde hair over her shoulder and passed the reins to the white-gloved footman who'd reached like an automatic mannequin.

They had horses! Pete squared his shoulders. Maybe he could get a job as a vet. He raced in after Cookie and approached the uniformed man behind the desk.

"A veterinarian, you say?" The man squinted at Pete.

"I left Nebraska a year ago to find work as a veterinarian in this part of the country. A few months back, my car and equipment was stolen. But I dream to take care of beautiful horses again." Pete leaned toward the man. "Please, do you have any work that I could do?"

The man stroked his chin and pursed his lips while Cookie stared at Pete in surprise.

Then Cookie stepped in front of Pete "And I'm an experienced chef.

"Have a chair and I'll be back in a few minutes." The man disappeared behind double oak doors.

"You never told me you're a vet." Cookie stared at him in awe.

"I'll explain later." Pete turned away from Cookie and ran his hands through his hair.

Pete and Cookie fidgeted in their chairs while they waited. When the man came back, he hooked his finger at Pete "Come on back to my office. My name is Mr. Bryan. I'm the manager here. We may be able to find some work for you." He gave Cookie a dismissive wave. "We don't have any openings for a chef, however."

"Either we both work, or neither of us works." Pete stopped in his tracks. "Surely you can find something in your kitchen for an experienced chef."

Mr. Bryan gave Cookie a reluctant nod, and they all headed to the back office

Mr. Bryan settled into a plush velvet chair behind a mahogany desk and tented his fingers beneath his chin. "Dr. Walters, the man caring for the horses is retirement age and not well. Now might be a good time to take some of the pressure off him. We have stable boys who feed, water, curry, and clean up after the horses. Your job would be to keep them healthy and oversee their care. Horseback riding, riding lessons, and carriage rides are important to our guests. We'll give you a try.

As for your friend," he faced Cookie, "what did you say your name is?"

"Ben, but everyone calls me Cookie. I managed and cooked at a small café at Blythe for more than a year, but I learned to cook in my parent's restaurant before that…"

Mr. Bryan held up his hand. "I'll take you over to Mr. Bouvier, Ben, to see what he might have for you. Then I will orient you both to La Quinta employment." He straightened a stack of folders on the desk. "Our clientele is, shall I say, used to certain treatment here, and we must maintain a sophisticated demeanor. We have many celebrities here, as you probably know." A quill pen rolled off the side of the desk and he swept it up in one fell scoop. "But we'll go over all that after we see Mr. Bouvier."

Two hours later, Pete and Cookie sat on a bench outside the resort with full stomachs and half their first week's pay, folded uniforms between them.

Pete rubbed a small gravel between his fingers. "Can you believe our luck, Cookie? You, an assistant chef—"

"For minimal pay." Cookie shrugged then grinned.

"Meals and uniforms." Pete lifted his crisp pants and shirt from the stack. "Laundered uniforms. And, Mr. Bryan didn't have to give us the advance."

"True." Cookie grabbed his uniform and stood. "Let's go check out those Sunshine Court Apartments he told us about. Section 14, right?"

"Right." Pete chuckled. "Cheap housing. Hope it's better than the flophouse I stayed in a while back."

Cookie laughed. "I'm sure it will be. At least it's close to the resort."

"And that meal was delicious." Pete rubbed his belly. "I might just move into that break room behind the kitchen."

Mr. Bryan dashed out the front door and raced past them to

a waiting black touring car. "Thank you, fellas. See you in the morning."

"Sure thing. We appreciate your kindness, Mr. Bryan." Pete and Cookie walked off in the other direction. When they rounded the corner, Cookie jumped and kicked his heels.

A smile spanned Pete's cheeks. That Cookie. So youthful. And yet he could kick his own heels.

What could be better than working at such a prestigious place?

## 21

Pete braced himself against the stable door as the last of the new guests trickled back to the main lodge. European royalty, movie stars, singers, and rich business tycoons—who wouldn't want to work in such opulent surroundings? Why, he'd moved up a notch in class. And he loved working with horses. The job was a true blessing.

Except... the pampered, spoiled clientele never appreciated any service provided. They treated him as subservient in a way the people in Blythe never had. He spent half his days picking up after them in their wake, tolerating their entitled attitudes as they never lifted a finger to do anything for themselves.

His jaw tightened. How could anyone treat another human like an unworthy servant?

It didn't seem to bother Cookie, on the other hand. "I'm learning so much from the chef," he told Pete. "He trained in France, you know. His cooking is so different from what I learned at home. Every day is a new experience."

Pete couldn't begrudge Cookie his happiness. Not when cooking mattered so much to him.

Although their work schedules differed, they often explored

Palm Springs together. They hiked into the hills and around the city where the fruit hung ripe for the picking from an abundance of trees.

"That was an interesting walk today, Cookie. No one should go hungry in Palm Springs, yet so many men wear hunger with hopelessness on their faces. I don't understand it." Pete fell back into step with his friend on the hot sidewalk. "So, Cookie, who have we seen today?"

"Well, Katherine Hepburn and Spencer Tracy were at breakfast today as every day." Cookie counted on his fingers.

Pete removed his hat and wiped sweat from his brow. "Yes, they're regulars." He grinned. "I brushed the coats of Gene Autry's and Glen Ford's horses this morning."

"William Holden asked for a double stack of my special blueberry pancakes." Cookie raised his arm in the air and brought it down in a victory force. "And I heard the reclusive Ms. Garbo was in the stables in the early hours."

Pete smoothed his hair and replaced his straw hat. "Yes. Ms. Greta Garbo with her beautiful Arabian mare. I spent half the morning brushing that luxurious mane."

Cookie nudged him. "Ms. Greta's or the horse's?"

"Ah, Cookie." Pete laughed as they approached the back entrance to the hotel.

Near the corner of the building, three watchmen shooed off a couple scraggly men toting bindles. Pete dragged his hand over his shaven face. How blessed he was to be here.

While many hobos wandered the streets, beautiful or handsome people dominated the population of Palm Springs. They owned the latest vehicles, the most expensive clothing, and opulent jewelry. They wore extravagant hairstyles and perfect makeup.

Yet California suffered from a severe drought, as did Kansas, Colorado, Texas, Oklahoma, Nebraska, New Mexico, and South Dakota. "The dust bowl states," as the newspapers called them.

On April 15th, Pete and Cookie ended their hike amidst a group of resort guests gathered in the parking lot.

A looming toothpick of a man stroked his beard. "I tell you, yesterday's dust storm was so severe I believe it a sign of the world's end."

"Could be." A shorter, pudgier man tapped the sidewalk with his cane. "Tons of dirt and dust blowing dense and dark for four hours. Couldn't even see my hand in front my face."

A pretty blonde with a braided up-do waved her hand to the side with a flourish. "My Henry said the storm swept across state after state, stranding motorists, and killing animals. Miles of destruction."

Pete turned to Cookie. "I hope my friends are all okay in Nebraska."

"I hope…." Cookie clamped his mouth shut and shuffled forward.

Pete furrowed his brow then trotted after him. What on earth happened in that boy's past?

Cookie paused at the bottom step. "I'm glad we're in California right now. Sounds like we got the least of it."

Pete opened the door. "Since the La Quinta Resort, as well as most hotels in Palm Springs, close at the end of this month, I hope I've saved enough money to last me a while."

"Who knew that no one comes here in the heat of the summer? They've got a nice pool." Cookie waved toward the cool blue water, towering palms, and umbrellas shading the lounge chairs. "I had to spend $2.48 for new shoes, after rent, I don't have much left."

"Don't worry." Pete turned toward the building. "We'll share what I have." A little money that wouldn't last long.

At the end of April, Pete and Cookie collected their last checks from the La Quinta and bid the other staff goodbye.

Mr. Bryan slapped Pete's shoulder. "Hate to let you fellas go, but with this awful summer heat and the dust bowl…" His face hardened. "I don't know what we'll all do if there's no relief. All those hundreds of dead birds and rabbits. The acres of destroyed crops... we've even had to hang wet sheets to keep it out of our home. Guess we should put some up here, too. If we'll even be able to weather this decline in business."

"We understand." Pete squeezed Mr. Bryan's hand. "Thank you for this opportunity."

What would they do next? It had been a fluke to find jobs in Palm Springs. Hundreds of men wandered day after day without work and waves of them rode the rails to California.

Cookie stuffed his hands in his pocket as they headed back to their rooms for the last night. "I still want to go to Hollywood."

Pete kicked at a stone across the porch steps. "Guess I'll come along, then." His stomach tightened. He'd have to hop another boxcar.

"The Southern Pacific trains run eight times a day out of Palm Springs." Cookie drew a folded schedule from his back pocket and handed it to Pete.

Pete stopped, opened the schedule, and read. "We can grab the next train to Los Angeles in the morning."

With a nod, Cookie stuffed the schedule back in his pocket. "Sounds good!"

Pete tossed and turned all night. He wanted to jump the train like a man, but what if he missed the ladder and ended up beneath the train? By breakfast, his stomach churned, and he couldn't eat.

"It'll be easier this time, Preacher, now that you know what to expect. Don't forget, you can tell how fast the train is moving by how slow the couplings grab. Listen to it." Cookie pointed to the track.

They inched their way out of the weeds, crouched like predators, searched for yard dicks, and timed the train's speed and arrival where they waited. As the noisy locomotive passed, a rush of steam from the huge engine lifted their hats. Pete reached up and pressed his down.

Cookie gestured to a boxcar a few cars back. "Go!"

They both ran full force. Pete grabbed the hook as it passed, lifted his feet to the ladder, and flung himself into the car.

Cookie landed right behind him. "Good job, Preacher." He slapped Pete on the back. "And this car even has cardboard. I can't believe we're all alone in here."

"What good is the cardboard?" Pete's voice shook. Had he really made a successful train hop again?

"It's great for sleeping and hiding. One of a hobo's best friends."

After many miles, the chugging of the wheels and the gentle rocking of the boxcar tried to lull Pete to sleep, so he decided to nap in the corner in a big cardboard box.

He fell asleep, but awoke to shouting.

A jack roller pressed Cookie's face against the wall of the boxcar with a gun to his head.

Cookie elbowed him in the side. "No, I won't jump! It would kill me!"

Pete lifted the cardboard and peeked out. This man had robbed Cookie and now wanted to get rid of him. He must not know someone shared the car.

He reached into his pack for his pistol and crept up behind them as the burly man shoved Cookie closer to his doom.

His knees knocking, Cookie clung to the edge of the open doorway. "Please. Let me live."

Pete pressed his pistol into the jack roller's back. "Drop that gun, NOW!"

The gun thudded on the floor of the boxcar, and Cookie jumped away from the edge of the door. He collapsed, his face drained of color.

Pete shoved the gun aside with his foot and faced the robber. "Sit and take off your shoes."

The man obliged. His lips quivered as he raised his chin. "What are you going to do to me?"

"After you jump off this train you won't need your clothes and shoes, but we can use them." Pete stood over the man, pointing the gun at his head.

"Please don't make me jump. You can have my money. Here, take everything I have." He reached into his pocket, pulled out a hand full of bills, and held them out to Pete.

"Now take the laces out of your boots." Pete stuffed the money into his pocket.

After he had the long, brown laces out of his boots, Pete reached down and took them from him. "Now lie on the floor on your stomach."

By this time Cookie had stood up next to Pete.

Pete handed him one of the laces. "Tie his hands together behind his back with this shoelace."

As Cookie fastened the man's hands, Pete secured his feet with the other shoelace. "I should roll you off this train, but I won't, you thief. In fact, you're worse than a thief. You would have killed my buddy. You better hope that somebody finds you here before you rot and begin to smell like the garbage that you are. Now let's see what else you have in your pockets." Pete checked the man's other pockets. "Here's more money." He handed it to Cookie.

Cookie stuffed the money in his pocket. "Let's check his boots." He plunged his hand in each, coming out with a fistful of money.

After Pete put his pistol back in his pack, he handed Cookie the other gun.

"I'd like to shoot this low life right now."

"Please, don't shoot me. I've got a wife and kids," the man blubbered. "Please, don't."

Cookie gave him a swift kick in his ribs. "You're not worth a bullet." He put the gun in his waistband and sat down, leaning against the back of the boxcar. "What are we going to do with him?"

"Does he have anything we need?" Pete lifted the handle of the man's bag with the toe of his worn leather shoe.

Cookie looked at him. "I have new boots. Do those fit you?"

Pete stuffed his foot in one, wincing as it caught in the tight leather. "Nah. They don't fit." He lifted the hem of the man's shirt. "All of his clothes would be too small for me, too."

"I don't want anything that weasel wore." Cookie scrunched his nose. "I've never been so scared in my life. If you hadn't come with that gun when you did, I'd be a dead man now. You saved my life, Preacher. How can I ever thank you?"

"No thanks needed. Hobos take care of each other, right? Isn't that the code?" Pete cast a glance over his shoulder at the still-blubbering man. Did the code include worthless robbers? Would he have been driven to steal now if Betty and Rose had still been alive?

"No, I mean it, man, I owe you my life. I'll repay you some day." Cookie shuffled over to the cardboard. "I don't know how, but I will. I swear it, Preacher, I'll repay you somehow. Man, I thought I was dead for sure. I almost peed my pants before I saw you creeping up on him."

"Forget it, Cookie." Pete followed him and picked up the cardboard he'd slept under. "You don't owe me anything."

"Yes, I do. And I'll find a way to repay you someday."

They sat side by side, leaning against the back of the boxcar. The rails rattled, shaking the trussed up man as his sobs eased into sniffles.

"Thank you, Lord." Pete whispered beneath his breath.

"What did you say?" Cookie leaned closer to Pete.

"Oh, I thanked God for your safety." Pete unclasped his hands.

"I've been doing that ever since you got the drop on that

man. And I kept asking God to save my life all the while that man had me in his clutches."

"Well, there you see, you don't owe me your life, you owe it to God."

"I know that, but I still owe it to you as well." Cookie's jaw flinched. "Do you think… this man … and we've got all his money now."

"We needed money, didn't we?" Pete gestured toward the thief. "God provided."

Cookie frowned. "But…" He shifted his weight, turning away from Pete. "I still say I owe my life to you."

Pete closed his eyes. He didn't want to argue about it anymore. He was blessed to be traveling in the company of a man who knew and loved God as much as he. God had provided.

"Where is Hollywood?" Pete asked Cookie.

"It's on the northwest part of Los Angeles. When we get off the train, we'll ask someone how to get there."

Pete combed his hair with his fingers. How did Cookie manage to live with such ease? He always assumed the best, in both circumstances and people. Once, Pete asked Cookie if it didn't bother him to not have firmer plans about where he would go next. He had answered, "I know God will take care of me. He's my father. You told me so, remember."

Cookie's simplistic faith touched Pete yet again. Now, he agreed. "Yes, God will send someone to show us the way to Hollywood."

As the train neared Los Angeles and slowed, the man on the floor raised his head. "Untie me and let me go. I'll never rob anyone again. I promise. Please let me go."

"You're lucky we didn't push you off the train with it traveling full speed." Cookie gave him a shove with his foot. "After we get off you can yell loud enough and someone will rescue you. That's better than you deserve."

They waited until the train slowed enough in Los Angeles. First Cookie jumped and then Pete. They rolled and ran.

"Hey!" A brutish voice yelled after them. A yard dick. "Stop, or I'll shoot."

They stopped, and the detective planted his boots in front of them. "You're under arrest for illegal rail transportation. Pay the fine or go to jail. How much money do you have?"

"How much is the fine?" Pete hitched his backpack higher.

"How much money do you have?" The detective pointed his pistol at Pete.

"We'll try to come up with enough money to pay the fine, sir, if you'll tell us how much it is."

"Don't get cute with me, you good-for-nothing piece of crap." The detective motioned with his pistol. "Empty your pockets, both of you."

Pete wished they had thought to hide some of the money they had. When they came up with a total of $17.00, the yard dick said, "Well, look at that. The exact amount of the fine. You boys are in luck. You won't have to go to jail." He snatched the money, turned and left.

"Just when everything was going well." Shoulders slacking, Pete stuffed his hands in his empty pockets. Guess that's what he deserved for stealing from the thief. He didn't want to go on being a hobo. He wanted to wake up from this nightmare that had become his life and find himself back in Grand Island, Nebraska with Betty and Rose.

"Come on, Preacher." Cookie paused steps ahead of him.

"Wait." Pete said. He slumped to the ground.

Cookie turned. "What's the matter? You don't want to go to Hollywood?"

"No, but I know you want to go." Pete breathed out heavy, flaring his nostrils.

Cookie sat beside Pete and faced him. "Maybe we need to lay back for a while." Cookie pulled on some grass. "I heard meals are only ten cents at a greasy spoon on Fifth Street. Maybe eating will make us both feel better."

"We don't have ten cents between us." Pete removed his hat and ran his fingers through his hair. "How are we going to get a meal?"

Cookie grinned. "I've been on the road longer than you have, Preacher. I've learned a few things. I have money in my shoes, but because they often check shoes, I also have money in my fly."

Pete's mouth flew open. Thank goodness Cookie had been smarter than Pete and hid some money! "Your fly?" he asked.

"There aren't many places the dicks or the jack rollers won't look if they get their digs into you, but nobody has thought to check there. I don't know anyone else who does this, but I cut a small slit on the side big enough to stuff a rolled-up bill into it and keep it from falling out. I've got a dollar in each shoe and a dollar in my fly."

Pete grinned. They were going to eat.

Cookie cornered a tall, dapper man. "Sir, could you please direct us to a restaurant where we might buy an inexpensive meal?"

The man nodded. "Fifth Street. If you take a left, go three blocks down, and then another left, you'll spot it on the right."

"Thank you, sir." Cookie lowered his eyelashes and dropped his chin, nodding back to the man.

When they reached the restaurant, Cookie headed to the bathroom to get his money.

They sat at a scarred wooden table teetering from leg to leg until Cookie folded a piece of discarded paper and put it under one of the legs. The smell of cigarette smoke permeated everything in the room. Their waiter, a stooped, old man with callused hands sauntered over to him. Weeks of grime must have been embedded in his apron.

"Two specials." Cookie pointed to the menu.

Though not delicious, the dry chicken and greasy potatoes eased Pete's hunger. After eating, they got a room in skid row for the night.

"Twenty-five cents each." Pete turned toward Cookie. "Thank goodness you had the dollars."

"Lay your cape on your pillow so you don't get head lice." Cookie undid his bindle and spread the blanket over his mattress and pillow.

Late that night, melancholy crept over him like a heavy burden. How could he express his feelings? Fatigue and hopelessness left him mute and breathless as silent tears fell onto his dirty cape. Who was he? Why was he wandering without a destination?

Pete pressed his fists against the mattress. He wanted to go home. But he didn't have a home. *Lord, help me.*

The next morning, Pete awoke in a better mood. He scratched his stubbly chin. "Now what, Cookie?"

"We ask someone how to get to Hollywood." Cookie grinned.

Pete shook his head. How could he have been lucky enough to find a traveling companion with such a great disposition? They bought ten-cent breakfast at the same greasy spoon with plans to hitch hike toward Hollywood. Pete dragged, having slept so little.

His enthusiasm for seeing movie stars did not measure up to Cookie's excitement, but he wouldn't begrudge his friend's greatest desire. With a forced smile, he hitched on his pack, and trudged along.

The acrid smell of car exhaust and constant rattle of traffic in the hot, dry city made Pete dizzy. Where could he find relief? Maybe an open space between buildings? Sadly, their brick walls stood back to back.

They wandered to a busy street and claimed a spot on the sidewalk. Cookie thumbed for almost an hour before an old

Model A Ford pulled over. "Hop in, boys." the driver said, "Where you headed?"

"Hollywood." Cookie beamed as he climbed into the back seat.

Before long, they arrived, finding no celebrities, but they did find gold-outlined stars embedded in the sidewalk bearing movie stars' names.

"There's Warner Brothers' studio." Cookie tugged at Pete's arm. "Let's take a tour." They spent their precious few coins for a ticket. Instead of John Wayne, a director filmed Rin-Tin-Tin, the amazing movie star dog.

On the way out, Cookie stopped an usher. "How could a fella get a glimpse of John Wayne?"

The usher shook his head. "Sorry, sir. Mr. Wayne is not currently in Hollywood. We don't expect him to return for several weeks."

"Ah. Thanks." Cookie's chest heaved as he headed back outside.

"I'm sorry." Pete slung his arm over Cookie's shoulder. "Where do you want to go from here?"

Shrugging, Cookie kicked at dry sand. The dust settled onto their pant legs.

Pete brushed a bead of sweat from his forehead. "You know, Cookie. I'm ready to find cooler country. Let's head north."

A couple hours later, they hid in brush with many other men, waiting for the northbound Southern Pacific Railroad. Pete's stomach churned, and his knees knocked.

"This train will be faster than the last one." Cookie leaned close to his ear and whispered. "So, gauge the speed as it approaches and act accordingly. Grab the handle fast. If it throws you against the car, hang on for all your worth until you can pull yourself back and jump into the boxcar."

Pete met his gaze. His face must have blanched. "I... um..."

"Don't worry, Preacher. It'll be fine." He patted Pete's knee.

"Now don't worry about these other guys. Get close to the train and take your turn when it comes. If the car is too full, fall back. You're not ready to ride the top. But in case you ever do end up on top of one of those cars, be sure to buckle yourself to the train in case you fall asleep or the train jerks."

Cookie held Pete's gaze. "That's why you'll see some guys wearing two belts. And in case I don't catch the same car as you, I'll catch one behind you and we'll be able to see each other. Watch my signals when to jump out. Okay?"

Pete nodded. He didn't trust his voice. If he didn't get killed hopping trains, it would be miraculous.

The longer they waited, the more his nerves rattled, until finally the whistle blew.

"Here she comes." Cookie stood. "Now watch me, and when I point to a car, run for it." They crept closer, watching for the yard dicks.

"Go!" Cookie yelled and pointed. Pete ran with the others, grabbed the bar, jumped on the ladder, and flung himself into the car. He landed against the man to his right.

"See, it gets easier every time, doesn't it?" Cookie spoke from Pete's left.

Pete said nothing. Young men, many no older than twelve or fourteen, sat all around him. Though most wore ragged clothes and unkempt hair, they held determined expressions on their scared, dirty faces. Instead, he turned his gaze to the glistening blue waves that met the cloudless horizon outside the open boxcar door.

They followed the ocean all the way to San Francisco. On the inland side, horses grazed on green grasses in deep canyons amid hillsides. Homes built on steep mountainsides amazed Pete. How could they assure their safety?

When they neared the edge of San Francisco station, Pete's hunger gnawed at him with such intensity that he jumped out of the moving train without angst.

Cookie jingled the change in his pocket. "Maybe we should go for the trash bins tonight. Save our money."

They found sweet rolls from a bakery a few blocks away, only slightly dirty, then approached a kind-looking grocer.

The man waved. "You fellas looking for specs?"

"Please." Cookie raced to the man's side.

"Got some peaches in the back. Hold on." The man disappeared into the store, and Pete relaxed. Maybe Cookie was right. It did seem to get a little easier.

After a short trip to Santa Rosa, their boxcar disengaged from the train.

"We're going to have to find a different car." Cookie nudged Pete forward. "Let's go."

Pete stood at the edge of the car and scanned the horizon. No sign of yard dicks. "I like jumping when the car's standing still."

He landed as two detectives rounded the corner. "C'mon, Cookie." Pete yanked Cookie's jacket.

The two took off running, avoiding capture, and hopped aboard another boxcar.

"When is this one going to stop?" Pete settled in a cardboard box as the train started moving. "We've been traveling almost two days."

"This must be a hotshot." Cookie pointed to the double set of tracks. "Hotshots don't stop at all the stations; they go right through to their destination. If another train is on the rail they want, it has to get out of their way."

"Well, I hope it stops pretty soon." Pete's stomach rumbled. "I've been ready to eat for a long time."

"Me, too," Cookie said. "But my guess is that this hotshot won't stop 'til it gets to Portland, Oregon."

"All I can say is, I hope it gets there soon." Pete swallowed three times, as though that might squelch his roaring hunger. Perhaps the scenery would help him forget.

Fog hung over the high mountaintops, and the smell of pine and fir in the warm sunshine reached his nose. The train seemed to slow as it rattled through great forests of giant Redwood trees.

After several hours, they passed a sign in front of spectacular waterfalls. Columbia River. Pete lurched forward. "The Columbia!" Pete shook Cookie awake. "That's the Columbia River running alongside us! Did you see those waterfalls? There's another one! We must be in Oregon now."

Cookie groaned.

"Wish we could jump off here and spend time along the river." Pete soaked in as much of the beauty as he could.

The train sped along past Multnomah Falls, Benson Bridge, Horsetail Falls, and lovely green valleys, lush with tiger lilies, lady slippers, and giant Douglas Fir trees.

Eventually, the terrain became tamer, yet still beautiful. Oat fields dotted the landscape. Vineyards graced the land. Waves of a large lake lapped against the shore close to the railroad tracks. Pete's head reeled with all the grandeur he had seen.

Eventually, the train arrived at the Portland station. As soon as they slowed enough, Cookie jumped out and Pete followed. A yard dick appeared out of nowhere and grabbed them both by the arm.

"Nice ride, boys?" He snarled. "Can you pay the fare to our fine city of Portland?"

Both Pete and Cookie shook their heads. The dick hand-cuffed them and prodded them to his vehicle. As he drove them to the county jail, Pete wrung his hands as best the cuffs would allow. Now, he was a convict. How humiliating to be escorted to jail.

How much lower could he sink?

On her first day back to school after the Christmas break, Jenny built a fire in the big wood-burning stove and brushed bark from the front of her woolen dress. She grabbed a cleaning rag and wiped away the layer of dust that had settled on her chipped oak desk in her absence. Then, she wiped the shiny, ceramic, red apple her parents had given her and placed it back in its spot on the corner of her desk.

She loved her parents, and she enjoyed her time at home, but it disturbed her to see how much Father drank. Had he always drunk that much and she didn't notice, or had his drinking escalated? And had Mother always walked on eggshells around him like she did these past two weeks?

Her sweater caught on the drawer handle, and she frowned as she freed it. She'd wanted to discuss the drinking with her mother, but the opportunity never seemed to be there.

Maybe the holidays made Father feel the need to drink more. Or maybe he was celebrating her homecoming. After all, he did lift his newly-filled glass to Jenny often, saying how nice to have her in the house again. What if he had problems on his job? She should have asked him if something bothered him. Why hadn't she?

Someone knocked, and Jenny lifted her head.

Frank Ross shuffled into the schoolhouse with his daughter Janet. "I wanted to make sure you got back okay, Miss Howe." He removed his hat. "Hope you had a nice Christmas with your family."

Jenny got up from her desk to shake hands with him. "Yes, I did, Mr. Ross. And I hope you did as well."

"Yeah, yeah. The Hermanns invited us to their house for Christmas dinner, and they put on a spread, that's for sure." He patted Janet on the head. "I wanted to thank you for the wonderful Christmas program. Janet's part made her so happy."

Jenny smiled at Janet, who clung to her dad's hand. "You did a wonderful job, Janet. You remembered every word!" She sat on a desk in the front row, and smoothed the lace collar on her navy blue dress "I'm so pleased to have Janet in my class. She's a bright student. Thank you for bringing her in early today."

Mr. Ross fiddled with a button on his coat. "It's cold out. Do you have enough wood for the stove?"

"Yes, Mr. Dixon filled the wood box yesterday. That should be enough. The older boys, Dennis and Harold, carry in the next day's wood at the end of each day. Thank you for asking."

"Well, I see other kids coming in now, so I'll say goodbye. Janet, you be good and do what Miss Howe says, okay?" He nodded to Jenny, replaced his stocking cap, and left.

Poor man. His gray relief-issue pants, the ragged cuffs on this coat, and the air of defeat in his demeanor... He must have not yet found employment.

It took a while for Jenny to settle the rowdy bunch of kids into their seats. She marked roll on a small tablet. "Does anyone know why Dennis isn't here today?"

The chatter died, a secretive sort of silent, and the kids

looked down, upward, or toward the window. "What happened? Where's Dennis? Harold, tell me why Dennis isn't here."

Harold dipped his chin further.

"Harold, what's wrong?" Jenny placed a light hand on his desk.

Harold met her gaze with a quivering lip. "Dennis is in jail. He stole some clothes from a store."

"Oh, no," Jenny whispered.

"He wanted Christmas presents for his mom and dad and his baby brother." Harold wiped his nose with his shirt sleeve.

"I'm so sorry." Jenny wanted to cry. Dennis' family needed new clothes. They collected relief, like most of the families in Kathleen Creek, but that didn't feed and clothe a family. The stiff, gray pants doled out by the county only branded the wearer as one of the desperate poor.

She cleared her throat. "But, let's get to work, children." Poor Dennis and the whole Benson family. What could she do to help?

As she passed her desk, she lifted a book and carried it to the front of the room. "As you remember, we finished reading *The Red Pony*, by John Steinbeck, before you left for vacation. Did you like that book?"

A chorus of "yes" came from the students, as Jenny knew it would. They cherished the fifteen minutes she read to them first thing each morning. Not only did it teach them the enjoyment of reading, none of the students wanted to be late for school.

"Starting today," Jenny said, "I will read from *The Farmer Boy*, written by Laura Ingalls Wilder. You will like this book as well. So, sit up straight in your seats, fold your hands on top of your desks, and I'll begin."

Although the day proceeded well, Jenny couldn't keep from thinking about Dennis, a bright and sensitive boy in the seventh grade. What would happen to him? So many young boys and girls in Minneapolis resorted to stealing in order to help their families. What would become of this country if the economy didn't improve soon?

During the noon hour, Tommy Lazar started a fight with one of the younger boys and Jenny had to break it up. "What happened?"

"Tommy hit me." Phillip rubbed his jaw.

"Is that right, Tommy?" Jenny nudged Tommy's shoulder.

Tommy clamped his mouth shut.

"Come with me." She linked arms with Tommy and brought him to the cloakroom. When out of earshot of the other students, Jenny squeezed his hand. "What's the matter? Why did you hit Phillip?"

"I don't know."

"Were you angry about something?"

He stuffed his fists into his pocket. "Yeah, I guess."

"What made you angry?" She brushed up against a wool coat and reset it on its hanger. So much hurt in that cherub face.

"I don't know."

"Did you eat all your dinner?" Could hunger be making him angry?

Tommy shrugged, his head down. "Yeah."

"What did you have to eat in your pail?" Jenny lifted his chin and made eye contact.

Tommy squirmed. "A sandwich and an apple."

"Okay. What did Phillip have to eat?" Was he jealous of Phillips lunch?

Tommy shrugged again.

"Tommy, answer me."

"I don't know." Tommy jerked his face away.

How could she get Tommy to tell her why he started a fight? "Did Phillip make you angry about something?"

"No."

"Then why did you hit him?" Jenny lessened the edge in her voice.

"I felt like it." Tommy whispered his answer.

Jenny pursed her lips. If only she knew the cause of his anger. She placed her hands light on his shoulders. "Tommy, you can't start fights at school, okay? Now you're going to have to apologize to Phillip. And then I don't want you to hit anyone again, understand?"

"Yes, Miss Howe." Tommy shuffled behind Jenny back to where Phillip sat.

"Go ahead, Tommy." Jenny prodded him forward.

Tommy ground the toe of his shoe into the floor. "Sorry."

"Okay, Tommy. Phillip, Tommy apologized to you. Can you tell him that you accept his apology and you can be friends again?"

"Okay." Phillip turned to Tommy.

"Now you boys can play outside until I ring the bell. It's cold so bundle up well. And, no more fighting." Jenny nudged both boys toward the door. "Students, you may all go outside for recess."

Later that same day, Tommy made Bonnie cry and couldn't give Jenny any reason for being mean to the little girl. The Tommy she knew didn't act this way. She needed to investigate this further.

That evening, Jenny knocked on her landlady's door.

Mrs. Dixon swept it open so fast, it set her wispy gray hair flowing behind her. "Hi, Jenny. Come in. What's wrong?"

"I have a student who's changed since before Christmas." Jenny followed Mrs. Dixon to her brown horsehair sofa. "Do you know if anything has happened in the Lazar family recently that would make Tommy so angry?"

"I don't like to gossip." Mrs. Dixon smoothed her apron. "But I can see that you need to know. His father ran off with the banker's secretary the day after the Christmas program."

Jenny gasped. "No."

"Unfortunately, yes. He hasn't returned, and he probably

won't." Mrs. Dixon crossed her legs and leaned forward. "I understand that Mrs. Lazar cries all day. Tommy is their only child. He has a good reason to be angry. Is he taking it out on you?"

"No, he's taking it out on the other students. Poor Tommy. He has to have some outlet for that anger. But, I can't let him continue to be so disruptive in class. I don't know what to do about it."

"I wouldn't know what to tell you, either. Poor child."

His distress carried on for several days. The students enjoyed the story of *The Farmer Boy*, and Tommy fought with the boys and picked on the girls. Jenny first made him stand in the corner, but that disrupted the rest of the students even more. Then, she made him sit in the cloak room area, but he made so much noise that it, too, became a disruption. Talking to Tommy's mother didn't help. Mrs. Lazar only wrung her hands and cried.

Mark didn't want to listen to Jenny's problem with Tommy, and he offered no advice. He only said that his father hired Mrs. Lazar to work at the bank because he had known about his secretary's affair with Mrs. Lazar's husband and felt he should have done something to stop it from going so far.

After a while, Jenny made Tommy stay after school as a punishment.

He came to life when the rest of the children were excused for the day. "I'll clean the blackboard, Miss Howe." "Should I sweep the floor, Miss Howe?" "What else can I do, Miss Howe?"

Tommy must get terribly lonely going home to an empty house after school since his mother had taken a job. Jenny worked alongside Tommy doing the small tasks she gave him, drawing him into conversation. "What do you like to do at home?" "What pets did you have on the farm before you moved into town?" "What games do you like to play?"

While Tommy seemed to love spending time with Jenny

after school, his disruptive behavior during class time continued. What could be the solution?

Still, the students thrived under her tutelage, and Jenny thrived on teaching their young minds. She loved her students, fed them as best she could, and prayed that the families would all be better off soon.

One day in the spring, after Jenny agreed to return the following year to teach the 1935-36 school year, Mrs. Dixon stopped Jenny outside her room and whispered in her ear.

Jenny sucked in a deep breath. "Did you say they paid Mr. Gordon, the teacher who taught before me, $65.00 a month?"

"Yes, that's right."

"Then why am I only paid $55.00?" Jenny's brows lifted and her eyes narrowed to slits. How dare they?

"I don't know, dear. I suppose it's because you're a woman." Mrs. Dixon pressed her lips together and shook her head.

"Well, that's not fair!" Jenny stamped her foot. "I deserve as much as they paid him."

"Well, you do a better job and spend more time on behalf of the students than Mr. Gordon ever did." Mrs. Dixon raised her eyebrows.

Jenny scowled. "Who made the decision to pay me less?"

"The school board." Mrs. Dixon folded her arms. "Mr. Bursch is the chairman."

"Well, I need to speak to Mr. Bursch." Jenny pivoted and went into her room.

Mr. Bursch added her to the April agenda. However, they adjourned the meeting before getting to Jenny's concern, tabling all other matters to the May meeting. Jenny fumed. No one wanted to deal with her issue.

At the May meeting, she made her argument. While no one spoke on her behalf, many parents in attendance showed support. The board approved a motion to table the decision until the June meeting.

On May 25th, following the dismissal of school, Jenny demanded the board members allow her presence when they announced their decision on June 29th.

In spite of her parents' arguments that she should come home sooner, Jenny stood her ground. If necessary, she would rescind her agreement to teach next year. Hopefully it wouldn't come to that. She wanted to continue to teach in Kathleen Creek with dignity.

Would that be possible?

2 4

"Have you ever been in jail, Cookie?" Pete chewed his lip. Humiliation rode high on his tight and uplifted shoulders as they plodded ahead of the yard dick to the Portland jail.

"Sure, it's not so bad. They feed you. Sometimes you have to work, sometimes not. The cots are usually clean. Cleaner than skid row, at least."

Pete nodded. Jail might not be so bad after all.

The detective led them into a cold, dirty room filled with a heavy odor of stale urine, and Pete winced. Maybe it would be that bad.

That night, they received a generous plate of hot beans and thick bread, and the next morning guards brought them into the courthouse to go before the judge.

An old man in a black robe shuffled into the room, plunked himself onto his throne, and banged his gavel. He heard one case after another without a pause.

As the cases progressed, the wrinkles in Pete's brow deepened. Had the judge made his determination before even hearing the cases?

When they brought Pete before him, the county attorney read the charge.

The judge peered at him over his wire-rimmed glasses. "I sentence you to serve ten days in the Multnomah County jail." He banged the gavel down. "Next case."

The same thing happened with Cookie. The guard brought them back to jail, and the steel door clanged closed behind them.

"Now what?" Pete massaged his temples.

"Do you want to play tic-tac-toe? I broke a tine off my fork last night." Cookie reached under his mattress and pulled out a small, metal piece ideal for scraping on the concrete floor.

Pete howled. "You are amazing!"

Cookie only grinned.

Time dragged, broken up by adequate food and reasonable sleep on the thin mattress. A lady came around with reading material. Pete selected several books from a tall stack next to his cot. He laid down and pulled the stiff wool blanket up to his neck.

"What did you get this time, Preacher?" Cookie cocked his head toward the books.

"Ah…" Pete sat up. "The *Bible*, *The Good Earth* by Pearl S. Buck, *Cimarron*, by Edna Ferber, and *Lost Horizon* by James Hilton." He pulled a weathered marker from *The Good Earth* and lay back down. He wasn't in the mood for conversation. When would they get out of here?

During their stay, Pete told Cookie a lot about his childhood, his parents, and his wife and daughter. He told him about losing his vet equipment and everything when his car was stolen. One night, they stretched out on their cots, and Pete studied a crack in the ceiling. "Cookie, tell me about your family."

"What do you want to know?" Cookie rolled on his side to look at Pete.

Pete waved his hand toward Cookie. "You know, where did

you grow up? What was your school like? Do you have siblings? What kind of things did you do at home? Stuff."

Cookie hesitated until Pete thought he had dozed off. And then he said, "I always liked fishing. I'm an only child." He yawned. "I played baseball in school." Another yawn.

When Cookie's soft snores drifted across the room, Pete rolled to his side. Since he'd known him, Cookie had talked about school, friends, and learning to cook with his mother. But what of his father? All he'd ever mentioned was that his father had taught him to cut meat. And he'd made no reference to where he'd lived. What was in his past that he didn't want known?

A few days later the guard released them. Pete slipped the straps of his backpack over his shoulders, a wide grin spanning his face. How joyful to be reunited with his possessions. Though he'd worn out his underwear and had only the shirt and pants he wore, he had purchased extra socks.

Pete lifted his face to the sun, then turned east, strolling off after Cookie.

"Ah, to be back in the great outdoors." Cookie half-skipped down the sidewalk.

"Wait a minute." Pete stopped and breathed deeply. Would he ever get the stench of that urine smell out of his system? Even his clothes smelled of it.

They found the Columbia River and followed the tracks. Along the way, Pete examined the unfamiliar botanicals for wild edible and medicinal herbs. He removed his pack as he searched for the right spot to enjoy the river.

They sat on a large, warm rock on the bank. Pete picked up a pebble and skipped it over the water. "I don't know why the river calls to me as it does. There's something about it. Do you feel it?"

"I don't know." Cookie scratched his greasy sun-bleached blond hair. "What do you feel?"

"Peace. A peace like nowhere else. It charges my batteries – helps me to go on." Pete threw out his chest and raised his arms wide. "You know what I mean?"

"I guess I don't really, but that's okay. I do like the river though." Cookie reached out and caught a bug between his fingers. "Should we try fishing?"

"Why not? We don't have anything else to eat." Pete found a small thin branch to use as a pole.

Using Pete's line, hook, and bobber, and the bug as bait, Cookie caught a steelhead trout.

"Ah, nice one. But I bet we could have better luck with good bait." Pete dug some worms and they fished another half hour with no luck.

Cookie stood with the trout. "C'mon, Preacher. This'll be enough."

"I wish we had a grill to cook it." Pete took his hoof knife from his jacket pocket.

"We don't need one. You'll see." They found a nice camp site. Pete gathered wood and built a fire while Cookie used Pete's hoof knife to scale and gut the fish.

As the flames licked the dried branches and leaves, Pete sat on a rock, his gaze narrowing until he'd focused on every tiny sparkle. Memories flooded him. Betty's vivacious smile and Rose's cherub grin. Railroad's infectious laugh. And then, the loud cracks from the barn beams as they collapsed. The screams from the animals.

Pete eased his grip on the branch he'd held in white knuckles. He turned over his palm, where a reddened indentation covered his lifeline. He couldn't think about all that right now. He couldn't lose focus.

Hot coals glowed red beneath the burning wood as Cookie prepared the fish. He cut a sturdy green stick and moved the burning wood to the sides, away from the coals. Next, he impaled the fish through its head and lodged the stick into the ground in the midst of the coals.

"We'll have grilled fish in no time," Cookie moved some of the burning wood closer to the fish and backed away from the fire.

"You never cease to amaze me!" Pete shook his head. He returned to the river's edge and sat on a log watching the water pass by.

Cookie came and sat next to him. As soon as Cookie sat, he let out a scream and jumped up. Shaking his leg, he yelled, "Snake!"

Pete jumped up as a small rattlesnake slinked away. "Did he bite you?"

Cookie nodded and dropped back down on the log. He rolled up his pant leg. His ankle swelled around a three-pronged hole.

Pete grabbed his hoof knife and held it in the fire for a couple minutes while Cookie rocked himself in his arms.

He knelt in front of Cookie, rested the ailing foot on his thigh, and made a cut across the bite.

With his mouth to the incision, he sucked out the venom. A bitter, acid flavor crossed his tongue, with a slight burning sensation. He spit and sucked, and spit and sucked the bitter, greenish-yellow venom until he had gotten it all. His tongue had gone numb. He stood and took a mouthful of water from his canteen, swished it around, and spit it out.

Cookie trembled. His breath came in short spurts.

Pete whipped his cape from around his waist and spread it on the ground beneath a tree as he tried to wiggle feeling into his tongue again. He grabbed his backpack for a pillow and helped Cookie off the rock.

"Lie down here. I think I got all the venom." He eased his friend to the cape. "Maybe some traveled into your system before I made the cut, but I don't think it would be enough to do much damage."

He had sucked snake venom from a horse once before, but never a human being. The horse survived. Hopefully Cookie would, too.

"How do you feel?"

"Scared." Cookie's voice quivered. He closed his eyes while Pete bowed his head.

*Dear Lord, please watch over Cookie. Don't let him die.*

When he opened his eyes, Cookie had curled into a fetal position with his hurt ankle jutting out.

"Cookie!" Pete patted his cheeks. "Don't go to sleep. I need to know you're okay."

"I'm only resting. I feel weak, but I don't know if it's because I'm scared, or if it's because of the venom. Young rattlers are more dangerous than older snakes."

"Be still, but try to stay awake."

"I'm okay." Cookie's voice shook. "Let me rest a while."

"How are you doing?" Pete crouched over him.

"You asked that." Cookie gave a nervous laugh. "I'm okay. I've studied snakes. That was a young Western Rattlesnake. Snakes release only some of their venom when they strike, but young ones are inexperienced, so they release all their venom. That's why they're more dangerous."

Pete picked up his hoof knife and wiped the blade on the grass. "Don't talk. Be still."

"I'm in your debt again, Preacher." Cookie lifted his head.

Pete grimaced. Cookie shouldn't thank him yet.

After a while, the color returned to Cookie's face.

*Thank you, Lord.* "Have a drink of water." Pete unhooked Cookie's canteen and handed it to him.

Cookie's hand quivered when he raised it to his lips.

The smell of the fish wafted to them, and Pete's stomach growled. He gathered large leaves from an ash tree and laid the cooked fish on one. Then, he brought half the white flesh to Cookie and helped him sit up against the tree.

"I have salt in my pack," Cookie pointed to his bindle.

The two men savored the succulent fish as Pete's gaze flicked between the fire and his friend. *Thank you, Lord, for this tasty meal. Please, spare this young man's life.*

Cookie's eyes closed briefly. He must be thanking God as well. Such a good kid.

At dusk, Cookie stretched. "I feel good. Strong enough to get up and move around."

Pete frowned. Were there any signs of distress? Didn't seem to be any.

"Wait a minute." He fished through his pack, took one of his clean hankies, and wrapped it around the wound.

"Look at me. Fit as a fiddle, thanks to you, Dad. You saved my life. I'll find a way to pay you back, Preacher." Cookie gripped Pete's arm as he helped him to his feet. "I swear someday I will."

Pete shook his head. It would do no good to argue.

The next day Cookie seemed okay, so they found a tower where trains stopped to take on water. Pete knelt at attention like a tightly coiled wire ready to spring as they hid in the brush. Luck favored them, and a train slowed as it approached the tower.

The Northern Pacific tender turned his back to put water into the locomotive. Pete crouched with his pack and faced Cookie. Not yet.

Steam spewed from the train as the wheels squealed back into service. Couplings clanged and one car after another jerked into motion.

Cookie pointed to an open boxcar a few yards back. "Go!"

Pete sprinted to the train. He ran alongside it, looking over his shoulder at the open boxcar.

When it reached him, he grabbed ahold, jumped onto the

ladder, and threw himself inside. Successful once again, with Cookie right behind him.

Pete gripped the floor. *Thank you, God, for letting us board safely.* When he stopped shaking, he lifted his head up. Four men, three women, and a little blond boy sat against the walls. The boy moved closer to his mother. "You can sit here, mister."

"Thanks." Pete sat next to the boy. Kid couldn't be more than six.

Cookie squeezed next to Pete.

They rode in silence for several minutes, except for the taps of Cookie's fingers against his trousers. He finally sat up straight. "If we're lucky this train will take us through Oregon, through Idaho, and into Montana before it stops again. It looks like another hotshot."

Pete nodded and rested his head against the wall. The staccato ca-lunk, ca-lunk of the wheels would easily lull him to sleep. Should he try to stay awake? What if someone else tried to rob them? Was his pistol handy?

One of the men snorted and gasped in his sleep. Surely, with so many people in the car, a robber would think twice about causing trouble. Anyone else wanting to board this train would have to ride on top of the car.

Pete shuddered. He would never be ready for that. It looked too dangerous.

He wasn't cut out for this life. When would he find a home? He wanted a family again.

The boy shifted next to him, snuggling closer to his mother. Pete clenched his teeth. He wanted to be close to a woman again. But what woman would ever want him now? Would he ever have anything to offer?

Dust particles danced in the air of the boxcar when the late afternoon sun flashed between trees alongside the tracks. Pete gave in to the rocking motion of the boxcar that flung the little boy's sleeping body against his side from time to time. Poor kid.

Poor family. Even at his lowest, Pete was more blessed than they were.

The train continued along at a fast speed on flat lands, but slowed almost to a crawl through some of the Rocky Mountain passes. Men stood at the edge of the car, their backs to the women, and urinated when the need arose. The boy's father did likewise and then brought the little boy to the edge and held onto him as he followed suit.

When Pete took his turn, he crowded toward the edge of the door to block the view of the females. Those poor women. How would they handle their needs? When the conductor stopped the train to take on water, the women jumped off and ran into the bushes.

The farther east they traveled, the drier the land appeared. The mountain sides turned brown and crisp. The Clark Fork River moved lazily along with only a trickle of water in places, where now, in late spring, it should have been rushing. Evidence of prolonged severe drought showed everywhere as even the Russian Olive trees drooped their leaves in apparent mourning.

The mood in the boxcar sobered, where earlier it had been quiet but contemplative. Now an aura of tension and unease filled the car. It would be even harder to find jobs if the farmers couldn't grow crops.

Pete drifted off to sleep. He awoke when metal squealed against metal followed by a shrill whistle loud enough to damage the eardrums. "Where are we, Cookie?"

"Um… Missoula, Montana." Cookie leaned his head out the door. "We better get off here and find something to eat."

"How can we jump in the dark?" Pete searched the terrain alongside Cookie.

"Watch him." Cookie pointed to a man who had lowered himself to the bottom rung of the ladder. "He's checking to see when the train has slowed enough." The man had a strong hold on the sides of the ladder, then let down one of his feet. He yelped when his foot came back and hit his behind.

"The train's still going too fast." Cookie stood back from the edge. "That's how to tell when it has slowed enough. It's too hard to tell in the dark, otherwise. When his foot doesn't come back up to hit him, it's safe to jump."

They all watched and waited. When the man jumped off, Cookie followed, calling out to Pete over his shoulder, "Go!"

Pete leapt and rolled as the others threw out their bindles and dove after them. He had landed safely once again. Did everyone else make it? Did the boy?

The blond head bobbed as he disappeared hand-in-hand with his father into the darkness. Good. They were safe. How difficult it must be to travel like this with a woman and child. If only he could have done something to help them.

Pete slung his backpack over one shoulder. "I'd like to go to Helena. Remember that guy at the jungle talking about a veterinarian, Dr. Hagerty, in Helena who was getting old? Maybe I could get on with his practice."

"Okay with me. We're not going to find anything to eat until morning, so let's go find out how to get to Helena." Cookie tightened his bindle and they began walking toward town.

They soon caught up with one of the hobos who had jumped from the train with them, a man with a long beard shining silver by the small sliver of moon.

"Excuse me, sir." Cookie came alongside the man. "Do you know if an eastbound train comes through Missoula that might take us to Helena?"

The man turned, almost hitting Cookie with the long stick tied to his bindle. He stopped and scratched his face. "I once't took a train from here going through the Rockies to Helena. As I recall, it came in the morning. Real early, as I recall."

"Thank you." Cookie raised his hand in a quick salute

"Yes, thanks." Pete bestowed a quick pat on the man's back.

The man kept walking.

"How about we spend a day here and catch the train tomorrow?" Cookie turned up the collar on his jacket.

"Sounds good to me." Pete hitched his pack higher on his back. "I'm ready for a break from traveling."

A few minutes later, Pete pointed to a comfortable-looking spot around the corner of a building at the edge of town, and the men sat shoulder-to-shoulder to sleep before the stores opened.

When Pete awoke, darkness surrendered to a pink sky in the east. Pete stood, awakening Cookie. The pink spread wider and higher, followed by a golden glow until a huge yellow orb rose, too bright to continue watching. How amazing the world was. And how comforting to know that this cycle of day and night, sunrise and sunset, would continue day after day. *Thank you, Lord.*

They explored the city of Missoula and bought breakfast for fifteen cents each, then purchased an onion and a potato for a nickel from a grocer, and got a free piece of sausage from a butcher.

Cookie wrapped the vegetables in his bindle. "We did well, Pete. Good contributions for tonight's Mulligan Stew."

Pete put the packaged sausage in his backpack. "Yeah, and those used coffee grounds from that café were quite a score. We'll be the hit of the fire tonight. Let's find a jungle."

They hiked along the river until they saw smoke and smelled coffee a few yards shy of the jungle. Someone leaned against a tree strumming a guitar. He nodded to the newcomers.

Another man turned over the stew pot. Cookie tossed him the sausage.

"Thanks." The man cut it up and put it into the can over the fire while Cookie peeled and chopped the onion. When he tossed it into the can, hot grease sputtered. Soon the fragrance of onion and sausage floated throughout the camp.

"Got a potato, too." Cookie diced it and tossed it into the

mix, along with his canteen of water. One by one the handful of men sitting around got up and added something to the stew. Cookie stood nearby in case something needed cutting or peeling, designating himself as the chef. Soon the mix included a tomato, a can of soup, three hot dogs, some peas and more water.

"Seems like a good bunch here so far." Pete grabbed his canteen and followed Cookie to the river's edge.

Cookie bent down to fill his canteen. "I like the guy playing the guitar. Maybe he'll play *Big Rock Candy Mountain.*"

Pete and Cookie claimed a huge cottonwood tree to rest against. The man with the guitar sang a song about why a hobo travels that Pete had never heard before. When he finished he played *Big Rock Candy Mountain.* Pete pulled out his harmonica and joined in while Cookie and some of the others sang along. Cookie's grin spread ear to ear.

More men and two women arrived at the camp, bringing carrots and a loaf of bread. Cookie added the carrots to the stew and laid the bread aside.

Pete watched the newcomers. Both women appeared to be with the stocky man who had the largest feet Pete had ever seen. What were those? Size 16, maybe? They settled against the trees next to the guitarist.

"Do you know *I've been Working on the Railroad?*" Cookie leaned forward and spoke loud enough to be heard over the din of people talking.

"Sure, kid." The guitarist strummed the first three notes and almost all of the men sang along.

The man with the two women sang with gusto. Was one his wife? Maybe one was his daughter. His heart twinged. Imagine Betty being homeless along with him. And Rose? He shook away the horrible vision. It was tough enough for a man. But a woman? And children?

Pete untied his cape, spread it on the ground, and lay down

with his head on his backpack. He needed to think pleasant thoughts. The river. A picnic with Betty and Rose. A soft, warm breeze on his face as he read to them. Rose playing with her doll. A melodic gurgle of the river as it meandered over rocks. Fishing with his father as a child. The smell of Betty's biscuits coming out of the oven.

After a while, Pete opened his eyes. One of the men shaved in front of a cloudy mirror tied in a tree. Another came up from the river with a wet shirt and hung it on a line strung between trees. The man with the guitar strummed on, singing softly at times and merely playing at others.

Cookie tended the stew, a bemused smile on his face. Pete sat up, one limb at a time. When had he last felt so comfortable and peaceful among a bunch of strangers? They shared a feeling of brotherhood–of family.

The corners of Pete's lips upturned in a wry grin. For now, he guessed these hobos were his family. Would he ever have a true family again?

A small, young man sat far away from the rest, a plaid newsboy cap pulled low and his back nearly doubled over. Poor guy hadn't joined the singers. After a while, he disappeared into the woods. Such a strange figure. Almost… lumpy, yet graceful.

When he reappeared, Pete's breath caught. Was it a young woman instead?

He sat up straighter. It was. A very young woman dressed in men's clothing. Was she alone?

Several minutes passed, and she held her stoic vigil. She *was* alone. She must be so frightened. Though her appearance befit a boy, her walk gave her away. She definitely had female hips. Where had she come from, and where did she plan to go?

Cookie came and sat next to Pete.

"Look over there. That figure." Pete nodded in her direction. "A girl."

Cookie's eyes widened. "A girl?"

"Yeah." Pete nodded. "Don't let anyone else know. I want to help her somehow."

"I know." Cookie continued to stare. "It can't be safe for her traveling alone. What if the wrong guy finds out she's a girl?"

"I'll try to talk to her, maybe when she eats." Pete furrowed his brow. "Is it okay with you if she travels with us so we can protect her?"

"Sure, you know it is."

They kept an eye on her as she curled up with a blanket and slept. More and more men arrived at camp. Most had something to add to the stew, but some did not. Quiet conversations took place, and all seemed respectful of the sleeping people.

Cookie tasted the stew, untied his spice bag, and seasoned the pot with salt, pepper, and some green herbs. He tapped his spoon against the side of the can. "Folks, we're ready to eat."

The young woman got up, reached in her bindle for a cup, and went to the fire to get some stew along with a few others. Pete stood next to her.

Cookie dipped Pete's stew and then hers.

Pete flashed her a winning smile. "Hi, I'm Preacher and my friend here is Cookie. What's your name?"

She tucked her chin into her collar. "Carl."

Such a faint voice. Pete lowered his own. "I'd like to eat with you. Is that all right?"

She kept her eyes toward the ground and walked to a far fallen log. Was she trying to distance herself from him? She sat at the far end of the log, almost hidden by a low tree branch. With hunched shoulders, she held her knees tight together, her cup shaking slightly in her small hand.

Pete sat next to her, but not too close. "I don't want to frighten you, but I know you're female."

The girl jerked her head and gaped. "I…"

Pete laid a light hand on her arm. "Don't be scared. I'm harmless. I want to help you. Where are you headed?"

After a long moment's hesitation, she bit her lower lip. "I need to get to Bismarck, North Dakota to my grandma's." She flashed a quick glance at Pete. "My parents said I need to find my own way because they can't feed all of us anymore." Her lips quivered. "My dad lost his job and my mom is sick. I have three little sisters. I didn't have any money so I decided to hop a train to Grandma's house." With her head still turned down, she wiped a tear from her eye.

"Cookie and I will help you." Pete smiled again. He had to help her relax. "How long have you been hopping trains, ah, Carl?"

Carl snorted a laugh. "Since two days ago. I got on a train at Spokane but I had to get off so I could use a toilet." She whispered the last word.

Pete nodded. "Riding the rails isn't always convenient. Have you been here since then?"

"I've been here since yesterday." Carl's voice quivered. "I'm afraid to get on a train again. I almost didn't make it before." She shuddered.

"I'm new to rail hopping, myself. I know what you mean." Pete took a taste of the Mulligan Stew, chewing slowly, giving the young girl a chance to relax around him. After a few moments of silence, Pete said, "It was brave of you to hop a train."

"A friend showed me how, but it's not as easy as he said." She took another spoonful of the stew.

"Cookie and I'll help you. Keep pretending to be a boy, but try not to walk away from any of the men who can see you. Walk behind them." They finished their stew in silence as "Carl" kept sneaking glances at Pete.

"How old are you?" The poor girl seemed ready to bolt, or cry, or something.

"Eighteen." She gnawed her lip. "No, not really. I'm sixteen. I don't wanna lie to a preacher."

"I'm not really a preacher, but it's never good to lie." Pete motioned to her cup. "Do you want more stew?"

"Is it okay to have more?"

"Sure, go ahead and get some more. I'm going to have more, too." They both helped themselves. Cookie followed them to the log.

"Cookie, this is Carl."

"Good to meet you, Carl." Cookie rocked on his heels as Pete and Carl sat.

Carl dipped her head, allowing her bangs to fall over her face. "You too."

Pete leaned close to her ear. "Cookie also knows that you're a girl."

She pursed her lips. "My name isn't really Carl. It's Carla."

"That's okay." Cookie sat. "We'll call you Carl so no one catches on. The train comes in at 7:45 in the morning. Are we going to be on that one, Preacher?"

"Yes, and so will Carl. He's going to Bismarck." Pete chewed his mouthful of stew. "He can tag along with us as far as Helena."

Pete and Cookie moved their belongings to a tree closer to Carla. The next morning, they got up early and waited for the train to leave the station.

While Cookie gave her a lesson on when and how to jump, Pete paid close attention. He needed a refresher course.

They hid in the brush close to the tracks along with several others. Cookie scooted forward. "I'll point out the car and yell go when it's time. Don't let the others bother you." He waved his hand over the bushes. "Several will hop on the same car, but you take turns. Carl, you get on first. Watch the people ahead of you and jump quickly. Preacher will be behind you and I'll be right behind him." He held up his bag. "Throw your bindle in first and then jump onto the ladder. Climb up and swing yourself in. You'll be fine."

Carla grimaced and gripped the short tree branch that held her bundle of belongings.

They waited for the whistle and the chug, chug of the steam as it escaped the engine. Then, they listened for the lumbering of the wheels on the track, coming closer.

Carla gripped her bindle with white knuckles, glancing at Cookie as she trembled. Finally, he pointed to an open boxcar. "Go!"

Carla ran faster than he or Cookie, but Pete caught up enough to get right behind her. A spunky girl, she got in line and ran alongside the car for her turn. She threw her bindle into the car, grabbed the handle by a narrow margin, and stumbled.

Pete grabbed her arm to assist, and she leapt on with him right behind her. He laughed. "I'm a little more experienced at this, but nervous as you." When Cookie fell in alongside them, he grinned. "Whew!"

Both Carla and Pete laughed, their eyes shining. They'd all made it.

They sat with their backs resting along the front of the car. Cookie leaned close to Carla. "Let me tell you about Kathleen Creek, Minnesota. There's the nicest river, where a big maple tree grows so close to the bank you could lean against it and fish."

Pete closed his eyes. Cookie had found someone else to hear the tale he'd told so many times. But as pleasant as Kathleen Creek sounded, Pete daydreamed about Helena. Would it be his new home? Would he be able to work for Dr. Hagerty?

Would he finally be able to settle down?

Later that night, Pete and Cookie huddled in the corner of the train.

Pete dropped his voice to a whisper. "Let's ride all the way to Bismarck. Make sure Carla gets there okay." He picked a fleck of cardboard from his trousers. "We can always double back to Helena."

Cookie nodded. "We can't let her travel alone."

Carla cried when Pete told her. "My mother prayed for an angel to travel with me. Wait 'til I tell her I had two angels. How can I ever thank you?"

They got off the train at Miles City and stopped at a mom-n-pop joint to eat and use a toilet. Hard stares followed her to the restaurant bathroom.

Pete frowned. Travel was much easier for men in that regard.

Since Carla had no money, Pete and Cookie bought her meal. Then they found a jungle to spend the night while they waited for the next train the following afternoon.

Unlike the comfortable environment of their last jungle, a tension hovered over this one, keeping Pete's nerves on edge.

Two men argued. A dog tied to a tree barked incessantly with no one paying attention to his needs. Someone boiled clothes in a can set over a fire.

Pete grimaced. Lice, the scourge of the hobo, boiled along with those clothes.

An older, inebriated man huddled with his hands over his head as three young boys picked on him. None of the other men in camp interfered. Were they afraid?

Pete squared his shoulders. He'd had enough. "Okay, guys, leave this man alone."

The three faced Pete: a bulky redhead with scores of freckles, a ruddy-faced blond, and a dark-eyed boy with black hair who said, "Who made you our boss?"

"This man is vulnerable right now. It's the same as picking on a child." Pete stepped forward. "Is that what you are? Bullies? Because you are bullying a man who can't defend himself. You, who want to think you are men, are bullying a child."

Two of the young boys hung their head, but the leader crossed his arms and slammed them against his chest. "Who are you to butt into our business?"

"My name is Preacher." Pete softened his voice. "Our Lord God and Father would not want you to act this way, and I'd bet your own father wouldn't either. Why don't you boys walk off your energy and give this man some peace for an hour or so." He met each of their gazes. "Be sure to come back for Mulligan Stew later this evening. Okay?"

The two followers tugged at the leader's arms. "Come on, Bulldog, let's go. Come on."

Bulldog shot Pete an evil stare and stalked off after them.

Pete gave the old man a pat on the shoulder. "Are you all right, sir?"

The man nodded.

"I'm glad they left." Carla whispered. "I thought they were gonna beat you up."

A pockmarked man with salt and pepper hair clapped Pete on the shoulder. He shook his hand with a firm grip. "Thanks, Preacher. I'm City Lights. I sure do appreciate the way you defused that situation. None of us knew how to handle it. Those three young guys have a lot of strength among them. We're puny old men who couldn't take them on in a fight."

"My pleasure. This here's Cookie," Pete pointed, "and my little brother, Carl." He patted her back, and she inched closer to him. A lie, sure, but now he could act protective without anyone getting suspicious. And Carla did sort of shadow him, although she seemed to like talking with Cookie when away from hearing distance of the others.

Once again, Cookie manned the Mulligan Stew pot. The young hobos had brought cabbage and carrots and laid them by the fire. Pete passed Cookie the soup bones and two dented cans of tomato soup. Another man arrived with wild asparagus and onions. The stew shaped up nicely, and two more men arrived with bread. Again, Cookie did his magic with seasonings and by dusk the stew's aroma announced its readiness for consumption.

After the nine people in camp had eaten, the three young men returned. They finished the stew without a word to anyone. Then they settled into an isolated spot and spent a quiet and somber evening. Pete backed up to a thick tree trunk and hummed to himself. Boy, he missed the guitar music from the other night.

Later, Cookie caught Pete by the arm. "You sure sounded like the preacher back home when you talked to those boys. You sure you're not a real preacher?"

"Yeah, right." Pete laughed with him. "But it worked didn't it?"

"That, it did." Cookie tipped his hat. "Good night, Preacher."

"Good night." They took a place on each side of the sleeping Carla. As Pete nested into the spot, he hugged his thin, frail arms. How much weight had he lost since leaving home? He'd certainly lost the bulk to stand up for himself in a fight. What would have happened if he hadn't brought up God? He tightened the twine around his waist once again. He didn't want to know.

They spent the next morning exploring Miles City, Pete with his backpack, Cookie with his waist bindle, and Carla with her bindle on a stick.

A group of little boys followed them with taunts. "You're a bum, you're a bum, everyone's a bum, bum." The boys carried sticks and slapped them on the ground behind the three hobos. They hooted with laughter.

Tears brimmed Carla's eyes.

Pete's jaw flinched. "Ignore them."

When one of the sticks poked Cookie's leg, he spun on his heels. "Hey!"

The children all screamed and tossed their sticks as they ran.

"You are pretty scary, Cookie." Pete doubled over with laughter.

Carla frowned. "Those kids laughed at us, treating us like we're freaks or something." Her tears spilled over.

"You've got to toughen up, Carla, or you won't make it out here living this life. You have to admit, we're not part of polite society right now." Pete dug out a handkerchief and passed it to her. "It's against the law to be a homeless migrant."

"Thanks. I've seen lots and lots of hobos in the past few years." Carla dabbed at her eyes and passed it back. "We lived near the tracks. Sometimes there's been so many men on one car that they can hardly all fit. Inside and on top. Old men and young boys hardly in their teens, wearing worn out shoes and dirty hats." She stood taller. "And, I'm not the only girl riding the rails. Many of them don't try to pretend to be a boy, either, like those two on the train the other night. I only did it because

I had to travel alone. My friend said I'd be safer if I dressed like a boy."

"I know." Cookie pulled at long grasses along the walk. Hot sun coaxed out the scent of weeds in the open meadow next to them, and the sweet smell of clover wafted toward them. Horses whinnied in the distance. "I've been catching rides for a couple of years and have seen a lot. Whole families trying to get where there's work. Some get separated and others don't. They leave messages for each other on water towers."

"Water towers?" Carla turned and walked backward in front of Cookie.

Cookie hitched his bindle higher on his hips. "Many have codes to tell where they're going next or where there's work. Stuff like that."

Carla resumed walking next to Cookie. "My friend said hobos have a code to tell them who's friendly and who will let them sleep in the hayloft or give them a meal, too. He wrote some of them down for me. I keep it in my pocket. I haven't had to use it yet, but I might have to someday."

"That's good." Pete chewed on a stem of wheatgrass. "We're not too far from Bismarck anymore. Does your grandma know you're coming?"

"Yeah, but she doesn't know when, or that I'm coming illegally as a hobo. I couldn't tell her. She'd be too worried about me." Carla adjusted her cap, pulling it lower over her eyes. "When we get to Bismarck you're gonna have to meet my grandma. She'll fix a real good meal for you, too."

They arrived in Bismarck that evening. Cookie tried to determine a safe time to jump off in the darkness, but it took a long time before he'd risk Carla's life. When he finally jumped, Carla threw her bindle and leapt after it. Pete followed behind her. They all managed a successful landing but raced for cover, being dangerously close to the station.

A yard dick's face appeared on the other side of a large bush. "Stop, police!"

"Run." Pete darted through the nearby trees, Cookie and Carla at his heels. Darkness aided their escape. When they stopped, Pete's side ached, and Cookie gasped for his breath.

Carla dropped to the ground and laughed until she cried. "We made it this far, and I thought, 'now we're gonna end up in jail.'" She rolled to her side and sat up. "I don't wanna be a jailbird while I'm still a teenager. My grandma would die of embarrassment. Coming to her house like a hobo is bad enough." She wiped her eyes with her sleeve.

Pete patted her shoulder. "We've made it. You don't have to worry anymore."

They started out on foot, walking half a mile toward Grandma's house before an old Ford slowed beside them.

"Hello!" A freckle-faced man with mussed hair poked his head out the window. "Do you folks need a ride? Kinda dark for walking."

"Yes!" Carla raced up to the car. "Yes, we do. Do you know Grace Henley? She's my grandma. We need to get to her house."

"Sure, I know Grace. Hop in. I'll take you there."

They climbed in and Pete smiled at the driver. "Thank you, sir."

A few minutes later, they arrived at the two-story brick house. "My sweet Carla." Even in curlers, the white-haired woman bore an air of elegance. She embraced her granddaughter, then Pete and Cookie. "I'm Grace. Thank you for bringing her to me." When she stepped back, she frowned. "Oh, but look at you all. What on earth have you been through to get here? And that hat?"

Pete rubbed grime from his cheek and drew in a deep breath. "We found this young lady on our travels, ma'am. Hopping freight trains with us, and pretending to be a boy. Took her under our wing and made sure she got here safely."

Grace pressed her hands against Carla's cheeks. "A boy? Oh, Carla." The wrinkles in her forehead sunk deeper. "And hopping trains? Why, I—"

"But Grandma, I'm here now." Carla sat on the oak bench in Grace's entry. She removed her hole-filled shoes, snatched off her cap, and let a gorgeous mane of thick, dark curly hair tumble around her shoulders.

Pete and Cookie's jaws dropped.

"What?" She giggled.

Grace linked arms with Pete and Cookie. "Well, I do thank you for bringing her to me. Let's have some tea, shall we? And I'm sure you're hungry. How does breakfast at midnight sound?"

Warmth filled Pete's soul. "It sounds great, ma'am."

They spent about a week in Bismarck helping Grace put up wood. On the sixth morning, she greeted them with a hug. "I so appreciate you both."

Pete raked his fingers through his clean hair. "The pleasure is ours, Grace. I'm happy to stay put for a while."

Cookie rubbed his belly. "Me, too. I haven't ate like this in a long time."

"We're fortunate that we're north of the dust bowl." Grace skirted around them and carried the teakettle to the cast iron sink. "They're calling that April storm Black Sunday, and this whole drought and dust storm situation the 'Brown Plague.' It has killed hundreds of infants, children and old folks already." She filled the kettle with fresh water and set it on the stove to boil. "Now the grasshoppers are coming in droves and eating the rest of the crops."

"I overheard a man say that the National Guard is spreading arsenic and molasses on the grasshoppers, trying to kill them." Cookie pulled out a wooden chair and sat at the table.

Pete nodded. "I heard that, too."

"I read that the government has hired rainmakers, trying to

make it rain." Grandma reached into a cupboard and brought out a large teapot.

"How can they do that?" Carla set plates on the table.

"They're going to fire off rockets of dynamite and nitroglycerine, I guess." All four shook their heads.

Following breakfast, Pete and Cookie repaired a broken section of the fence surrounding Grace's yard.

"I'm eager to head toward Helena." Pete reached into the box of nails and drew out a long one. He drove it deep into the wooden post.

"I don't want to go back west." Cookie held the next board steady while Pete grabbed another nail. "I've never been east. I'd like to see what it's like out there. Why don't we go east?"

Pete drew in a deep breath. "Cookie, I'm tired of traveling. I want to settle down somewhere. Find a home. Practice veterinary work again."

"They have horses and cows in the east, too." Cookie's jaw twitched.

"I'll think about it. In the meantime, we need to wrap this up so we can get that porch rebuilt."

When they finished the fence, Cookie removed rotted porch boards while Pete roamed town for unused lumber.

As the sun rose higher, a line of trees towering over a few tall buildings turned to shadows on the eastern horizon. Was Cookie right? Should he continue east and try to find a practice there somewhere?

He longed for rushing water to give him peace. Where was that river Cookie always talked about? Kathleen Creek. Minnesota. Due east from here. Maybe three hundred miles or so? He could go with Cookie one more time and see that river. Should he?

While they rebuilt Grace's porch, she showed her deep appreciation with wonderful meals. Her tiny garden yielded radishes and lettuce, and her few scrawny chickens provided eggs. With her sewing and mending, she bartered meat from the butcher and flour from the mill owners.

On the night they finished the porch, Carla brought Pete and Cookie a glass of cold water, and they sat on the steps.

Ice tinkled in the glass as she passed Pete's to him. "Thank you for getting me settled with Grandma. It will be such a help for her to have someone around." A frown flickered across her bright face. "But I do miss my family."

Pete drained half the glass. "I feel guilty eating all that food she works so hard to secure, but I'm grateful for it. And for the soft bed we've enjoyed this past week."

Cookie nodded. "Me, too. Very grateful, indeed."

Carla took a tiny sip. "I suppose with the porch complete, you're ready to move on. Where are you headed next?"

Pete grinned at Cookie. "East."

They set out the next morning. While passing through Fargo, North Dakota, Cookie doubled over with cramps. "I've got to get off, Preacher. I've got to go."

The train hardly slowed enough before they made their jump. Pete raced after him. "Cookie?"

Someone jerked his arm, and Pete groaned. The yard dicks.

Cookie poked his head out of the bushes. Pete flicked his hand to him. Why wasn't he hiding?

With his hands on his hips, Cookie emerged beside them. "If you take him in, you take me, too."

As the yard dick shuffled them along, Pete looked down the bridge of his nose at Cookie. "You didn't have to do that."

"Hobos watch out for each other, remember."

Pete shook his head. This was getting old.

They stood behind the iron bars as the door clanged shut. "Why didn't you go on without me?" Pete furrowed his brow.

"We're a good team. Besides, if you've got a buddy watching your back, you're safer."

Pete nodded. It made sense. "You're a good friend, Cookie."

"I owe you." Cookie punched his thin pillow and lay down.

The next day they stood, in turn, before the Cass County judge, a balding man with a round face and wispy white mustache. To each, he recited, "I hereby pronounce you guilty of unauthorized use of railroad transportation and sentence you to fifteen days to be served working on a state highway crew."

"Well, at least we'll eat regularly." Cookie grinned as the deputy escorted them back to their cells.

Pete creased his brow. Yet another delay to him getting on with his life.

Over the fifteen days, the hot sun burned into their flesh as Pete and Cookie shoveled gravel alongside other men building the highway.

"I hoped to gain a little weight, but I'm working off every bit of the food they feed us." Pete re-tied his twine belt. "I've gotten so skinny my own mother wouldn't know me."

"I'm getting soft. This will build up my muscle again." Cookie flexed his arm.

"How can you always be so positive about everything?" Pete winced at his own disgusted tone.

Cookie studied him for a few moments. "'God did not give us a spirit of timidity, but a spirit of power, of love and of self-discipline.' You read that to me from the Bible, Preacher. Don't you remember? I do. I've thought about it a lot."

Pete's heart lurched. How could this young man, really still a boy, humble him so? Cookie called *him* Preacher, yet he taught Pete about trusting God.

When they finally left with their sparse belongings, Cookie pointed to a newspaper lying on the street. "Look, it's July already." He bobbed his head to the right. "East?"

"East." Pete grinned. "How about Kathleen Creek? I want to see that spot on the river you always talk about."

A cloud passed over Cookie's face. "I want to go further east. But you should go to Kathleen Creek. I know you'd love it."

Part ways? Pete frowned. "Let's head in that direction, stop off at Kathleen Creek for a bit, and then we can continue east. I'd hate to leave without you."

"I'll think about it." Cookie walked a few paces ahead of him. He spun, a slight quiver in his lips. "Preacher, it's been great traveling with you, but right now we want different things. I'm not done seeing the country, but you want to settle." His chest heaved. "You'd like Kathleen Creek. You should go there. Sit by the river and decide if you want to stay."

A large, black locomotive spewed steam at the depot a short ways off, readying for takeoff. Cookie looked at the train, and then back at Pete. "I'll grab that train going southeast, but I'll know where to find you. Joe the butcher is a mean old cuss but he'll feed you. He'll give you something to eat if you tell him to read Hebrews 12."

Pete caught Cookie's arm. Why wouldn't he at least stop by the river first? "Won't you come with me? I'll hate splitting with you, Cookie, but the river is calling to me. I need to go there." The train whistled. Cookie extended his hand then withdrew it and put both arms around Pete. He squeezed him in an enormous hug. "So long, Preacher."

"God go with you, my friend." Pete's voice came out hoarse. "I'll pray for you."

The clangs of the rail came closer together, the train moved faster and faster. A tear glinted from the corner of Cookie's eye as he turned to run for it.

Fourth of July fireworks had lit up the sky as soon as the sun disappeared and thundered well into the morning. Pete's eyes burned from lack of sleep. Sweat poured from his forehead and rolled down his neck, soaking the back of his shirt. The boxcar felt like his grandpa's sauna.

He tried to stay cool by standing in the open doorway of the fast-moving Soo Line car, keeping his balance with one hand against the door frame while swaying and rattling over the rails. Cookie promised he'd find cooler weather in northern Minnesota. Maybe it would be cool when he reached his destination, but it certainly wasn't yet.

Now, what all had Cookie told him about Kathleen Creek? *You can sit against an old maple tree and fish or read or think with a nice cool breeze on your face.* Those words drew Pete, but Cookie's other words spoke more urgently. *Joe the butcher is a mean old cuss but he'll feed you. He'll give you something to eat if you tell him to read Hebrews 12.*

How many days had Pete been on this train? And when had he last eaten? His weak legs buckled when he stood, and he fought regular dizziness. In another hour, he'd be there. He sat to conserve his energy, keeping his legs in the car.

The verdant scene passed by with maples, oaks, ash, cotton-woods, and a variety of other trees creating dense forests. Everything wore a layer of dust from many storms. Brown, crispy hay spotted dry fields. And the corn... would it amount to anything without rain?

Once, the train stopped to add water next to a sign on a corn field fence. *First six rows for hobos, the rest is mine.* What had Rail-road so often said? *People are good.*

Even facing north, the hot breeze burned his exposed skin to the point of near blisters. He should rest a while. He scooted against the wall inside the boxcar. At least he was alone and had his pick of the space. Soon, perspiration ran down his face and back and he could hardly breathe. He had to move back to the doorway. The next stop would be Kathleen Creek. Not much further.

Oh, for another bath. He'd taken one in the river the night before. Irrelevant now, with all his sweating. He'd washed his hair, shirt and pants only three days ago so maybe they didn't look too bad. As they neared the town, he shook his head. Why did it seem so important to look his best when meeting Joe, the Butcher?

The train slowed. The whistle blew. Then the sign appeared. *Kathleen Creek.* Pete slipped his pack on and crouched at the door of the car, weak with hunger. Why did he let himself go so long without food? It wasn't the same without Cookie.

Pete made the jump and darted into the bushes. Were there no yard dicks here? After several minutes, he headed toward a wide and inviting main street. Canopies covered the wooden boardwalks in front of the shops. Cars, horses, and buggies lined the streets. What a nice place to live.

As usual, people kept a wide berth around Pete and averted their gazes. For some reason, it bothered him today.

A shrill scream drew a crowd of people to the sidewalk several feet ahead of him.

Pete ran after them. A whimper and howl accompanied the wail.

He worked his way through the crowd to a little girl with shiny brown curls. She knelt next to a puppy lying in the middle of the street behind an ice wagon.

"Help him." She lifted her chin, her lips quivering. "The wagon ran over him. He's hurt!"

A man and woman tried to help her stand. She pushed them away. "Somebody has to help him."

A young man in a blue uniform approached. "I'm so sorry. Something spooked them. That's why they backed up on the dog. I'm sorry. I'm sorry."

"Let me through." Pete pushed his way between a young couple. When people saw him they stepped aside. Did they think he was contagious? He held back his snarl, knelt by the dog, and dropped his pack. The crowd went silent.

Trails of tears stained the girl's cheeks. "Can you fix him? Please?"

Pete examined the Bernese Mountain puppy with his hands, crooning to him as he did so. "What's his name?"

"Max." She let out a shaky breath.

Pete lifted the dog's chin and examined its teeth. "What's your name?"

"Mary. Is he going to be okay?"

A man and woman, obviously Mary's parents, came up behind her and laid their hands on her shoulders.

Pete inwardly groaned. How could he convince these people he had no intent to harm their daughter? That he was a man, like them, who'd once had a family and a beautiful little girl of his own?

Pete squeezed the dog's hind leg, and it yelped as his fingers ran over a sharp point. "Max has a broken leg, Mary. Otherwise he seems to be okay." He faced the crowd. "Can someone bring me a wire hanger, wire cutters, some cotton cloth, and some tape? I'll put a splint on it and his leg will heal fine. He'll be running around and getting into trouble again, in no time at all, Mary." He smiled at her.

"I'll go." The man holding Mary's shoulder turned and left.

"I'll go, too." Mary's mother faced the woman standing next to her. She motioned for the woman to hold onto Mary for her.

Pete blasted a breath through his nostrils. Good grief! Did he look that scary?

The crowd remained. No one spoke while they waited for the supplies.

Pete caressed the black, brown, and white puppy. "You're a good boy, Max." He leaned close to the dog's ear. "You'll be well again, soon. A bit of pain and limping, but you'll be up running again in no time." As he tried to stretch out his leg, he banged his ankle against a wheel. "Can someone move that ice wagon so we have a little more room here?"

"Yeah, sure, I can move it." The young man snapped to attention. "I'm so sorry." He drove the wagon ahead, settling the team at the side of the street. A fine team, like Mike and Maddie.

The girl's father returned with the supplies. Pete set the leg and wrapped it in cotton batting. He cut two pieces of wire, and using them as splints, bound cotton and tape around the leg.

"There now, Max." He helped the dog stand. "You can go run around again. You'll get used to one back leg in a splint, but it won't be forever."

He ruffled Mary's hair. "See? He's fine. Now Mary, don't baby him by carrying him around. Let him run. He'll limp a little at first, then he'll put weight on it. In about four weeks you can take off the splint, and he'll be as good as new."

"Thank you." Mary reached for her beloved pet with one hand and wiped away the last of her tears with the other.

"You are welcome. You have a beautiful puppy." Pete smiled. "Take good care of him."

"I will, mister." Beaming, she kissed the dog's nose.

Pete put on his backpack, swaying a bit as he did. Mary's father gripped both Pete's hands and helped him stand. "Thank you very much. You did a great job and it means a lot to our daughter. What can we do for you?"

"I need something to eat." Pete brushed his hair from his eyes. "I've traveled a long way with no food."

A small whiskered man in a black wool fisherman's cap and dirty white apron waved to Pete from the edge of the crowd. "Come with me. I have hot stew."

Pete shuffled to his side.

"I'm Joe." He squeezed Pete's frail fingers in his strong ones.

Pete's breath caught. Cookie's Joe?

Joe led Pete to a cedar picnic table in the shade behind the meat market across the street. It *was* Cookie's Joe. "Have a seat and I'll bring you some stew." He disappeared into the back door, letting the screen slam behind him.

Pete rested at the table until Joe returned with a steaming bowl and two hot buttered biscuits. He set them on the table with a spoon and whisked back toward the door. "I'll get you a glass of milk."

"Thank you, Lord." Pete picked up a biscuit and took a bite. The warm butter rolled over his tongue and slid down his throat. Heavenly. Oh, if only Cookie were here. Pete could thank him for telling him about Kathleen Creek and Joe. He took another bite and had the biscuit eaten when Joe returned with the milk.

"I hope you like rabbit stew." Joe set the glass in front of him.

Pete nodded with his mouth full.

"I made the stew, but my wife Dolly made the biscuits." Joe sat at the table. "We're the butcher and the baker in town. She runs the café part of this operation. We both do the cooking. and she does all the baking. What's your name?

"Pete."

"Where do you hail from, Pete?"

"Nebraska."

Joe took off his wire-rimmed glasses, found a spot on the hem of his apron, and wiped them clean.

"This is delicious stew. Thank you." Pete wiped his mouth on his sleeve, and drank the last of the milk. "This was the best food I've had in a long time. Please tell Dolly that I love her biscuits."

"Do you want more?"

Pete gaped. He had never been offered seconds before. And Cookie called Joe a mean old cuss. This man was anything but mean. "Joe, I thank you most kindly for the offer but I'm afraid my stomach is not used to that much food at one time anymore." He burped. "Excuse me. If the offer is still good, I'd like to come back this evening."

Joe picked up Pete's dishes and nodded. "Knock on the door."

Joe's shoulders stooped as he disappeared through the back door. Such a heavy burden. Why was he so sad?

Cookie had told him to walk north on Main Street to reach the river so Pete headed north. When he reached the Crow River Pete closed his eyes and breathed in the song of water rustling over rocks and the memories it brought back to him. He felt as if the river was feeding his soul and he didn't want to move. But Cookie had told him about a special place a mile west so he turned and continued walking.

He recognized the spot as soon as he saw it. A huge maple tree grew so close to the river that roots appeared on the bank. Pete dropped his pack next to the tree and sat in the cool of the shade, leaning against the wide trunk. The gurgling, moving water of the river mesmerized him. He relaxed and let the sound of the water envelope him with its healing power.

As Pete sat with his eyes closed he felt as if he had just released a years' worth of burden. Like he had found a home. Was it possible that people here might trust him? Could he redeem himself with the people of Kathleen Creek?

What could he do for Joe? He found a fishing pole and fished for two hours, catching a good string of fish. By that time the sun was low on the horizon and the mosquitos were out in full force.

When Pete knocked on the back door of the meat market, no one answered. He opened the screen and knocked again. Still no answer.

An automobile pulled up to the front of the cafe and a man and woman got out of the car. Pete approached them and said, "Excuse me, I wonder if you would be kind enough to give Joe a message for me. I'm not presentable enough to go into the café."

The woman pulled her chin back and wrinkled her nose as she looked Pete up and down. The man said, "Certainly, I can do that. What's the message?"

"Tell him that Pete has a string of fish for him. I'll be at the back door. Thank you." The man nodded and they walked into the café, the woman moving to the opposite side of the man from Pete.

In only a few minutes Joe came out. "Come in," he told Pete. When they were both inside a small entryway that had a table and two chairs along the wall Pete handed Joe the string of fish.

"Well, thank you, Pete. Let me get you something to eat." Joe brought out a bowl of thick wild rice soup, two slices of buttered bread and a glass of milk. "I have orders to put up, but just knock in the morning if you're still around," Joe said.

Once again Pete wondered what was making the man so unhappy.

## 2 8

Jenny Howe, like everyone else, ran out to see why someone screamed with such panic. She stood on the outside edge of the crowd as the hobo splinted Mary's puppy's leg.

The man's abundant facial hair obscured his age, but his gentle manner touched Jenny's heart as it hadn't been touched in a long time. His voice, a tender but authoritative tone, sounded younger than middle-age. His ragged clothes hung loose on him. The tall, skinny body must have once belonged to a bigger man.

When he looked up to request that someone move the wagon, the sun caught a glint of compassion in his blue eyes. Jenny's quick intake of breath matched a time when she saw the same flash of brilliant blue in a bluebird's flight. She couldn't stop looking at him.

His long fingers expertly worked his makeshift supplies, while comforting both the patient and Mary with loving, soothing words. This was no ordinary hobo. Why was he homeless?

"I'm waiting for you, Jenny!" Mark revved his engine.

She pulled herself away and hurried to Mark's shiny, new Cadillac.

"Why were you keeping me waiting?" Mark shifted into gear and tore out of town, kicking up gravel and dust in his wake.

Jenny shook off his childish actions. "A hobo put a splint on Mary's dog's leg. The ice wagon ran over it. That man splinted the leg like an expert with a wire hanger, cotton, and tape"

"How do you know he did it expertly? Maybe it won't even work."

"He knew what he was doing. He first gave the dog a thorough examination and found the broken leg and fixed it." Jenny sat back against the seat. How wonderful that Mary's beloved dog would be okay again.

"What would a hobo know about examining a dog?"

"I don't know." Jenny loved Mark, but sometimes his condescending attitude irritated her. How could she be passionately in love with him when he wouldn't grow up? All he wanted to do was play and have fun. Especially since he could afford to spend much more time away from earning a living than most people. His parents probably spoiled him even as a little boy.

She smoothed her hand over the luxurious leather seats. How lucky she should feel to be the recipient of his wealth and time. After all, Mark was driving her home so she didn't have to take a train to Minneapolis.

After a good long distance, Mark slowed the car. "We should stop for dinner before I take you home. Where would you like to eat?"

"You choose a place."

"It's a little out of the way, but it would be nice to eat at Captain's Cove on Lake Minnetonka. A lot of wealthy business people eat there."

"That's okay with me." Jenny shrugged.

Mark wrinkled his nose. "I'm taking you to one of the most

expensive eating establishments in the area and it is only 'okay' with you?"

"Mark, you know that money doesn't impress me as much as it does you." Status and wealth – those were the important things to Mark.

"Money should impress you. Look at all the people who have nothing right now." Mark jerked his hand in the air. "Are they happy? No, they're miserable. Do you want to be miserable? Do you want to be living off the county like so many of the people around us?"

"No, of course I don't want to be miserable or unable to feed myself. I see misery all around me. Most of my students' fathers are unemployed and on relief. Even the farmers can't make it anymore. But money isn't the most important thing in the world, either."

Mark strummed his thumbs on the steering wheel, glanced at his reflection in the rearview mirror, and checked his teeth. Then he smiled. "I haven't told you about the week I spent up north at the Wellington's cabin with Kenny and Buzz. We fished almost every day. I caught six walleyes the first day and three the second..."

Jenny faced the side window. How could he drone on about fishing with all the misery that surrounded them all the time? Most of her students came to school hungry. Jenny pulled the collar of her jacket close around her neck and shivered.

"Jenny, did you hear what I said?" Mark slapped his hand on the steering wheel.

Jenny flinched. "What?"

"I asked you when you're coming back to Kathleen Creek." Mark's voice held an edge.

"Oh. Well, I won't come back any sooner than I have to. My parents are already upset because I stayed here so long after school closed for summer."

"Oh, yeah, you wanted to be here for the school board meeting." Mark nodded.

"Yes, I did." Jenny's pitch raised an octave. "They have treated me so unfairly."

"Well, you're a woman. You don't need as much money as a man."

Jenny's jaw dropped. "Mark, I deserve to be paid the same as a male teacher. What makes you think I don't need as much money? I pay as much for room and board. I need clothes and food like Mr. Glover did. I work as many hours as Mr. Glover did, maybe more."

"You don't have to yell at me, Jenny. I'm not the one who treated you unfairly." Mark lowered his right shoulder and drew his body away from her in mock defense.

Jenny made tight fists, the veins in her neck raised. "But you've got the same opinion as those idiotic school board members!"

"Well, you stood up for yourself and got the same pay, so why are you still so mad about it?"

Jenny sighed. Sun glinted off Mark's polished, shining dashboard. How could this spoiled, only child ever understand? Take a deep breath. Unclench the teeth. Soften the tone. "If not for some of the parents and my threat to not come back, I don't think they would have agreed to it."

"Well, I'm glad you'll be coming back." Mark reached over and squeezed her hand.

As his new sporty coupe carried them closer to Minneapolis, Jenny's heart pounded harder. Her mother would ask again, "Has Mark proposed?"

Her parents thought Mark the perfect husband for her. His impeccable taste in cars and clothing impressed them. Every time mother wrote, she asked when it would happen and not if.

Jenny wanted to marry and have children, but did she want to be married to Mark? He was handsome, rich, and sometimes charming. But he could also be irritating, crude, self-absorbed, controlling, and immature.

Did she love him? Maybe.

Did he love her? She didn't know. He had never told her he loved her.

He was thoughtful, considerate, a good kisser, and a gentleman who never tried to go too far with her. If she didn't marry Mark, who would she marry? Maybe she wouldn't. Would she remain an old-maid school teacher? She shuddered.

"Do you realize how old you are, dear?" her mother had asked. "You don't want to end up like Aunt Ellen, do you?"

Jenny shook her head.

Her mother clucked her tongue. "I'm sure your dad's sister never thought at your age she would end up a miserable old maid. But year after year she became more irritable. Negativity rendered her a person no one could love. You watch that doesn't happen to you, honey."

Jenny yawned. "Mark, I'd like to nap for a while. Is that okay with you?"

"Go ahead." Mark glanced toward the rearview mirror. "I'll wake you when we get to the restaurant." He ran his fingers through his hair. One of the many irritating habits that made Jenny cringe. He was so stuck on himself. Yes, he was handsome. But did he have to preen about so?

Jenny closed her eyes. Staying in Minneapolis would have yielded better pay. She might have found love. Why did she always make bad life choices?

Yet how could she call teaching in Kathleen Creek a mistake? She loved her students, especially Janet Ross. How could she not adore that sweet little girl, by far the youngest in her class? She loved holding her on her lap while she read each morning and helping her with her coat. Would she ever have a daughter she could care for like that? A little girl she could love? And, of course, she'd want at least one son as well.

Yes, her students needed her, but she needed them, too. She needed an outlet for her affection. She yawned. Fall couldn't come soon enough.

When Mark called her name, Jenny blinked free from her sleep.

He grinned. "Look at that big smile. What were you dreaming about?"

"Hmmm?" She rubbed her eyes and sat up straight. She couldn't tell him, nor could she forget the hobo's brilliant blue eyes looking at her with passionate love.

A hobo! What was wrong with her?

## 29

The July night air cooled, and Pete headed along the river toward a park shelter. He lay beneath the shelter on the crisp, dry grass, covered his arms with his cape, and shielded his face with a bandana. Hopefully that would ward off the mosquitos buzzing constantly around him. As usual, his pack served as a pillow and his head protected his life's possessions. Even here, his safety wasn't guaranteed. His months on the road had taught him to be cautious.

The next morning dawned bright and sunny. Pete leapt up and explored the area. The grass crunched dry and brittle beneath his feet. What might be growing wild? What could he bring to Joe? Could anything be harvested for medicinal purposes?

Tiny little, red, wild strawberries lay on the ground, ripened by the sun and heat. What fortunate timing, to find them before the birds discovered them.

Ordinarily the strawberries would be his breakfast, but were there enough to bring Dolly some, too? He tied his cape around his waist, lifted the hem, and collected them. The further into the brush, the thicker the strawberry patch became, so he dug a clean bandana from his pack and poured the berries into the middle of it. Had he picked enough to make a pie? Maybe not.

Pete put the berries into his hat and carried it with one hand while he picked more berries. There. That should do it. Now, what other plants and trees were in the area?

He could tap the pines for resin. And maybe he'd come back for rose hips when the wild roses bloomed. Did that mean he intended to be here that long? The thought made him smile. Maybe he would.

Mid-morning Pete knocked on Joe's screen door.

Joe's eyes lit up. "I thought you'd maybe moved on."

"I've been picking strawberries." Pete handed him the hat of tiny red berries. "Dolly might want to make a pie."

"She'll be so happy with these. I'll bring them to her right away. Sit down. I'll see what we have in the Yesterday Box for you."

"The Yesterday Box?"

"Ah, yes, well the Yesterday Box is a bread box that we put all the baked goods into that are left at the end of the day. We only serve fresh in the café. We give yesterday's away. I'll see what we have. Do you want a cup of coffee to go with it?"

"I would love a cup of coffee! Haven't had a cup in a long time."

"Black?"

"Yes, please." Pete's face warmed.

"Make yourself comfortable. I'll be right back."

The screen door slammed behind Joe, and Pete laid his pack on the ground. Soon the door opened, and a large woman came out with a tray and his empty hat.

"I'm Dolly and you must be Pete." She placed a cup of coffee and a plate of two donuts in front of him. "I understand you love coffee." She laughed, her voice loud and her energy high. "I could kiss you for bringing me those wonderful, tasty little strawberries."

Pete grinned at the graying woman with the sensible bun atop her head. Her clean-washed face held a fine layer of perspiration. And the twinkle in her eyes... this feisty woman could likely take a kidding as well as dish it out. "I haven't had a kiss in a long time." He lifted one side of his face and pointed to his cheek.

"Now what would Joe say if I kissed all the young men who come here wantin' a bit of food? Oh, what the heck, you're not much older than our son." She reached down and gave him a peck on the cheek. "There now."

A glint of a tear formed in the corner of her eye. Pete frowned. What did he say?

"Thank you," Pete called after her as she retreated with haste.

Joe came out a few minutes later with a coffee pot and refilled his cup. He sat across from Pete. "What did you say to Dolly? She had herself a bit of a cry when she came in. She tried to hide it, but I knew."

Pete broke off a piece of donut and popped it in his mouth. "She gave me a kiss on the cheek and said I wasn't much older than your son."

"Oh, that explains it." A shadow crossed Joe's face. "Our son left home over a year ago, and we don't know where he is. It's been hard on Dolly. We worry he might be ridin' the rails, homeless."

"Is that why you feed the hobos? You hope someone out there is feeding your son?"

"You might say that. We only started doin' that after we thought our son might be need'n a handout somewhere." Joe brushed away a fallen maple leaf from the table. "Before that I used to turn away anyone asking for food. You might say I was different then. I used to drink a lot, and that made me mean."

Pete finished his donut while Joe stared toward the table. Why had Cookie called Joe mean? If Joe had quit drinking and changed before he started feeding hobos, then... Cookie seemed to know so much about Kathleen Creek. "What's your son's name, Joe?"

"Ben. Benjamin Joseph Harrison. Have you met him somewhere?" The quick hope in Joe's eyes panged Pete's heart. Was that what made Joe so sad?

*They call me Cookie but my name is Ben.* Could Cookie be Joe's son? "I've met a lot of men these past six months. Most of them don't even share their names." Pete took a sip of his coffee. "They go by nicknames." How could he get their hopes up? Even if Cookie was their son, he could be anywhere with no way to reach him.

Pete stood and put his pack and hat on. "Thank you again for the food. God will bless you for what you're doing."

If Cookie was Joe and Dolly's son, could he possibly get word to him that his father changed and his mother needed to see him?

Pete rounded the building of the meat market and headed toward the river with his cape flapping along his side with each step.

"Hello, mister." Mary pulled Max in a little red Coaster wagon in front of the mercantile.

Pete waved and crossed the street. "Hello, Mary. Hi there, Max. How are you doing today?" He leaned over and checked the splint, caressing the dog.

Max wagged his tail and kissed Pete's face.

"Max likes you." Mary giggled.

"I like Max too. He's a beautiful dog." Pete slipped his fingers between the dog and his collar. Still room to grow. "Where did you get him?"

"My daddy got him for me for my birthday. I'm six. I'm going to go to school when summer is over."

*When I'm six I'm going to go to school and learn everything.* Sweet Rose. Pete smiled at Mary. Why wasn't he doubling over in pain at the memory? Mary's mother rushed out of the store.

She took hold of Mary's arm and wrinkled her nose at Pete "Come on in."

"Goodbye, mister." Mary balked as her mother pulled her into the store along with the wagon and Max.

Pete winced. How scary he must look. He tried to keep his dark hair short by cutting it himself, but he could only comb his hair with his fingers. His beard had grown way too long. He had bathed and washed his shirt in the river before catching the train to Kathleen Creek. But, with the heat in that railroad car, did he smell bad now?

He sniffed at himself as he looked down at his pants, worn thin and held up with twine. He had taped the loose soles of his shoes to the uppers so they wouldn't flap. Yeah, he probably did look scary to some people. But he'd treated their dog. Couldn't they see that he was harmless?

His chest swelled from anger and breath came in spurts. When had he ever found such rage? He sat on the bench outside the mercantile door. Why did Mary's mother offend him so easily? People had treated him like that since he began riding the rails. This was no different.

Yet it felt different. He wanted the people of Kathleen Creek to like and trust him. This *was* different.

Two young women approached along the boardwalk talking. They passed him with only a quick glance. The pretty blonde said to her friend, "Glen looks at me, but when I look back at him he looks away. I know he likes me. How do I get him to talk to me? He's so shy!" They entered the store together.

A farmer and his wife came up the boardwalk from the other direction. They flinched at Pete, then she faced her husband. "Now don't say a word about me being in the family way again. I don't want any gossip about too many children." They, too, went into the store.

Two young boys came running by. The bigger boy said, "You keep Dave busy at the candy counter, and I'll swipe the comics."

Pete gripped the bench. He was invisible to these people. It didn't matter what they said in front of him, because he was nobody. They could reveal their secrets and think nothing of it. He got up, adjusted his pack on his back, and continued toward the river.

When he reached the feed mill he passed two shaded benches on each side of the doorway. Maybe he should escape the sun for a bit. People had said it'd been a record-breaking hot summer, and it sure felt like it again today.

Not long after he settled himself on one of the benches, a man drove up in a new automobile. He wore a suit, vest, and tie with an expensive-looking watch chain hanging from his pocket. His stride announced his importance to the world. Another man came out of the building and accosted the rich man. "George, please …"

"I'm sorry, Chet." The rich man dodged the man. "We cannot extend your loan. I told you that at the bank yesterday. I'm truly sorry. Now, if you'll excuse me."

The banker pushed the man's hand off his arm and walked into the mill. The rejected man sat on the other bench, covered his face with his large hands, and wept.

He didn't seem embarrassed that Pete could see him crying. It truly was as if Pete had become invisible. No one *wanted* to see him. If they did, they might feel obligated to *give* him something or help him in some way.

A mother and three young girls came out of the mill followed by a clerk carrying two fifty-pound flour sacks, each with a different print bag. He loaded the sacks into the back of an old pickup. "You take care now, Mrs. Hermann."

Pete heard the youngest girl say, "I want you to make my dress from the pink flour sack."

The mother pursed her lips. "I'm sorry, honey, but I can only buy two sacks of flour. The price went up to $1.89 a sack. I have to make dresses for Bonnie and Tammy from that fabric.

Bonnie's red dress will fit you, and you can wear that to the wedding."

The little girl cried. "I'm sorry, honey," the mother told the desolate child. "You'll look real pretty in Bonnie's red dress."

Pete couldn't help staring. The little girl reminded him so much of Rose. She even sounded like her.

She must be about a year younger than Mary. As an only child, and the mercantile owner's daughter, Mary probably had lots of dresses. She might have grown out of a pretty dress that would be perfect for that little girl to wear to a wedding.

Back in Grand Island, where people trusted him, Pete could have put in a word with a family like Mary's. They would have been happy to share with a less fortunate child.

Pete stood and turned toward the river.

The screen door slammed, and his ears pricked.

"Somebody's got to do something about Tommy," the banker said. "Yesterday he shot that cap gun right under my window when I had a client with me in an important meeting. He does it to irritate me. Ever since his pa left, he's gotten into mischief whenever he can. His pranks are going to lead to something worse, I tell you. Somebody's got to do something about him!"

Pete left the mill and strolled toward the river, his hands swinging at his side. The birds sang lovely songs, the hot breeze warmed his face, and the green trees danced around him. Still, everything had a layer of dust from the dust storms that had come all the way here from the southwest.

Dust, hobos, and mischievous boys. All the things society could do without. Poor Tommy. Wonder how old he was. Was he the kid stealing the comics? Did he spook the horses that caused Max's accident? Pete would have to keep an eye out for him.

Pete grimaced. Who was he kidding? How could he help Tommy when he couldn't even help himself to a decent living? He was nobody.

## 30

Pete stopped across the street from an ornate house. A young man sat on the front porch in a wheelchair, his shoulders slouching and head hanging. Another troubled soul?

The man pushed long, dark hair from his face and waved. He dropped his limp hand back into his lap and looked down.

"Hello," Pete called.

The man jerked his head up. "Hello." He waved again, with enthusiasm.

"Beautiful summer day," Pete strained his voice loud enough to carry across the street, "but it sure is hot."

"Would you like some lemonade?"

Pete blinked twice. Well, that was unexpected. "Yes, thank you." As he crossed the street, the man called to someone inside. A young woman came out onto the porch, but when Pete reached him, she had retreated back into the house.

"Sit." The man bounced in his wheelchair, his smile reaching every part of him.

Pete took a chair across from the man, and the woman appeared with a tray of glasses.

"I'm James Davis." He touched his chest, then pointed to the young woman. "This is my sister, Katherine."

Ah. The woman who'd asked a friend how she could get 'Glen' to pay attention to her.

"Have a glass of lemonade." Katherine nodded to the tray.

Pete reached for a tall foggy glass glistening with sweat on the outside. "Thank you, Katherine. I believe I saw you at the mercantile earlier today."

"I don't remember seeing you." She drew her eyebrows together and cocked her head.

"My name is Pete. And thank you, James, for the invitation. It feels good to sit and have a cold beverage." He took a long drink and breathed out deep appreciation.

"I have to get to ironing. Will you excuse me?" With that, Katherine went back into the house.

Pete took another drink, letting the cool, sweet, and sour taste linger in his mouth a few seconds. "I'm new in town. What's there to do around here?"

"Not much." James sounded depressed. "'Course, I can't participate in anything, so I don't pay much attention."

"Have you been in a wheelchair all your life?" How difficult it must be for a young man to be so confined. No wonder he looked so sad.

James turned the chair and faced Pete. "No, I had polio a few years ago."

"What do you like to do for fun?"

"I don't have much fun."

"What did you do before you had polio?"

"I played softball and football and went skating and hunted."

All the things he couldn't do now. A pain of sympathy crept into Pete's chest. But, he had an idea. "Do you like to play cribbage?"

"I do, but I don't usually have anyone to play with." James shrugged.

"I have time. If you have a board, let's play."

"Wow, I'd like that." He leaned forward. "Katherine!"

She came running into the porch, deep worry lines on her forehead. "What's wrong?"

"Nothing. We're going to play cribbage. Will you please bring the board out here?"

Pete smoothed his long beard. Such a handsome young man. Maybe about twenty-five.

They moved a small table between them, and James arranged the board. "You go first, Pete."

"Okay." After sorting his hand, Pete discarded. "15 – 2, 15 – 4 and a pair for six holes."

"Ten for me." James moved his peg.

Pete quirked his brow. How had he counted so fast? "What?"

James laid out the cards. "15-2, 15-4, and three of a kind is six for 10 points."

"Are you a math genius or something?"

"I've always been good at numbers." James grinned.

"You could have a job as an accountant." Pete said.

James ducked his gaze.

Pete played on without further comment until James had won both games. He stacked his cards on the table. "Better get going. I've enjoyed our time together, James. Can I stop in again sometime?"

"Any time. I'm always here." James grimaced.

"Thanks again for the lemonade." Pete shook James' hand and picked up his backpack. He walked a few paces with a spring in his step. How wonderful it felt to be useful and to give James a few minutes of happiness. "By the way," he turned back, "what do you know about the Hermann family?"

"They live three miles outside of town. North, over the bridge. On the right." James pointed. "Gunther Hermann is a good farmer. What do you want to know?"

"I saw Mrs. Hermann and her daughters at the mill. The

youngest girl reminded me so much of my own little Rose. I can't stop thinking about her, that's all."

Several minutes later, Pete arrived at "his spot" by the river. What a great day. He'd found someone to befriend other than Joe and Dolly. Obviously an intelligent young man, James could be productive given the opportunity. Maybe Pete could help him.

Now, to find Tommy and see if he could do something for him. Kids who lived in towns usually didn't have enough chores to keep them busy, and if his father was gone, his mother probably worked all day. Tommy was probably left to his own devices. He'd ask Joe about him.

"Sure doesn't sound like I want to leave Kathleen Creek any time soon, does it?" He settled against the maple tree. And that little Hermann girl. Maybe he could figure out a way to get her a new dress, too.

By mid-afternoon the sun made Pete sleepy, so he spread his cape on the ground and took a nap. When he awoke, he settled once more against the tree. What could he find for Joe to pay for his next meal? While he had seen raspberry and blackberry bushes, the berries had not ripened, nor had the blueberries or chokecherries.

The river ran past him, bringing a hint of sound to the serene, beautiful place. Wait. What was that moving? He stood for a closer look. A snapping turtle moseyed up the bank. Soup!

He ran to the edge of the brush, found a stick, and loaded his pistol. The turtle pushed its armored shell forward with hind legs as its long outstretched neck moved a horny yellow beak from side to side.

When the turtle reached the top of the bank, Pete poked it. "Come on, you. Grab hold of that stick."

It clamped down with its vise-like jaw.

"There you go." Pete pulled the hammer back on his pistol and shot the turtle in the head. He grimaced at the bloody mass almost severed from the body. "I'm sorry, big fella, but we need you for the soup pot."

He put away his revolver, picked the turtle up by his scaly tail, and headed toward town.

Joe beamed. "He'll make a fine pot of soup. Sit down and I'll bring you something to eat." He returned with a cup of coffee and a donut. "Dolly's frying you some fish. We had a run on it at noon today, but we saved some for you in case you came back. We've had five fellas here today asking for food. They finished up the soup."

As Pete ate the donut and enjoyed his coffee, Joe sat with him at the picnic table. "All those other guys eat and move on. Nobody ever brings us fish or berries or turtles. Or comes back the next day. What's your story, Pete?"

"No different than the others. Riding the rails by circumstance. No money to settle anywhere. Relying on the good graces of folks like you to keep me alive." Pete gripped his cup. "This coffee tastes so good. Thank you."

"I'll get you a refill." Joe left and came back with the coffee pot. "The fish should be ready soon."

Before long, Dolly appeared with a tray of food. She set a plate full of fried fish and potatoes in front of him, along with a slice of strawberry pie. She added a fork and knife, salt and pepper shakers, and a napkin. "Here you go, dear."

Pete's eyes widened. Fried fish and fried potatoes! Strawberry pie! Dolly treated him like a paying guest. No one had ever given him a napkin with the food he panhandled. He had such a lump in his throat that he couldn't speak.

"You enjoy now." Dolly left him.

"Thank you, Lord, for this wonderful meal and the people who provided it. Bless them. Help me to be a blessing to them. Amen." With that he placed his napkin on his lap, sprinkled his food with salt and pepper, picked up his fork and knife, and ate like a gentleman in a fine café.

Satiated, Pete lounged around town. He hoped to see Tommy, but no young boys that fit his description came into the vicinity. A middle-aged woman passed by with another, younger woman. "James is a smart boy. But he's depressed. He doesn't try anymore. He sits there looking gloomy, and he's short with his sister when she tries to read to him. And his father doesn't give him the time of day. If only his father could see how bright he is…"

Pete stood straighter. He could help. With his shoulders squared, he returned to James's house, finding the young man on the porch with the cribbage board sitting next to him.

James waved and smiled as Katherine came out with two glasses of lemonade and disappeared inside. "Come on. Let's play again."

When Pete played the first hand, James pointed. "Sixteen points."

Pete chuckled. "Wait a minute now. How do I know you're not cheating by giving me a lower score?"

"I would never cheat!" James said in all seriousness.

"I'm teasing you, James. I know you wouldn't cheat." Pete stacked his cards in his hand. "I'm impressed by your mathematical skills. What does your father do? Is he as smart as you are?"

"My father works for the railroad. He's gone most of the time." James took a long drink of his lemonade. "My mother died a few years ago. Katherine stays home because of me. I feel sorry for her."

"Katherine is a beautiful young woman. Does she have a beau?"

James shuffled the cards. "She's stuck on Glen. He delivers our ice. But he never asks her on a date or anything."

"How about you? Are you interested in anyone?" Pete swatted a mosquito away and took another sip of lemonade.

"Me?" James scoffed. "I never get out of the house. Besides, who would be interested in a cripple?"

"Are you healthy otherwise?" Pete drained his glass.

"I'm okay besides that."

"There is someone out there for you, James. You are more than your legs, you know."

James hung his head and dealt the next hand. Pete won the first game, and James won the next two.

"One more?" James gathered the cards.

"I'd better be off. But soon." Pete gave him a hearty handshake. "Thanks for the lemonade."

Back in town, Pete sat on the bench in front of the barber shop. While Kathleen Creek seemed like a great little place, many of the people appeared to have serious problems. How could he help them? He was supposed to be a vet, yet he was no longer a vet. Did he have any other skills? What was he? Who was he? What could he do with his life?

As he continued in his reverie, a little boy raced along the boardwalk toward him. He stopped in front of Pete. "Hello, mister."

"Hello, young man." Pete smiled at him.

The boy's mother caught up to him. She grabbed his hand and jerked him away from Pete. "Haven't I told you to stay away from tramps? They're dangerous!" Her face twisted in distaste as she dragged the little boy away.

Pete hunched over, resting his chin on his fists. Was he deluding himself into thinking he could be a productive part of this community? The sun dipped lower in the pink horizon. He needed to claim his spot beside the river for the night. By the time he reached the bank, the light had waned to a weak gray and mosquitos abounded. He found a flat spot and covered his body against the marauding insects.

With a deep breath, he closed his eyes. *Help me know what to do, Lord.*

## 31

Pete awoke in the early morning to buzzing cicadas, and already the sun bore down hard on him.

His life stretched ahead with no purpose. Could he do anything to help James or Tommy? Probably not. He had hoped the people in Kathleen Creek could accept him, but he didn't belong here anymore than he belonged anywhere. Even the gurgling laughter of the river mocked him.

His stomach growled. Joe and Dolly had treated him well—better than he deserved—but he didn't want to burden them further.

He got up, filled his canteen from the river, and trudged up Main Street to the end of the block until he reached the Merriweather Hotel and restaurant. The railroad depot loomed across the street. Should he move on? Where would he go?

He slinked around to the back of the restaurant. Maybe he'd find something edible in their trash container. A slightly burned flapjack sat near the top. He had eaten worse. As he gulped it down, his chest heaved. Wonder what delicious item might have been in Dolly's Yesterday Box.

The Merriweather had a long open porch looking across the

street to the depot. Pete sat there in a comfortable rocker with sweat rolling down his face. This kind of heat and humidity meant haying time. Maybe he could hop a train and get on at a farm for a day. Or maybe he should see if any farmers around here needed help.

The Hermann farm. North of town. Maybe they would need help. With renewed purpose, he retraced his steps through Main Street, avoiding Joe and Dolly. It might be too hard to leave if he saw them again.

He continued northward with the fierce heat on his shoulders and his pack weighing heavy. A cloud of dust roiled up from beneath his shoes. He came to a fallen log alongside the road beyond the bridge and sat for a rest and a drink of water.

He removed his straw hat and wiped his brow with his sleeve. As he bent his arm, the elbow of his shirt ripped. The other elbow had torn through earlier and his collar had worn to the backside. If only he had another shirt.

After a brief respite, he hiked a couple more miles until a farm appeared on the right. It must be the Hermann farm.

As he approached the neat farmyard with paint-chipped buildings, he passed a pitiful field of withering corn. A dog greeted him in the driveway, wagging its tail. "You must have a happy family, little guy." Pete bent down and stroked his ears.

Laughter erupted inside the house as he knocked. The oldest girl, with two long braids, came to the door with two younger blonde girls behind her. She wrinkled her nose. "Mama, it's a tramp. He probably wants something to eat."

Pete waited until her mother came to the door. "I wondered if you need help with haying or with something else. I'd like a job."

Mrs. Hermann wiped her hands on her apron. "Don't you want something to eat?"

"After I work." Pete's stomach growled. Cinnamon and bacon smells emanating from the kitchen made his stomach lurch. Oh, to say yes to breakfast right then. But no, he'd work first.

Mrs. Hermann toyed with her apron strings. "My husband's behind the barn, down in the long grass with a heifer. It's having a tough time calving. You can go talk to him."

Pete hurried behind the barn. Mr. Hermann snapped his head up and frowned. "I gott no time for you now. I gott a heifer trying to calf and she's not gettin' da job done." Sweat drenched the small man with a thick mustache and round face.

Lying on her side, the young Holstein opened her mouth and bawled, low and long. Her body clenched in pain.

"How long has she been in labor?" Pete removed his hat, laid his pack aside, and squatted next to the Holstein.

"Found her dis mornin'." Mr. Hermann wiped perspiration from his brow. "I'm about to pull it vit dis rope."

"Can I take a look first?" Pete scooted closer to the animal.

Mr. Hermann cocked his head.

"I've done this before." Pete laid a light hand on the cow. "I'd like to check her out. See if I can determine the problem."

Mr. Hermann moved aside with a clenched jaw. "Alright. Der ain't no vet since old Doc Harold up and died."

"I'll need a bucket of hot water and some soap. And do you have antiseptic?" Pete removed his shirt. When Mr. Hermann returned with a bucket of water, a bar of soap, and a bottle of iodine, the whole family followed.

Pete poured iodine in the water and lathered his arms. He lay on the ground and put his hand into the cow. "The calf's head is back and there's not much room in there to turn her around. And she's bone dry."

"Can't ve yust pull it out?"

Pete shook his head. "Pulling her out without first getting the head around would break the heifer's pelvis. Do you have a cord about as thin as twine?"

"I have a cord in the house." Mrs. Hermann ran to get it.

Pete doused the cord in the antiseptic water and tied a loop in it. He washed and lathered again and then inserted his arm once more. Holding the noose, he searched for the calf's head in the small space, pausing during the cow's periodic contractions.

He braced his legs against a tree stump and reached with all his might. His fingers brushed the calf's jaw and tiny teeth. "Ah. There it is." He slipped the noose into its mouth. "Thank you, Lord."

The slipknot tightened as he yanked the thin twine. With a good hold onto her lower jaw, he handed the end of the cord to Mr. Hermann with his other hand "Keep a gentle tension. If you pull on it while I guide the head, it should come around. Tug when I tell you. Don't jerk it."

He braced his hand against the calf's shoulder. "Now a gentle, steady pull." Finally, the head moved. "Good. Keep going. Still gentle. It's coming around."

The neck straightened against his arm. He let go of the shoulder and grabbed the little muzzle, guiding its head until it rested on the fore limbs. "Okay, stop."

"Oh, don't hurt the baby." One of the girls pressed up against him. Her mother shushed her.

"She'll be fine." Pete flashed a smile over his shoulder then faced Mr. Hermann. "I have the noose over his head now. Wait for another contraction and then pull when I tell you."

With the next contraction, the head and the rest of the body slid out into the world. The little calf lay glassy eyed and unmoving on the floor.

One of the girls gasped. "Is she dead?"

Pete cleared the mucus from her mouth, blew down her throat, and performed chest compressions. After a few moments the calf sucked in a deep breath and jerked her legs.

"She's alive!" The girls all squealed.

Pete brought the female calf to her mother's nose. The mother's ribs heaved, but when the calf brushed against her face, she nuzzled and sniffed this new life. She struggled to her feet and licked the calf all over until it tried to sit up.

Pete beamed. New births were always such a blessing. He brushed the grass and dirt from his body. A jump into the river would be so nice about now. And a drink of water. Every muscle in his body ached.

Mrs. Hermann and her stair step daughters huddled around the calf, oohing and aahing while Mr. Hermann beamed like a proud papa.

Mr. Hermann gripped Pete's shoulder. "I'm beholden to you. Vat did you say your name vas?"

"Pete."

"Tank you, Pete."

"Yes," said the others. "Thank you, Pete."

Pete smiled and nodded. "You're very welcome." Such a nice family.

"I'll fix you something to eat now." Mrs. Hermann turned toward the house.

"Thanks." Pete picked up his hat and pack. He filled the basin from the outdoor pump, and using the big bar of soap next to it, he scrubbed his face, neck, arms, and hands. He wiped himself with a towel hanging over the side of the bench. Then he found a shady spot alongside a shed, put on his shirt, and sat.

Mr. Hermann joined him.

"I'm looking for work." Pete ran his fingers through his wet beard. "Do you need help putting up hay?"

"I could use a man. Dat young man on da nex' farm dat helped me before took off for college last year and didn't come home. Gott a summer job in Chicago vere he goes to school." Mr. Hermann swatted at a fly with his hand. "His folks ain't too happy 'bout dat. It leaves us bote vitout help. I mowed hay yesterday, and it should be ready to load tomorrow if dis dry vedder keeps up."

He lowered his gaze to the ground. "Can't pay you, but Lavinia's a goot cook and you ken sleep in da barn."

Mrs. Hermann came out with a glass of buttermilk and a plate covered with a towel. "Thank you, ma'am." Pete took a bite of the hot German potato salad. "This is delicious. I see why your husband says you're a good cook."

Mrs. Hermann smiled shyly, pushed back a long stray strand of brown hair, and returned to the house.

"So will you stay, then?" Mr. Hermann asked.

"I want to go down to the river, but I'll be back this evening if that's okay with you." Pete dug his fork into the potato salad and took another bite.

"That's good. Lavinia will have supper for you, so come up to da house if I'm not outside."

"Thanks." Pete finished eating and left. The sun burned high in the sky with blistering heat.

As usual, time spent along the river provided the tonic Pete needed and left him feeling refreshed, like salve to his soul. Maybe he should visit Joe and Dolly. Wonder if they saved him some turtle soup. He could check later. Yawning, he lay on his cape beneath the maple tree and read from Betty's poetry book. Before long, he laid the book on his chest and fell asleep.

In early afternoon, Pete tapped on the screen door of the meat market.

Grinning, Joe came outside with a tray of food and set a bowl in front of Pete. "The turtle soup was a hit with our customers today. Dolly made sure we saved some for you." He set down a plate of biscuits and a glass of milk, along with silverware and a napkin. "I'll bring you coffee when you're done with that."

"Thanks."

Joe flicked his palm and ducked back inside.

As Pete finished, a frail, withered man came to the back

door, rags hanging loose on his shoulders. "Do you think there's some soup left?"

"I don't know. Knock on the screen door." The man was surely too old to be riding the rails.

Joe came out, gathered up Pete's empty dishes, and winked at Pete. "Have a seat, Martin, and I'll bring you something."

Pete scratched his head. Wonder what that meant.

Joe came out with a bowl of potato soup for the man. No bread. No milk. No napkin. No coffee. Just potato soup.

"Thank you, Joe." The man lapped up the soup, nodded to Pete, and left.

Pete stood.

"Wait." Joe went in and brought out a cup of coffee. "Martin lives outside of town. Like most folks, he's come on hard times and needs a handout once in a while. I don't mind."

"You're a good man, Joe." Pete sat at the table again.

"I wish Dolly thought that." Joe's face darkened. He shook his head as he placed the coffee in front of Pete.

"Doesn't she want you to feed hobos?" Pete lifted the steaming cup to his mouth.

"Oh, it's not that." Joe dropped onto the bench across from Pete. "She blames me for Ben leaving. And she's right. It was my fault. When I got to drinking I was too hard on the boy. Didn't realize it until too late. Dolly and Ben tried to tell me. But the bottle spoke louder than they did. It took Ben leaving to wake me up."

Pete's breath caught. If only he could do something for him. "Have you heard from Ben?"

"Last Christmas we got a card from him postmarked California. He only signed his name. At least we knew he was alive and remembered us. That helped."

California. Surely Cookie was their Ben. "He's young. The young men do well out there." The corners of Pete's lips turned up as he pictured Cookie hopping the trains. "They're strong and fast. I'm sure Ben is well. He's probably working for some farmer. He'll probably come back home someday and he'll be so grown up you'll hardly recognize him."

"I wish I could believe that." Joe brushed his hand over his face. "If he doesn't come home soon, I don't know what will happen to Dolly and me. We used to be so happy. Now she sleeps in Ben's room and only talks to me about the business. Nothing else."

"I'm so sorry for your troubles." Pete gulped the rest of the coffee.

Joe got up from the bench as if the world weighed him down. He picked up Pete's empty cup and shuffled through the door. Pete's heart ached for the sweet man.

If only he knew for sure if Cookie was their son. The evidence sure pointed that way. Maybe he could give them some peace of mind.

3 2

---

Late afternoon loomed in front of Pete like a vacuum. Nothing to do, no one to see, and nowhere to go. Well, except the possibility of playing cribbage with James. Having a job and place to sleep comforted him, but he didn't want to go back to the Hermanns' yet.

Maybe he could find Tommy. Where might he live? How old was he? What did he look like? Pete walked south toward the Merriweather Hotel porch. As he passed the barber shop, he came to a window with a small table of newspapers. When had he last read the news?

Inside, a rotund man stood behind the man from the feed store. The banker, Pete recalled. The barber wore wide suspenders and shirt sleeves rolled to his elbows. Freckles spotted his bald head. Was he kind or stern?

Laughing, the barber draped a cape around the shoulders of the banker. He seemed to have good humor.

Pete wiped the sweat from his forehead and went into the shop. "Good afternoon." He smiled at the barber. "Would you mind if I read the paper?"

The barber's brows lifted, but he nodded and turned back to the banker. "Now, George, what were you saying?"

"The average husband is so conceited because he thinks he scored a triumph when his bride accepted his offer to support her for life." The two men laughed together.

Pete smiled at George's clever remark and sat in one of three waiting chairs. He grabbed a copy of the *Kathleen Creek Courier*. The front page headline read, *Feed Shortage in Sioux County*.

Pete rested the folded paper in his lap.

*Because of the acute feed situation existing, 500 head of cattle may be purchased in Sioux County under the terms of the government purchasing program. Owners wishing to dispose of excess animals may do so. First consideration will be given to cattle that would likely starve before next spring.*

What a depressing article. Pete turned the page. The paper contained much advertising, sports news, funeral reports, and several columns on nearby small-town activities. Pete shuddered when he read about a home that had burned to the ground, but thankfully there were no fatalities.

A theater offered a showing of *The Count of Monte Cristo*. Pete fingered the hole in his pocket. It would be nice to see the movie if he had 25 cents admission. But, of course, he did not.

He folded the newspaper, laid it back on the table, and waved at the barber. "Thank you."

The barber tossed him an absent wave. "George, I don't know what I'm going to do about these aching feet."

As he left, however, Pete walked with a lighter step. It had felt good to read a newspaper again—a current one, instead of parts of old newsprint being used as bedding in the hobo camps. It made him feel more human.

The barber's hearty laugh had warmed him. And… Pete knew what could help his aching feet. He stepped a bit faster, heading toward the wood's edge where yarrow grew. If the barber placed it inside his shoes, it would help relieve foot pain.

After tucking his harvest in a bandana, he stopped to play cribbage with James.

As usual, Katherine brought them a glass of lemonade as soon as Pete stepped onto the porch.

"So, what shall we discuss today?" Pete shuffled the cards as James set the pegs.

"Birds." James pointed to a chickadee chirping in a nearby spruce tree. "I much enjoy bird watching."

"I do, too." Pete shielded his eyes from the sun. "My favorites are the tiny wrens because of their long and lyrical birdsongs. You should have seen some of the different birds I saw in the south and west during my travels. Road runners and—"

"Oh, tell me. Tell me." James lurched forward.

After two losing rounds, Pete expressed his thanks and walked away. Someone whistled behind him. Grinning, Pete glanced over his shoulder. Was it really James?

He waved goodbye to his smiling friend. Could having a friend make that much difference in a person's life? Maybe next time he visited, he should dig out his harmonica and see if James would like to play it.

Back at the Hermanns' farm, Pete washed his shirt and socks in the basin by the pump and draped them over the clothesline. He sat against the shed in the shade and massaged his feet. While many of the hobos he'd encountered complained about their feet, Pete had been fortunate. He kept his socks clean and aired his feet when he could. Whenever he found yarrow, he put some in his shoes.

Pete took out the bandana with his harvest from earlier. The lack of rain had dried the leaves and flower heads a bit already. He'd bring it to the barber after it dried completely.

What was the barber's name? Would he be appreciative?

Pete looked up. The oldest Hermann daughter stood near him, fingering a plaid ribbon that tied the end of her braids.

"Mama said I should bring you this lemonade because it's so hot out."

"Thank you. And thank your mama for me." Pete accepted the cold glass with a smile. He took a long drink. "Mmmm. This really hits the spot."

The girl rocked on her heels.

"What's your name?"

"I'm Tammy. My next sister is Bonnie and my baby sister is Olivia. He's Rusty." Tammy pointed to the dog standing next to her.

Pete held the cool glass against his warm cheek. "I understand you'll be attending a wedding soon. Who's getting married?"

"My mama's sister. Mama didn't think she'd ever find a husband being so plain and all, and she thinks she trapped a man to marry her."

Pete chuckled. An innocent revelation certainly not meant for anyone outside the family to hear. "I'm sure your mama is happy for her sister."

"She says she made her bed and now she has to sleep in it." Tammy twisted the hem of her skirt. "So she's happy."

With another chuckle, Pete handed Tammy the glass. "Thanks again."

"I'll bring you some supper when it's ready." She ran into the house.

Pete untied his bandana and spread the yarrow leaves and tiny white flowers over it. He pulled the bandana into the sunlight, yet sheltered from the wind. Then he leaned his head back against the rough, weathered siding of the shed and closed his eyes.

"I brought you some supper, mister."

He sat up with a start.

Tammy handed him a plate piled high with roast beef,

mashed potatoes, and green beans. Then she reached into her pocket for a fork. With a smile she returned to the house.

Except for the flies that kept landing on his food, Pete thoroughly enjoyed his meal. When he finished eating, the sun had moved, so he tied up his herbs and put them back in his pack. He made a trip to the outhouse, and when he came out, he found Mr. Hermann, collecting his plate. "Thank you for the good meal."

"Lavinia is a good cook." He sat in the shade where Pete had sat earlier and indicated a spot next to him. "The hay will be ready to load tomorrow. What there is of it. It's a sad crop, with no rain." He rubbed his shoe over the crisp brown grass. "If we don't get rain soon the corn will go to ruin, too. We can't keep the animals if we don't have feed for them." He shook his head and eased up. "We'll start after milking in the morning. You can sleep in the barn tonight. Lavinia will send out a quilt." With his head hanging, he walked to the house.

The sun dipped behind the trees and the sky became crimson, forecasting another hot, sunny day. Pete went to the barn and checked on the eight milk cows, a few hogs, and the chickens already roosting for the night. They all looked healthy in spite of the drought and feed shortage. "Time for me to go to bed, too."

Behind him Mrs. Hermann cleared her throat, "I don't know if you'll need this tonight but a cover is always a comfort." She handed him a well-worn, patchwork quilt.

It did, indeed, make Pete's night more comfortable.

The next day dawned even hotter. "It's almost a hundred decrees already. Hottest year on record," Mr. Hermann said.

Pete fed the animals while Mr. Hermann milked the cows. After a quick breakfast, they headed for the field with a hayrack hitched to the team.

Mr. Hermann and Pete worked side-by-side lifting forks full of hay onto the wagon as the horses moved along the windrows every few feet with Mr. Hermann commanding them to "Hup" and "Whoa." Heat shimmered visibly in mid-air, and both men coughed frequently from the dry dust rising up from the ground. The sun burned Pete's aching back.

Mid-morning, Mrs. Hermann drove to the field bringing fresh water, coffee, and biscuits still warm from the oven. A welcome break. He rested his tired body in the relief of a shade tree amidst the sweet fragrance of curing hay and beautiful birdsongs drifting from the trees.

Pete reaped the harvest of the earth—the labor of plowing, disking, dragging, seeding, fertilizing, mowing, raking, and loading all coming to fruition. What a warm feeling of accomplishment.

In another hour, with the hayrack heaped full of hay, Mr. Hermann jumped onto the wagon and drove the team home. Pete sat alongside him, dangling his feet almost to the ground. Back at the barn, Pete climbed into the hot, stuffy loft to trip the hay fork and spread the hay. Mr. Hermann operated the pulley as the horses pulled each large fork full of hay into the loft.

At noon they ate fried potatoes, sausage, and creamed peas. As soon as they finished eating, Mrs. Hermann left the room and returned with a blue chambray shirt. "Gunther's father recently passed away. Some of his clothes will fit you, Pete. Try on this shirt. You can't keep working in this sun with your shirt split open in the back like that. You have a terrible burn." She pressed a jar into her husband's hand. "Gunther, put some of this Noxzema on Pete's back."

Pete's threadbare shirt had, indeed, split, and his scorched back burned. He removed the rags, and Mr. Hermann spread some of the salve on his back. "Thank you kindly, both of you." Pete fastened the buttons to the almost new shirt. A perfect fit. "And thank you for the good meal."

Mr. Hermann capped the jar. "Let's rest an hour and then we'll go back to the field."

Pete went to his spot on the north side of the shed and stuffed the old shirt in his pack. A cool healing already soothed his back.

Sooner than he'd like, Mr. Hermann came out of the house. He filled the water jug, corked it with a corn cob, and soaked the burlap wrapped container. "The water on the outside evaporates and keeps the inside water cool." He slapped his hand against the cork once more before moving toward the barn.

Pete harnessed the team and brought them out of the barn. Together, he and Mr. Hermann hooked the horses to the wagon and headed back to the field.

The sun scorched the earth as it had all week. Dust from the dry soil roiled high behind the large hoofs of the horses and Pete tied his bandana over his nose. In the next field, the corn withered under the heat. Pete could only pray for rain like everyone else.

Once again, Mrs. Hermann arrived with refreshments mid-afternoon. By suppertime, they finished loading the last load into the hayloft. Pete's eyes drooped, and his back burned.

Mrs. Hermann set a supper table in the shade beneath a huge maple tree. "My stars! It's like an oven in the house." She dabbed at her hairline as she and her daughters brought out dish after dish. "At least here we have a slight breeze."

They had pork chops, mashed potatoes, gravy, cucumber salad, yellow beans, bread, butter, and milk. After giving thanks, Pete ate until he couldn't eat any more.

"How is your sunburn?" Mrs. Hermann asked.

Pete rubbed his sore neck. "I didn't want to complain, but it still burns pretty bad."

"We'll put more Noxzema on it." She bustled into the kitchen and returned with the cream. Once again, Mr. Hermann spread it on Pete's back. Oh, how these people humbled him.

Pete helped Mr. Hermann bring the cows from the pasture, and then he fed the other animals while Mr. Hermann milked the cows. That night, while Pete settled himself in the hay to sleep, he fidgeted to find a comfortable angle that didn't aggravate his sunburn. How kind the Hermanns had been to him. What could he do to help their family? They struggled like most families, yet their generosity knew no limits.

The crowing rooster awakened Pete and he saw Mr. Hermann already milking his cows. Pete went to check on the calf he helped deliver—the one the girls had named Pricilla.

"Aww, look at you, Pricilla, nursing in contentment." She'd soon be weaned from her mother, poor thing. He walked back to Mr. Hermann. "I'm so grateful to your family for your kindness, and I'd like to be more helpful to you. What can I do?"

"Will you help Tammy and Bonnie pick potato bugs today?"

"I'd be happy to help."

At breakfast Pete chuckled as the girls groaned, "Do we have to?"

After the meal, Mr. Hermann gave Pete and each girl a syrup can with a few inches of kerosene.

"Go down each row and use this paddle to knock the bugs off each potato plant into the pail of kerosene." Mr. Hermann handed them each a wooden paddle. "At the end of each row, dump the bugs in a pile to be burned later." He gave Pete a can of kerosene. "You'll use this to refill the pails for the other rows."

Pete donned his straw hat and each girl wore a bonnet with a wide brim to protect her from the sun. Still, the overbearing heat forced them to take frequent rest stops under a nearby oak tree.

During one rest, Pete helped Tammy retie her bonnet. "I heard you start school soon. How old are you girls?"

Tammy stood straighter, her already rosy cheeks flushing. "I'm ten, and going into the fifth grade. Bonnie's—"

"I'm eight. Third grade." Bonnie danced between them.

"And Olivia?" Pete shook the dust out of his straw hat.

"She starts first grade this year." Tammy took Bonnie's hands and twirled with her.

Bonnie grinned. "We get to ride to school in a horse-drawn bus. I can't wait for September."

"Yeah," Tammy said. "We love our teacher, Miss Howe."

By late morning, he'd learned that Tammy liked to read and Bonnie liked to draw. Neither liked to pick potato bugs, haul water to the garden, carry in firewood, pull weeds, gather eggs from the chicken house, or wash dishes.

"Do you girls like anything?" Pete chuckled.

Bonnie scratched her chin. "We love to help daddy make ice cream."

"Our favorite thing in the whole world!" Tammy rubbed her belly.

Bonnie mimed eating with a spoon. "Yes. Our favorite thing."

"It is sooo good," they said in unison.

"Maybe your daddy will make some again soon." Pete winked.

They both shook their heads. "He only makes it on special occasions."

Pete opened his mouth. Should he tell them he'll have a birthday soon? No, the Hermanns had done enough for him already. But the girls sure made that ice cream sound good.

They didn't finish picking bugs from all the rows until late afternoon.

"Good job." Pete trudged with the girls back to the house.

Just as they rounded the corner, Mrs. Hermann came out. "Wash up. Time to eat."

The hot, nutritious food and the hard work had reinstated his strength and good health. If only Pete had a family of his own like this one, he might forget his past.

Mr. Hermann expressed his gratitude for Pete's help, and after eating, Pete again asked what else he could do.

Mr. Hermann gave him a long look. "Don't know what you

can do for us anymore than you already did. 'Course, on a farm there's always work to do. Can't harvest corn yet. Wheat will be next, if it ain't burned up by then. You rest now. We'll talk more in the morning."

Early the next morning Pete heard Mr. Hermann in the barn milking already. He got up quickly and asked, "How can I help you today?"

"Maybe Lavinia can use help in the garden. The girls haul water to it and that's an ever' day job. I got to work on my grain binder today. Get that ready. Always something to do on the farm."

He picked up his three-legged stool with one hand and the pail of milk with the other, then moved to the next stanchion. "Come on, Millie, move over. And keep that tail out'a my face."

As Pete walked away, Mr. Hermann called to him. "Lavinia'll have breakfast ready soon as I'm done milking."

Pete wandered behind the house. When he found the huge garden, he shook his head. Terribly dry. He carried some pails to the pump. By the time Tammy announced breakfast, Pete had watered a quarter of the garden.

"How can I thank you for watering the garden?" Mrs. Hermann poured coffee into Pete's cup.

"This breakfast and the Noxzema is more thanks than I need. I'll finish the rest of the garden after breakfast."

Tammy jumped up to start clearing the table as soon as everyone finished eating. "If Mister Pete waters the garden, can I go swimming with Frannie today?" She tugged at Mrs. Hermann's sleeve. "Remember she asked me? Her mom is taking their kids to Long Lake to swim and have a picnic today. Ple-ease?"

"You have to bike over to Frank Ross's first and bring them some bread and a jar of canned beef." Mrs. Hermann passed her a basket.

"Okay. What should I tell Mrs. Ross this time?" Tammy bent down and tied a shoelace.

"Tell her that your mama thought they might like these." Mrs. Hermann re-tied the ribbon on Tammy's braid.

Tammy tossed her braid behind her back and turned toward the door. "Okay, but she'll know we're giving it to them because they're so poor."

"Listen, Tammy," Mrs. Hermann reached for Tammy's hand and bent close to her daughter, "The Ross family moved to that farm too late to put in a garden, and Mr. Ross hasn't been able to find a job. They don't have money to buy flour to make bread. We're their neighbors, and God wants us to help our neighbors. Okay?"

"Okay, Mama." Tammy flung a sheepish look toward her mother.

"And I guess since Pete is doing your job today, you can go swimming. You better thank Mr. Pete." Mrs. Hermann poured hot water into the dishpan and handed Bonnie a dishtowel.

"Thanks, Mr. Pete." Tammy ran to call her friend, while Mrs. Hermann smiled after her happy daughter.

Olivia stood in the doorway with a wistful grin. She might have enjoyed swimming, too.

Mrs. Hermann ruffled her hair. "Shut the screen door before you let all the flies in, honey."

Pete's heart ached, yet he smiled. How wonderful it would have been if Rose had lived.

Would he ever have another daughter to love?

After Pete finished watering the garden, he attacked the weeds. Being of use made him almost feel at home. First Joe, Dolly, James, and now the whole Hermann family. He was making friends. Could the community of Kathleen Creek learn to trust him? Could he someday have a veterinary practice here? A tingle of excitement pulsed through his chest.

By supper, Pete had hauled many full wheelbarrows to a dump site behind the barn, creating a high pile of weeds.

Mrs. Hermann didn't stop smiling all through supper. "Now, Pete, when we haul water to the garden, only the vegetables will soak it up, not the weeds."

"If you would like, tomorrow I can hoe around those plants. Loosen the hard soil for you." Pete dabbed his mouth with a napkin.

"That would be wonderful! I'm going to can green beans tomorrow." Mrs. Hermann passed the potatoes to her husband for a second helping.

"I can pick beans for you." Pete took another bite of roast beef. Succulent, savory, tender, and hard-earned. "Unless, Mr. Hermann, you have something else you'd like me to do?"

Mr. Hermann shook his head.

The next day when Pete came in for the noon meal, his heart warmed. All those quart jars filled with green beans lined up on the counter… How good it felt to help in a small way. After supper, he still wore his wide grin. "Mrs. Hermann, what can I do for you tomorrow?"

Her eyes lit up. "I'm going to make dill pickles. You can carry up empty jars from the basement. I'll have to wash them."

"I can wash jars while you make the dill pickles, if that will help," Pete offered.

"You wouldn't mind doing that?" Mrs. Hermann quirked her brows.

"I washed a lot of dishes on the road, Mrs. Hermann. I want to help any way I can."

The next day, after he helped Mr. Hermann with chores, he went down to the basement and carried up several boxes of dusty Mason canning jars.

He washed the jars while Mrs. Hermann mixed up a batch of bread. She kneaded the dough with gusto, pushing, turning, and even slamming the dough around on the table. An exhausting job, for sure. Then, she set the large round pan of dough in the sunny east window and covered it with a lightweight towel.

She handed Pete a bushel basket and sent him into the garden to pick cucumbers. When he brought the filled basket into the house, she'd sterilized the jars. "Set the basket on the chair," she said. "I'll get some dill."

"Can I start scrubbing these cukes?" Pete held up a short, thin one.

"Sure, if you want. Use that brush there on the sink. Cold water is okay." She left and returned with a bouquet of aromatic fresh dill. "Well, Pete, I can't wait for my girls to get old enough to be as much help as you are to me today. This day-long job will be done before noon."

She set the dill on the end of the counter. Then, she brought the pan of bread dough into the kitchen, dumped the dough onto the table, and slashed it into six even chunks with a long butcher knife.

Next, she took several bread pans from the cupboard, greased them with lard, shaped each chunk into a loaf, and filled the pans. She placed them in the same sunny spot to rise and resumed the pickle-making.

Mrs. Hermann called Tammy into the kitchen later and handed her a bucket of green beans and cucumbers along with two loaves of bread in a flour sack. "Take these to Dorothy Ross."

"Can't Bonnie go this time?" Tammy whined. "I always have to go."

"Bonnie's too young. Tammy, God will bless you for doing this generous thing for a neighbor. You must do it with a joyful heart. Do you know what that means?" Mrs. Hermann leaned down and placed her hand on Tammy's shoulder.

"No." Tammy held her mother's gaze.

"It means you should be happy to do something good for someone else. You should smile when you hand Mrs. Ross this food, and be glad that we can help them. Mr. Ross feels so bad that he can't work and earn money to buy food for his family. If his neighbors didn't help them, they wouldn't eat."

"But, Mama, sometimes Mrs. Ross cries when I give her the food." Tammy's eyes misted.

"I know, honey. She's grateful." Mrs. Hermann wiped her daughter's eyes with her thumbs. "But it's easier for her to accept help coming from you than if I brought it to her. Do you understand?"

Tammy took the bucket and the flour sack with a sigh. "I guess so. And I'll remember to bring back the bucket and the sack, like always."

Mrs. Hermann clucked her tongue. "That poor family, Pete. Three little ones, no job, no garden, no animals. The Callens keep them in milk, the Larsons keep them in eggs, and I try to keep them in bread and a few other things that relief doesn't provide."

She tucked pieces of dill into each jar packed with cucumbers. After adding a boiling vinegar solution, she wiped the lip with a clean towel, laid a sterilized lid on the rim, and fastened a ring around the top. Finally, she handed the last jar to Pete to tighten. "I'll need to run into town and buy some more jar lids."

She had moved the jars of green beans to the basement shelves earlier, and now the counter displayed rows and rows of beautiful, green, dill pickles. Pete placed the last jar next to them. "Mrs. Hermann, you have a rare gift, to create such beauty and nutrition for your family. It is a blessing to play a part in it."

Mrs. Hermann nudged him aside and put six loaves of nicely raised dough into the big oven to bake. "Now, Pete, let's sit in the shade and have a cup of coffee. Tell me, is your back better now?"

"It is." After a brief rest and conversation, Pete paused by the door. "I'd be glad to go into town and pick up those jar lids for you. I have a letter to mail, and I'd like to check on Max." And take the yarrow to the barber.

"Wonderful, Pete." She scrawled a list on a piece of paper. "Have Rosemary Johnson put it on my slip at the mercantile. That's Mary's mother."

Pete hurried to town, entered the mercantile, and approached the post office window. "Good morning," he said to Mary's mother. "I'd like to mail this letter, and then I have an order for Mrs. Hermann. She said to have you put it on her slip."

Mrs. Johnson examined the letter. "I see you've affixed the three-cent stamp as required. I'll make sure it gets out, and I'll have Mr. Johnson get those lids for you right away."

Pete's mouth twitched. He had very few of the stamps left.

"I'd also like to check on my patient." He rested his folded hands on the counter.

She furrowed her brow. "I'm not sure I understand."

"Max." He held his hand about two feet from the floor.

"Oh." She blinked. "Do I know you?"

"My name is Pete. I'm afraid I don't know yours." He extended his hand.

"My name is Mrs. Johnson. I'm the postmistress."

"Are Mary and Max home?" Pete stuffed his hands in his pockets and rocked on his heels.

Her shoulders heaved. "David!" When her husband came to her she jerked her thumb to Pete. "This man wants to see how Max is doing. He splinted his leg a few weeks ago, remember?"

"Oh, of course. Pete, isn't it? I'll get Mary and Max. They're playing in the house." As David turned to leave, Mrs. Johnson added, "And he needs three boxes of jar lids for Mrs. Hermann."

"Mister Pete!" Mary raced toward him. Max came behind her in an awkward run. When Pete squatted in front of him, the dog licked Pete's face. He still wore the splint.

Mary twirled her skirt. "Is Max's leg healed now?"

"Not yet, Mary, but Max is growing so fast right now that I want to make sure this hasn't gotten too tight for his leg to grow." Pete felt around the splint. "I'd like to remove this and put on a new splint. Could you get me the same materials we used before, Mr. Johnson?"

Mary paced as Pete removed the splint and massaged Max's leg. When Mr. Johnson returned, Pete put on the new splint. "There, now. Max's leg is fine again for a few weeks."

"Okay." Mary's eyes twinkled. "Thank you, mister."

"You are very welcome, Mary. It makes me happy to help him." The two ran back into the attached house.

David stood behind Pete and offered his hand. "You have my thanks as well. I'm beholden to you. Is there anything I can do for you?"

With David's help, Pete stood. Hmm. Maybe there was something. "I understand Mrs. Hermann's sister is getting married."

"Yes. The last weekend of next month. Lavinia bought lace the other day for a dress she's sewing for one of her girls."

"Well, Olivia, the youngest, won't have a new dress for the wedding." Pete brushed dust from his trousers. "She's quite heartbroken about it. I wonder if maybe Mary has outgrown one of her dresses that she might give to Olivia."

"You want one of Mary's old dresses?" Mr. Johnson tapped his finger against his chin.

"Yes, I do. The Hermanns have been very good to me. I'd like to do something special for them. I know this would make the whole family happy." Pete followed David to the front of the store. "I believe that if Mary's recently outgrown something it would fit Olivia. It would be a new dress, you see."

David reached for jar lids on a shelf near the counter and put them in a bag. "We can find something. I'll have Rosemary look through Mary's clothes. Can you come back in about an hour? You can pick up the lids then, too."

"Yes. Thank you so much."

Pete strolled to the barber shop. The stubby bald barber hummed to himself as he swept hair from the floor.

"Hello, sir." Pete dodged the hair as he approached the barber. "When I was reading your newspaper a while back I overheard you say your feet hurt. I find yarrow to be extremely helpful in alleviating sore feet if you keep some in your shoes." He held the packet out to him. "I found some and dried it for you. I hope it helps."

The barber accepted the packet with a slack jaw and a quirked brow. Pete turned to leave. "Enjoy this nice day, sir." The barber still held a puzzled stare, saying nothing.

Pete puffed out his chest as he headed toward the river, stopping to rest briefly on one of the benches in front of the flour mill. It felt good to help someone. People came in and out, still ignoring him as if he were invisible. They all seemed like nice people if one could become acquainted.

At the Davis home, Pete found James sitting on the porch as usual. Poor guy. Did he ever do anything else?

"Pete!" James gave him an enthusiastic wave.

As Pete climbed the porch steps, James held out his hand. He squeezed Pete's fingers and shook with gusto.

"Do you play a musical instrument?" Pete reached into his pack.

"No, but I like music."

Pete put his harmonica to his lips, and played *Back in the Saddle Again.*

"That sounded great!" James smiled. "I wish I could play a harmonica like that."

"It's easy. All you have to do is practice until you know where each key is and then go from there. Want to try it?" He held the harmonica out to James.

James hesitated then took the instrument from him and blew. When a sound came out, his eyes widened.

Pete grinned. "Keep going. It'll take you a while to get used to it."

James tried again. "That was fun." He held it out to Pete.

"You keep it for a while. I don't need it right now." Pete stood. "I've got to go now, but I'll be back so you can play me a tune."

As he strolled away, Pete swung his arms at his side, falling into rhythm with the breathy notes James made with the harmonica. He headed back to the mercantile. As soon as he opened the door, Mr. Johnson met him with two wrapped parcels. "Here are the lids and the dress. Rosemary demands that you don't mention to anyone where you got it. I'm sorry about that, but she only allowed it that way." He smiled as he handed Pete the package. "Mary always looked so charming in this dress. It's red. I'm sure Olivia will love it."

"My thanks to both you and Mrs. Johnson. Tell her I will honor her request. This will make a little girl very happy." He put the package under his arm and headed toward the Hermann farm.

When Pete reached his spot along the river, he stopped, slid his fingers under the tape, and peeled back the wrapping paper. As he held up the red velveteen dress, its pleats unfolded. Betty had made Rose a similar dress. He could picture her twirling around, her face aglow. *I'm pretty!* Instead of the usual sharp pain, gentle warmth filled Pete's heart. This dress would make Olivia very happy.

He re-wrapped it, put it in his pack, and continued toward the Hermann's farm.

The Johnsons had been kind. Did they trust him a little?

As the summer heat bore down upon Minneapolis, Jenny's thoughts remained much of the time on the homeless man and his brilliant blue eyes.

He'd held such compassion for Mary's injured puppy. The way he took over the situation exuded knowledge and authority. When he'd used his slim, gentle fingers to examine the dog and splint its leg, he'd shown expertise. Why did he wander around without a home, obviously penniless? And why did she keep thinking about him?

She'd had a good time with Mark on the Fourth of July when he took her to Lake Minnetonka. They'd joined his friends for a day of boating and picnicking. She'd enjoyed the cool water and gentle breeze that had made the scorching day almost comfortable. His usual charming self, Mark had been thoughtful in many little ways that made the day even more special.

He brought along her favorite brand of root beer and rubbed Noxzema on her shoulders when they turned pink. He'd acted proud to show her off, and she felt as proud to be with him, unhappy to see the day end when Mark brought her back to her parents' house.

It had felt good to sit in the boat with Mark's arm around her as he flirted with her, his laugh livening the whole party. Later that evening, they danced on the beach to music from the docked boat.

Mark twirled and dipped her in flamboyant movements, then held her close to slow, sensuous music. He'd hummed in her ear as he slid his cheek around to meet her lips with his. A warm, sweet, and loving kiss. But no passion. Not like the hobo's kisses in her dreams.

Jenny sighed. Mark appeared to be attracted to her. To her knowledge he didn't date other women, and they had been together for almost a year. It was time for the next step. But did she even want to marry him? And why had he not proposed? Did he, too, want more passion in their relationship? Or, did he think being a husband and a father would hinder his constant play time?

The hobo hadn't seemed like a playboy. Wonder what he looked like beneath all that facial hair. Was he still in Kathleen Creek? Doubtful. Would she be destined to wonder about him the rest of her life and never know more?

On the morning of August 16th, Jenny picked up the daily newspaper and promptly dropped it. "Plane Wreckage of Rogers and Post." Not Will, her favorite comedian. Could it be true?

Her breath hitching, she read on. Will Roger's airplane had crashed in Alaska.

His face splashed on the front page of the newspaper—that crooked grin and lock of hair dangling in his eyes. Jenny wept. Good thing Mark wasn't with her. He would laugh. For some silly reason, the hobo came to mind. He would understand and comfort her in her sadness.

PETE SAT IN THE KITCHEN, tapping his fingers under the table. He couldn't figure out when and how to present Olivia with her new dress. It would be only a few more weeks until the wedding. What reason would he give them?

Mrs. Hermann took her coat from the rack and wrapped it around her. "I'm headed to town."

Pete caught her at the door. "Might I ride along with you? I want to say hello to Joe and Dolly."

"Of course." She slipped her worn leather purse over her shoulder. "The girls will want to go, but there's room. I'll only be there long enough to buy a few things, if that's okay."

"Sure."

In town, Pete knocked on Joe's back door.

Joe sauntered out, smiling. "Nice to see you, Pete. With so many men coming to the door today I only have a little soup left..."

"No, no. I only came to say hello. Thank you, anyway. I've been helping the Hermanns on the farm and I've been eating well. How are you? How is Dolly?"

Joe leaned closer. "Well, I don't mind telling you this, and I wouldn't tell many others, although anyone who sees Dolly today would know it anyway."

Pete frowned. "What's wrong with Dolly?"

"Today is Ben's 18th birthday, so she's been crying all day. No matter what I say it doesn't help. She even called Tommy in from outside and made Mickey Mouse pancakes for him, crying all the while. She always made those for Ben on his birthday, even after he was a grown boy."

Mickey Mouse pancakes! Cookie had said his mom made Mickey Mouse pancakes on his birthday, ever since they took him to see the Mickey Mouse movie Steamboat Willie. That was the proof Pete needed. Cookie was Joe's son. Should he tell Joe?

He needed time to think. "Um... nice to see you, Joe. Give my best to Dolly. I hope she feels better tomorrow."

He hurried to the car and reached it as Mrs. Hermann did. They rode home in silence, with Pete staring out the window.

How could he tell Joe and Dolly that he knew Ben? Would they be angry he hadn't said anything before? Would it make them feel better if they knew Ben was okay? He didn't want to hurt them for the world. Or would they feel worse to know that Ben was a hobo? If only he knew what to do.

"I got the grain binder ready." Mr. Hermann wolfed down the last bite of his macaroni and cheese. "Some of the wheat heads are starting to drop."

"What does that mean?" Mrs. Hermann took her husband's plate away and poured another cup of coffee for him and Pete.

"It's too dry. I think it's ripe enough to harvest. If we don't harvest now it's all going to be on the ground." Mr. Hermann gulped down his coffee.

"I'll help if I can." Pete hastened to finish his own coffee.

Mr. Hermann nodded. "I'm going over to the neighbors after dinner and see how their wheat is faring. It's early, but if they're ready to harvest now too, we ken do our threshing together." He rose from the table, put on his hat, and went out.

Mrs. Hermann dropped into the chair next to Pete. "We're worried about the corn. Last year we had to make silage or it would have all burned up. Looks like we will again. At least we had enough moisture early that we did get some crop, although we won't have enough feed. We'll have to pare down. Those poor farmers southwest of us have nothing. I heard from neighbors that they're leaving their farms and heading west to California." She clicked her tongue, stood, and cleared the dishes.

Pete wiped his mouth on his napkin. "Thank you again. What else can I do for you, Mrs. Hermann?"

"Oh, I don't know." She carried the dishes toward the kitchen. "Rest a while. I'm sure you're tired. Tammy and Bonnie can help me clean up."

Pete yawned. Rest sounded wonderful, but Tammy and Bonnie must need some, too. In fact, Mrs. Hermann probably felt just as tired. But, he did as Mrs. Hermann suggested.

Pete hardly had time to lie down when Mr. Hermann returned in his Model A Ford. "We checked Larson's wheat and went over to Callen's. Both the same thing. We all need to harvest quick or we lose it all. Let's get the team ready."

All afternoon, Mr. Hermann drove the team and pulled the grain binder that cut the wheat and tied it into bundles. Pete grabbed the bundles as they chugged out of the grain binder in windrows, and he set them up onto their dry stubbled ends into tipi-like shocks. They could be threshed after a couple days of drying.

After the men spent hours of back-breaking work, Mrs. Hermann appeared with the car. Mr. Hermann directed the horses to a shady area along the edge of the field and stopped them. The men joined Mrs. Hermann as she carried a basket to a large cottonwood tree and spread a blanket beneath it.

They drank the water she had brought in a large jar. Then Mrs. Hermann poured coffee into three cups and served meatball sandwiches, which both Pete and Mr. Hermann ate with gusto. When they finished, Mrs. Hermann frowned. "I didn't have enough sugar to make a cake today. And I don't have a nickel to buy even a pound." She held out the thermos. "But at least we have coffee."

Pete's heart went out to her. So much need these days.

Mr. Hermann waved his hand toward the team. "Lavinia

brought water for Jack and Jill. You know, the horses. Would you drive the car out to them and give them a drink?"

He drove slowly over the wheat stubble until he reached the two sturdy draft horses and removed the two pails of water from the car. Of course, each horse emptied a full pail in only three deep draughts, but at least Pete could give them that much relief. He put the empty pails into the car and returned it to the clearing where Mrs. Hermann waited with her basket.

"I'm glad you're here to help Gunther." She handed him the basket.

"I'm glad I'm here, too." He put it in the passenger seat and climbed out. "Thank you for dinner."

She slid behind the wheel. With a smile, she waved to Pete and then to her husband. A while later, she came back with their supper.

After they ate, Pete finished cutting the wheat and shocked the grain while Mr. Hermann milked the cows.

What a blessing to have such long days of sunlight enabling them to work so late.

"It's been a good day's work, even if the harvest was slim." Mr. Hermann slapped Pete on the back.

Pete gritted his teeth. Oh, the sunburn! "Yes, it's been a good day's work." *And thank you, Lord, for this good day's work, the good food, and especially for this good family.*

Pete's neck and face warmed. Were those tears in his eyes?

He pulled out his bandana and faked a sneeze in order to wipe his face without notice. He must be getting soft in his old age.

The following morning Mr. Hermann caught Pete by the arm after breakfast. "I'm going to Larson's today to help with the wheat harvest. Would you feel comfortable cleaning the barn?"

"Sure. Happy to do it." Pete put on his straw hat and followed Mr. Hermann out the door, careful to not let the screen door slam.

As Pete first cleaned the cow gutters and the horse pens he thought about Joe and Dolly.

Pete needed to see them. What should he tell them about Cookie? That he had been a good friend and he was a fine young man?

Cookie's Christmas card had meant so much to them. Even a brief word or short visit might reassure them. Could he get word to Cookie somehow that his parents needed to see him? That Joe had changed and was no longer a mean old cuss?

That's what he'd do. He'd find a way to tell Cookie his parents need him to come home, even for a visit.

If Cookie came home, Joe would become like the man in the

Bible welcoming home his prodigal son. What a joyous reunion that would be.

The Bible! What else did Cookie say about Joe? *He'll give you something to eat if you tell him to read Hebrews 12.* Pete frowned. He'd forgotten to tell Joe that. What did Hebrews 12 say? Pete could hardly wait to look it up in his Bible.

As soon as Pete finished cleaning the barn he washed up and had a drink of water. Then he headed for his pack in the hayloft. When he pulled out his dusty Bible, he grimaced. How long had it been since he last opened it? *Hebrews 12.* The chapter addressed discipline. He read it twice. Now he understood Cookie's and Joe's family dynamic. Evidently Joe had been a strict disciplinarian and unfairly so.

So why did Cookie want him to bring this chapter to Joe's attention? Pete read it again, pausing at verse seven. Ah. Cookie wanted Joe to know he understood his father disciplined him for his own good. He turned back to the Bible. At verse eleven, he read, "Now no chastening seems to be joyful for the present, but painful; nevertheless, afterward it yields the peaceable fruit of righteousness to those who have been trained by it."

Pete closed the Bible and laid it on his lap. Wow! Cookie had sent him to his father with an apology. He'd meant for Pete to tell Joe that he understood, that he respected him for it. He'd wanted Joe to know he forgave him.

"I have to tell Joe." Pete jumped up, the Bible slipping off his lap. "I have to tell Joe and Dolly."

He slid the Bible under Olivia's dress and fastened the clasp of his pack. He'd give her the dress tonight. He could hardly wait to see her reaction.

Tammy peeked into the barn. "Time to come eat. We'll be at the picnic table."

After the meal, Pete slid his pack over his shoulder. "I have a letter to mail. Unless you have something pressing, I'd like to go into town this afternoon."

Mrs. Hermann picked up several plates. "No, that's fine. Gunther won't be back until late today. He thought they would harvest Callan's wheat when they're done at Larson's."

"Well, then thank you for the good meal." Pete started toward town. He'd mail his letter first, a short note to Pastor Jim and Karen telling them of his whereabouts and letting them know he was alive and well.

He paused at his spot along the river. The noon-time sun beat savagely against his body, and the maple tree beckoned. After a long drink from his canteen and a swipe of his sweaty brow with his shirtsleeve, he relaxed in the relative cool of the shade. After several moments of peace, he set off again.

He passed James's ornate house, finding the porch unoccupied. Maybe he'd stop in on his way back to the farm. Finally, he reached the mercantile.

Spots formed before his eyes as they adjusted from the brilliant sun to the dim interior of the store. Mr. Johnson helped a customer in the back, and Mrs. Johnson stood inside the gated post office speaking through the doorway. An older, frail woman faced her, fanning herself with a large paper fan.

Pete waited on a chair in the front window.

The older woman glanced at him, and her padded shoulders stiffened before she turned back to Mrs. Johnson. "What I mean is that Dave works too hard. And it's a shame you couldn't have more children so Mary would have a playmate."

Mrs. Johnson shuffled a stack of envelopes and placed them in a basket. "Keep your voice down—"

"There's no one here." The older woman waved her hand over the room. "You could be a bigger help in the store if you gave up the postmistress job."

"No!" Mrs. Johnson's voice shot back quick and sharp. "I am the Kathleen Creek Postmistress and I'll not give that up. As it is, my arthritis makes it almost impossible for me to get around in the store some days. It's better for me to handle the mail."

"Well, the day may come when you can't do that anymore, either." The older woman adjusted the hairpin holding her coarse, gray hair to her head. "You could sit behind the cash register as well as that post office window."

Pete winced. Such criticism.

"There are many business proprietors in town, but only one postmistress." Mrs. Johnson's lips pursed. "Can't you see how much prestige that gives us? I intend to keep my position as long as I can."

Mr. Johnson strolled into the room then halted. "Oh, I'm sorry to interrupt your conversation, Mother. Rosemary, did the raisin order arrive yet? I told Mrs. Olson we'd have the order by now."

"I haven't seen it." She sighed heavily as her mother-in-law followed Dave toward the back of the store. "I tried to tell her..."

Pete slumped in his seat. He didn't want to embarrass Mrs. Johnson, so he left the store. His letter could wait.

As he crossed the street to the meat market, the train whistle blew. Maybe some hobos would jump off here, and Pete could ask if they'd seen Cookie. He hurried toward the depot and ran to the back end of the train.

What luck! Two hobos jumped off and ran to the side. Pete followed them into the bushes.

A wide grin spread over one hobo's face. "Preacher!"

Even greater luck. What were the odds of finding someone he knew? "City Lights! Great to see you! You too, Birdsong!" Pete embraced the frail, dirty men. "Hey, have either of you seen Cookie lately?"

A yard dick latched onto Pete's arm. "Okay, you scum bags. I saw you jump outta' that boxcar. All'a youse. You're under arrest."

"He wasn't on the train." Birdsong glared.

The yard dick planted a clout on the side of Birdsong's head with a blackjack, striking hard enough to buckle his knees.

Not jail again. Not now. Pete needed to tell Joe and Dolly about Cookie. He needed to give Olivia her dress before the wedding.

As the yard dick prodded them along, his shoulders heaved. He'd better wait and tell his story to the judge. He held Birdsong up as they stumbled over the tracks, across the street, and down the block to the jail house.

Pete tightened his grip on Birdsong's body.

"Move!" The yard dick prodded him with his club.

City Lights put Birdsong's other arm around his neck and helped support his weight so they could move faster.

Pete pounded his frustration into the sidewalk with every step. The judge would let him off. He'd have to when the others vouched for him.

The yard dick shuffled them into the jail.

"Judge comes in the morning." The jailer showed them to a large cell and slammed the iron door with a clang.

Pete spent the rest of the afternoon and evening sitting cross-legged on a cot. His brow furrowed. Why had he let his guard down at the rail yard? How had he let himself get caught? And what would Mr. Hermann think when he didn't return that evening?

Deep creases covered Birdsong and City Light's brows as well. So frustrating to be in their present situation.

The next morning, an officer escorted them into a court room paneled in rich mahogany. Two tables and four chairs faced a raised platform spanning the front of the room, with long pew-like benches filling the rest of the space.

An officer stepped forward. "The Honorable C. J. Haney."

A plump, pink-faced, heavyset judge with thick-rimmed glasses walked into the courtroom with an air of supremacy. He climbed three steps and sat in the large black leather chair facing them. Without looking up he called, "The State of Minnesota, County of Sioux versus, ah, Birdsong?"

Birdsong jumped from his seat and stood before the judge, his chin raised. "Yes Sir."

"Do you have a last name, Birdsong, or is that your last name?" The judge peered down his nose at him.

"Just Birdsong, Your Honor." He squared his shoulders and clasped his hands behind his back.

The judge cleared his throat. He turned pages from a file. When he lifted his head, his lips twitched. "You are hereby charged with illegal railroad transportation. How do you plead?"

A gangly young man in a cheap light grey suit with hair hanging in his face sauntered forward from one of the tables. "Wilfred Peterson, Your Honor, Assistant Sioux County Attorney representing Mr. ah, Birdsong. He pleads guilty, Your Honor."

Birdsong faced the stranger.

"Do you agree with that plea, Mr. Birdsong?" The judge pushed his glasses higher on his nose.

"Yes, I'm guilty, Your Honor," he pointed, "but Pete wasn't on the…. "

The judge raised his hand. "We'll get to your friend's case in due time. Inasmuch as you plead guilty to this charge, I remand you to the county jail for thirty days. Next case."

City Lights received the same sentence.

When Mr. Peterson pled guilty on Pete's behalf, Pete objected. "Your Honor, I did not come into town on that train. I merely ran into some friends. The people of Kathleen Creek will vouch for me. Joe and Dolly, Mr. and Mrs. Johnson, Mr. and Mrs. Hermann…"

The judge's shoulders slumped. "Mr. Peterson, what have you to say about this?"

The red-faced attorney stood. "I, um… I don't know, Your Honor."

"Mr. Peterson, did you not consult with your clients before this arraignment?" He glared at the young attorney.

"No, Sir, I was only given their files moments ago." The young attorney shifted from side to side.

The judge drew his eyebrows together, then faced Pete. "Tell me, Dr. Walters, are you employed?"

"I am presently employed by Gunther Hermann and reside with him and his family north of town."

"Have they paid you in cash?"

"No, Your Honor, room and board." Did he look like a hobo? His hair was still a bit long, but he wasn't dirty as Birdsong and City Lights.

The judge shrugged. "Do you have five dollars?"

"No, sir." Pete poked the hole in his pocket.

"If you are not gainfully employed, do not have a permanent residence, and do not have five dollars in your pocket you are considered a vagrant." The judge closed Pete's file. "I hereby charge you with vagrancy. The penalty is nineteen days' incarceration or a fine of $25.00." The judge removed his glasses and rubbed the bridge of his nose. "Will your employer pay the fine for you?"

Pete chewed his chapped lower lip. The Hermanns might if they had the money, but of course, they did not. Even if they did, he couldn't ask them. "No, Your Honor."

The judge tapped his gavel. "Then it is the decision of the Court to remand you to the Sioux County Jail for nineteen days. Next case."

As the deputy sheriff led Pete back to his cell, he gave him a friendly pat on the shoulder. "You won't be here long. The feds are hiring men to dig firebreaks in the Chippewa National Forest up north. The county gets paid for every man they bring up there to work, They'll make good money on you. The yard dicks get a piece of the action for every hobo like you they bring in. Today isn't your lucky day."

It sure wasn't. Nineteen days! And it couldn't have come at a worse time.

The next day, a different deputy shoved Pete, Birdsong, City Lights, and another hobo into a two-door Model A Ford Sedan. To Pete's chagrin, the overweight sheriff told off-color jokes most of the long drive to northern Minnesota.

Hours later, they entered a heavy forest where the exhilarating scent of pine filled the air and tall trees obliterated the sun. Pete held his cap across his chest as if they had entered another world, a hallowed place. Pine needles softened the floor of the forest and made for a smooth, quiet ride with the exception of a barely discernable crunch beneath the wheels. No one spoke.

They soon entered a clearing with about a dozen large tents to the left and three chuck wagons to the right. Men unloaded from a few other vehicles and fell into line with them.

The forest echoed with dull ax thuds and a buzzing circular saw in the distance. Machinery engines rumbled, heavy chains rattled, and men's loud voices boomed. A smell of smoke drifted from the west.

The deputy delivered his charges and their papers to a string-bean of a man with dull red hair and a ruddy complexion. His shoulders curled forward over a concave chest, and he leaned from his waist. While his posture indicated weakness, his hard, gray eyes and small, cruel mouth spoke otherwise. He spat tobacco juice to the ground. "New jailbirds, you will not be shackled, but make no mistake. This is a chain-gang. You'll be digging a firebreak around a fifteen-foot diameter circling the perimeter of the lookout tower being built up ahead. You will do as you're told."

"No talking." The redhead gave a menacing glare. "A relief station is over there." He jerked his thumb to the left. "Do your business now, because you won't get another chance for a while. Then follow me. You'll be given a shovel and start digging. Is that clear?"

Pete stood in line for the facility and then took possession of a sharp-nosed five-foot shovel. Redhead herded them into the bed of a pickup truck and drove deep into the woods. They bounced up and down over a rough dirt road until Pete's buttocks burned. His head jiggled on his neck, and he scrunched his shoulders. A guy could get a spinal injury on a road like this.

An occasional "Timber!" pierced the air, followed by a loud crash.

The truck came to an abrupt halt. Redhead got out and bellowed, "Turn every inch of this ground. Any questions?"

No one spoke.

"Form a row from here to here." Redhead paced off fifteen feet. "Now, you jailbirds and CCC men have to work together, but I'll keep an eye on you jailbirds, so don't try nothing funny."

Soft ground lay beneath the heavy layer of pine needles. Good thing, because it made it easier for the thin soles of Pete's shoes to push the shovel into the ground. City Lights worked to the left of Pete, and a young CCC man worked to his right.

"My name's Oliver," the CCC man said.

"Pete."

"What you in for?" Oliver lodged his shovel into the ground with his foot.

Pete turned over a pile of soil. "Vagrancy."

"I rode the rails for a while before I got on with the CCC." Oliver leaned over to pick up a large pine cone. He twirled it around in his hand. "Why don't you give that a try?"

"I'm too old for the Civilian Conservation Corp." Pete paused to wipe his brow with his sleeve.

Oliver froze. "Oh."

"Stop talking and keep working," Redhead yelled.

With Redhead out of earshot, Oliver held out his covered hands. "They didn't give you no gloves?" He unearthed a June bug, stomped on it a couple times, and continued digging.

"No." Pete's shovel hit a hard root, and he tried to cut into it to no avail.

"They give us all gloves." Dry leaves crunched beneath Oliver's feet. "You'll have blisters before the day's over."

"Probably." Pete's palms already burned.

Oliver leaned closer. "I'll see if I can get some for you tomorrow."

"You can do that?" Pete gaped. How odd this stranger would so quickly offer kindness. People were good. Just like Railroad. And Mr. Hermann.

"I'll try." Oliver plunged his shovel into the dirt.

A boss man came along the line after a couple of hours and blew a whistle. "Break time!"

Like the other workers, Pete found a shady spot beneath a tree and sat with his back against it. A bearded blond man gave everyone a dipper of water from a bucket.

After a few minutes the boss blew his whistle again. "Break over!"

When Redhead moved out of range, Pete learned about Oliver's home in Oklahoma, his parents and siblings, and his adventures on the road. Though Pete liked the eighteen-year-old boy, some quiet time would be nice.

The kid even followed Birdsong, City Lights, and Pete in the chow line and sat next to Pete while they savored the delicious meal of juicy roast pork, fried potatoes, savory brown gravy and peppered corn.

Oliver aspired to own a horse ranch someday. He had grown

up on a ranch and he didn't get along well with his father, so he left to make his own way in the world. Poor kid probably hadn't had anyone to talk to for a long time.

After supper, Redhead herded the "jailbirds" to the edge of the camp. "This is the jail tent. You'll stay here 'til morning. I'll be right outside, so no funny stuff."

Pete claimed a cot, removed his shoes, and lay down. His back ached. His right foot hurt from pushing the shovel into the ground with inadequate footwear, and the blisters on his hands burned. His whole body hummed with fatigue.

Body odor loomed in the hot, stagnant air around him. Surely Pete contributed to it. He closed his eyes and released a huge breath. Finally, some freedom from Oliver's battering voice. He did manage to come through with a pair of gloves for Pete right after their meal. The boy had a huge heart but his non-stop talking...

He missed Cookie. If only he'd been able to tell Joe and Dolly that their son was okay before his arrest. And when did Mr. Johnson say Mrs. Hermann's sister was getting married? He couldn't remember. He had to get home to give Olivia her dress. And he needed to remove Max's splint. Why, oh why did this happen now?

And his pack. It had been such a part of him for so long. If only he had the comfort of Betty's poetry book or the Bible.

City Lights lay on the cot next to Pete's and Birdsong's cots. Other small groups of people straggled in, each with their own "prison guard." At first, the tent remained silent. Then hushed conversations escalated into argumentative noise until Redhead came in to demand quiet.

Even here, the mosquitoes found Pete with their high pitched buzz as soon as the sun hid behind the landscape. He reached into his back pocket for his bandana. No, he'd wiped his sweat with it for too many days. Better not cover his face with it. He put it back in his pocket and swatted at the blood-sucking insects until he fell asleep.

A few days later, Pete pulled City Lights aside. "Do you find it odd that Redhead has relaxed with each passing day?"

City Lights shrugged. "Ah, he thinks we're happy for the good grub and the safe cot. Why would we try to leave?"

Pete rocked his shovel in the soft ground. For most of the incarcerated men that might be true. But those men didn't have the Hermanns to worry over. Could he go back to them after being released? What would they say to him? Should he confess that he had been arrested?

Pete became acclimated to the long days of hard work. On the sixth day, he cried a single tear, realizing his birthday was the day before. So much for celebrating another year of life. It hadn't been a good year anyway.

On the eighteenth evening, Redhead beckoned to Pete. "A car will be arriving for you right after breakfast in the morning."

Pete said goodbye to Oliver before they parted for their tents, wishing him well. Sleep eluded him like a kid on Christmas Eve. If only he could drift off so morning would come faster. Tomorrow, he would to be on his way to Kathleen Creek—his home.

Would the Hermanns welcome him back?

3 8

<hr>

In early September Mark came to Minneapolis to bring Jenny back to Kathleen Creek.

"Let me tell you about all the things I've done this summer." He started the car as she climbed in. "Swimming competitions, fishing contests—you should see the monster catfish I caught. I won so many prizes that…"

Jenny inwardly groaned. Had he worked at all this summer? Did he not even have to worry about making money? How well did she really know him? As he prattled on, Jenny toyed with the hem of her shirt. What could she say to him? Her life dulled in comparison. She had attended weekly concerts in the park with her parents. One day, she visited the county fair with a friend. She'd gone to movies and shopped with various girl-friends, but he wouldn't have been interested in that. While his activities were active, hers were not. With so many differences, were they compatible for marriage?

She'd not spent much time with Mark since then. Preparing for the new school year had kept her busy. The students and parents welcomed her back with exuberance and appreciation. Now, aside from her doubts about Mark, she only worried over the frequent antics of Tommy Lazar, who'd spent the end of the last school year avoiding his work and disrupting the class. While she could understand his continual anger, she couldn't help him.

The economy must have worsened since the end of the last school year. The children had lost weight, their clothes looked more worn, and the oldest student, only 13, had quit school to go off on his own. People in town believed he had become a hobo like thousands of other young kids. Her heart ached with the sadness of it all. She would continue her practice of the year before, making stew twice a week for the student's noon meal. In her free time, she would knit warm hats and mittens to give them at Christmas.

What else could she do?

During the long ride back from Chippewa National Forest, Pete propped his head against the window of the car. While the deputy driving rarely spoke, he whistled the Carter family song "Can the Circle Be Unbroken" until Pete's head ached. Wonder if he'd get mad if Pete asked if he knew any other songs.

Tall spruce trees and clear blue skies whisked by, but Kathleen Creek occupied his thoughts. Had he found a home there?

Certainly he couldn't stay with the Hermanns forever. Could he be a vet again?

Long after dark, when they reached the county jail, the officer on duty returned Pete's pack and cape. A smile spread across Pete's face. He was home.

The gaslights along Main Street lit his path as far as the river where the moonlight took over and led him to the maple tree. There, he dropped his pack and stood at the edge of the dark water.

Its song warmed Pete to his bones. A welcome home.

He bowed his head. *Dear Lord, thank you for this spot, and for my release. Thank you for the Hermanns and for Joe, Dolly, and Cookie.*

As the rustling river soothed him, he untied the cape from his waist and laid it on the ground beneath the tree. With his pack beneath his head, he fell into a restful sleep and awoke in the morning with renewed vigor and a voracious appetite. On his way to the meat market, he whistled, though when he neared it, he stopped. He needed to approach the subject of Ben. But how?

He knocked on the back door, and Joe came out smiling.

"I'm glad to see you. Thought you'd moved on." Joe opened the door wider. "Gunther Hermann came in and said you disappeared. He was concerned about you because he expected you to come back. That's been a few weeks ago." Deep creases spanned his forehead. "Well, I guess it's your business what you do, but I have to tell you, Gunther was worried."

"Joe, it's good to see you, too." Pete brushed his long hair from his eyes. "I got picked up for vagrancy. I couldn't pay the fine, so I had to serve the sentence digging a firebreak in the Chippewa National Forest."

Joe shook his head. "You must be hungry. I'll get you something. Sit."

Pete removed his pack and sat on a bench at the cedar table. Before long, Dolly brought coffee and a cinnamon roll. "Joe's frying some eggs and potatoes, but I wanted to say hello. I'm glad you're back. How are you?"

She seemed to really care about him. It brought such a lump to Pete's throat that he had to swallow before he could answer. He would have to tell them together about Ben.

Dolly patted his arm. "I've got customers. Gotta' go, but welcome back, Pete."

In only a few more minutes Joe came out with a hot plate of eggs, potatoes and toast. He started to leave, but Pete cleared his throat. "Joe? I need to talk to both you and Dolly privately. When would be a good time?"

Joe hooked his thumb in his apron pockets and rocked on his heels. "Come at eight, after the café closes." His shoulders heaved. "You can't tell me now?"

"No. You and Dolly should be together." Pete picked up his fork.

"Is it about Ben?" Joe's eyes moistened.

"I can't tell you until tonight." Pete stabbed his potatoes.

With that, Joe went back inside.

When Pete finished eating, he crossed the street to the mercantile.

Mrs. Johnson sat at her post. "Can I help you?"

"I came to remove Max's splint."

"Oh. David! Pete's here to check the splint." Mrs. Johnson sifted through a stack of letters.

Mr. Johnson rushed in with Mary and Max

"I'm sure Max's leg is all healed now, so I'm going to take off his splint. Is that okay, Mary?" Pete knelt to her eye level.

"Are you sure he's okay now?" Her curls bobbing, she clasped her hands in front of her.

"I'm sure he is." Mr. Johnson handed Pete a pair of scissors, and Mary clapped as he removed the splint.

"Max, you can run around as good as new now." Pete stroked the dog's perky ears.

Max rewarded Pete with kisses all over his face, making both Pete and Mary laugh.

"Good to see you folks again, but I must be off." Pete nodded to Mr. Johnson, grabbed his pack and headed toward the Hermanns.

Pete rushed by James's empty rocker. Curious why he wasn't sitting outside, but better get straight to the farm.

When Pete reached the Hermann's property, the horses

nickered. Rusty ran barking down the driveway with his tail wagging.

"Look at you, all excited to see me." Pete stooped and hugged the Collie. "Such a wonderful welcome."

A cold sweat ran down his back. "I hope the rest of the family will be this happy to see me." They both continued up the driveway to the farmyard.

Olivia squealed. "Pete!" She raced to the clothesline where Mrs. Hermann stood pinning a sheet.

"Well, I'll be." Mrs. Hermann pursed her lips. "You've come back, have you?"

Not the warm welcome Pete had hoped for.

The odor of fresh silage tickled his nostrils, and he exhaled, long and hard. "Mrs. Hermann, I got arrested for vagrancy that day I went into town. Judge Haney sentenced me to nineteen days. I had to serve the time because I couldn't pay the fine."

Mrs. Hermann's face paled like a window shade opening to the sunshine. "Oh, Pete, I'm so sorry." She dropped a wet sheet back into the basket. "Come, sit in the shade. You must be thirsty. Are you hungry? I can make you something."

"A cold drink would be wonderful." He slipped off his pack and sat next to Olivia under a nearby tree. Tammy and Bonnie joined them.

"Where were you?" Tammy whined. "We wanted you to come back."

"Something happened and I couldn't return until now. I came back as soon as I could."

"I'm glad you did," Bonnie said.

The other girls nodded as Mrs. Hermann brought a glass of cold water and a sandwich for him.

After drinking and eating, Pete puffed his cheeks. "What is Mr. Hermann doing today? I smell silage."

"We made silage last week. The neighbors helped us until we got ours all in. Now they're filling the silo out at the Larsons' farm." Mrs. Hermann waved her hand eastward, past their own cleared field. "Now Gunther will work to help them until it's all done. I don't know what we'll do without shelled corn for our feed this winter, but at least we'll have silage for the cattle."

"I'm sorry I couldn't help." Pete stuffed his hands in his pocket and ducked his gaze.

"Well, something else always needs doing." She brushed a bead of sweat from her forehead. "Gunther might not say so, but he'll be glad to see you." She picked up Pete's empty glass and plate and gave them to Tammy. "Honey, take these in the house, please. I've got more sheets to hang."

Mrs. Hermann went back to the clothesline. Pete sat for a few more minutes and then put his pack in the barn. He didn't want to assume his welcome until he heard it from Gunther, but he would do what he could until then.

Across the yard, a row of gleaming white sheets hung from the line, and past them, the cattle barn loomed. Mr. Hermann had milked alone this morning. Pete rushed to Mrs. Hermann's side. "Have you washed the cream separator yet?"

"No." She frowned.

"I can do that," he said. "Are the parts still in the milk house?"

Her face brightened. "Yes, they are. Go ahead, Pete. Thanks."

"I'll help you." Olivia skipped along to keep up with Pete's long stride.

She carried the milk pail while Pete brought the empty cream can and metal pieces into the milk house.

Pete washed and Olivia dried, then Pete hung the hanger-like rack of discs. He covered them with a cloth to keep the flies away and turned the milk pail and cream can upside down.

As they left the milk house, Olivia put her hand in Pete's. Another lump formed in his throat. Her smile almost broke his reserve.

Olivia raced off to play, and Pete went into the barnyard to check on the animals. The cows grazed way off in the back pasture. Hogs rutted in the mud and chickens wandered the yard pecking for bugs and worms. Jack and Jill stood by the fence nuzzling each other.

What else might he do? Maybe the eggs? Pete found a basket and went into the hen house. He brought the filled basket to the back porch and washed the eggs.

"My stars, you are most helpful, Pete." Mrs. Hermann came into the house wiping her hands on her already wet apron. "Thank you. Now, if you don't mind, would you empty the wash water while I fix dinner for us? Tammy will show you how."

"Sure." Pete followed Tammy to the side of the house where the hand-cranked washing machine sat in the shade on the dry lawn. He hadn't seen a manual wooden machine in many years. Betty'd had an electric model that took a lot less work. But they'd lived in a town with electricity, a luxury that hadn't yet reached the rural areas.

A pang of sympathy struck Pete's heart. Poor Mrs. Hermann. Even if Tammy and Bonnie helped by cranking the agitator, Mrs. Hermann still had to hand-crank the clothes through a wringer several times and hang them on the line to dry.

Tammy waved her hand in front of his face. "We always dip the rinse water with these pails and water the flowers around the house with it. We dump the wash water into the bushes behind the house. Mama says the bleach keeps the weeds down."

Olivia hurried up behind them. "I'll bring the scrub board and the clothes stomper into the porch."

"I'll bring the soap and the bluing and the clothes stick." Bonnie raced after her sister. She paused for a few moments and caught her breath. "I hate washday, but I like it better in the summer when we can do it outside."

Pete dipped some of the pails half full of rinse water for the flowers. He dumped the remaining water from the tubs and washer into the rest of the pails. "Where does your mother keep the tubs and wringer rack?"

Tammy pointed to the back yard. "We store them behind the house under the eaves and cover it all with a tarp to keep them clean and dry. But Daddy helps Mama do that."

"I bet we can do it." Pete helped them carry everything except the washer behind the house and arranged it all under the eaves. He led them back to the washer. "Okay, girls. Here's what we'll do. Bonnie, you hold on to this leg, right here at the base. Tammy, you take the one across from me, and Olivia, you hold on to this one. We'll go a few feet and then rest."

They picked up the heavy machine. After several starts and stops, they got it behind the house, set it in place, and covered it.

As they returned to the front yard, Mrs. Hermann set a basket of food on the picnic table. "My goodness, Pete. Have you already put away the washer?" She beamed.

All three girls smiled. "And we helped." Olivia danced around her mother's feet.

"We've helped a lot!" Bonnie joined her.

Mrs. Hermann's eyes twinkled. "Well thank you all for the work you've accomplished today. Tammy, Bonnie, Olivia, and Pete."

He nodded to the pails. "Can I water the garden for you after we eat?"

"That would be great, Pete. Thanks." With the girl's help, she filled their plates.

"We'll help water the garden, won't we Tammy?" Bonnie took a huge bite of bread.

"Mm-hmm." Tammy nodded, her mouth full of German potato salad.

"Me too," Olivia said.

With another smile, Mrs. Hermann met Pete's gaze. How wonderful to see acceptance and friendship.

But what would Gunther say about him returning?

Pete and the girls spent most of the afternoon pumping and hauling water to the vegetable garden while Mrs. Hermann canned tomatoes. So much work to farm and raise a family. While he had no desire to be a forever farmer, his desire for a family rose passionately in his chest. What would Rose have been like at Olivia's age? Sunny and cheerful, like Bonnie? Extra helpful like Tammy? Was it possible that he was missing her a little less?

When the hot sun lowered, Pete ventured to the barn. Mr. Hermann would return soon. He'd better bring the cows in and feed them.

He had closed the stanchions on the eight Holsteins and put silage into the manger when Mr. Hermann's car rattled into the yard.

Pete remained in the barn, out of sight, his heart pounding and his lungs constricting. By the time Mr. Hermann came into the barn, Pete had measured the oats and linseed oil into the slop barrel, readying it to add skim milk for the hogs, and had gathered the rest of the eggs from the hen house.

"It sounds like the sheriff directed your plans last month."

Mr. Hermann gave him a wry grin. "Thank you for coming back. I can sure use your help." With a nod, he grabbed his stool and pail, settled alongside the first cow, and began milking.

Pete released his breath. He went into the milk house to arrange the discs into the separator bowl. When he returned, he reached for the almost full pail of milk in Mr. Hermann's hand and handed him a clean, empty one.

"I'll separate." Pete waited, but Mr. Hermann held the pail tight.

When Mr. Hermann cocked his head, he added, "I grew up on a farm. Did plenty of separating in my youth."

"Well, sure then." He passed over the pail.

After they finished, Mr. Hermann let the cows out and headed into the milk house. He poured some of the cream into a pitcher and the rest into a can submerged in a tank of cold water.

"Pete," he passed over the pitcher, "bring this to the house. I'll slop the hogs before I come in."

"I put the oats and linseed oil in the barrel already."

Mr. Hermann nodded.

Tammy rushed in. "Mama's going to churn butter so she needs some cream."

Her father took the gallon jar she'd brought. Using a big dipper, he filled the jar with the thick, rich cream.

Pete followed her to the house with the pitcher of milk and basket of eggs.

After supper, Pete found Mrs. Hermann alone in the kitchen. "I wanted to ask…" He rubbed his tired neck muscles. "Has your sister gotten married yet?"

She dried the last pan and hung it on a high nail. "The wedding is next weekend."

Pete wiggled his toes. "Olivia is sad because she doesn't have a new dress to wear, so I'd like to give this gift to her."

Mrs. Hermann's eyes widened. "You bought Olivia a dress?"

Pete grinned. "I worked for it. I'm quite sure it will fit her."

"My stars! She will be so thrilled." Mrs. Hermann pressed her palm against her chest. "I guess it's okay to give it to her. I'll tell Gunther first."

"Great." Pete retrieved the package from his pack. When he came into the house, the family sat around the table facing the door. Pete cleared his throat. "Mr. and Mrs. Hermann, girls, I'm grateful to all of you. I know Olivia would like a new dress for the up-coming wedding, and that has been a challenge for your family. So, while this gift is for Olivia, it is also a gift for the rest of you, because I know it will make you all happy. Right, Tammy? Right, Bonnie?" He handed the package to Olivia, whose eyes shone bright and smile widened.

As soon as the red fabric peeked into view, the girls "oohed" in unison.

Olivia's jaw dropped, and the package fell to her lap. "It's beautiful!" She covered her lips with trembling hands. "Can I try it on?"

"Yes, go try it on." Mrs. Hermann took the dress by the shoulders and carried it across the room to the stairs. "I'll help you." As they left, the other girls followed.

"That was good of you." Mr. Hermann led Pete to a rocking chair in the sitting room.

Pete gave him a modest nod. When Olivia came downstairs to model the dress, Mr. Hermann clasped his hands and whispered, "My princess."

Olivia threw her arms around Pete and hugged him. "Thank you, Mr. Pete. I love it."

His heart melted like butter in the hot sun. "I have an appointment in town this evening, Mr. Hermann, but, if it's okay, I'll be back later tonight or in the morning."

"Yeah, yeah, you come back. We haul manure tomorrow." He took his eyes off Olivia long enough to glance at Pete. "And call me Gunther."

"And call me Lavinia." Mrs. Hermann patted Pete's arm. "You're a good man."

Pete put his pack on his back and started toward town, his stride long and purposeful. Joe waved from behind the screen door as Pete approached.

How would he find the words? "Lord, guide me," he whispered.

"Dolly," Joe called. "He's here."

Dolly burst outside, wringing her hands. "Do you want to talk here or do you want to come into the café?"

"Will we be interrupted out here?" Pete pointed to the table where they'd fed him so many times.

"We might." Joe jerked his thumb toward the back door. "We'll sit in the back by the open window. It's coolest there with the breeze coming in."

Pete followed Dolly past bright red chairs and benches over checkerboard tile to a corner booth while Joe locked the door behind them.

Dolly glanced toward the kitchen. "Do you want some coffee or something to eat?"

"No, thank you." Pete set his pack by his feet and slid into the booth.

Dolly scooted in across from him. She leaned forward. "Is it about Ben?"

"Yes, Dolly, it is." Pete steepled his fingers on the table as Joe sat next to her.

"Tell us." Joe draped an arm over Dolly's shoulders. "No matter what it is, tell us."

"The Mickey Mouse pancakes. That confirmed it."

Dolly gasped, almost breathless. "Do you know where he is? Is he okay?"

"I don't know where he is, but he's fine." Pete spun the sugar bowl in his hands, then straightened the salt and pepper shakers. "Well, let me start at the beginning."

Pete pushed the sugar bowl against the wall. "I last saw him in early July, healthy, strong, and happy."

Dolly released a long, loud sigh as Joe patted her arm.

"I met Ben in a little town called Blythe on the border of California last February. I took a job washing dishes and he was the fry cook." Pete brushed a few crumbs from the table into his hand and shook them out over the floor.

"A fry cook?" Dolly's brow creased.

"He's a pretty fair cook." Pete chuckled. "We became good friends. After we had some money in our pockets again, he wanted to go to Hollywood to meet John Wayne, so we headed west together. In Palm Springs, we both got jobs at a resort. Ben worked as assistant chef and I took care of the horses. We saw many movie stars there, but Ben didn't see John Wayne."

Joe snatched a paper menu from behind the salt and pepper shakers and fanned himself. Was the man about to cry?

Pete flattened his palms on the table. "The resort closed for the summer, and by then Ben wanted to move on. He told me that he likes the freedom to go where he wants, and do what he wants. He's learning so much from the people, places, and different work experiences. He hopes someday he'll know who and what he wants to be."

Tears streamed Dolly's face, and she sopped her tears with the hem of her apron. "Please, continue."

"We traveled to Hollywood and saw Rin-Tin-Tin, but we still didn't get to see John Wayne." Smiling, Pete shook his head. "Then, we went to North Dakota, and after that, Ben wanted to see the eastern part of the country." He reached across the table and squeezed Dolly's hand. "He told me about the river in Kathleen Creek and suggested I come here."

Dolly's tears flowed even harder. Joe hugged her shoulders and kissed her forehead.

Pete's breath caught. How his heart ached for them. "He said there was a butcher at the meat market that would feed me if I told him to read Hebrews 12."

"Hebrews 12?" Joe quirked his brow.

"Yes, Hebrews 12."

Joe scratched his stubbly chin. "What did he mean by that?"

"I read it, and I think I know." Pete swallowed. "It's a message for you, Joe."

"Get the Bible, Mother." He nudged Dolly toward the edge of the bench.

"I have my Bible right here." Pete picked up his pack, found the chapter, and handed it to Joe.

Joe puffed his cheeks. "…lay aside…patience…endured…consider him…for whom the Lord loveth he chasteneth, and scourgeth every son whom he receiveth.…"

Pete could quote the rest. "'If ye endure chastening, God dealeth with you as with sons; for what son is he whom the father chasteneth not?'"

Joe jerked his chin up. "He's telling me he forgives me." With that, he broke into sobs, and Dolly comforted him.

After a few moments, Pete took the Bible. "Here's more: 'But if ye be without chastisement, whereof all are partakers, then are ye bastards, and not sons. Furthermore, we have had fathers of our flesh which corrected us, and we gave them reverence; shall we not much rather be in subjection unto the Father of spirits, and live?'"

Pete closed the Bible as Joe and Dolly embraced and cried together. After they drew apart and all three dried their tears, Joe placed his hand over Pete's. "Pete, you are our angel. Ben sent you here to deliver this message. Thank you."

"You'll never know how much this means to us." Dolly's voice quivered. "Even though we don't know where Ben is, we know that he's all right—healthy and happy—and that's good enough. I wish with all my heart he would walk into this café someday soon, but we can wait easier now."

"I'm surprised Ben knows the Bible well enough to have chosen this passage as a message for me." Joe traced the embossed words on the worn leather cover.

"Ben always did like the Bible stories I read to him. And he took his Bible with him when he left." Dolly dabbed her puffy eyes with a napkin. "I'm so glad to know that he reads it."

"This calls for a celebration." Joe stood. "I'll make the coffee. What kind of pie do we have left, Dolly?"

She scrunched her forehead. "Lemon, I believe. Or chocolate. I'll go check."

Joe went to the kitchen and soon returned with three empty mugs. "Coffee's brewing." He picked up the Bible again, thumbing through it to Hebrews 12. "Pete, why didn't you tell me about this Bible passage sooner?"

Pete ducked his gaze. "That first day after I treated Max, you offered food without me asking. Later, it didn't seem necessary and I forgot about it until I realized that Cookie was your son. He had told me long ago that even though everyone called him Cookie his name is Ben. But I called him Cookie like everyone else. He never told me his last name, and he didn't tell me that this was his home town."

"Did he say anything else about me?" Joe gripped his empty mug with both hands.

Pete laughed. "Yeah, he called you a mean old cuss. That puzzled me because I never saw you that way."

Joe chuckled and shook his head. "I wish he could see the man I am now. When he left, I had a loud wake-up call to change my ways."

Dolly came in with the coffee pot and a tray holding three servings of chocolate pie. "You have changed, Joe, and I'm proud of you for it. If Ben can forgive you, so can I."

She put her arms around her husband and kissed him. Tears leaked from Joe's eyes as he held her tightly.

After enjoying the pie and coffee, Pete put away his Bible

and slung his pack over one shoulder. "Well, I'll be off now. We're going to spread manure early tomorrow morning, so I better get some sleep."

"Can I give you a ride to the farm?" Joe scooted closer to Dolly, forcing her to the edge of the booth.

"No thanks. The moon is still bright." Pete gave him a sideways grin. "It's a good walk."

It was too late to stop in to visit with James, but when Pete reached the river, he sat with his back against the maple. Might as well luxuriate for a while. Joe and Dolly seemed so happy. Perhaps they'd reconcile. It certainly had been an emotional time. They were such good people. If only Cookie would come back—even for a short visit—it would be healing for them all.

Where was Cookie now? How far east did he go? Maybe he liked it there. How long would he keep wandering?

At one of the hobo jungles, the talk had turned to President Roosevelt's New Deal programs, specifically the Civilian Conservation Corps dubbed CCC, a public works relief program for unmarried, unemployed, men ages eighteen to twenty-three. "It started less than two years ago and it already has camps all over the United States," one of the men had said.

"Camps?" Cookie had asked.

"Yeah, they have over 500,000 men living in those camps." The man reached in his bindle and withdrew a worn brochure. "Here."

"Maybe I could cook in one of the camps. Somewhere like Minnesota." Cookie scanned the brochure and handed it back to the man. "I like the woods."

The man stuffed the brochure back in his bindle. "How old are you, Cookie?"

Cookie's face had sobered, crestfallen. "I won't be eighteen until this summer."

Pete sat straighter. Cookie is eighteen now. Would he have

signed up for the CCC program? Surely, that's what he would have done. Maybe Pete could find him after all.

Pete's grin deepened but faded as something shrieked overhead. An owl flew low, its wings spread wide, and Pete laughed. Might it be a sign that he should search for Cookie?

He got up and headed toward the farm. Mrs. Johnson might know where he could send letters. His pace quickened. He would find Cookie and tell him that Joe had changed.

Pete had tucked himself into a soft pile of hay in the barn with a plan. But his stamps were gone. He would need money for postage. Sleep found him before he could figure out how to earn it.

The next morning after breakfast, Lavinia beckoned Pete to the back porch. "I have something for you." She bent and picked up a pair of almost-new Red Wing work boots. "It looks like your feet are about the same size as my father's. Those shoes of yours are about to give way completely. Try these on."

"Really?" Pete slipped them on and stood. He took a few steps. "They're perfect! How can I thank you enough?"

"Don't we have a pair of Dad's pants and a belt, too, Lavinia?" Gunther came up behind his wife.

Lavinia's eyes bulged. "I'm sure we do." She took off back into the house. In a few minutes she returned with a pair of jeans and a brown leather belt. "These should fit you."

"I… I don't know… what to say." Pete bit his lower lip as tears brimmed his eyelids. What could he say that would be thanks enough? He brought the clothes to the barn, along with his worn out shoes. After untying the twine he used as a belt to hold up his ragged pants, he slipped into the jeans. The substantial feel of almost new denim delighted him. He added the belt and made a few turns. New clothes. How wonderful they felt.

He put clean socks on and then tied his new boots with deep satisfaction. "Thank you, Lord." Tears rolled down his cheeks. "Thank you, thank you."

The horses whinnied. Gunther must be hitching them to the manure spreader. Pete hooked his thumbs into the waist of his jeans and snickered. Look at him, the hobo, too dressed up to work with manure. Feeling foolish, but following his instinct, he put his old pants on, rolled up his new jeans, and put them in his pack. He fastened his new belt around them.

Gunther frowned as he approached. "You don't like the new ones?"

Pete's cheeks warmed. "They're too good for shoveling manure. I'll change later." They laughed heartily.

Gunther tossed a pair of rubber boots to Pete. "We need boots for this job." His shoulders still shook with laughter.

While Pete put on the old rubber boots, Gunther backed the spreader up to the manure pile outside the rear barn door.

Then, still chuckling, he handed Pete a pitchfork.

A week after returning to the farm, Pete went into town. The world looked glorious! Vibrant crimson and bright yellow leaves fluttered to the ground, and the river took on a silver hue as water slid over rocks worn smooth from years of wear. Blue jays and cardinals flitted from tree to tree, landing on the ground to feed. Goldfinches called to each other. Pete couldn't stop smiling.

Unfortunately, a dust storm had come through the day before, and a new thin layer covered everything. He had seen the cloud in the distance and had yelled for help as he snatched clothes off the line.

Lavinia and the girls had all come running. They had barely managed to get all the clothes in the house before the storm reached them.

Pete stood inside the house with the family as the dust seeped through cracks around the windows. Such force. It would be hard to believe without actually seeing it.

Now, as he walked along the river Pete imagined the dust that must have blown alongside it. So much dirt now covered the trees, shrubs, and grass. Thick clusters of red-orange blossoms hung on the sumac branches, coated with dust as well. Fall was almost here. Then, winter.

His good mood waned. What would he do with himself? Would the Hermanns have enough work to keep him on? He had no desire to hitch or ride the rails. He wanted to stay in Kathleen Creek. How could he make that happen?

When Pete approached James's house, notes from "Back in the Saddle Again" drifted with the light breeze. The Gene Autry theme song sounded great! How could James have become so proficient in such a short time?

James stopped playing and waved. "I can play a few songs. I love this harmonica!" With a jubilant grin, he played "Happy Days Are Here Again" and then "All of Me."

"James, how did you learn so much in so little time? Are you sure you never played before?" Pete sank into the chair next to him.

"No, I didn't. But I play so much that my mouth gets sore. Here, you'll want this back." He held the instrument out.

"No." Pete shook his head. "You keep it."

"I've missed you, Pete." James' voice held a smidge of hurt.

"I've missed you, too." Pete dipped his chin. "I came into town about a month ago and had planned to stop in to see you. However, I got arrested for vagrancy and shipped off to the north to a work camp." He frowned. "I got back a week ago, but we've been busy on the farm. I'm on my way now to make a quick trip to the mercantile." He leaned forward. "I have only about a half hour to visit today."

James rested the harmonica in his lap and held open the door for Pete. "Let's go inside. I'm sure sorry you got arrested."

"That's one of the risks of a life riding the rails." Pete followed him into the house and down a dark hall to a solid oak table.

They played a quick game of cribbage in the dining room,

and when Pete left, James gave him a hearty handshake. Seemed his feelings had been soothed.

In town, Pete waited on the bench outside the mercantile until no customers remained inside. Then he approached Mrs. Johnson, who sat on a stool behind the post office window. "May I help you?" Her tone indicated she'd rather not.

Pete stepped forward. "Mrs. Johnson," Pete softened his voice, "as the highly qualified postmistress of Kathleen Creek I know you must be a discreet and trustworthy person."

Mrs. Johnson gaped. "Well, yes."

"That's why I've come to you." Pete folded his hands on the counter and held her gaze. "I need assistance, and you are the only person in town who can provide discretion in this matter."

Mrs. Johnson brought her shoulders back. She actually looked attractive when she smiled.

"How may I be of assistance to you?" Sincerity now dripped from her voice.

"It goes without saying that this must remain between you and me." Pete leaned closer.

She nodded.

"Joe and Dolly have been good to me. Their son is a close friend of mine, and I want to help them find him." He dropped to a whisper. "However, I don't want to get their hopes up. You understand the importance of confidentiality, I'm sure."

"Of course." Mrs. Johnson set aside the stack of mail she'd been sorting. "You know Ben Harrison?"

"Yes. I believe Ben may be at a CCC camp, probably in Minnesota. I want to write to him in care of those camps until one of the letters finds him."

"I see." She drummed her fingers on the counter.

"That's where I must rely on your professional connections, Mrs. Johnson. I don't have the addresses."

"Oh, I'm certain I can find them for you." She pointed to a

thick folder on a far counter, stuffed with papers. "Do you have a letter written yet?"

"I have, but I don't know where to send it."

"One CCC camp isn't far from here. It's up in the Brainerd area. Another of our patrons corresponds with his son there." Her grin widened. "I can get that address for you right now." She hopped off the stool and cried out as she stumbled forward.

"Are you okay, Mrs. Johnson?" Pete hurried to the open doorway of the postal area.

"I'm fine. Call me Rosemary." She gingerly put her weight on her right foot until she could walk on it. Then she navigated two steps with some difficulty. When she appeared in the window again, she flipped through the pages of a file and copied the address as if nothing had happened.

Such pride. Pete took the address from her.

"If you have the envelope, I can mail it today."

"That brings me to yet another problem." Pete stuffed his hands into his empty pockets and turned them out. "You see, I don't have money for the envelopes or the stamps. I hoped you or Mr. Johnson might have some work I can do to enable me to purchase what I need."

"I see." Rosemary met his gaze, then lowered hers to his feet.

"I'm working for Mr. Hermann on his farm, but I only get room and board. I can't ask them for wages." He stuffed his pockets back into his pants. "And I don't have much free time for another job, but maybe you can think of something I can do on Sundays or on rainy days."

She propped her chin on her fists. "You can't ask Joe, I suppose."

"No, because I don't want him to know what I'm doing."

"Riiiight." She closed the folder with the addresses. "Well, I'll talk to David about it."

Pete put the address into his pocket. "Guess I'll be seeing you, then. Thank you, Rosemary."

She sighed. "It would be a shame to not start on your project today since you already have a letter and an address. I'll float you a stamp. I'll start a slip for you and you can pay it later. Do you need envelopes?"

"I'm afraid I do." He removed the letter from his pack.

She passed him the envelope, and he addressed it.

"What nice penmanship." Tracing her fingers over the letters, she scooted the envelope through the glass. "I'll send that out right away."

"Oh, Pete," she called as he turned to leave. "Did Olivia like her dress?"

He beamed. "Oh, did she ever love her dress! That gift made the whole family happy. I honored your wish to remain anonymous, though."

Her eyes twinkled. "That's wonderful. Maybe I can find a few other items I can donate to Olivia. They must be struggling with this drought."

Pete headed to the door. "I'm sure the Hermanns would appreciate any help. That would be kind of you."

A woman came into the store. Rosemary winked as she waved goodbye to Pete.

Pete whistled as he jaunted out of the mercantile. How great it would be to get Cookie to visit his parents. And how nice that Rosemary was opening up to generosity. What a beautiful September day!

"I know you." A feminine voice came from behind him. He turned to face a curvaceous brunette with glorious green eyes.

"You fixed up Mary's puppy's leg." She stepped in front of him.

"My name is Pete." He tossed his hair out of his eyes. "And you're right. I did splint Max's leg, which is all healed now. But I didn't meet you that day."

"I was leaving town when the accident happened." She

extended her dainty hand. "My name is Jenny Howe. I'm the school teacher here."

Miss Howe. No wonder Mary was so excited. "It's nice to meet you, Jenny Howe. I know several little girls are eager to start school. Especially Mary. She's six now, you know."

"I know. She's a special little girl. She'll learn easily." Jenny glanced over her shoulder. "Nice to see you again, Pete." With that, she pivoted and crossed the street as a man rushed toward her with a deep scowl.

"I've been waiting for you, and you're wasting time with that bum." He threw an accusing glare Pete's way.

Jenny took the man's arm and spun him, walking fast with her head down.

Angry, unintelligible words traveled to Pete's ear. Who was this guy to her? Married women were not allowed to teach school, so he couldn't be her husband. Her fiancé? Her brother? It didn't matter.

Yet her pleasant personality, pretty face, soft voice, and appealing figure stayed on his mind all the way back to the farm like a warm, sweet breath. Hopefully he'd see her again.

But Gunther kept him busy on the farm over the next few days, and Lavinia busied herself with wedding preparations.

Tammy, Bonnie, and Olivia woke up so giddy on the day of the wedding, they literally jumped up and down. They took turns on a stool while Lavinia curled their hair with a rod she heated on the stove. She admonished each of them in turn to be still, or they'd get burned.

By early afternoon, all three modeled their dresses and polished shoes for Pete.

"Look at you, Tammy. Your rosy cheeks complement that lovely dress. And you, Bonnie. Such beautiful curls framing your face." He took Olivia's hand and twirled her. "And you, Miss Olivia. A vision in that dress."

The girls all blushed. "Thank you, Mr. Pete."

Gunther and Lavinia looked handsome as well, with her floral hat and his Sunday suit and tie. Before they left, Pete caught Gunther's arm. "Don't rush back. I'll do the milking tonight."

Gunther patted Pete on the back. "You're a good man."

The next couple of weeks found everyone busy as usual. While the girls went to school, Gunther and Pete fell into a comfortable routine of farmer and farm hand. Pete brought in the cows, and they both milked. While Gunther fed the animals and cleaned the barn, Pete separated the milk and washed the separator. Lavinia served a daily breakfast of eggs, bacon or ham, and potatoes, having fed the children earlier, and then supplied coffee and biscuits for lunch.

Pete plowed fields, hauled water, sharpened sickle blades and cleaned the barn and chicken house. He gathered eggs, hauled in firewood and hauled out ashes. After breakfast each day, he picked cucumbers, tomatoes, beans, melons, squash, and peppers, and dug beets, carrots, and potatoes. In the afternoons, he hauled canning jars into the kitchen and the canned vegetables into the cellar, along with potatoes, squash, and carrots.

He spent the evenings picking rocks from the fields, throwing down silage and hay, harvesting oats, and hauling straw.

One day he put on his old pants and shirt and borrowed Lavinia's laundry tub and scrub board to wash his new clothes. She gave him soap and helped him carry hot water from the reservoir. After that, she left her set-up in the yard every wash day for him to use at the end of the day. Then, he emptied the water and stored everything under a tarp alongside the house.

When Pete's farm tasks left time for daydreaming, his thoughts turned to either Cookie or Jenny. Almost every evening he chose an address from the long list of CCC camps Rosemary had supplied him and wrote at least one letter.

While she hadn't found work for him yet, Rosemary said

they'd have something for him to do later, and until then she tallied the stamps and envelope costs on a slip. Every few days he mailed the letters, with return address of "Preacher." A few letters returned from various CCC camps marked "Addressee Unknown."

Pete tried to time his visits for after school hours, but he never ran into Jenny Howe again, much to his disappointment. He always stopped in to say hello to Joe and Dolly, who were on good terms again, although they still missed Ben.

Pete lived one day after another in a wavering, foggy hope. Would he ever find Cookie? Would he be able to practice veterinary work again? Would he find love again?

What did his future hold?

One day as Pete left the meat market, Jenny exited the bank and walked toward him. Pete's breath caught in his throat, and he stopped in his tracks.

She smiled when she reached him. "Hello, Pete." Her sweet voice carried so much cheer. "Nice to see you again. How are you?"

He pressed his pocketed hands against his thighs. Oh, to take her in his arms and keep her by his side for the rest of his life. He returned her smile. "I'm fine, Miss Jenny. It's nice to see you, too. How is school this year?"

"School is going well. I have good students in all eight grades. Tommy Lazar is the only one giving me any trouble."

Tommy Lazar. Pete nodded. "I once overheard someone say he's a bit of a scamp. Since then, I've wondered about him."

"Oh, that's putting it mildly." Frown lines creased her porcelain face. "His father left a year ago and he's been troubled ever since. He used to be such a sweet boy. He's an only child and his mother works in the bank so Tommy's left on his own most of the time."

"Where do they live?" Pete shifted his pack to the other shoulder.

"That little yellow house across from the Catholic Church." She pointed. "Do you have children?"

"No." His heart lurched. How he missed Rose. She would have loved to have the kind, beautiful Miss Howe as her teacher.

"Well, it was nice seeing you again." She began to cross the street toward the mercantile. Then, over her shoulder, she said, "Some of the parents are going to be at the school house on Saturday helping the students plant trees alongside the road. If you're interested in helping, why don't you come?"

"Maybe I will." Pete fought off the silly grin creeping across his face as she turned away. "Maybe I will."

He caught his reflection in the hardware store window. Long, stringy hair, straggly beard, and dirty clothes. He would only embarrass Jenny by showing up. How could he go to the schoolhouse looking like a hobo?

He dropped down onto a bench in front of the shoemaker's shop. He needed to think. Was Jenny being friendly, or did she feel the same attraction? Why would she invite him if she wasn't curious about him? But, he had nothing to offer her. He couldn't even buy her a meal at the café.

A bitter laugh caught in his throat. He was kidding himself if he thought she'd have anything to do with him.

The sun slid behind a cloud, making the late afternoon as pale and gloomy as Pete's mood. He skulked back to the farm, his pack heavy on his shoulders. Why did he continue to carry it all the time? Certainly it was safe at the farm. It wasn't like he had money. He didn't need his gun or his sewing kit. His new jeans had a pocket to hold his handkerchief and hoof knife, and his shirt had pockets for the letters.

He liked to collect berries and medicinal herbs, but he had already picked most everything along his usual path.

Maybe if he left the pack at the farm, he'd look less like a hobo. And, he'd take more yarrow to the barber someday soon. Then he'd ask him for a haircut and shave. Maybe then, he'd look good enough for Jenny. And, maybe he could do something about Tommy Lazar. She'd surely appreciate that.

Saturday, Pete did not go to the school to help Jenny. While Tammy washed up for supper, he asked her if she knew the wayward Tommy.

"He's mean."

"How is he mean?" Pete leaned against the door jamb and crossed his legs.

"He pulls my hair and fights with the boys." She scrubbed dirt from under her fingernails.

"Why does he fight with them?"

Tammy pumped cool water over her arms. "No reason at all." She dried her hands with a towel. "He's mad all the time."

"Do you think he's sad?"

"No." She frowned. "He's just mad."

"I think he's sad." Bonnie came behind them for her turn at the basin. "I saw him crying by the outhouse one day. But he yelled at me to go away."

Pete leaned toward her. "Do you know why he cried?"

"No." She dropped the soap, and Pete picked it up.

"What happened in school that day?" Pete handed her the bar.

"I don't remember." Bonnie soaped her hand.

"That's okay. Thanks for telling me that." He handed Bonnie the towel.

Pete waited until Olivia and Gunther took their turns before he stepped up to the dry sink and washed. If only he could learn more about Tommy. What was going on inside that poor kid's head?

Over the next few days, Pete made occasional trips to town, but learned nothing about Tommy. He did play cribbage with James a few times.

The young man's harmonica repertoire now included many more popular songs. In fact, he seemed like an entirely different person than the sullen fellow with no self-confidence Pete had first met. He also appeared to be less reliant on Katherine. Wonder whether Glen had talked with her yet.

One day in town, Katherine met Pete when she came out of the meat market.

"Nice to see you out and about, Katherine." Pete stopped.

"I have to be home more than I like, but my own things keep me busy, too." She adjusted her hat. "I ran out of yarn and can't find the right color. I'm so frustrated! It's my friend Glen's birthday soon. I wanted to make a scarf for him, but it looks like I won't finish in time."

"What color yarn are you looking for?" Pete moved closer.

"Blue. It will look nice with his blue eyes." Katherine's cheeks turned a bright pink.

Pete's jaw clenched. Betty had said the same about his sweater.

"How soon do you need the yarn?" Pete tapped his toes on the boardwalk. He could give her the sweater. It would lighten his pack, for sure.

Katherine sighed. "His birthday is next week."

He scraped his teeth across his bottom lip. He had to. "I have a partially-finished sweater made from blue yarn. You could pull it apart if it's the right color for your scarf."

"You do?" Katherine lifted off her heels then settled. "Where is it? Can I see it?"

"It's in my backpack at the Hermann's farm, but I can bring it to you in a few days." He gestured north with his thumb.

"I can drive out there with my father this evening when he gets home." Katherine gushed the words. "Is that okay?"

"I'm sure that would be fine." Pete grinned. "You know where they live?"

"Sure. I'll see you this evening. Thanks so much, Pete." She pirouetted and skipped toward home.

Pete chuckled. Sure, soon as he'd left his pack behind, he'd needed it. Hopefully the sweater would be the right blue.

Back at the farm, a bolt of pain struck his heart. Did he really want to give Betty's sweater away? Did he want to let go of the painful memories of Betty's frantic knitting before she died?

Yes. It was time.

That evening, when Mr. Davis drove into the farmyard with Katherine, Pete brought the sweater to her with peace.

She covered her mouth, stifling a squeal. "That's perfect! Oh, thank you! Are you sure I can have this? I can pay you a little."

"No, you don't need to pay me. My wife had been making this for me before she passed away." Pete's burden lifted with the words. "She would be glad to know you have it. Glen's birthday scarf will make him very happy. He seems like a shy kind of guy."

"He's very shy, at least with me." She darted a glance toward her stern-faced father.

"I do thank you, Pete." Mr. Davis started toward the car. "Come on, Katherine."

"That was a nice thing to do," Lavinia told Pete. "It must have been difficult to part with that, since it's probably the only thing you have left of your wife's." Her eyes held a gentle question.

"I didn't need it, and Katherine did." Pete went back to the barn, his heart bruised and the familiar lump filling his entire throat.

---

JENNY FINGERED the gold chain around her neck. Why had she invited Pete to come help plant trees on Saturday? Why was she attracted to him? "I'm making foolish choices again," she said aloud to the empty school house. "I'm attracted to a hobo, for goodness sakes! How much sense does that make?"

Yet he no longer looked so much like a hobo. Good boots, a clean denim shirt, jeans that fit, and a leather belt. But she didn't know anything about him. Why hadn't he shown up on Saturday? Maybe he was married. Why had she invited him?

How irrational she was to be attracted to someone like Pete. What would her father say?

Yet her parents' opinion mattered less than her subconscious as Pete dominated her thoughts. Where did he sleep? Was he still in town? Had she offended him by asking him about children? Hopefully not. Oh, that she would see him again soon. But many weeks passed without a sight of him.

PETE CONTINUED to send letters for Cookie to different CCC camps in Minnesota. When they finished work early one Friday, he once again told Gunther he needed to go to town.

"Got a hot date?" Gunther gave his soulful laugh.

"I wish." Pete shared the laugh, but his heart couldn't match it. Not with visions of Jenny on his mind. He found his soap and towel in his pack. Then he tied a pouch of yarrow to his belt. "I'm going to get a haircut and have a shave," he sing-songed as he trotted down the driveway toward town.

At the secluded spot along the river, Pete quickly slipped nude out of the bushes into the deep, cold water in a shaded spot below low-hanging branches, as was his routine. He washed his hair and body with the thin sliver of soap, then dried off. After he dressed, he laid the soap on a stump and spread the wet towel on a bush to dry. He would pick them up on his way back to the farm. Hat in hand, with a spritely step and his yarrow hanging along his side, he continued to town.

He waved to Dolly as he passed the café and crossed the

street toward the barbershop. Once more, he studied his reflection in the shop window before going in. This was how people saw him. Long unkempt hair and long beard. The barber waved, so he went inside.

"Good morning. Did that yarrow help your sore feet?" Pete surveyed the empty shop.

"Oh, my, it helped a lot." The barber took a few paces around the room. "See? Do you have any more?"

"Yes, I've been collecting it and drying it for you." Pete untied the pouch that hung from his waist and handed it to him. "I guess I didn't introduce myself before. I'm Pete."

"Well, thank you kindly, Pete." The bald freckled head shone as the barber half-bowed. "My name's Rueben." He untied the pouch and smelled the contents. "Ahh. My feet thank you, too."

He pointed to Pete's hair. "Can I do something for you to show my appreciation?"

"I sure would like a shave and a haircut." Pete grinned.

"I happen to be free at the moment. Have a seat in my chair." Reuben grabbed a cape and draped it over Pete's shoulders with a swish. He lowered the chair as far as it would go, then lathered Pete's face with Burma Shave Cream. "This will be a pleasure. I don't often work on such a volume of hair and beard as this. Do you want to keep your moustache?"

"No, I want to be clean shaven." Pete squared his shoulders.

"Now, tell me, where are you from?"

"My home was Grand Island, Nebraska, but I'm looking to make my home hereabouts." Pete relaxed into the chair. "Circumstances put me in the league of other wandering working men, but I want to settle down."

"Interesting." Rueben notched the chair up a bit, then shaved beneath Pete's chin. "Guess you've heard about those the CCC camps and President Roosevelt's New Deal…"

"Yeah. I'm too old."

When Rueben slapped Pete's face with an intoxicating liquid, he snickered. "This is Bay Rum, the newest after-shave on the market. What do you think of it?"

"I haven't smelled this good in years." Pete laughed.

"Now, how do you want your hair cut?"

Pete scratched his smooth chin. How had he used to wear his hair? "Short in the back and above the ears on the sides. Leave the top long enough to comb to the right. You can see where my part is."

When Reuben whipped off the cape, he spun Pete so he faced the mirror. "What do you think?"

Pete blinked and gaped. Without the long hair and beard, the scar on his neck stood out for all to see. But he was used to that, and it had tamed over the years. Except for the white untanned areas outlining his earlier beard and moustache, he looked good.

"The tan line will fade now that it's fall."

Tears formed in Pete's eyes. He looked much younger than he did with the beard and long hair. He ran his fingers through his short, thick hair. His natural curl had bounced back, and though somewhat sun bleached on top, it still shined dark and brown. "It looks good, but I don't have a comb." He winced. He shouldn't have said that.

"Here, take this." Rueben handed him a comb.

Pete flushed. "Thank you. Do you have a container for the yarrow so I can have my bandana back? I use it for collecting herbs."

While Rueben found a bowl, Pete studied his new look. Would Jenny even recognize him now?

"Thanks again, Reuben."

Rueben swept the hair into a dust pan. "Come back again and thank you for the yarrow. Bring more whenever you can."

Pete bounced down the street like a new man.

Rosemary leapt from her stool when he entered the mercantile. "Why, Pete!" Then, she wrinkled her nose and frowned. "I have more returned letters for you."

"Well, I consider it progress when I cross one more off my list." Pete handed her the three new letters. "Maybe one of these will find its owner. Can you put it on my slip?"

"Of course I can." Rosemary smiled.

"Let me know when I can work it off." Pete tipped his hat.

Rosemary nodded and waved.

Pete would find Cookie. He would help Tommy. Maybe he would get to know Jenny better.

He might even make Kathleen Creek his home.

———

Jenny paced in her bedroom. Had Pete left town? The thought put such a hollow feeling in her stomach. Maybe she should ask someone about him. When her landlady needed to go to the store for baking powder, Jenny offered to do the errand for her. She took the landlady's quarter to the mercantile. There, she wandered around the store, the can of baking powder in her hand. When the other customers left, she approached Rosemary.

"That hobo. I think his name is Pete. Is he still wandering around?" She tucked her chin into her chest to hide her warming neck and cheeks.

"Oh, my, yes. Pete is a good friend of mine." Rosemary lifted her chin and sat taller on her stool. "You should see him now that he's clean-shaven. Why, you'd hardly recognize him. He's downright handsome. He's been working for the Hermanns all summer. Why are you asking, dear?"

"I wanted to give him an update on Tommy Lazar, that's all." Jenny's cheeks warmed even further.

Rosemary chuckled. "Well, I'll tell him you asked after him."

"Oh, no, please don't do that. Please don't say anything."

Jenny grabbed her skirt with both hands. "As long as I know he's still around, I'll wait until he asks again. All right?"

"Whatever you wish, dear."

Jenny handed her the quarter and rushed out of the store. Surely Rosemary wouldn't tell him. But wait. How did they become such good friends? From what she had heard, Rosemary Johnson considered most people beneath her. What a strange turn of events.

So Pete had been working for Tammy's family all summer. Would he stay here? And he cleaned up. Maybe he didn't want to be a hobo any longer.

How could she manage to see him again?

4 2

Pete headed toward Tommy's house. Though he'd hoped to catch a glimpse of Jenny on the way, the large, Gothic-style Catholic Church on the corner captured his attention instead. Had it really been almost a year since he'd been inside a church? How he missed that part of his life!

Crisp red and orange leaves crinkled with each step through a whole block of colorful trees. Finally, he reached the lot where Tommy's house sat back from the street.

A young boy in the yard threw rocks into a tree as a woman with corn-colored hair opened the screen door. "Tommy, come on in. Supper's ready."

Tommy gave one last ferocious hurl. Then he ducked his head and kicked at the leaves on the ground as he made his way into the house.

Pete's jaw tightened. Clearly, the boy was troubled. How could he help him?

His stomach growled. Maybe he should visit Joe and Dolly and something would come to mind. Before Tommy's hard luck, what things might have brought him joy? Had he liked to fish or play ball? Maybe he'd raced in the fields with the other children or enjoyed games of cribbage with his father.

A few minutes later, when he knocked on the back door of the meat market, Joe met him with a smile wide as his face. "You must be my friend Pete, but it's hard to tell with all that hair gone." He offered a warm handshake. "Time for you to stop knocking out here. Come into the café." He led the way across the sawdust-covered floor.

Pete dusted off his pants. He had stopped wearing the cape around his waist a few weeks ago and washed his clothes only a few days ago. It had been a long time since he had sat in a café with the public.

Joe turned and waved. "Come on. Dolly will want to see you, too."

Pete followed with tentative steps.

"Sit here so we can visit." Joe motioned to the end stool at the counter and approached Dolly, who served food to a family in a booth. When she finished with them, he whispered something that made her jerk her head up.

When she met Pete's eyes, she hurried toward him. She wrapped her ample arms around Pete as he stood. "My Petie! I'm so glad to see you. You should come more often. The Hermanns keep you too busy. What do you want to eat? Joe, bring him a menu."

Pete frowned. How could he pay for a meal?

"Never mind the cost." Joe handed him the menu. "For you, it is on the house. Anything you want."

Dolly set a cup of coffee before him. "Do you know what you want?"

Pete took the menu. Chicken pot pie, beef steak, pork chops, all for ten cents. Fried ham, hashed meat, and fish balls for five cents. Baked beans, bread and butter… So many delicious offerings. But, how could he? "Don't you have any soup left?"

Dolly laughed, her eyes wide and bright. "Petie, my darling

boy, order whatever you would like and we'll fix it for you. You're not a hobo asking for a handout anymore. Any friend of Ben's is a friend of ours. What sounds good to you?"

Pete traced a finger over the menu. "Well, when you put it that way, how can I refuse? I'd like the crispy fried chicken with French fries and lettuce salad."

While he waited, he arranged the salt and pepper shakers and lined his silverware in a row. Around him, the other diners chatted and laughed over their meals. No one stared. No one wrinkled their nose and moved away. Did the haircut and shave make that much of a difference? Of course, the clothes the Hermanns had given him matched what the other customers wore. Maybe now he could blend and become a member of the community after all.

Joe and Dolly seemed so happy to have him in Kathleen Creek. Rosemary, too. And the barber. He really did belong. As he left, he caught Dolly by the arm. "Thank you so much for the meal."

After supper, Pete stopped in to see James, and Mr. Davis waved from their porch. "Pete, I thank you for teaching James how to play the harmonica."

"I didn't teach him anything." Pete took the seat opposite James, who set up his cribbage board. "I handed him the instrument. He taught himself. I knew he's a mathematical genius, but I didn't know he was a musical genius, too."

Mr. Davis squinted at James as if seeing him for the first time. "A mathematical genius?"

"He could easily get a job as an accountant when this economy improves. He might even be able to do a company's books at home."

Mr. Davis gave James several pats on the shoulder.

James ducked his head.

"Or, with his musical talent, he might play for dances." Pete winked.

"I'll give you your harmonica back now, Pete." James handed him the instrument. "Thank you so much for lending it to me."

"I told you to keep it, James. It's a gift to my friend." He passed it back. They played a quick game, and Pete lost.

"But now I have to get back to the farm. Nice to see you, Mr. Davis." He shook hands with both men and left. Hopefully his words made some impact on James' father.

On his way back to the farm, Pete passed Katherine and Glen sitting on a picnic table. Her father was home, so she had a few minutes to herself. Chuckling, Pete pretended to not see them.

Back at the barn, Pete wanted to write more letters to Cookie, but he couldn't write without a lantern. Gunther thoughtfully provided kerosene. Still, he couldn't risk another barn fire. His letters would have to wait.

He lay back in the hay under the comfort of Lavinia's quilt. How cold the nights had become. Did Tommy have a quilt? Did he have anything to play with? Back in Nebraska, a boy about Tommy's age had walked around the neighborhood with his slingshot. What was that kid's name?

Pete sat upright. That was it! He'd make Tommy a slingshot and teach him how to use it. Of course, he'd have to ask Mrs. Lazar for permission. Didn't she work at the bank? After the farm chores tomorrow, he'd find the perfect tree branch. He smiled as he lay down again. He'd spent so many wonderful days with his father shooting cans off a fence with slingshots. What a great outlet for Tommy's anger. Pete could teach him to practice on cans and to only kill for a reason. Never for anger or for fun.

---

By November 1st, the crops had all been harvested. The dust storms increased with the newly-plowed fields around the countryside, requiring Lavinia to delay her laundry several times.

Three weeks earlier, Pete had cut two Y-shaped branches from a hickory tree to use for slingshots for Tommy and himself. They had now dried sufficiently for him to finish the job.

Gunther gave him a used bicycle inner tube for the bands, and Pete cut pieces from the tongues of his old worn out shoes for the ammunition pouches. When he finished, he had two beautiful, new slingshots.

He picked up a rock and tried one out, aiming for a particular spot on the fence. It worked well. Maybe tomorrow he could give one to Tommy.

The next day the whole family picked apples. Pete worked fast and when they finished, he touched Gunther's shoulder.

"I need to go into town, but I'll be back in time for milking.

"Pete, you work hard every day. Don't hurry back for chores. I can do it. Come back when you want to. Enjoy the rest of the day."

"Thank you. In that case, I will not return for supper." Pete grabbed the slingshots and the letters addressed to Ben. He went to the bank and approached the blonde woman at the teller station.

He drew a deep breath. "Mrs. Lazar?"

The blonde woman tilted her head, spilling hair from behind her ear. "Yes. I'm Mrs. Lazar, Can I help you?"

"My name is Pete." He extended his hand. "I've been working at the Hermann farm all summer. Joe and Dolly at the Café, and the Johnsons at the mercantile, know me. I made Tommy a slingshot. With your permission, I'd like to teach him how to shoot at targets and maybe hunt for squirrels with him."

"Why would you want to do that?" Mrs. Lazar's eyebrows arched.

"Miss Howe mentioned that Tommy seems troubled, and

since my daughter died, I would enjoy spending time with a child again. I could spend late afternoons and Sundays with him, if it's okay with you."

"Let me think it over." Her brows unfurled. "Maybe you could come to the house on Sunday afternoon and we can talk."

"That sounds good. I'll be there about one o'clock."

Pete's shoulders slumped, but he wasn't surprised. After all, Mrs. Lazar would want to ask others about him.

Across the street from the bank, Glen stood at the back of the ice wagon. He looked up as Pete approached him.

"Hello." Pete extended his hand. "You don't know me, but I'm a friend of James, Katherine's brother. My name is Pete."

"I'm Glen." He wiped sawdust from the tops of the large ice chunks. "I saw you when you fixed Mary's dog's leg."

"Would you maybe like Katherine to be more than friends?" Pete stepped aside as an ice pick rolled past his feet.

Glen's face reddened from the tips of his hairline to the bottom of his neck. "I don't know what to say to her most of the time."

Pete knelt and picked up the ice pick. He handed it to Glen. "I overheard Katherine say she thought it romantic when a man reads poetry to a woman. All you have to do is let a book do the talking." I don't have a poetry book."

"I have the perfect book. One I read to my wife before she passed away. I'll bring it to you." Pete's chest caught, but he had to do it.

Glen scratched his head. "Why would you give me your book?"

"I like Katherine, and she deserves to be happy." Pete grinned as he started off toward the mercantile.

Glen called after him. "I'll be at the gas station most of the day. I help out there on weekends."

Pete waved. "See you tomorrow."

Once more, Pete left for the mercantile with mail for Cookie.

Rosemary met him at the window with a smile. "More letters?"

Pete nodded. "I sure wish one of them would find him. Do you have any mail for me? I'm expecting a letter."

"No." Rosemary turned back to the mailbox counter. "Nothing for a Pete Preacher."

"Oh, Preacher is the nickname that Ben knows me by. My name is Peter Walters."

"Oh, my goodness!" Rosemary dropped her stack of mail. "I have some letters for a Dr. Peter Walters. Is that you?" She slipped off her stool and cringed at the first few steps. Limping, she retrieved the letters from the back side of the mailboxes and handed them to him. "I should have known. Pete... Peter. I'm sure glad you claimed them. So, you're a doctor?"

"A veterinarian, but let's keep that between us for now, okay?" He flipped through the envelopes. One came from Pastor Jim, one from an official government address, and two that only said, "Cookie."

Pete gasped! He dropped down onto the window seat and slit open one of Cookie's letters.

*Dear Preacher,*

*I sure hope you are still in Kathleen Creek. And if you're there, you know by now that Joe and Dolly are my parents. I didn't tell you because I knew you'd try to talk me into going home.*

*I joined the CCC on my birthday, and here's the thing. You're only supposed to join if your Pa is unemployed. As you know, mine is not. Since I call you Dad anyway, and since I owe you my life, I gave them your name as my step-dad. I said your address is General Delivery, Kathleen Creek, Minnesota. This means that you'll get a check every month from the government for $25.00. We get paid $30 a month but $25 has to go to our family. I want you to have it. I get everything here, including clothes. I want you to buy the tools you need to do your vet work again. Maybe you can rent a house and get a car eventually.*

*<u>Do not give the money to my parents.</u> Pa would only drink it up and Ma has money from her parents. She is doing okay in the Café. I have the rest of my life to help them. I want to help you now. I owe you that. You can make a new start. Some day when you're a rich doctor you can make it up to me. Ha ha.*

*Please, write to me as soon as you get this letter so I know the money will find you. Let me know how Ma and Pa are. I'll write to them after I hear from you.*

*Your friend, Cookie*

*P.S. They call me Cookie here too. I work in the kitchen.*

Although he had used only "Cookie" on the envelope return address, he included his full name and address inside the letter. Pete read it twice. How could he believe what he read? Then he opened Cookie's second letter.

*Dear Preacher,*

*I haven't heard from you yet and I'm worried you won't be getting the checks if you're not in Kathleen Creek. In case my first letter got lost, I'm sending you another. I'm at a CCC camp in Blackduck, Minnesota and I like it here. We get everything we need and get paid*

*$30 a month. But, we only get $5 and the rest has to go to our family if our father is unemployed. I gave them your name as my step-father and they're sending the checks to you to the Kathleen Creek post office. You should have one check already.*

*I want you to use the money to start over with veterinary work. Please let me know that you got this letter and the check. Do not give the money to my parents. I want you to have it. Please write to me right away.*

*Your friend,*

*Cookie*

Again, Cookie included his full name and address at the bottom. Pete folded the letter and put it in his shirt pocket and opened the envelope from the federal government. A check for twenty-five dollars with his name on it. He inhaled deeply and slowly blew out his breath. Wow! Twenty-five dollars! He could buy a speculum and a float, and file Jack and Jill's teeth.

Twenty-five dollars every month? He could pay Rosemary what he owed her at the post office. And buy Jenny supper at the Café. Why, he could pay for a place to live. But how could he accept this money?

He folded the check and put it in his other shirt pocket. He patted both pockets. Twenty-five dollars!

Several minutes passed in a trance. Then, he sat straighter. What had Pastor Jim and Karen had to say?

Ah! Pastor Jim and Karen had been pleased to hear from him and were happy to know of his safety. Alvin and Emma had a beautiful baby boy and named him after Alvin's father. Alvin clerked at the hardware store and seemed happy with it.

The letter went on with more news from Grand Island, but Pete couldn't stop fidgeting. He put it in his back pocket to finish later, rushed out of the store, and headed back to the bank. Hopefully it would still be open.

"God bless you, Cookie." With a thalump-thalump his long,

quick stride carried him over the wooden boardwalk. He dashed kitty-corner across the street.

Mrs. Lazar greeted him with a nod. "Back already?"

"Yes, ma'am." Pete passed her the check. "I'd like to open an account, please. Deposit fifteen dollars, and I'd like the rest in one-dollar bills."

As Pete stuffed the ten one-dollar bills in his front pants pocket, he stood straighter. They couldn't arrest him for vagrancy now.

He left the bank with a satisfied smile.

"I have to write to Cookie." Pete turned north on the boardwalk. "I have to tell him to come home for a visit."

A passerby creased his brow. He must have heard Pete. That was okay, because Pete was used to strange looks. But... how long had it been since he'd had one? With his better clothes, a clean-shaven face, and shorter hair, people now treated him kindly. He sprinted to the post office. It felt great to be part of the community.

"Rosemary, I have to answer one of these letters right away. Do you have a sheet of paper and an envelope I can use?"

Rosemary nodded.

He grabbed the pen on her counter. "How much time do I have before you close?"

"We close at four-thirty, but don't hurry." Both heads turned to the wall clock. Four twenty-five. "I'll post your letter when you're done with it." She limped back to her stool. Pete scrawled quickly.

*Dear Cookie,*

*Please forgive me for the short letter. The post office is about to close. I will write a longer letter this evening and send it soon. Thank you for the check. I've cashed it because I really do need the money, but I will have to think on whether I can continue to claim this money before I cash the next one. I am happy to hear you are doing well.*

*Your good friend, Preacher.*

When he handed Rosemary the envelope, he winked. "Look who I'm sending it to."

Rosemary brushed her finger over the name and gasped. "You found him?"

Pete leaned closer and dropped his voice. "Those letters from 'Cookie' are from Ben. That's his nickname because he's a cook."

"Isn't that something?" Rosemary's eyes twinkled, then filled with disappointment.

Pete took a single pace back. Why was she upset? Oh, wait. She couldn't help look for Ben anymore if he wasn't sending his daily letters. Maybe he could think of something else.

"I'll never forget how you've helped me find him, though." Pete fingered the dollars in his pocket. Finally, he could pay her back. But should he wait? Would she accept it? Besides, should he even keep the money? Should he give it to Joe and Dolly?

"And now I need another favor. Will you please keep this confidential until Ben writes to his parents? I don't want them to hear about him from someone else. Ben promised to write them after he hears from me." He squeezed her hands. "I'm going to write him a long letter tonight. I didn't want to keep you from closing. Know that I so appreciate you, Rosemary, and all you've done to help me."

Rosemary tightened her grip on his fingers. "Of course I'll keep your confidence, Pete. You know I will."

"I do, and I thank you again. I'll let you know how it all turns out." As he left the store, he patted the money once more, letting his gaze linger on the café. He couldn't face Joe or Dolly yet. He needed to think about the money.

He hurried north without stopping to visit James.

When he reached his spot by the river, Pete stopped to sit against the maple tree. He took out both of Cookie's letters and read each of them again. How wonderful that Cookie was in a good place. He seemed to be happy. Pete tilted his chin toward heaven. "Thank you, Lord."

Cookie sincerely seemed to want Pete to have the money. While Pete did save Cookie's life that day in the boxcar, and undoubtedly when he got snake-bit, Cookie didn't owe him anything. Pete would have to clear that up with him, for sure. But, what if he did keep the money each month? What would he do with it? He leaned his head against the tree trunk and closed his eyes.

He'd buy a speculum and float first of all. Then he'd buy a surgical kit and a medical bag. Over time, he'd keep buying vet equipment until he had all he needed. Then, he'd save enough money for a used car. When he had enough clients, he'd rent a room or a house and set up his practice. Cookie's money could give him a new start.

"Yahoo!" Pete raised both arms and waved them overhead. "Yahoo! Thank you, Lord."

But that wouldn't be fair to Cookie. He was working for that money. He said Pete could make it up to him one day. Could he?

Pete scratched his chin. What if he said he wouldn't take the money? He couldn't send it to Joe and Dolly. Maybe he could put it in the bank for Cookie. Or he could set up a practice and pay Cookie back in the future. *Lord, what should I do?*

Pete jumped up and headed to the farm.

"I know I said I wouldn't be back for supper, but my plans changed," Pete told Gunther when he went into the barn. "I have to write a letter before it gets dark, but then I'll do the separating."

"I checked the lantern for kerosene but you haven't lit it." Gunther cocked his head.

"I don't like lanterns in the barn. They can be dangerous." Pete's arms prickled. Hopefully Gunther wouldn't ask him to explain why.

"I have lanterns morning and night doing milking and

chores." Gunther stepped closer, planting a light hand on Pete's arm. "You afraid of fire?"

"I guess I am." Pete hated to admit it.

"You can write your letter in the house after supper in the lamplight."

"Thanks." Pete grabbed the other three-legged stool and patted one of the cows on the rump to move her over. The two men worked in silent partnership until only one cow remained. Pete grabbed the heavy can of milk while Gunther took care of the last cow.

"Go ask Lavinia how much milk she wants for the house before you separate." Gunther called as Pete carried the can to the milk house.

Pete filled the jars. He'd finished separating when Gunther came in, grabbed the can of skim milk, and went out to feed the calves and hogs. Pete carried the milk into the kitchen and returned for the separator parts. By then Gunther met him, and they washed up at the dry sink. When he sat at the kitchen table to eat, warmth spread over Pete. They'd accepted him as a member of the family.

"Pete needs to write a letter after supper, Mother." Gunther took the seat next to Tammy. "Do we have paper and envelopes?"

"I have a tablet and envelopes." Pete placed his napkin on his lap and let his eyes take in the bounty of meat balls, spaghetti, peas, cucumber salad and hot, fresh rye bread. "But, I would appreciate being able to sit at the table in the lamp light to write it."

"We do our homework after supper." Tammy bounced in her chair. "You can sit with us.

"I like to color." Olivia picked up a pea with her fingers and plopped it in her mouth.

Lavinia sighed. "Olivia, please use your fork."

"I have to read a book." Bonnie pointed to a leather-bound volume behind her on a small table.

"My goodness, will there be room for me at the table?" Pete grinned and winked.

In unison, all three girls said with a definite tone, "Yes!"

So when they finished, Pete retrieved his tablet, pencil, and envelope from his pack and brought it into the house. He took out his hoof knife and sharpened his pencil. After collecting the shavings in his hand, he dumped them in the kitchen trash can.

While Tammy and Bonnie dried dishes, Olivia brought Pete into the dining room. "You can sit here." She claimed the chair next to him.

Gunther brought a different kerosene lamp into the dining room and set it in the middle of the table. He lit the wick, replaced the glass globe, and turned the small, metal dial to bring the wick up higher for maximum light. "Remember, girls, no talking when you're doing school work."

Pete's heart soared. Such sweet girls, all grinning at the pleasure of sitting around the table with Mr. Pete while they worked.

*Dear Cookie,*

*I am blessed to be in Kathleen Creek, with its beautiful fall trees and the gentle rushing river. The Hermann family has blessed me further, permitting me to work on their farm. They've welcomed me as a cherished friend, and provided me food and a place to sleep. The farm work is hard, but pleasant, and I so enjoy being of help to this family.*

Pete drummed his pencil eraser against the table, and Bonnie looked up from her book. She giggled, and Tammy nudged her.

Chuckling, he averted his gaze.

*Joe has changed since you left. He's kind, not at all the mean cuss you described to me. When I first arrived, a strain existed between Joe and Dolly, but they've since reconciled and found a piece of happiness*

*—a piece, since they cannot be complete without you. They miss you, Cookie. Please write to them.*

He rolled the pencil between his lips. Should he address the money issue? Maybe not yet. He needed time to pray, think, and discern what God wanted him to do.

*Thank you again for the money, Cookie. It is such a blessing to walk around town without fear of being arrested for vagrancy. But, we'll talk more about it later. Please, please write to your parents.*

He signed his name, addressed and sealed the envelope, and got up from the table. Tammy, Bonnie and Olivia smiled.

"Good night, ladies." His voice came out squeaky. So much gratitude, but how could he possibly express it. Oh, what a blessing to be a part of this family.

A dark cloud passed over his heart. He didn't deserve such love and support. They didn't know his terrible past. Would he ever dare to tell them?

44

On Saturday Pete rushed out with Gunther to start the chores, Cookie's letter burning in his pocket. "I must get to the post office first thing this morning."

Gunther nodded.

After breakfast, Pete dressed in his heavy coat and trudged through the white blanket toward town. They'd had their first snowfall the night before. So soon. Pete dreaded the on-coming winter. What would he do with himself? Could he stay on at the Hermann's farm all winter? Would they keep him on?

He did have Cookie's money, but could he keep it? If he did, how soon could he afford to live on his own?

A scream reached Pete's ears as he neared the park. A young girl shrieked as Tommy pulled at her braids. "Let me go!" she yelled.

Pete raced to the scene. "Let go of her hair, Tommy."

The boy released the braids and scowled. "How do you know my name?"

"I know your mother." Pete stepped between Tommy and the girl. "My name is Pete. I'm going into town. Will you walk with me?"

Tight-lipped and with darting eyes, Tommy shifted from one foot to the other. After several long moments, he dragged his feet toward Pete. When he reached him, Pete walked on. "I saw you in your yard one day."

Tommy cast him a quick glance.

Pete swung his arms at his side. "I'm new in town, and I hoped we could be friends."

Another quick glance.

"What do you like to do for fun, Tommy?"

The boy shrugged.

"Have you ever shot a slingshot?"

"No. My dad was going to …." Tommy clamped a hand over his mouth.

Pete grinned. He'd been right about the slingshot. "I recently made a couple. Would you like to do some target shooting with me?"

"Can I?" A flicker of light shone in Tommy's eyes. "But I gotta' ask my ma."

"Of course. Your mother invited me to come to your house tomorrow. I'll bring the slingshots with me."

"Great!" Tommy skipped ahead a step.

Pete caught his sleeve. "But I don't want to hear that you're pulling little girls' braids anymore, okay?"

"Okay."

They walked along in silence until they reached the mercantile. Pete planted his right foot on the bottom step. "I'll leave you here, Tommy. See you tomorrow."

"Bye."

Rosemary grinned and waved. "Another letter?"

Pete passed her the envelope addressed to Ben Harrison. "Yes. Thank you so much for your help and for keeping my secret."

"I am the postmistress. That's my job." She winked.

"Oh, you're doing much more than your job. I feel so

honored to have your friendship, Rosemary. And how is Mary liking school?"

"She is doing very well. Miss Howe says she is one of the brightest pupils."

Pete nodded. "That doesn't surprise me. And how is Max?"

"Max mopes until she gets home from school. And he knows when it's time. He sits and waits by the window, and you should see his tail wag as soon as he catches sight of her. Oh, hello, Fred. Excuse me, Pete."

"I'll see you later, Rosemary. Thanks again."

At the gas station, Pete handed Glen the poetry book. Glen quickly slipped it into his jacket without looking at it and glanced side to side.

"Poetry isn't just for girls, Glen." Pete chuckled. "Many men write poetry and many men read poetry. I used to read that book to my wife all the time."

"Thanks." Glen ducked his head.

"Good luck, Glen." Pete waved goodbye. As much as he would have liked to visit with Joe and Dolly, Pete headed straight back to the farm. After half a block, Jenny Howe walked toward him on the arm of the same man from earlier.

When they met, Jenny's face lit up. "Hello Pete. This is Mark Weston. Mark, this is Pete… "She bit her lip. "I don't know your last name."

"Just Pete." A handshake seemed unlikely, so he nodded to the scowling man.

Jenny gave him a sweet smile. "Okay, 'Just Pete', we met Tommy a few minutes ago, and he said you're practicing with slingshots on Sunday. I haven't seen that boy so happy since before his father left. That's so nice of you to take an interest in him."

Mark tugged hard on Jenny's arm.

She frowned. "Goodbye, Pete."

Mark's angry voice drifted back to him. "I told you before…."

Pete shook his head. Why would Jenny want to spend time with someone like Mark?

---

ON SUNDAY, Mrs. Lazar welcomed Pete into their living room, where a plate of cookies sat on a tray. "We're going to have refreshments first. Do you want lemonade, Tommy?"

"Yeah." Tommy sat in a lump on the sofa next to his mother and downed the beverage while she and Pete sipped their coffee.

"So, Pete, tell us how you came to be in Kathleen Creek." Mrs. Lazar re-filled his cup.

"I traveled to Dallas in the hopes of moving there." He took another sip, letting the warm, bitter liquid wash over him. "Soon after I arrived, my car was stolen and everything in it. And after that, a street gang robbed me of all my money."

Pete dipped his chin. "I had nothing, and I needed employment, but there was nothing available in Dallas. So, I rode the rails to find work."

"You were a hobo?" Tommy lurched forward.

"I was." Was. Pete clutched the leg of his pants. Was he no longer a hobo? He didn't look like one anymore. And it had been months since he'd hopped a train.

Tommy's faint voice pulled him out of his fog. "What did you say, Tommy?"

"Can we go shooting now?" He bounced in his seat.

"Mrs. Lazar?" Pete downed the rest of his coffee.

"Go ahead, but be careful." She squeezed Tommy's shoulders and gave him a kiss on the forehead. "Do exactly what Mr. Pete says, okay?"

"Okay, Ma. Come on, Mr. Pete." Tommy raced out the door.

"Thank you for the coffee, Mrs. Lazar." Pete followed Tommy out the door.

Pete led Tommy west past several houses until they came to a wooded area on the outskirts of town. He produced the slingshots, and Tommy skipped a few paces.

Pete laughed. "Now Tommy, remember always that this slingshot is not a toy. It is a weapon, like a gun. It can kill. Are you old enough to have such a weapon and use it responsibly?"

Tommy nodded.

"This weapon will last you a long time if you take good care of it. Don't leave it out in the rain or snow. Don't leave it out in the sun, either." Pete traced his thumb over the handle. "This is hickory wood, rubber bands, and a leather pouch. It is important to take good care of the slingshot so it lasts a long time, understand?"

Tommy nodded again.

"No matter what you use as ammunition in your slingshot, it will hurt or kill whatever it hits. So you have to be sure that there are no people or pets in your line of fire." Pete knelt to meet Tommy at eye level. "Never shoot at a person or a pet with this, understood?"

"Okay."

"No matter how mad you get at someone, or how mad you get at the world, you never, ever, shoot at a person or a pet."

"Okay."

"Now, let's find a target." Pete scanned the clearing. "See that boulder next to that big oak tree?"

Tommy's gaze darted. "Yes! Yes, I see it."

"Now watch me." Pete held the handle of the slingshot with his right hand and put a rock in the leather pouch, holding the stone in place with his thumb and forefinger. He stretched the rubber bands back until taut, aimed at the rock, then let go. The stone pinged as it hit the rock.

"Wow! You hit it!" Tommy picked up a small rock. "Let me!"

It took Tommy several tries, but eventually he hit the rock. "Bulls eye!" he yelled, his hands in the air.

"Good job!" Pete clapped. "The more you practice, the better you'll get. It's fun to set empty cans on a fence and try to knock them down."

"Let's go find some!"

Tommy's enthusiasm energized Pete. He hadn't felt like that in almost two years. Not since Betty and Rose died. "Let's do it."

"I bet Mom has some empty cans." Tommy led the way, and Pete had a hard time keeping up with him.

They spent the rest of the afternoon shooting stones at empty cans set along a fence outside of town.

"Tommy, it's getting late. We need to get you home."

Tommy's face sobered. He opened his mouth, but clamped it shut when Pete dipped his chin.

"Okay."

"I had a good time today, Tommy." Pete tucked his slingshot into his pocket. "I hope we can be friends."

"I had a good time, too, Mr. Pete." Tommy extended his hand for a shake. "I'd like to be friends. Can you come over again?"

With a grin, Pete accepted the hearty handshake. "I work for Mr. Hermann and don't have a lot of free time, but I'll try. What time do you get home from school?"

Tommy put his head down and muttered something.

"What did you say?" Pete placed a light hand on his shoulder.

Tommy huffed. "School gets out at 3:30 but I usually have to stay after."

"Are you getting special help with something?" Pete tipped up Tommy's face.

"No, I get detention." Tommy winced.

Laughter erupted from deep in Pete's chest. "Well, if you can stop getting detention and get home early enough to get your homework done, maybe I can get here before it gets dark on some days."

Tommy stuffed his hands in his pockets. "Okay."

Pete started toward Tommy's house. Hopefully he'd made a difference in the boy's attitude.

As soon as Tommy walked in, he plopped on the couch next to his mother. "You won't believe it! We set up all those cans and I hit them…" He turned to Pete.

"Can I keep the slingshot for a few days? I'll take good care of it."

"Yes, Tommy." Pete leaned against the door jamb. "You can keep it forever. I made it for you."

"Wow!" Tommy's dark green eyes widened. "You made it for me? How come?"

"Well, I saw you throwing rocks into a tree one day, and I decided you'd be good at shooting a slingshot, so I made you one."

"Wow!" Tommy hugged the slingshot to his chest, and his mother mouthed, "Thank you," above his head.

"I have to go." Pete waved to them both. He *did* have a good time with Tommy. He *did* want to be his friend. And maybe he *could* make a difference in his life.

At least, Pete hoped so.

45

After his time with Tommy, Pete stopped to play a few games of cribbage with James and listen to him play the harmonica. What a marvelous player James had already become, much better than Pete, even with his years of experience. James was, indeed, an extraordinary young man.

That evening, Pete wrote a letter to the Haver-Glover Laboratories in Kansas City, Missouri ordering a speculum and a float, but didn't seal the envelope until he could enclose a check. The next morning, he brought the letter into the house with him.

After breakfast, and after the girls left for school, Pete stopped Gunther before he got out the door. "I have something to tell you. You, too, Lavinia."

Gunther sat back at the table, and Lavinia took the chair beside him.

Pete took the place they'd set for him that morning. "This is my story. I'm a veterinarian. I had a practice in Nebraska, but after my wife and daughter died, I decided to move to Texas. However, on the trip there, someone stole my car with all my money, all my vet equipment and supplies, and everything except for what I had in my pack. That's when I started hopping trains and taking any work I could get to survive."

Lavinia clicked her tongue against her teeth.

Gunther's eyes widened, "A horse doctor!"

Pete nodded. "You know that both Jack and Jill need their teeth filed and you can't do it. I can't do it either without the proper equipment." He held up the envelope. "I received some money in the mail last week, and I want to order the equipment. I need to go into town to use a telephone to make a call to Kansas City, Missouri, to place the order."

"Yes, yes." Gunther jerked his thumb toward town. "It will be good to get those teeth filed so they can eat good again. Go ahead, go to town to use the telephone. Please."

Pete walked into town and made the call from the mercantile. He wrote the check, and mailed it, then whistled as he left for the farm again.

The next morning Pete scooted back away from the table and looked at Mrs. Hermann. "I'll help you get the washing set up. It's easier now that it's in the porch. Is the water hot enough yet?"

"I think so."

Pete carried the hot water from the boiler and poured it into the washing machine. He pumped enough cold water for both rinse tubs and turned to go.

"Bring your clothes to me and I'll put them with the others." Lavinia said.

"You don't have to do that. I can do them." He took another step toward the door.

"No, you bring them to me. They can go in with Gunther's clothes."

"That's so good of you." Pete went to the barn and changed. He brought his shirt, pants, and two pair of socks to Lavinia.

She sifted through the pile. "Where's your underwear, Pete. You don't have to be shy."

He ducked his gaze. "I don't have any underwear. They wore out long ago."

"Oh, my stars!" Lavinia covered her mouth with her hands. "That won't do. I'll find some of Gunther's father's underwear for you."

She hurried upstairs.

Should he wait, or should he go?

Before he could decide, she came back downstairs with an armload of clothes. "Here's a few things I'm sure you can use." She handed the whole armload to Pete. "Go now. Put on some underwear. It's cold."

When Pete reached his spot in the barn, he spread the stack of clothes out over the feed bins. So many clothes! Pants, shirts, undershirts, briefs, socks, long johns, winter coat, scarf, cap and leather chopper mitts with wool liners. He tore off his worn jeans and shirt. He had forgotten how good underwear felt. He finished dressing in his new clothes, and with a new bounce in his step, he went to find Gunther.

It only took Gunther a few hours to spread the news of Pete's veterinary training. After Pete filed Jack's and Jill's teeth, other farmers either called the Hermanns' asking for "the doctor" or they drove into the Hermann's yard to ask if "Doc" would come and treat some ailment.

Pete apologized to Gunther when he took time to do the vet work, but Gunther only beamed like the proud father of a successful son. "You go. We can do without you. They need you. Go."

People tipped their hat to Pete. Tommy proudly announced to everyone that Dr. Pete was his friend. When paid in eggs or meat or grain, Pete brought it to the Hermanns. A few times, he earned cash.

Joe and Dolly announced to everyone that Pete had found Ben for them. They proclaimed that Ben was a cook at a CCC camp in northern Minnesota and would come home for a visit as soon as he could. In Cookie's next letter to Pete he wrote:

*Dear Preacher,*

*I hope you are well. I've received a lot of letters from both my mother and father since I wrote them. It's nice to be in touch with them again. My father sure sounds like he has changed since he quit drinking. Thank you for taking my message to them. I'm in your debt once again.*

Pete grimaced. Would Cookie never stop feeling like that?

*Not to mention, I received a letter from you. I appreciate that you tried to find me. I'm so thankful everything has worked out.* Not as thankful as Pete was, for sure.

*My parents have written of your veterinary service to the farmers in the community. I'm so pleased that the money has helped so many in the community. It's my hope you've not mentioned to my parents that I sent it.*

Pete folded the top of the letter over. He hadn't mentioned anything to Joe and Dolly, but he so wished he could tell them of their son's generosity.

*I am working hard and getting fed and clothed good. If you think that cooking for two hundred boys isn't hard work, you should try it some time. (I say boys because some of the guys here aren't older than fourteen, even though they're supposed to be at least eighteen). This camp is run by the Army and they treat us like soldiers.*

Pete laughed. Imagine the free-spirited Cookie obeying orders like a soldier.

*The boys have to be up at five in the morning, and have one hour to clean up. Six o'clock is breakfast. Then the flag assembly includes news and assignments. Everyone gets into their trucks, and they take off for the day.*

*Of course, since me and the other chief cook have to make breakfast for all of them, I'm up at four o'clock to cook and serve the breakfast and pack lunches for the guys to take with them. I still have to do the flag assembly, but when the boys leave in the trucks, me and my assistants get back into the kitchen to supervise KP duty (KP is punishment for the guys who mess up) and cook supper for the whole gang again. Since we have to get up so early, my crew gets a one-hour break during the day. I usually sleep then.*

Pete shook his head. And he thought he worked hard.

*The trucks return to the camp at four in the afternoon. They have one hour to shower and be at the mess hall at five for supper. Classes begin at six and last until nine o'clock. At ten it is lights out.*

Classes? Pete arched his brow.

*You wouldn't believe all the classes they teach here. The two classes everyone has to take when they first get here are Hygiene and Letter Writing. Some of the boys haven't been to school much and can't even write. We are encouraged to write to our families every week. They teach a lot of other classes here and everyone has to take one. I'm studying biology right now.*

*Write me back.*

*Your friend, Cookie*

After reading the letter, Pete secured a nice diamond willow branch to make a cane for Rosemary but had trouble finding time to carve on it. While the major farm work had lessened somewhat now during mid-November, there was always something to do. Farmers worked on their equipment and their buildings, with daily chores ever present.

But Gunther liked to rest after his noon meal, so Pete used that time to whittle off the bark and sand the bare wood. After applying two coats of varnish in the back porch of the house, he told the family it would have to dry for several days. At their mother's warning, the girls all agreed to leave it alone.

The day finally came when Pete walked into the mercantile with a beautiful diamond willow cane. He had fashioned a curved handle from a branch that grew out of the side. The handle had a natural hook at the end.

"Rosemary," Pete hid his grin as he approached the window. "I know that you're not tall enough to reach things on those top shelves. I've wanted to do something special for you, since you've been such a good friend to me, so I made you a hook for reaching those things. Will you accept this gift with my most sincere gratitude?"

Rosemary looked at the gleaming yellow wood with the intriguing raised diamond pattern and frowned. "It's a cane."

"It *can* be used as a cane." Pete traced his hand over the hook. "But its main purpose is to be a jewel in your hand as you gracefully reach for that box on the top shelf. This is made from a diamond willow tree. It's considered quite a rarity in Nebraska where I come from."

Rosemary reached for the stick and slowly swiveled it around. "It *is* beautiful. You made it yourself?"

His grin escaped. "Yes, I did. I made it specifically for you. I hope you will accept it with my most sincere thanks for what you've done for me."

"Oh, I only did my job. And you paid me for the supplies and the stamps. You don't owe me anything." Rosemary tested the height as it stood on the floor next to her. A perfect estimation.

"It is a gift of appreciation."

"It must have taken you a long time." Rosemary ran her fingers along the smooth surface and traced some of the diamonds.

"It took a while."

A woman that Pete didn't know entered the store, walking past them. She stopped when she saw the cane. "Oh, how beautiful! My grandfather had a stick like that. He said the Indians make them as gifts. They're supposed to bring long life."

"My friend, Dr. Pete, made it for me. It is beautiful, isn't it?" She faced Pete. "Thank you. What a thoughtful gift."

"I hope it brings you long life." He pulled a list from his pocket. "While I'm here, I need to pick up some turpentine, mineral oil, and tincture of iodine."

"Of course, and I also have some letters for you, Dr. Pete."

4 6

As soon as Pete had his purchases in hand, he sat on the bench outside the store and eagerly opened the first envelope. Another check from the government. He folded it, tucked it away, and patted his pocket a couple of times with silent thanks. His third twenty-five dollars! The other letter came from Cookie.

*Dear Preacher (Or should I say Dad?)*

*Thank you for your letter. I'm glad to know that you have a good family to be living with. I'm also glad you like the maple tree by the river as much as I do. Some day we might share it.*

*You asked about the camp. We have thirty men each to seven barracks, a field hospital with a dentist, a mess hall, an education building and a rec room. We have indoor plumbing with hot showers and flush toilets. Most CCC camps don't have that, because they are built to take down and move often. This camp is permanent because there is so much work to do in this area. For example, we clean the forests after the lumber companies cut everything, but left behind stumps and branches. Many of the guys here are also cutting trails, and building bridges, campgrounds, and state parks. The U.S. Forest*

*Service is in charge of the work we do, even though the Army is in charge of us, if that makes any sense.*

*Since these guys are so young, a few older guys have to teach them how to use the equipment. We have lots of guys come back to the doctor during the day with injuries. One kid cut part of his foot off with an ax.*

Pete winced. As bad as life had been for him in the lowest points, he'd never had it so difficult.

*We heard a lot of hard-luck stories on the road, but I've heard even more here. The typical kid here comes in at least ten pounds under-weight and is from a large family. The only way to keep them from starving is the money the government sends home to them each month.*

*Even with all the hobos we saw out there, I didn't realize what bad shape this whole county is in until I came here. There is no work for the men. President Roosevelt saved this county with this CCC program! Who knows what the families with no young men are doing for money. I guess I can now understand the young women we saw on our travels who sold their bodies for a quarter.*

*Well, anyway, I hope you are well. I am doing great.*

*Write soon,*

*Your friend, Cookie*

Pete's spirit soared. How lucky he was in Kathleen Creek, living and working with a family like the Hermanns when so many men couldn't. His heart sang. With Cookie safe and happy, and another check to deposit in the bank, he felt almost giddy.

Pete's friendship with Tommy bloomed. And finally, one day he ran into Jenny.

"Oh, Pete." She waved him down from across the street as he left the mercantile. "Tommy has only received detention a few times lately. What a difference you've made in his life."

Pete's chest puffed. "I'm glad to—"

"Let's go, Jenny." Mark dragged her away.

Another day, he passed her outside the school. "Hi, Jenny."

Her eyes brightened. "Hi, Pete."

Mark grabbed her arm and dragged her away again. Why was he so set against Pete talking with her? Oh, to see more of her without Mark.

He did, however, see more of Mrs. Lazar. She moved next to Pete one day after she sent Tommy on an errand when he arrived. "I'm sure you know that my husband left me."

She leaned closer, her long, blonde hair brushing his shoulder. "It's no secret that he left me for another woman over a year ago. I never filed for divorce because I never had a reason to. But last week, I saw the lawyer and started divorce proceedings."

Pete blinked. What should he say? "I hope that goes well for you, Mrs. Lazar."

"Please call me Henrietta. I wanted you to know about my divorce because I didn't want you to think of me as a married woman."

A married woman? Pete's brow creased. "I only think of you as Tommy's mother." What was she getting at? When was Tommy coming back?

"Well, I'm more than Tommy's mother, Pete." Chuckling, she winked. "I'll soon be a single woman again and ready to date."

Pete choked back a gasp. She wanted to date *him*. He hadn't seen that coming. "I'm not ready to date yet."

"Hasn't it been almost two years since your wife died?"

Was she batting her eyelashes at him? Pete stifled a groan. "Yes, but that doesn't mean that I'm ready to date."

"Well, I will be ready to date soon, and I like you a lot." She punctuated her declaration by caressing his arm.

"Okay. Thanks for telling me. I'll wait for Tommy outside." Pete hurried out the door.

In truth, he *wanted* to date, but he wanted to date Jenny. If only he knew whether she felt the same.

Thanksgiving Day arrived, a day of feasting and fun in the

Hermann household. The Frank Ross family joined them for roast duck dinner, and Lavinia sent them home with a box of food. Then, only a week after Thanksgiving, the townspeople geared up for the holidays, displaying Christmas decorations on the gaslight poles.

One day in town, Gunther pointed to the red poinsettias and garland hanging from a post. "Now Pete, while our town got electricity a few years ago, they can't bring themselves to convert to electric street lights. Our city pays Jake, an old man, to light the gaslights every night and snuff them out in the morning."

Pete grinned. What a quaint, perfect town.

The second week in December saw the second snowfall of the season. On the way home from school, Tommy ran alongside Pete, huge white flakes collecting in his red hair. "Miss Howe asked me to play the part of Joseph in the school Christmas program. You'll come and see me in the program, won't you, Dr. Pete?"

"Of course I will. I'm proud of you, Tommy." Pete ruffled the boy's hair, sending the snowflakes fluttering to the pristine white ground. "Miss Howe must like you to give you such an important role."

"She said she's proud of me, too. I don't fight anymore, and I haven't had detention in a long time. I want to be like you, Pete. I told her that."

"I'm honored, Tommy." Pete's voice squeaked.

When he stopped at the post office, Rosemary had another letter from Cookie.

*Dear Preacher,*

*I'm glad you had a good Thanksgiving. I guess we did too, but it took a lot of extra work making a special dinner for our young guys. But I was glad we did. Most of them were lonesome for their families. The special dinner (and a day off from work) brightened their spirits somewhat. You might think we eat like a bunch of lumberjacks here, but we don't. We set our tables with tablecloths and real china, glasses, and silverware. The guys can eat as much as they want, and many of them are putting on the weight they lost before they got here.*

*You asked about entertainment. The guys don't go out to work on Saturdays. They clean their bunks and wash their clothes. Saturday nights, we can walk six miles into Blackduck and go to a dance or a movie. Some people in town like the CCC guys, and others don't. I saw a sign in a store window that read,* No Dogs or CCC Allowed.

*On Sundays, traveling ministers lead us in a service, or a truck will take us to town to church. We have a lake next to our camp, and we can go boating or fishing. We have activities in our rec room too. Sometimes we have boxing matches.*

Pete smiled. Sounded like Cookie might even be having a little fun.

*I am getting as good as my mother at making bread since we bake one hundred loaves a day to feed this crew. We even have some guys cut wood for our cooking stoves and the heating stoves in the barracks. Believe me, it's a full time job.*

*On a sad note, one of my friends here, Goon, (everyone has nicknames) was out looking for a lost man (that's one of the things CCC guys do). Somehow Goon ended up falling through the ice and drowned. No one knows how it happened, but they didn't find him until the next day. We're all sad about it.*

*Take good care of yourself,*

*Your friend,*

*Cookie*

Pete tucked the letter in his pocket. It must be hard for those young guys to be so far away from their families. Yet Cookie seemed to be doing well.

After supper, Tammy handed a folded piece of paper to Pete. "A note from the teacher, Dr. Pete."

"For me?" Pete's eyebrows shot up. He took the sheet of paper.

*Dear Dr. Pete...*

"Read it to us!" Olivia jumped up and down.

Bonnie nodded, and even Gunther and Lavinia leaned forward.

"All right." Pete cleared his throat. *"Dear Dr. Pete, I would like your assistance with the live farm animals for the Christmas program. Can you meet with me at the school house at three-thirty one day this week? I appreciate any help you can provide. Sincerely, Jenny Howe."*

Lavinia handed him a tablet, pen, and ink. Bonnie and Olivia stood over him. "Dear Miss Howe." He winked at the girls. "I will be there at three-thirty. It will be my pleasure to help you with the animals. Sincerely…" He frowned. How should he sign it?

"Dr. Pete." Bonnie giggled.

Tammy took the note with a smile of importance. "I'll get this to Miss Howe first thing in the morning."

The next afternoon, Pete changed into clean clothes. Snowflakes piled on his shoulders as he strolled to the school house. He arrived as the squealing children left, dancing around him on the white sidewalk. Jenny smiled and waved from the door. "Come in, Pete. Thanks for your willingness to help."

He paused at the steps. Would it be proper to be alone with her? The school house did have windows, and they were planning a school event.

She outlined her plans. "My first question is where to get the animals."

Pete took a pencil and tablet from her. "Well, Mr. Barthel could bring goats, and Mr. Kottke could provide sheep and lambs." He scrawled at the bottom of her page. "The Andersons have a few camels, and the Bregenzers raise rabbits."

A half-hour later, Jenny closed her notebook. "Thank you so much, Pete. I do appreciate all your help. Especially with the delivery. I cannot imagine how difficult that will be to manage."

"It will be my pleasure." Pete handed her the pencil. "Anything for the students."

During the next few days, Pete informed Jenny which farmers agreed to loan their animals. This necessitated, of course, a lot of time together that Pete thoroughly enjoyed. Did Jenny like his company as well?

A week before the program, Mark Weston drove into the farm yard. He rolled down his window. "Pete, get in the car. We're going for a ride. I want to talk."

"Why?" Pete pointed to the snow-covered picnic table. "Can't we talk here?"

"You don't want this made public." Mark nodded to the seat.

"Fine." Pete got into the car. What could Mark possibly want?

Mark drove a short distance up the road. "A cousin visited me over Thanksgiving. He's from Nebraska, and he knows who you are. He told me how the people ran you out of town after you burned down a farmer's barn with all his animals inside."

Pete's face turned stone cold.

"What would Jenny say if she knew the truth about you?" Mark's words stung like the strike of a rattlesnake.

"I… um… well…" Pete gritted his teeth. "What do you want?"

"Leave Jenny alone. She's mine." Mark's face twisted into a snarl. "Tell her you can't help with the Christmas program."

"I can't do that." Pete clenched his fist between the car door and the seat. "She's counting on me."

"Find someone else to do it, or I'll tell everyone what I learned about you." Mark put the car in gear. "In fact, why don't you find a different town to hide in?" He made a U-turn and dropped Pete at the farm.

When he climbed out of the car, Pete's legs buckled. He stumbled to the back of the shed and collapsed against the wall. How could he possibly defend himself? While it had been his decision to leave Grand Island, the community did drive him out with their contempt for him. And he did burn the barn down with his careless drinking. He had no defense for the truth.

Pete's pulse raced. What would Jenny think if she knew the truth? She wouldn't want anything to do with him.

And Tommy! He wanted to be like Pete. He'd hate him now.

The Hermanns treated him like a son. They wouldn't trust him anymore.

And all the other farmers who called upon him as their vet. They wouldn't want him in their barns after they knew about his past.

Memories from Grand Island came rushing back: the cold stares, the harsh words. Pete dissolved into tears. "Oh, God," he whispered, "what am I going to do?"

Olivia came out the back door and skipped toward him, her blonde curls bouncing.

He had to get away. "Olivia, tell your Daddy that I went into town." Tears streaming, he ran down the driveway. He needed the river. But when he got there, he couldn't stop. He needed Joe.

Pete burst into the meat market, out of breath. "Pete, what's the matter?"

Joe held Pete by both arms and shook him. "What's wrong?"

"I've lost everything. Everything." Pete gripped his right temple with his palm.

"Come upstairs. We'll talk." He led Pete upstairs to their living room. "What did you lose?"

How could Pete explain?

"What did you lose, Pete?" Joe's voice, so caring, gentle, and loving triggered more tears. He handed Pete a hanky and rubbed Pete's shoulder. "Nothing you tell me would shock me, Pete. I'm a good listener, and it will stay between us."

Pete gnawed his lower lip. How could he tell Joe? But then again, how could he not? What else did he have to lose? Even if he left town, Mark would tell everyone about him. Joe and Dolly would hear anyway.

"Mark Weston came to me today and told me to leave town. If I don't, he'll tell everyone about my past."

"What about your past?"

Pete puffed his cheeks. "I lost my wife and daughter within days of each other. The anniversary of my daughter's birthday, I drank during the night in a farmer's barn while treating his horse for pneumonia." His shoulders shook. "Somehow, I must have knocked over the lantern and caught the barn on fire." After another deep breath, Pete wiped his wet cheek with his sleeve. "I slept so sound that I didn't wake up in time to get the animals out of the barn. I almost didn't get out myself."

Joe gripped his arm. "Oh, Pete."

"The farmer lost everything, and the townspeople shunned me. I had to make a new start. Find people who would trust me again. I thought I had found it here in Kathleen Creek. But, now I've lost that, too."

With a slight twitch of his jaw, Joe steepled his fingers. "You didn't drink after that?"

Pete shook his head.

Joe blinked several times. "As I see it, drinking caused the mistake you made, right?"

Pete nodded.

With a light touch to Pete's arm, Joe made circles with his thumb. "As long as you remember that, you're not likely to repeat the mistake, right?"

Pete nodded again. "But no one will trust me if—"

"Now, that isn't entirely true, Pete." Joe pointed his finger at his own chest. "People make allowances for each other because they've all made their own mistakes. If you prove you don't go to the bottle as soon as things get tough, people forget."

"But Mark will make everyone see the worst of it." Pete massaged the bridge of his nose.

"Maybe Mark wants you out of the way because Jenny might like you better than him." Joe chuckled. "Are you sweet on Jenny?"

"A little." Pete swallowed. "But, I don't have anything to offer her. I don't know if she could ever be interested in me."

"Mark must think so, or he wouldn't be so eager to get rid of you." Joe slapped him on the shoulder. "You know, Pete, this depression isn't going to last forever. In another year or so you could have your own practice again. Don't give up on us. We need you here."

Dolly gave a loud squeal from downstairs. Laughter followed. "Ben, Ben, you've come home!"

47

Both Joe and Pete ran down the steps into the café. Cookie had wrapped Dolly in his arms.

Tears covered her cheeks in unabashed joy. Joe joined them, as customers wiped tears away. After Cookie's parents released him, they stood back.

"Pete is here." Joe stepped aside.

"Preacher!" Cookie lunged for Pete and engulfed him in a hug.

"Preacher?" Joe and Dolly both quirked their brows.

"That's what we called him in the jungles." Cookie laughed. "He always read his Bible, gave advice, and helped people. It's good to see you, Preacher."

Pete hugged him again. "It's good to see you, too, Cookie."

"Here, sit at this table." Joe indicated chairs. "What can I get you? Are you hungry? Dolly, bring them some coffee to start with."

Pete slid into the seat. "How long will you be here?"

Cookie took his place opposite Pete. "The CCC gave us time off for the holiday. I get two weeks."

The two men ate a roast beef dinner with Joe and Dolly stopping at their table as often as they could.

Joe even closed early. "Pete, I insist you spend the night with us so you and Ben can catch up."

Pete caught the flicker of worry in Joe's face before he disappeared. Joe wanted to keep an eye on him. Still, what a joy to spend time with Cookie. He called Gunther to let him know that he wouldn't be back until morning.

When Joe and Dolly went to bed, Cookie and Pete went downstairs to the closed café so they wouldn't keep Joe and Dolly awake. It felt good being together again.

Toward dawn, Cookie broke down with his own tears. "If you hadn't told me that my father quit drinking, I wouldn't be here today. I can't believe the change in him. Drinking is a terrible thing. It destroys both the drinker and everyone around him."

Pete knew that to be true. The dreadful flames filled his mind, lapping up the barn while the animals screamed. The accusations and disdainful glares. Drinking was a terrible thing. Mark had certainly brought that point back to light. With a grimace, Pete faced the window. What could he do about Mark? How soon would the whole town know his past?

Cookie's words blended to gibberish.

"I'm sorry, Cookie. What did you say?"

"You're deep in thought, Preacher. Is everything all right?"

Pete forced a smile. "Sure. The money I get every month has made all the difference in my life. If my clients paid me, I could probably have a practice again." He turned away from the window and met Cookie's eyes. "I'm going to start saving for a car as soon as I have a few more vet tools and supplies. I don't know how I'll ever repay you, Cookie. This should be your money, not mine."

"How many times do I have to tell you?" Cookie shook his

head. "I have everything I need right now. I want you to have the money."

"I should be putting it in the bank for you." Pete backed away from the table.

"The only thanks I need is for you to establish a practice here in Kathleen Creek so when I come back home someday, you'll be here, rich and happy. Then you can help me get established in something. Fair enough?"

"It's a deal, my friend." Pete squeezed Cookie's hand as they shook on it. "We'd better get some sleep. I have to work tomorrow." The first rays of morning sun peeked through the window. "I mean, today."

Both men slept late, but Dolly had bacon and eggs ready for them when they came downstairs. "I heard noises up there, so I knew you'd be down soon." She set hot plates in front of them, then leaned down and kissed Cookie on the forehead. "I still can't believe you're here."

After breakfast the men arranged for another visit, and Pete took off for the farm. To his chagrin, he arrived after chores.

"Did you have a nice visit with your friend?" Gunther tugged the milk pails toward the barn.

"I sure did. I'm sorry I missed chores, but we sat up and talked until dawn."

"Well, I think we'll cut wood today. The snow is not too deep yet." Gunther trudged a few paces forward. "Better dress warm."

Pete wore the long wool underwear and wool socks Lavinia had given him, along with the heavy winter coat, scarf, fur-lined cap with earflaps, and leather chopper mitts with wool liners. They hitched the team to the wagon and drove through the pasture until they entered an area of ash, boxelder, maple, and cottonwood trees. "Do you know how to use the cross-cut saw?"

"No."

"Here, you take one end and I take the other. Never push. Just pull. Like this." Gunther set the saw blade against a log lying on the ground. "Did you get hold of that handle? Good. Now, I pull and you keep the saw straight." He moved the blade across the branch and created the first cut. When the saw passed through, he nodded. "Now you pull."

Pete eased the saw through the branch creating a deeper cut. They pulled it back and forth until the log fell in two pieces. The strenuous movement kept Pete's blood circulating, with the exception of his fingers and toes. With a lot of stomping and flexing, Pete kept them warm as well.

By noon, Pete's back ached, but they had a wagon filled with cut and split, wood. They headed home to a delicious, hot dinner and an hour's rest. Then, they hitched the team again and cut more wood until milking time, with only a short mid-afternoon break for coffee and sandwiches Lavinia had sent with them.

Pete couldn't worry over Mark's threat until he herded the cows home from the pasture. But then, it weighed heavy on his shoulders. What options did he have? He could leave. But where would he go? Besides, he didn't want to leave. And who was to say the same thing might not happen in another town?

If he stayed, then what? Would Mark really tell everyone about him? Of course, he would. Then what would happen? Pete cringed. That scene at the café in Grand Island… Everyone looked at him with angry eyes and pinched mouths, shaking their heads in accusation. The people ignoring his greetings, looking away from him as if he disgusted them.

He couldn't go through that again.

How could he convince Mark not to spread his story around? What did Mark want? To leave Jenny alone.

Give up Jenny? How could he? Why… Why, he loved Jenny. Each time they had met to discuss the Christmas Program, he'd fallen deeper. Jenny might feel the same way.

But how would she feel after Mark told her about him?

She'd never trust him. An unreliable man, "run out of town." To be seen with him would bring her shame.

It was unfair. He'd changed. But how could he convince anyone of that? Who would trust him? Certainly not the farmers.

Dizziness covered him as Mr. Donaldson's words came back: *"I'll not be calling on you no more, Doctor Walters, no siree! Not one farmer will trust you now, Doctor. Not a drinking man who doesn't know his responsibilities. No siree! You got no business here, Doctor. Go!"*

"Why are you standing there like that? Are you sick? You don't look good." Gunther peered into Pete's eyes. "Close the door, Pete."

Pete obeyed then steadied himself against a support beam.

"No, you don't look good." Gunther took Pete by the arm and led him to the house.

Pete numbly followed.

"Lavinia, Pete don't look good. I think he's sick. It's cold in the barn. Can you put him to bed in the house?"

Lavinia took Pete's arm. "I'll put him in Olivia's room. She can sleep with the girls. Come, Pete. Do you have a fever?" She placed her hand on his forehead. "You don't feel feverish. Do you have a cold? Is it your stomach?"

He managed to shake his head, but she dragged him up the stairs and into a bedroom decorated in pink and purple. Dolls and a teddy bear lay on the bed. "Let me help you with your coat."

She removed his outer clothes and his shoes. "I'll leave you to finish undressing. Get into bed. I'll go downstairs and get you something hot." She removed the toys from the bed and turned down the covers.

Pete didn't deserve the love being heaped upon him. He broke into loud, pitiful sobs.

"Oh, Pete." Lavinia rubbed his arm. "Where do you hurt? Do you need a doctor?"

Pete could only shake his head.

"I'll get Gunther." Lavinia hurried out of the room.

Shame washed over Pete. Crying like a baby! And how could he explain it? He had to calm down. By the time Gunther tromped up the stairs, two at a time in his heavy boots, Pete's breathing had slowed.

"What's the matter, Pete? Do you need a doctor?"

"No, I need a good night's sleep. I'm sure I'll feel better tomorrow." Pete stood straighter. "Don't worry about me."

The creases in Gunther's forehead deepened. "Were you at the saloon last night?"

"No." Pete leaned against the bed. "We spent the whole evening at the café and upstairs at Joe and Dolly's. But we talked 'til dawn. Maybe I'm worn out. I'm sure I'll be fine tomorrow. I'm sorry."

After a few moments, Gunther turned to go.

Lavinia lingered. "What would you like? Coffee? Something to eat?"

"I'd like to sleep, if that's okay."

She fluffed his pillow. "Okay. You sleep."

"Thank you." As she closed the door, Pete crawled under the sheets and closed his eyes.

The crowing of the rooster woke him. Where was he? Oh, right. He had slept all night in Olivia's bed. And where had the poor girl slept?

He got out of bed and slipped a leg into his pants. A glass of milk and a sandwich sat on the table next to the bed. He gulped them down and went out to help with chores.

Gunther sat on a stool milking a cow. His face lit up when Pete approached. "How do you feel?"

"I'm fine." Pete grabbed the other stool and moved to the

next cow down the aisle. They milked in silence until Pete took the can to separate.

Gunther came in, cocked his head toward Pete, and grabbed the skim milk. He met Pete's gaze again and shuffled out the door.

Back to life on the farm. Pete smiled.

But wait. Back to life until Mark told his secret. His shoulders heaved. What should he do?

They spent the morning working in the woods with the cross-cut saw, cutting dead and storm-damaged trees. White vapor escaped with each breath. Rabbits played nearby and the calls of crows and chickadees filled the air.

In the afternoon, they brought out the circular buzz saw, powered by a one-cylinder gasoline engine mounted on a wagon chassis. They cut the logs into pieces, and by evening they had another wagon load of wood.

All day, each of the Hermanns' furtive gazes darted toward Pete. Over supper, Lavinia patted his shoulder. "Pete, Gunther and I talked about how cold it must be in the barn at night. We decided it's time you slept in the house. Olivia is happy to move in with the other girls. She'll sleep with them again tonight, and tomorrow we'll get an extra bed. After supper you can bring your belongings into your room and no one will touch your things. I've removed Olivia's things so the room is all yours. You'll be comfortable there."

Pete opened his mouth then clamped it shut. How could he accept their kindness? After swallowing, coughing, and clearing his throat, he took a deep breath. "I'm, ah…" He cleared his throat again. "I'm grateful. Thank you."

He kept his eyes in his lap until he could lift his fork with a steady hand. Then he finished eating without making eye contact with anyone. Lavinia tried to keep table talk going, but the conversations fell flat, shallow, and disjointed.

"If you don't mind, I'm still very tired." Pete pushed his plate back and stood. "May I be excused?" He held his tears until he made it to the barn. How could he leave the Hermanns? But what would they think of him if he didn't?

It took a while before he could go back into the house with his pack. The family all raised their chins when he came into the kitchen. He nodded and he went up the stairs to his room. His own room! A comfortable bed to sleep in every night. A safe place for his belongings. Though he didn't deserve it. *Thank you, Lord.*

But how long would this last? Maybe Mark had already told Jenny about him. The long and restless night offered no solution, and he finally fell into a listless sleep.

The next morning Pete professed to feeling fine and sleeping fine. He thanked them again. They cut firewood all day again, eager to bring in enough wood before a heavy snowfall. After supper, Pete went into town to see Cookie.

"I thought you'd be here last night." The lilt in Cookie's voice faded.

"I thought I'd give you one night with your parents, or your friends, before I descended upon you again."

"I'm glad you're here. We're going to have a sleigh ride." Cookie grinned. "If you didn't show up, we'd a'come and picked you up. You won't know any of my friends, but you'll get to know them soon enough. Morrie has the sleigh. Here he comes now."

A noisy crowd of laughing young people pulled up in front of the café, parking beneath the gaslight. Cookie and Pete jumped on. In the semi-darkness, a female voice whispered, "Come sit here, Dr. Pete."

"Okay," he whispered back. He slid into the seat and faced the woman. Jenny! But where was Mark? Not onboard at least. For tonight, he'd relax and enjoy the camaraderie as they rode out into the countryside, singing and laughing.

Even in her heavy coat, Pete dwarfed Jenny. A hint of

lavender wafted up when he leaned closer to hear what she said. Every time she laughed, a tingle shot through his belly. Sweet Jenny—humorous and fun, and so beautiful in the moonlight. Oh, how he wanted to kiss her.

When the driver turned the team toward town, the wind hit their faces. Jenny shivered. Pete hugged her and pulled her closer. She settled into the fold of his arms as if she belonged there. Now, he really wanted to kiss her. Excruciating.

The noise in the sleigh settled to soft whispers as the passengers snuggled closer. They drove past snow-laden tree branches gleaming in the moonlight. An owl hooted, and far in the distance, the eerie yips of a pack of coyotes interrupted the peaceful clip-clopping of the team.

Someone started singing "Oh Mighty God," and others chimed in until they pulled into town, as noisy as they left it.

Morrie glanced over his shoulder. "Cookie, you and Pete want to get off here? I'll bring the others back to where I picked them up."

Pete dragged himself away from Jenny.

Her hand lingered over his arm. "Come to the school house tomorrow afternoon."

Her whisper sent tingles coursing through him. "Okay."

Mark would likely kill him, but how could he say no?

He hopped off after Cookie, waving his goodbyes to the others. After he and Cookie entered the closed café, he paused at the foot of the steps. "How come Jenny Howe came there alone?"

"Jenny rents a room from the Dixons'. They invited her to come with them." Cookie winked in the dim light. "How do you know Jenny? You two looked pretty cozy."

Pete stuffed his hands in his pockets. "I'm helping her organize some live animals for the Christmas Program."

"Be sure to invite me to your wedding." Cookie snickered.

"I don't have anything to offer Jenny." Pete's cheeks warmed. "How can I even start a courtship with her?"

"Preacher, you've got to get on with your life. We'll get rain one of these years and the farmers will get back on their feet so they can pay you. This won't go on forever. You better grab onto her and hold on so someone else doesn't snatch her up. You looked good together."

If only that was all he had to worry about!

Pete called the Hermanns and stayed the night with Cookie again. He returned the next day in time for chores, and they spent the day cutting firewood, the two men working together like a well-seasoned team.

But for how long?

Two weeks before Christmas. Pete and Gunther continued to cut more firewood. Mark's threat still hung over Pete's head like an anvil.

Beautiful quiet snow peppered oak leaves that hung tightly to their branches when they should have fallen long ago. Those leaves didn't cave in. Would he cave in to Mark's demand? What would happen if he told Gunther about his past? He grabbed the other end of the cross-saw and pulled in tandem with the good, honest, understanding man on the other end. Should he tell him?

"I have to go into town late this afternoon." Pete jumped back as the dead branch fell. He would meet Jenny, as promised. At least he knew that much.

Gunther nodded, and shortly after their afternoon break he put the saws on the wagon. "We can call it a day."

They brought the wood home, and Pete hopped off the wagon. "Gunther, I hate to not help unload, but I don't want to be late." He took off down the driveway. By the time he got to Jenny, frostbite nipped at his fingers and toes. He hovered next to the wood stove at the back of the school house for a long time.

"I forgot that you don't have a car." Jenny came up behind him, her lips pressed thin.

"I'm saving for a car." Heat crept up from Pete's neck to his ears.

"I wanted to have everything in place for the program Friday night." Jenny moved things around on her desk. "The kids are so excited. They've worked hard on learning their recitations." She tucked hair into her dark, full bun at the back of her head. "Tommy is proud that he can play Joseph. He keeps telling me you're going to be here to watch him."

"I know. He talks about it every time I see him." Pete took off his snow-damped hat and placed it on a table near the stove. "He says he hasn't had to stay after school lately."

"I've never seen such a change in a student. Your friendship with Tommy turned him into a different kid. He idolizes you, you know." Jenny tipped up her chin as if she, too, idolized him. He took a step closer to her and put one hand on her shoulder. Would she back away?

Her breath quickened with his pulse, and the corners of her mouth curved upward. With his other hand, he cupped her face She stepped closer, close enough for him to lean down and brush her lips with his. She didn't move.

The scent of sweet vanilla danced between them, and Pete tasted a hint of cinnamon on her soft skin. He caught his fingers in the wispy strands of gingerbread-colored hair that had escaped from her loose bun. Her gray eyes glistened with tears. Had she, like Pete, waited for this moment? Dreamed of it, even?

She tugged him closer, and he wrapped her in a tight embrace. With a sigh, she wound her arms around him as he deepened the kiss.

So perfect. And everything he thought it would be. If only

Pete could hold her like that forever. If he could have her close always. Marry her.

Mark's face flashed in his mind, and Pete released her. What would she think when Mark told her about his past?

He straightened and squared his shoulders. "Do you need help with anything else?" Inwardly wincing at his business-like voice, he took a few paces back from her.

Tears hung at the corners of Jenny's eyes. "I hoped you'd help me put up the curtains." A deep frown tainted her lovely face.

The lump Pete had carried in his throat for weeks tripled in size. His jaw twitching, he swallowed. "Sure, where are the curtains?"

She brought out a coil of wire and sheets fashioned with rod pockets. "I'd like to hang one side there," she pointed, "and the other over by that shelf."

He tapped a hook into the wall and looped the wire around it then helped her thread the curtains. When they finished, he attached the wire to the other wall. "That should work well." With a wry grin, he passed her the hammer and wire cutters.

"Thanks for your help, Pete." She carried the tools to a basket on her desk.

"Anything else?" He held his breath and unbuttoned the neck of his shirt. He needed to get out of this room.

"No, we're ready for the program. Is everything in place for bringing in the sheep?"

Pete nodded.

"I hope it works out well. They've never had live animals in the school house before. At least sheep won't make quite the mess other animals might."

"It will." Pete crossed the room and donned his hat. How he hated to leave, but it was best. "I have to get back for chores. I'll see you at the program. Good luck with everything."

He lingered at the door. Though his pounding heart demanded he kiss her again, he forced himself to turn and leave.

All the way home the memory of the kiss kept him warm.

Jenny liked him. If he left town, he would have no chance of a future with her. But if he stayed, Mark would tell her everything, and he'd lose her anyway. How could he win in this situation? *Lord, tell me what to do.*

At the farm, Pete grabbed a barn stool. He milked in silence next to Gunther, a comfortable sharing of duties, as usual. At supper, the children led the table conversation about the upcoming Christmas Program. Excitement ran high as they each recited their piece for the others.

Olivia stumbled over her words. "The stars shine... the stars..."

Bonnie giggled. "The stars shine bright in the heavens tonight."

"The stars shine bright in the heavens tonight, and the... the..." Olivia frowned.

"And the moon glows high overhead." Tammy patted her hand.

After supper, Pete emptied the water from the icebox and dried the separator parts that Lavinia washed. Then he retreated to his room to write a letter to Pastor Jim and Karen.

On Friday, Pete penned the designated program animals outside the back door of the school house and dashed back to the farm for chores, supper and dressing for the evening. He crowded into the car with the Hermanns as they rode to the school house. Lavinia held her special Red Velvet cake in an aluminum pan on her lap. Each of the girls wore the dresses they had worn for their aunt's wedding, except now long, brown stockings had been added to keep them warm.

They had only been in the school room a few minutes when Mark swaggered up to Pete. "I thought you'd be gone by now." He spoke quietly through clenched teeth.

Pete narrowed his gaze. "I needed to help with the program."

"I'll give you three more days." Mark smirked. Guess he thought he'd won.

Pete's shoulders slumped. And Mark probably had won. Now, where was Jenny? Ah, yes. Behind the curtain with her students. He went out to ready the animals for their manger scene.

After the program, Pete safely penned the animals again and returned inside for food and fellowship. Mark stayed at Jenny's side the rest of the evening, though she cast several frowning glances toward Pete.

Once, Pete raised his eyebrows and his hands as if to say, "I want to talk to you, too, but I understand." At the end of the program, he met her by punch bowl. He gave a stiff nod to Mark and flashed her a quick smile. "It was a wonderful program, Miss Howe."

Tommy rushed up beside them, dragging Pete forward in the line for refreshments. "Did you see me, Mr. Pete? Did you see me?"

Pete ruffled his hair. "You did a great job, Tommy. Those other kids seem to like you."

"I don't fight with them anymore." Tommy fidgeted in his costume as his mother came up behind them.

"I'm proud of you, Tommy." Pete knelt to his eye level. "The only time you should fight with someone is if you're protecting someone else."

"I know, you told me that." Tommy gave him a dimpled grin.

"It's a good thing to remember."

"Oh, I forgot to get a cookie. And I want another piece of cake." Tommy ran back to the table, leaving his mother alone with Pete."

Pete chuckled. "He's a good kid, Mrs. Lazar."

"He needs a father." She gave Pete a hard pat on the arm.

Pete wiggled his toes in his shoes. How could he respond to that?

"Pete, I tell you, it was a good program." Farmer Kottke caught him by the elbow.

As Farmer Barthel pulled him away, Pete gave Mrs. Lazar a short wave. He'd worry about her later. For now, he needed to figure out what to do about Mark and Jenny.

That night, when he lay in bed trying to sleep, his eyes popped open. *David.*

He bolted upright. David? What David? The owner of the mercantile? Pete scratched his chin. Why would he think about him?

He fumbled beside his bed for his lantern, his hand coming to rest on his worn leather Bible. Wait. David in the Bible? King David had many enemies who threatened him. He'd also committed terrible transgressions and rose to be a man loved by God.

Pete jumped out of bed, lit the kerosene lamp, and picked up his Bible.

Psalms. That's what he wanted. The words that David had used when he felt the same kind of anguish that Pete felt. He found the page and read until he could no longer stay awake. He closed the Bible and blew out the light. He knew what he had to do. *Dear Lord, please give me your protection and blessing. And give me courage.* With that, he fell soundly asleep.

After only a few hours of sleep, he woke to a festive Saturday, the first day of Christmas vacation for the girls. As soon as they finished breakfast, they asked to be excused and ran upstairs to play in their room.

As Gunther rose from the table, Pete tugged at his sleeve. "Can we sit for a few minutes more? I have something I want to tell both of you."

Gunther sat again. "Would you like a little more coffee?"

Pete held out his cup. "Sure. Thanks."

Lavinia poured the rest of the coffee for Pete, herself, and

Gunther, and put the pot to the back part of the stove. When she sat opposite him, she leaned forward. "What is it, Pete?"

"I told you about my desire to move to Texas after my wife and daughter died, but I didn't tell you the whole story. I'd like to tell you now."

"Okay." Gunther sipped his coffee, and Lavinia rested her elbows on the table.

"Almost two years ago, my wife and daughter both died days before Christmas." Pete's hands trembled and he set his cup down on the table. "Last December, during a terrible snowstorm, I got called out to a farm to treat a horse with a bad case of pneumonia. I started drinking earlier that evening." He lowered his gaze. They would hate him within minutes. "It would have been my daughter's sixth birthday that day, and I had a hard time dealing with my memories. I spent the night in this farmer's barn to keep an eye on his horse. Late that night, I took the lantern from the hook and went to check on the other animals in the barn. Then I must have set the lantern next to me and went to sleep. At least, that's what I think happened." Pete took a deep breath and interlocked his fingers. "I had a bottle with me and had kept drinking."

"Oh, Pete." Lavinia reached across the table and squeezed his hand.

Pete pulled away. He didn't deserve her affection. "The next thing I knew, the barn had caught fire. Flames spread quickly, and the fire blocked the back door." His voice cracked. "I couldn't get the front doors open because snow had drifted high against the door."

Pete trained his focus on the grains of the table. After several labored breaths, he pressed his palm against his forehead. "I almost passed out with the smoke, but I broke a window and got out. The animals all died, and the barn burned to the ground.

"Those shrieks and screams... the flames, lapping at the

wood... I..." Pete's voice dropped to a whisper. Tears fell unchecked. "They lost the farm. She was in the family way with their first child."

Lavinia sniffled.

Pete wiped his face with his handkerchief and blew his nose. "After that, none of the farmers called me for vet services. They didn't trust me anymore. I couldn't take the guilt and the shame so I left Grand Island for a new start." He pressed his spread palms on the table as though that would steady his quivering hands. "The rest I already told you."

They sipped their coffee in silence. Finally, Lavinia cleared her throat. "Why are you telling us this?"

"I wanted you to know the truth. You trust me. You've invited me into your home. I wanted to be totally honest with you. You deserve that." He stood. "Gunther, Lavinia, if you want me to leave, I will. I don't want to. I've grown fond of all of you, but it's up to you. I'll leave you alone to talk about it."

He put on his coat and hat and went to the barn.

With his face skyward, he dragged open the barn door. "Lord, be merciful on me." But such a huge weight had lifted off his shoulders. What happened next was in God's hands, but like David, he had asked for God's love and mercy. God loved him enough to give him that. He climbed to the hayloft, picked up a hay fork, and threw down hay for the cows.

He'd finished and climbed down from the loft when Gunther came into the barn. "What happened to the farmer and his wife?"

"They live in my old house. He works as a clerk in the hardware store." Pete let out a long, deep breath. "They had a beautiful baby boy. I've kept in contact with my pastor and his wife, and they've kept me updated."

Gunther sat on the bench along the wall, whittling a long stick. Pete paced along the opposite wall. What would Gunther say?

Finally, Gunther lifted his head. "I think we will make ice cream. We have ice in the ice house. I'll bring some cream into the kitchen and ask Lavinia to mix up a batch while we get the rock salt and ice ready in the ice cream mixer." He jumped up and hurried out the barn door.

"What should I do?" Pete called after him.

"Take your turn crankin' the handle with the rest of the family."

## 49

Jenny pressed her palm against the school house window frame, the fog from her breath creating a large circle on the glass. Her plan to get Pete's attention had certainly worked. Better than she'd anticipated, actually.

She'd felt nervous, about seeing Pete again, but she did not expect the song in her heart as she greeted him at the school house that day. Oh, the sight of him, clean-shaven and dressed in new clothes and boots. His short, wavy hair shined. A tiny shiver traveled up her arm. The feel of his hair in her hands, clean and soft as she had raked her fingers through it when they'd kissed. If only she could jump into his arms and stay there forever. What was the matter with her?

She found him so intriguing. Like the bad scar on his neck. Maybe a burn? Without his long hair and beard, it was more noticeable. She had wanted to ask him about it, but never found the right time. She managed to maintain a professional demeanor in spite of her yearning heart, as they discussed what animals would work best, where she might borrow such animals, and how it would all come together for the program.

The more he helped her, the more she fell in love with Pete. Yet he held her at a friendly distance.

And then, that last visit. Her arms around him, his hands cupping her face. Jenny stepped away from the window and carried a stack of books from the back desk to a front shelf. What would her parents say? They would be horrified. They would insist that she come back to Minneapolis immediately and get her head on straight.

After all, hadn't she lost her mind? She knew only a few things about Pete. He'd been a veterinarian, he'd taken it upon himself to mentor a troubled boy, he worked as a farm hand, and Rosemary Johnson called him her friend. That all said a lot about what kind of man he was. Yet so many questions remained unanswered. Was he, or had he ever been, married? Did he have children? Where did he come from? What about his parents and siblings? And... how did he feel about her?

She didn't feel it appropriate to ask those questions while they worked on the Christmas program, yet they plagued her during her free hours and kept her from sleeping. She had made excuses for not seeing Mark the last two times he asked her out, but she couldn't continue to do that without him getting suspicious.

She couldn't help but find Mark coming up short in comparison to Pete. She now knew she didn't love him. She couldn't feel such a strong attraction to Pete if she loved Mark. She'd have to tell Mark at some time, but not right before Christmas.

When Pete sat next to her on the sleigh ride, she hoped he couldn't hear how hard her heart pounded. Had he realized she'd melted when he'd pulled her closer to him? She thrilled at his deep bass voice as they sang together and felt a twinge of disappointment when the driver announced he'd drop Pete and Ben off first.

And then, she'd invited Pete to come to the school house.

Oh, that kiss. His lips so soft and warm, and the kiss so

tender it made her head spin. He'd reached for her and held her while her heart turned to mush. At first, she'd thought he didn't ever want to let her go, but after his abrupt release, he'd practically pushed her away. What had happened? Had he remembered that he was married or something?

What had she done wrong?

And then, the Christmas program itself…

Attendees heralded it a great success, the live animals a popular added attraction with Pete's assistance. After the program, when Jenny mingled with the parents and other guests, Mark stuck by her side like a cockle burr, an irritant she couldn't get rid of.

Not only that, but he had his hand on her back, shoulder, or arm. He kept taking her hand in his, as if claiming her as his property.

Across the room, she thought Pete had glanced her way a few times. Who could tell, with that pesky fly buzzing close to him all evening? Mrs. Lazar certainly seemed to stake her claim to Pete. Between her and Mark, Pete had only gotten close enough to congratulate Jenny once after the program.

Yet, the earnest look in his eye heartened her. He did seem to want to be closer, to talk with her, and to be with her. At least his kiss had said as much.

She was right in her feelings. She knew it. But the sliver of doubt crept back in. On Sunday, they crossed paths at church for a brief moment in the back hallway near the bathroom. He caught her as she swept by. "Can I see you this afternoon?"

Her cheeks warmed. "I…" Could she get away from Mark? She'd find a way. "Okay."

After dinner Pete met her at the schoolhouse. "Would you like to go to the Merriweather for coffee and pie?"

She gave him a warm smile as he took her arm.

They strolled through the warmest air of the week as soft

snow came down about them. Pete requested a window seat, and they both ordered coffee and pumpkin pie.

"So, Jenny," Pete twirled his spoon in the swirl of whipped cream topping. "Tell me about your family and your hometown."

"I grew up in Minneapolis, Minnesota where my parents still live. I'm an only child." She paused and played with the crumbs of her crust. What else should she tell him? That she'd failed in two serious relationships but she thought she loved him? Yeah, right.

"I'm an only child as well." Good. Pete filled the silence. "And how long have you taught at Kathleen Creek?" He seemed to savor the pie as though he hadn't tasted it before.

Jenny's shoulders relaxed and a wide smile spanned her cheeks. "Two years. I love the students and so enjoy my job. What about you?"

At the next table, two people stood to leave. Maybe that would permit the privacy he needed.

"I'm from Grand Island, Nebraska. And Jenny, I need to tell you my story." He swallowed, and her heart went out to him. What terrible things had this man lived through?

"I was married once, with a beautiful daughter, Rose." His lips quivered. "I lost them both to tragic, early deaths. And I... well, a year later, I needed a new start. I headed out to Dallas with all my veterinary equipment. Almost as soon as I arrived, someone stole my car, and a gang robbed me of my money. I was left with no choice but to ride the rails until I could find work."

She shook her head. "Oh, Pete. I'm so sorry."

He drummed his fingers on the table. There was more to the story, she was sure of it. What was Pete not telling her?

His blue eyes softened. "Anyway, enough about me. I should congratulate you again on the wonderful Christmas program." Laugh lines gathered at the corners of his mouth. "My favorite part was the runaway sheep. Everyone in that audience got a good laugh."

"That they did." She laughed with him and then sighed. "I suppose you noticed that Mark Weston seemed tethered to me all evening."

"Yes. I didn't know your relationship, so I thought it best to not interfere." Pete rubbed his hands under the table. He must be so nervous. Jenny longed to reach out and steady them.

"Last year I dated him a few times. Nothing serious." She shrugged. "This year, he seems to think I belong to him. He asked me to go sleigh riding with him tonight, but I told him I had other plans. The Dixons think I should marry him." With a toss of her hair, she scoffed. "Not that he's asked me. He likes to play a lot."

"What do you mean by 'play' a lot?" Pete frowned and took a bite of his pie.

"He's always going on hunting or fishing trips or to out-of-town baseball games. He can get away whenever he wants to go. His family has money, and Mark makes good money, but he's too immature for a serious relationship with anyone."

His fork mid-air, Pete leaned forward. "Do you like him, though?"

"Not really. He thinks he's better than other people. I don't like that about him."

Pete's scowl cut Jenny to the heart, though it softened at her words. He must like knowing she didn't approve of Mark's behavior, especially how terribly Mark had treated him before he had his haircut and got a shave.

As they left the hotel restaurant, Pete stumbled over the last step. She slipped her fingers into his, and he faced her, pulling away. "I still need to tell you something. Where might we talk privately?"

PETE SHIVERED in the severe cold. Jenny must be freezing in her thin dress, even with her heavy coat.

She blinked up at him, her frosty breath swirling around her dainty face. "Would you like to help me clean up the school house? It was too late after the program to do much."

"Sure." Pete followed her down the path. With the guise of helping to clean, they could be alone together without the appearance of impropriety. When they reached the school, he built a fire in the stove. They took down the curtain and wire, swept the floor, and re-arranged the desks. Then they sat on top of the desks closest to the stove. Pete slipped Jenny's tiny fingers between his callused ones. "I like you a lot, Miss Jenny."

She put both hands in Pete's and squeezed. "I like you a lot, too, Dr. Pete."

Pete's breath caught. Oh, how he wanted to kiss her. But first, he had to get through the difficult talk. He cleared his throat. "Jenny, I need to tell you something."

Deep wrinkles creased her forehead. "What is it, Pete?"

"Everything I told you about me is the truth. But there's more." He cleared his throat again. "When my wife and daughter died, I soothed myself by drinking." Her gaze hardened, and he held up his palm. "I know I shouldn't have. Believe me, I learned that lesson."

His chest tightened. "One night, I helped a friend with a sick horse. Stayed overnight in the barn, since poor Gertie had pneumonia."

Her eyes widened, and Pete puffed his cheeks. "The horse, I mean. Gertie was the horse."

He fanned his face and blasted out another puff of air. "I had a lantern. Carried it with me to check the animals, and I... I..." He gulped loud when he swallowed. "I must have set the lantern down in the straw. I was still drinking, and I... I..."

Her face. So stoic. What was she thinking?

"The animals were trapped. By the time I woke, I couldn't

get them out. Snow had blocked the door to the barn and…" Was she even still listening? With one final heave of his chest, he closed his eyes. "I got out a window. Alvin, my friend, and his wife… they lost everything. So I left town." He swung his feet, striking the desk with his heel. "I signed over my house to them and took off for Dallas. There. That's my story."

Jenny sat icily still. Then, she pulled her hands from his and got up from the desk.

Pete reached after her, but she moved away from him. With her back to him, she bowed her head. What else could he say? She sure wasn't talking. Should he wait?

After several long, silent minutes, Pete got his coat. "I'll go then. If you never want to see me again, I'll understand." He put on his hat and drew it down over his eyes. "I haven't had a drink since, and I don't intend to ever have another one. I'm a good vet, Jenny. I want to set up a practice here in Kathleen Creek as soon as I have enough money to buy a car and rent office space. I want to have another family someday."

No answer.

"Goodbye, Miss Jenny. I'll put out the fire."

"Leave it. I have papers to grade."

"Goodbye." Pete closed the door behind him.

The bitter wind cut through him like a sharp knife. It took his breath away as he fled from the school house. He'd hoped that Jenny would accept his past with the same forgiveness as the Hermanns. Well, that hope was smashed to smithereens! She would probably never speak to him again.

Marrying him would bring shame to her. She would be as ostracized as he might soon be. Mark would make sure that the whole community learned his story. He couldn't blame Jenny for not wanting anything more to do with him.

As he raced on past the meat market, Dolly waved from the porch. "Pete! Pete! Did you forget you planned to visit with Ben today?"

Pete stopped in his tracks. He had forgotten. He met her on the porch as Joe came up behind her. They both wore worried frowns.

Joe touched his arm. "Are you all right, Pete?"

"I guess so." Cookie would leave soon, and he didn't want to ruin their happy days. "Are you ready for me to beat you in another game of cribbage, Cookie?"

"You bet." Cookie tossed Pete his sideways grin.

They played two games while Joe and Dolly sat at the table, talking. Suddenly the bells of the Catholic church rang, fast and loud.

"Sunday at six? Something's wrong, Joe!" Dolly leapt up. At the same time loud voices called to one another on the street.

"The school house is on fire!" someone yelled.

"Jenny!" Pete dropped his cards on the table and hopped to his feet.

"Jenny?" Cookie scooted out of the chair.

"Jenny's in the school house!" Pete grabbed his coat and ran fast as he could. As soon as he reached the school grounds, he tapped a woman's shoulder. "Where's Jenny? Where's Jenny Howe? Has anyone seen Jenny?" He nudged his way through the crowd. Was she among the many people standing around watching gray smoke escape from the back of the building?

Pete fought dizziness. Smoke escaping from every crack in Alvin's barn. He shook his head.

Jason Dixon stood at the front of the crowd.

Pete shook his shoulder. "Where's Jenny?"

"I don't know." Jason swiveled his head. "I haven't seen her."

"Jenny's in there!" Pete ran to the door.

"You can't go in." Someone grabbed him and held him down.

"Jenny's in there!" He jerked himself free. When he opened the front door, the heat blasted him backward. He got up and crawled into the smoke-filled building. "Jenny! Jenny, where are you?"

Animal screams filled his ears as smoke filled his lungs, yet Pete heard faint church bells ringing and fire truck horns moving closer.

Pete kept as low as possible and searched by her desk. "Jenny!"

He made his way down the aisle of desks to the back of the room toward the stove. "Jenny!"

He tried to hold his breath. Smoke burned his eyes.

If he didn't get out of there, he would die. The door! He must be close to the back door.

He crawled a few feet further, but his world went black.

## 50

Jenny had been happy when Pete asked her out for pie and coffee, and she didn't even mind the bitter cold as they strolled arm-in-arm to the Merriweather. He'd seemed nervous, as though he resented the presence of other customers, and when the people at the nearest table rose to leave, definite relief crossed his face. Did Pete have a problem with people?

When Jenny expected Pete to talk about his relationship with her, he changed the subject. Yet, at the schoolhouse the day after the sleigh ride, when he'd had taken her hand and said he liked her a lot, it almost took her breath away. She'd wanted Pete to take her in his arms and kiss her again. But terror struck her heart when Pete said he had something to tell her because it echoed the day Jed had said the same. She didn't want to hear what Pete had to say. She wanted to run out of the school house.

His words sounded like an echo in a large empty drum that reverberated back to her, taunting her choice to pursue her attraction to him—her inability to make good choices.

He had nothing to offer her but more disgrace for her parents. They would not be able to withstand another onslaught of gossip and disgrace. She was, after all, their only daughter in whom they had such hope. How could she do that to them again? She should have known she'd make another mistake.

And Pete, being a drinker—her mother would never let her go through what she'd had to endure with her father's drinking. Pete had said he hadn't had a drink since, but was that true? Could Jenny trust he wouldn't drink again?

She'd tuned out his insistence that he'd changed. She didn't want to hear any more. Couldn't stand to hear any more. How could she have been so wrong once again?

And to face Mr. or Mrs. Dixon? They'd ask about her date with Pete. What could she say?

When she heard the school house door close, she had collapsed into a puddle of tears at her desk. By the time she finally stopped crying, the fire had gone out in the stove, and she no longer wanted to grade papers. Wrapping her scarf around her swollen, red face, she put on her coat and went out the door.

She'd reached her room unnoticed. Dropping onto the bed in her clothes, her total emotional exhaustion brought a deep sleep of escape in no time at all. When she awoke to a foreign noise, she blinked several times and bolted up. The church bells? But it wasn't Saturday night…

The darkness outside her window alternated with an orange, flickering light some distance away. Many voices yelled at once. Did she hear someone calling her name?

She jumped up and raced to the window. The school house was on fire! She threw on her shoes and coat, hurried out the door, and ran down the block. She had to shove her way through the crowd to get to the front.

Ben waved and pointed. "Pete's in there."

Over the noise of the crowd and the fire, someone yelled her name.

"I'm here! I'm here!" She clutched the buttons of her coat.

"Oh, no! Pete thinks I'm in there. He thinks I'm in there! Somebody get him out! Get him out!"

The volunteer firemen broke down the back door and found Pete lying face down. They moved him to the grass and hovered over him.

"I found a pulse!" One of the firemen waved to the crowd. "Someone call the doctor."

"Bring him to the Catholic Church. It's the closest." Joe lunged forward. With Ben and several other men, he carried Pete across the street. Jenny rushed in behind them as they laid him on the carpeted floor. Soon, Dr. Rushford came with his black bag, and the crowd of people parted to make room for him.

The Hermanns burst into the church.

"Is Pete okay?" Lavinia covered her tear-streaked face.

"We will pray. Surely he will be." He draped an arm over his wife's quivering shoulders.

As Dr. Rushford knelt at Pete's side, Jenny wrung her hands and cried.

Lavinia gasped labored breaths. "Oh, my Pete. Dear, sweet Pete."

Ben fell on his knees at one of the pews. "Lord, please watch over our friend, Preacher. Send a blessing of healing over him, and please, permit his full recovery."

The room buzzed with several conversations going at once until the priest burst in. "If you'll all take a seat I'll conduct a prayer service." People filed into the pews, and he took his place at the front of the church.

Mark burst in. "Pete Walters started the fire himself. I saw him coming out of the school house before the fire. In Nebraska they ran Pete out of town after he burned down a barn with all the animals in it. Now, he did it again."

"What do you mean? Pete didn't set the school on fire!" Jenny leapt from her pew and stomped her foot.

Gunther stood. "Pete told us all about what happened in Nebraska. It was an accident. He had been drinking, but he hasn't had a drink in a year. He's worked for me for six months and I'll vouch for him any time. He is so afraid of fire that he won't even light a lantern in the barn! He did not start the fire!"

"I don't believe Pete started the fire, either." Rosemary Johnson thumped her cane on the floor and pulled herself to her feet. "Dr. Walters is one of the kindest, most considerate men I have ever known. He cares about people. My position as postmistress of this town prohibits me from revealing everything I know, but I can tell you, he is not the kind of person who would burn down the school house!" Nose pointed upward, she faced several directions in the room. "I mean it. Dr. Pete's a good man!"

Mrs. Lazar and Tommy stood next. She wrapped an arm around her weeping son's shoulders. "Dr. Pete has mentored my son and made a huge difference in his life—in our lives. He teaches Tommy the things a caring father would teach him if he had one. He would never burn down the school that he tells Tommy is so important in his life."

Ben stood. "You know me as Ben, but Pete knows me as Cookie. He is my best friend. I know him better than anyone in this room. He saved my life—twice. I've lived with him and worked with him. He's not the kind of man that would burn down a school house."

The sheriff raced in, stopping when he reached the front of the church. He rocked on his heels with his thumbs in his waistband. "I have a witness who said he saw Pete Walters leaving the building before the fire. And I understand he has a history of starting fires."

"Now wait a minute." Joe clenched his fists. "Pete has been with us for the past two hours."

The sheriff shook his head. "I have a witness who claims that he saw Pete leave the school house less than an hour ago."

"If he set the school on fire, why would he go back in to rescue me?" Jenny stalked a few steps forward and faced the crowd. "He thought I was still in the school house. I told him I had papers to grade."

"Who is your eye-witness, Sheriff? It wouldn't be Mark Weston, would it?" Joe scowled, and all eyes turned toward Mark.

"As a matter of fact, it is." The sheriff scratched his chin as Mark shuffled a few paces toward the back door. "How do you know that, Joe?"

"Because Mark was blackmailing Pete, trying to get him to leave town, but it didn't work. I guess he thought he could pin this on Pete and get rid of him that way." Joe slammed his fist against the back of the pew. "Trust me, Sheriff, Pete came to our house about two hours ago, and he would never set fire to the school house. Mark is your fire starter. I hope Pete makes it, or Mark will be a murderer."

Mark shook his fists at the crowd. "The people in Grand Island, Nebraska ran him out of town. Do you want a man like that living in Kathleen Creek?"

Ben walked over to Mark, puffed out his chest, and planted his hands on his hips. "I understand that you think you know what happened back in Nebraska that would make people in this community mistrust my friend Dr. Pete."

Mark stepped closer, right up to Ben's face. "What else is there to know other than this "hobo" got drunk and burned down a barn full of animals? How do you explain that?"

"Oh, I wouldn't try to deny that." Ben sidestepped him and turned to the crowd. "Shouldn't Mark, of all people, know that men sometimes drink to excess and make mistakes? Like the one you made that night you drank too much and ran off the road with Lettie in the car with you. How is her leg, by the way? I heard she never did walk the same after that." He faced Mark again. "Dr. Pete made one of those mistakes that he regrets. But you can't undo a mistake like that, can you?"

"What does that have to do with anything?" Mark lunged at Ben, and a couple of men restrained him.

"Well, what you don't know is that Pete felt so bad about *his* mistake that he signed over his own house, his team of horses, and his buggy, to that farmer and his wife, and left to start life over in a new town."

A collective murmur spread through the church.

"How do you know that's true?" Mark wriggled against the men who held him.

"Pete didn't tell me." Ben stood straighter. "He wouldn't have ever told me. He's too good a man to brag about that. But I bunk with a guy at the CCC camp from Grand Island, Nebraska. He saw Pete's name on one of the letters he sent me, and he told me all about what Pete did—the drinking, the barn burning, and the huge personal sacrifice Pete gave to make amends."

Mary stood up in her pew. "Dr. Pete saved my puppy!"

Everyone laughed.

"I'd trust Dr. Pete to come back to my farm any day." A wispy man in bib overalls said in a loud voice. "He's a super vet!"

"Me, too." Mr. Barthel yelled out. "Dr. Pete is welcome in my barn any day."

"I don't know what kind of a vet he is," Rueben, the barber scooted to the edge of his pew and stood, "but he sure knows his medicinal herbs. He brought me yarrow that cured my sore feet. He has my vote!"

Glen stood and stammered. "Pete, ah, helped me..." He sat down, his face red, his hands shaking.

"He's coming around!" Lavinia waved her hands over her head. "Pete's coming to!"

Jenny knelt beside him while everyone crowded around her. Pete's eyes fluttered, then widened. "Jenny!"

"I'm fine, Pete." Her tears dripped into his hair and rolled down his forehead. She wiped them away as more spilled from her eyes. "I wasn't in the school house."

Mark lunged through the crowd and waggled his finger at Pete. "You started the fire. You did it in Nebraska and you did it here."

"No." Pete tried to sit up. "I—"

Jenny placed her finger over his lips. "Shhh… Rest, Pete. We know you didn't do it."

The sheriff snagged Mark's arm. "Mr. Weston, you're going to have to come with me. I'm taking you in for questioning."

"Jenny, please…" Mark reached for her.

She blocked his view with her palm and kept her gaze trained on Pete.

"Doctor, can we take Pete home now?" Lavinia tightened her coat.

"He's had a lot of smoke inhalation." Doctor Rushford snapped the clasp of his bag. "But he's conscious and looks like he'll be okay. He'll need lots of rest for a while, but you can take him home."

People trailed out of the church. Jenny and Lavinia helped Pete sit up while Gunther went to get his car.

"Everything will be fine." Jenny kissed him on the forehead. "It will be just fine."

Pete stayed in bed for a day before Cookie came to visit him. Next, Joe and Dolly came to see him. Then Jenny came, worried that he wouldn't recover. He assured them that except for some coughing and feeling fatigued, he felt fine.

When the room cleared, Jenny moved to his side. "Pete, I'm sorry I acted the way I did when you confided in me about your past. Your drinking made me hesitate." She gripped the bed rail with white knuckles. "My father is an alcoholic, and I know how much it affected our whole family. I don't want that for my children or for me. If I thought you would drink again, I wouldn't want to see you anymore."

"Believe me, Jenny, I don't plan to ever drink again." He scooted higher in the bed, reaching back to adjust his pillow.

"My dad has said that many times, but when any difficulty comes along he heads for a bottle of whiskey." Her eyes glistened.

"That's not me." Pete's head fell back against the headboard.

"That's good, Pete." Jenny reached for his hand. "You're a good man. I knew that from the first time I saw you. I can trust my instincts again. You need rest, so I'll leave you now." She gave him a squeeze and released him. "Get well."

The next day, the Hermanns still insisted that Pete rest. Midday, a new, shiny, black Ford drove into the yard.

A tall, lanky man in a black and gray herringbone suit strolled up the walk. Gunther let him in, and he clomped up the stairs to Pete's bedroom.

"Hello, Pete. I'm Mr. Farnsworth." He stuck out his hand and caught Pete's in a hearty shake. "I own the car dealership in St. Cloud. A lot of people have come to me asking if there isn't a way I can provide you with a car. Seems like you're a right popular guy in these parts."

Mr. Farnsworth twirled a set of keys. "I have an almost new Ford V-8 Sedan that I had to repossess. It's in good condition. I could let you have it for a small down payment and $5.00 a month. Could you handle that?"

"I…" Pete's jaw dropped. Lots of people were trying to help him? Why? "Why are people asking you that?"

"I don't know for sure myself." Mr. Farnsworth winked. "I understand you've helped a lot of people in this town, and now they want to help you."

"I haven't done anything." Pete tugged the sheets closer around his waist.

"That's not what I hear." Mr. Farnsworth dangled the keys in front of Pete. "Do you want the car?"

"Yes, but I don't have any money for a down payment."

"Can you swing $5.00 a month?"

Pete's head swam. Could he? With the money Cookie had sent him… "I could give you $5.00 a month." Why was this happening?

"Okay. I don't make a habit of this, but since I want to keep my customers happy, I'll forego the down payment." Mr. Farnsworth put the keys in his pocket. "People seem to think you're a reliable risk. I'll have my man bring it here for you. Mr.

and Mrs. Johnson paid for the first tank of gas. It's nice to have so many friends." He shook Pete's hand and then left.

Lavinia came back into the room with a basket of cleaning supplies. "Are you buying a car, Pete?"

"It seems as if I am. What's going on? He said a lot of people want me to have a car. I don't understand it."

She chuckled. "You have a lot of friends in this community."

"Why? I thought no one would want to have anything to do with me once Mark told them about my past. Surely, they all know now, don't they?"

Whisking a cloth duster over the windowsill, she whistled a breath. "They also know what you did for the farmer and his wife whose barn burned."

"How do they know that? I've never told anyone." Pete cocked his head from side to side, cracking his neck joints.

"Ben found out from someone he works with. He told everyone at the church when you were still unconscious." She lifted a picture frame from the dresser and dusted under it. "A lot of other people talked about what you've done for them."

"But I haven't done anything."

With a huge grin, she dusted the top of his forehead. "Well, they say you have. The people here trust you, Pete. You don't have anything to worry about."

Pete laughed. Maybe he had done a few good things. How could all this have happened? Jenny's good graces came because he tried to rescue her. Now he had a car so he could take her on dates, and he could drive to his vet clients instead of walking. *Thank you, Lord.*

Later that day, James's father drove into the yard. He met Gunther as he walked up to the porch. "Hello, Gunther. I need to see Dr. Pete."

"Go on upstairs." Gunther waved him into the house.

With a furrowed brow, Pete sat up straighter. "Hello, Mr. Davis."

"I was out of town the night of the fire, but I understand this community learned a lot about you that night." Mr. Davis sat on the chair Lavinia offered him. Then she left the room.

Pete hung his head. "Ah, yes—"

"You've become the town hero."

Pete jerked his head up. "Hero? I didn't save anyone. Jenny wasn't even in the school house."

Mr. Davis scoffed. "Nonsense. I understand you have a bad history that resulted in quite a fear of fire."

Pete nodded.

"Yet, you ran into that burning building. Not many people would do that." Mr. Davis leaned forward and rested his elbows on his knees.

"I thought Miss Howe was in there." Pete pulled the quilt up and folded his arms on it.

Mr. Davis twirled his hat in his hands. "You must think quite of bit of her."

Pete's cheeks warmed.

"Well, that's not the reason I came to see you." Mr. Davis stood and walked to Pete's bedside. "I came to thank you. My son talks about you a lot. You brought James out of a depression that had me really concerned. I didn't know what to do for him. But your friendship brought him out of it. I should have thanked you earlier."

"No thanks are necessary. I enjoy him. He helped me a lot too. When I first came to town, most people wouldn't even talk to me, but he did." Pete swallowed. "My hobo persona scared people off, but not James. He saw me for who I am, not who I looked like. He's a good guy, and a smart, capable guy."

"So I'm learning, thanks to you." Mr. Davis sat on the edge of the chair. "I also discovered that the reason Katherine is so happy lately is because you showed a certain young man how to win her heart. Glen spends a lot of time at our house lately, which makes all of us feel better. I am in your debt for a lot of reasons."

Pete's grin traveled all the way to his eyes.

"Well, you probably know that my wife died a few years ago. I don't know if you knew she was a milliner, a hat-maker." Mr. Davis raised his hat toward Pete. "She had her shop in that building next to the barber shop. Since she died I haven't had the heart to do anything with it. It sits there empty." He lowered his head. After a few moments of silence, he looked up again and cleared his throat. "I understand you could use an office for your veterinary business. The front would work well for that, and it has living quarters in the back."

Pete gaped. He took in a deep breath. "How much rent?"

"Well," Mr. Davis stroked his chin. "I've had a few people— more than a few people, really--suggest that you need a helping hand in order to get your practice up and running again. They seem to think you're an asset to this community, and they want you to stay around. If you'd be willing to clean it up and make good use of it, I could let you have it for the cost of utilities for the first year. After that, I'd have to charge you rent. How does that sound?"

Pete swallowed hard again. Twice. "I can't believe it! How can I thank you enough? A place of my own again! Thank you so much." He pumped Mr. Davis's hand up and down. "When can I move in?"

"As soon as you want to. I brought you the keys." Mr. Davis reached in his pocket and handed him the keys with a smile. "Now I won't have to worry about squatters moving in. I had to kick them out a couple times. That's a hard thing to do when you know somebody's got nothing, but you can't trust your property to people you don't know anything about." He began to leave the room, but turned back with a wink. "Now you'll have something to offer to that pretty little school teacher."

Dizziness overcame Pete. What had happened? Had the

earth spun and tossed him into the land of good and plenty? No, this was a God thing. "Thank you, Lord!"

Lavinia came upstairs with a curious grin on her face. "Why the big smile, Pete?"

"Mr. Davis is giving me the use of his building for a year without rent! I'll have an office and living quarters! Can you believe it?" Pete's smile faded. He'd no longer live there and help on the farm. Would she be disappointed?

"Oh, Lavinia." He took both her hands in his. "I'll miss being here with you and your family. I can still come and help Gunther some of the time. You've been so good to me. I don't know how I can thank you."

"Gunther will miss the help, and the girls will miss you. And I'll miss you, too, you big lug!" She laughed. "But, I'm happy for you. You need a practice of your own, and it's always nice to have a place of your own. Mr. Davis is doing a wonderful thing. Good for you."

Yawning, Pete slipped further into the bed. A car, and now an office and home! He sat up. Could he afford all that? He'd have to buy gas for the car, utilities for the building, payment on the car, and he'd have to install a telephone.

Cookie's money would be eaten up in no time. Most of his clients had only paid him in food so far. He'd need that, too, because he'd have to feed himself. Working for the Hermanns and being fed and cared for might have been an easier life than having a vet practice.

He lay back down again and closed his eyes, but Jenny's bright face came to mind. Maybe they could be married someday and have a home filled with children.

Excitement bubbled up into his chest and spread into a smile on his lips. He needed to get up from the bed. He could hardly wait to move into town and start his own practice again. He'd find a way to make the finances work.

Two days later, Christmas Eve arrived. After breakfast, when

Pete went back into his room, he found a brown, three-piece suit lying across his bed. On top of it, a crisp white shirt. A tie lay next to the clothing, and a pair of dress shoes stood on the floor. Lavinia! How could he ever thank her enough?

Everything fit perfectly. And now, he had nice clothes for the Christmas Eve service. How could he have found such good friends?

Cookie came to see Pete later that morning. "I'll be going back to camp the day after tomorrow, Preacher." He passed Pete a miniature burlap bag. "Some of Mom's special Christmas candy. I want to thank you for letting me know about my dad. I can't believe the difference in him. We've become close on this visit, and I'm so grateful to you."

"You have terrific parents, Cookie. I hope you never forget that." The words caught in Pete's throat as he wrapped his fingers over the candy. "I'll keep an eye on them for you since I'll be living across the street from them. If they ever need help, I'll be here. But it's me who can never thank you enough for the money to get started in my vet practice again. When you're ready to come back home, I'll set you up in whatever you want to do. I am truly in your debt, my dear friend."

The two men hugged, and Cookie squeezed extra hard. "I'll see you in church tonight, right?"

"You bet! I'm escorting Jenny to the candlelight service in style." Pete beamed. "I have a new suit, a new car, and a beautiful woman on my arm. What more can I ask?"

That night Pete studied himself in the mirror. He looked like a new man. He could hold his head up now. The people in this community cared about him and trusted him with their animals. Jenny loved him. Maybe someday he'd have another little girl like Rose.

Pete fell to his knees at the edge of the bed. So many blessings. "More than I deserve," he whispered. "Lord, thank you for everything you have given me here in Kathleen Creek. I don't deserve all this love and kindness, but I thank you for it. Thank you for forgiving me my mistakes and helping me to not drink again."

Pete gripped the bedrail. "Thank you for helping me to forgive myself and get over my grief enough to open my heart to loving again. Thank you for Jenny. Thank you for friends like the Hermanns, and Joe and Dolly, and Cookie."

Tears streamed his face. "Thank you for saving me from the fire. Forgive my sins and guide me in my new life here in Kathleen Creek. In Jesus' name, Amen."

He stood, wiped his cheeks and looked in the mirror again. He was truly a new man.

Lavinia called upstairs to the girls. "Daddy has the car warm. Come downstairs. We're leaving."

Pete followed them as they bounced step to step in their fancy dresses.

"Can I ride with you, Mr. Pete?" Olivia caught his sleeve when he reached the bottom stair.

"Pete has to pick up Miss Howe." Lavinia swatted her after her sisters. "You ride with us. We'll see them at church."

Pete winked at Olivia, and she rewarded him with a wide, toothless smile. Olivia was sure growing up.

Pete's car barely warmed by the time he reached Jenny's driveway. She wore a beautiful blue dress beneath her dark blue woolen coat and a warm, but stylish hat to match. She admired first Pete, then his car, her eyes twinkling and dimples showing.

Inside the church, people on both sides of the aisle smiled as they marched, arm in arm, up the aisle to the pew where the Hermanns already sat.

Pete shot her a knowing glance. Maybe soon, they'd walk down that aisle again.

As they slipped into the seats, the organ played the first notes of "Hark the Herald Angels Sing."

Pete opened the hymnal to the right page and moved it

slightly to the left. Jenny reached up and took hold of her side of the book. They moved closer to each other as they sang.

His heart burned with a raging hot flame he'd never thought possible.

This was the way they'd share the rest of their lives—close, each holding up one end of whatever came their way.

THE END

Dear Reader,

I hope you enjoyed this story. The Great Depression has many lessons for us today if we only care to look back and remember them. The hobos who were the migrant workers of that era helped to save this country by their hard labor, harvesting crops for the rest of America being paid only pennies.

Yet, it was the generosity of the American people who understood their circumstances and helped the hobos survive by frequently providing them with work, food, and shelter. And, of course, hobos helped each other along the way the best they could.

It was by honoring God's commandment, "Love thy neighbor as thyself," that helped get us through that devastating time. But the biggest reason our country survived that era was the programs that President Franklin Delano Roosevelt's administration created and implemented, mainly the Civilian Conservation Corps (CCC) and the Work Program Administration (WPA).

I hope you will give this book a good review and tell your friends about it.

God bless you.

I'd love to hear from you. Email me at www. connielounsbury.com.

Connie Lounsbury